The Amygdala Hijack

Colin T. Nelson

Rumpole Press of Minneapolis, MN

Printed in the United States of America

September 2015

Rumpole Press of Minneapolis, MN

Dedication

To my grandmother,
Gunilda Pauline Nelson,
Who introduced me to mystery stories

Also by Colin T. Nelson

Reprisal

Fallout

Flashover

Up Like Thunder

Acknowledgements

As usual, I could not have completed this story without the help of many people who generously gave me their advice and time.

My wife, Pam, gave me ideas, support, and while she's my toughest editor, she's also my biggest cheerleader. Kurt Huver, Crime Scene Investigator at the Hennepin County Sheriff's office educated me about blood stain analysis and suggested plot ideas. My reading/editing group who gave me so much time and made wonderful suggestions includes: Mike Austin, David Epstein, Marilyn Curtis, Kathleen Neaton, Mary Stanton, Carol Epstein, and Jessica Austin. My editor, Jennifer Adkins, gave more than the usual amount of effort for me and the story. Thanks to all of you!

Laws are spider webs through which the big flies pass and the little ones get caught.

—Honore de Balzac

The most dangerous criminal may be the person gifted with reason but with no morals.

—Martin Luther King, Jr.

Chapter One

Murder victim Mina Jensen never had a funeral; was never buried, cremated or even properly mourned. Ted Rohrbacher, a former criminal lawyer, received a call from her husband and Ted's childhood friend begging for help. In a frantic voice, Dan Jensen said, "There's a good chance I could be charged with killing my wife." Since Ted knew the victim also, he was hesitant to even talk with Danny. Years ago, Ted had been a successful prosecutor, but after the disaster that ruined his career, Ted had vowed never to go back into a courtroom or do criminal law again. He didn't even read the crime news.

When Ted protested, Dan turned on the guilt. "I'm innocent. Mina and I had our problems, but I couldn't do something this gruesome. You're the only friend I can turn to."

"Dan, I told you: I'm not taking cases like this anymore. I don't want to go into a courtroom again if I can help it. I can refer you to—"

"Just talk to me. I'm scared."

Their history went back to the high school hockey team. Also, Mina was a cousin to Ted's wife. So when Dan had married Mina, the relationship became even closer. Ted had finally relented and agreed to at least meet with Jensen.

Ted waited for him now in his office in the newest steel and glass building along France Avenue, south of Minneapolis. Two years ago he'd joined a boutique law firm that specialized in tax and estate planning—basically making wealthy people richer. After years in criminal work, Ted felt calm and peaceful for once. He was in his early forties and still had time to build a significant and lucrative practice.

Estate planning was slow, dominated by filling in the forms, and once he'd learned the law, these were routine cases that Ted could do with his eyes closed. Fine by him.

In his office, he felt hermetically sealed inside and could look through the floor-to-ceiling glass to see over the roof of the Galleria shopping mall. Rain clouds drifted toward him from the north and colored the air pewter. That caused the sumac bushes along the edges of the parking lot to glow bright green.

While waiting for Dan's appointment, Ted booted up his Google calendar and saw that he was scheduled for a lengthy meeting with an elderly couple who wanted to set up a trust to insulate their wealth from estate taxes when they died. Most of his work was like this: holding the dry hands of his clients to assure them their money would remain in their hands. The phone buzzed quietly, and the receptionist's silky voice said, "Daniel Jensen is here for his appointment."

Ted reached for his father's blue blazer from the hanger behind the door. Ted had inherited it after the old guy's death a few years ago. Even with Ted's muscular shoulders, the jacket fit uncomfortably—like the memory of his father. His death had left unresolved problems.

The blazer covered an expensive white shirt and a Ralph Lauren silk tie, which he tightened against his neck. Ted left his office, turned into the hallway, felt the soft cushion of the carpeting, and came out to the small lobby. It was decorated in tan tones with aluminum panels to create privacy. The architect the firm had hired referred to it as "Frank Geary does a law firm." To Ted, it just seemed cold. The receptionist nodded her head toward the man sitting in one of the chairs. Dan Jensen was squeezed between its arms and looked relieved to be able to get up.

Ted's wife, Laurie, and her cousin, Mina, were very close. But Ted had not done much with Mina and didn't know her well. Neither had Ted seen Dan since Dan's business started getting busier. Ted hadn't seen him for a few years. The change was startling.

Dan had worked as an MP, military police, with the army in Afghanistan during the war. Ted wasn't sure what he'd done while over there. Although Dan was still broad in the chest and handsome, the rest of him looked worn out. His stomach sagged and his head hung forward as if it was burdened by some weight. His clothing used to be tailored and expensive. Now he wore sloppy jeans and a red golf shirt that was stretched out at the collar, exposing a tan line where the neck met the chest.

"Thanks, Teddy. I really need help on this." Dan gripped Ted's hand tightly. In spite of the cool air in the office, sweat glistened across Danny's face. He swiped it with a bare hand.

Ted led him into a dimly-lit conference room behind a sage-colored glass wall. In that sanctuary, it was quiet. Ted could smell the over-stuffed leather chairs that surrounded a long table.

"Coffee, water?" Ted offered. He called to get two bottled waters from the kitchen in the back room. When a clerk returned with the water, Dan hunched over the table with a tan file folder in front of him. He removed a crumpled paper from it. Ted set the sweating bottle on the table. Dan pulled it toward himself, leaving a streak of moisture across the wood. He shoved the paper toward Ted.

Before he read it, Ted studied Dan. His face looked heavy, as if there was too much skin for the size of his face, and he had intense blue eyes that darted around the room. He hadn't shaved for several days—probably not from stylish considerations.

"This isn't me," Dan protested.

"Slow down." Ted raised his palm toward him and picked up the paper. It was wrinkled like an old newspaper and Ted spread it on the table to flatten it out. It was a formal complaint, drafted by the prosecutor to initiate a criminal case. As he looked at it, Ted's chest tightened. He'd sworn that he'd never do this work anymore. It was too painful.

The complaint was labeled, "State of Minnesota, Plaintiff, versus Daniel J. Jensen, Defendant. District Court, Fourth Judicial District." His date of birth was listed as July 17, 1972. That was followed by several paragraphs of facts that alleged what the prosecutor thought Danny had done that made him guilty of a crime. The last portion of the complaint read:

Offense

Count 1: Murder in the Second Degree (Felony) Minn. Stat. #609.19, Subd. (1), #609.11

That on or about May 10, 2013, in Minnetonka, in Hennepin County, Minnesota, **Daniel J. Jensen,** while using a firearm or other dangerous weapons, caused the death of Mina Jensen, a human being, without premeditation but with intent to effect the death of that person.

When Ted had finished reading, he looked at Danny and tried to hide the revulsion that he felt. Even after years of representing criminals, Ted found some cases were so upsetting that he still had a hard time believing humans could act the way they did. This was one of those cases. Unlike on the TV news, where murders shared time with cartoons and ads for underarm deodorant, when Ted had practiced criminal law it brought him face to face with reality and death. Sometimes it was too real—especially when he'd known the victim. He couldn't work on this. Besides, the case was impossible to win.

Ted noticed the complaint had not been stamped by the clerk of court. It hadn't been formally filed. Technically, Dan wasn't charged with a crime—yet.

"What am I gonna do?" Dan lifted his head and grinned in a weak fashion. His teeth were new: white and straight. "A detective named O'Brien gave it to me. Said he'd like to see me pay for what I did."

"This is serious. If it gets charged the maximum penalty is forty years in prison." Ted could see the fear in Dan's eyes.

Dan's chest sagged against the table. "O'Brien told me they were still investigating, but that he knew I was guilty."

Undoubtedly, the press was all over this one. Lots of spilled blood tended to do that.

Ted sighed. "Mina was my wife's cousin, for God's sake. Ethically, I can't take this case." He folded the complaint and pushed it over the table toward Dan. It gave Ted an easy way out.

"But I'm innocent. Can't you defend me then?"

4

How could a lawyer refuse an innocent man? Ted looked at his watch and decided to at least listen to him. Ted said to him, "Okay. Let's start with the alleged facts." Ted retrieved and unfolded the complaint. He started to read. "The police say that you called them and thought your wife had been killed. They met you at your house at Lake Minnetonka and found blood spatters on the wall of the bedroom, lots of blood on the floor in the outline of a human, a bullet lodged in the wall, and streak marks of blood across the floor."

Dan nodded.

"But you didn't call right away."

"I wasn't sure—"

Ted interrupted him. "And you had several domestic problems with your wife prior to this. Neighbors had called the police several times, and your wife had even told her friends that she was afraid of you, and that you owned several guns."

"Well, yeah. I needed them when I worked in Afghanistan. But. . ."

"The preliminary forensic testing of your clothing indicated the presence of lots of blood—your wife's blood."

"I can't explain that."

"What?" Ted jerked back in his chair.

"See, I passed out. Mina and I were fighting and drinking, I admit that, but then there was someone else in the bedroom. I don't know who, and I don't know how he got there, but the fight switched to him and me. I snapped or something, because I can't remember anything after that."

"You don't know anything about this?"

"I mean, I saw it when I woke up, of course. But I didn't do it. I've got some problems from my time in the war, but I *couldn't* do something like—this. She was my wife." His eyes moistened with tears. "You know me."

Ted took a deep breath. He thought of Mina. Bright and cute and always pushing the envelope in life. When the family had called Laurie about Mina's death, both she and Ted cried. Several days later when Dan had called Ted, he told Laurie about it.

She'd asked him, "How can you even think of representing someone who could have killed my cousin?"

"I'm not going to. But any good defense lawyer knows everyone is entitled to a strong defense."

"Of course, but you can't get involved."

"I don't want to and I won't," Ted assured her.

Now, sitting in front of Dan, Ted wondered how he could avoid the case. He'd have to be honest with Dan. It would be tough, and there might be nothing anyone could do to get Dan out of trouble—even if he was innocent. Ted felt sorry for him. Printed on the bottom of the complaint but unsigned so far was the name Sanford Rogin III, an experienced and tough prosecutor. Ted had worked with him in the past and didn't like anything about the guy. The evidence against Dan looked bad. Ted would send him to a competent criminal defense lawyer and be able to face Laurie and the family later.

Setting the complaint on the table, Ted changed the subject. "What did you do in Afghanistan?"

"I was in military police, and they sent me there for four—count 'em, four deployments. We provided security for the civilians posted there. I got extra pay for hazardous duty. But finally it really messed with my mind."

"What's the problem?"

"Post-traumatic stress disorder. I'm seeing a shrink at the VA hospital, but I don't think it's working. Trouble is, they don't have any magic pills to make it all go away. Sometimes I just snap." He looked up at Ted. "So, you'll take my case, huh?"

"What happened?" He could smell English Leather cologne on Dan—something too old for a guy his age.

Dan's eyes poked all around the room, and he kept looking over his shoulder at the door to the lobby. "Teddy, I didn't imagine it'd be that bad in Afghanistan. I was only a cop, after all. Then one day my best friend suddenly blows up from an IED. I see his body come apart in large chunks and the blood splatters all over my face." Dan paused to watch Ted's reaction, and then said, "And it got worse after that." Dan's body jerked and he started to hyperventilate. A wheezing sound came from deep in his chest. "I can't tell you—"

Ted jumped up and yelled for the receptionist to bring more water. She rushed in with another bottle of mineral water. Danny gulped it so fast that he started to choke. In five minutes, he had recovered.

Danny gasped. "You should see my psych reports."

Ted didn't say anything, but he thought about the case. He felt a tingling in his stomach. He had to admit there were some tempting legal aspects. Then he thought of his wife. "Danny, I'm not sure that I'm the right lawyer for you."

"I know I can't pay a lot right now." Dan's eyes, rimmed in red, bored into Ted. Sweat stained the shirt in the middle of his chest.

"Huh?"

"I know it looks bad. When I got back from over there, I started my own security firm here. I've made a ton of money. Unfortunately, there have been a few tough spots. But we've got some equity in the house. I'll get it out to pay you."

"Danny, it's not that," Ted lied. So that's why Danny had come to Ted—he couldn't afford any other lawyer. Ted stood and moved beside Danny and patted his shoulder. In Ted's mind he pictured Dan's big house on Lake Minnetonka where the murder had occurred. "I just think a different lawyer would be better for your case."

Dan leaped up from his chair and slammed it backward. "I need you right now. I'm more scared than I ever was in Afghanistan."

"Okay." Ted patted the air with his palms to calm down Dan. Ted softened his voice. "I remember the prosecutor from years ago, and maybe you could cut a deal."

"No," he yelled. "I didn't do it."

Ted sighed and turned to look out the window. A breeze lifted the leaves on the linden trees around the parking lot. It looked like they were waving at him, warning him. He felt the tingling in his stomach again. He knew what it meant. What if Dan was really innocent?

Ted thought of Laurie, and with the knowledge that he'd have to face her and the family about the case, Ted decided to help Danny

—but only temporarily. He would at least look into the mental illness aspects and see if that could help Dan. Then as soon as possible, he'd try to get the prosecutor to drop the case. "All right. I'll check into things," Ted assured him.

Dan's case was certainly unusual, and that intrigued Ted. After all, he had never seen one like it in his entire career. Even though Danny could be charged with second degree murder and the case against him seemed strong, the prosecutor had a major problem with the evidence to prove his guilt. It was also the reason there hadn't been a funeral or a burial for Mina Jensen—no one had found her body.

Chapter Two

The next morning, Ted drove his convertible Mercedes into northeast Minneapolis. He would need professional help to look into the case. When Ted turned onto Marshall Avenue, he approached a row of new townhouses. Several large blocks of granite grew out of the ground in front of the houses, each piece carved into a beautiful sculpture. He called them the Stonehenge of Marshall Avenue.

Samantha Carter lived in the third house on the left.

Years ago, he had worked with her when she was a Minneapolis homicide detective and Ted was in the prosecutor's office. After twenty years, she'd qualified for a pension, which she grabbed and went into private investigation. Now she was a single woman who was divorced from the father of their two children. When her sister had been killed by a boyfriend, Sam had also raised two of her sister's children while holding down the job as a cop. All the children were grown now and usually didn't live at home anymore. But sometimes, between college enrollment and jobs, they dropped in for a few weeks at a time for the free food and to wash their clothing.

He parked and walked the few steps to her door. As usual, she was late. As he waited, Ted thought of one thing that made working with Sam difficult—she often acted like his mother and lectured to him. Maybe he should get back in the car and forget everything. Laurie had called shortly after the meeting with Danny. Ted had told her that he'd temporarily represent him but couldn't take the case.

"What the hell?" she shouted. "I thought you told me—"

"He hasn't been charged yet. I'm just going to check on a few things for him. His mental health, for instance. If I find something in his defense, I can approach the prosecutor to get the case thrown out right away."

"Ted, don't do this."

"Don't worry. I'm meeting with Samantha Carter. Maybe she can work on that." He had felt his chest tighten in preparation for another fight with her. They were the only couple he knew who had remarried after a divorce. Ted didn't want to upset the balance for any reason.

"I'm sorry," she apologized. "It's just that I'm so upset about Mina. Get home early. Matt wants to talk about colleges." Her voice had dropped to a lower register. One that she knew could hook him. "And I want to see you."

He knocked on Sam's door a third time, and the sound of a saxophone floated through the front window. Samantha played jazz with a small combo in town. She wasn't a professional musician, but she always said, "At least people pay to hear us play." He heard her slither down the scale, bending notes as the solo came to an end. Even without her back-up group, the music made the skin on Ted's neck tingle.

She yelled from the back room. "That you, Teddy? The doors always open for you."

She stepped into the room. "Hey, T-man." Sam brought energy with her into the room. Unlike most people who saw the world in grays, Samantha saw the world in Technicolor. She was in good shape, but now into middle age, her weight had started to drop lower on her body. Although she wasn't beautiful, her smile and personality overwhelmed most people who met her. Today she wore a golden wig.

Ted noticed the four African masks that guarded either side of the fireplace. Between them was a portrait of a young African girl. Her face glowed while a tear streaked down her cheek. Ted cocked his head to the side while he looked back at Sam's hair. "Color du jour?"

"Hey, when you're as cool as I am, everything's always golden."

"Meaning you got up late and didn't want to mess with your hair."

"At least I got more of my own that you do." She unsnapped the alto sax from the neck strap and set it on a small stand near the couch. From her pocket, she brought out a metal cylinder and capped the mouthpiece carefully, as if the horn were an extension of her body. "I want to be ready for a gig we got at the Dakota. Coming up soon. Still having trouble memorizing those diminished scales."

"What scales?"

Sam chuckled. "Never mind. Lots of sharps and flats. To you, it'd sound like Arabian hootchie-cootchie music."

"If anyone knows hootchie-cootchie, it's you."

"Don't laugh. I was famous once."

"Oh?"

"Yeah. Remember the song by the rock group Traffic? 'The Low Spark of High-heeled Boys'? That was me on the sax part."

"That was you? Why didn't you stay in the business?"

"Discrimination. Not race, but gender. All the producers wanted women for was to sing and look pretty. Instrumentals were for the dudes."

Ted looked at the saxophone Sam had propped on a stand. Various levers and rods ran down the length of it while bars and buttons popped out from the tangle of metal at unexpected places. It looked complicated, but overall it sparkled in golden colors.

Samantha offered him a seat and changed the subject. "I thought you were dead," she said. "Haven't heard from you for months. Then I get this crazy e-mail." She leaned so close to his face that he could smell her vanilla perfume. "I've seen the news coverage of the case. Were you out of your mind when you said yes to this one? Or was it the big bucks?" Her eyes probed around his face.

Ted told her the case intrigued him and he felt sorry for Jensen. He shook his head. "But I'm not taking the case."

"Uh huh. I know why you're up here with me. You're tempted by this one, aren't you?"

"How can you tell? All right, there are some things that are slightly interesting. What if I found something that the prosecutor would listen to and give Danny a break? Wouldn't take much of my time, but it would help him."

"You're not telling me the truth."

"What?"

"You're bored making the big bucks now, and you'd like to get back in the action." Her eyes probed around his face.

"Never."

She grinned, which split her cocoa-colored face around a white smile. She stood up and went into a small office next to the living room. She came out cradling a file folder. "Where do you want to start?"

"Let's talk to the shrink."

"Just be careful, Teddy. Don't bet all your money on this one," she lectured him.

That irritated him. "Don't worry."

She lifted an umbrella out from behind the couch. Then she led him out the front door, closed it, and secured the door with two locks. She looked at his new Mercedes. "Law business is good, huh?" She got into Ted's car. They started for the appointment Ted had set with Dan Jensen's doctor.

Sam bent forward to look at the sound system. "What have you got here?"

"Okay, I know you won't like the music selection."

Her eyes opened wide and showed brown orbs with an unusual gold shading around the edges.

"We've been through this before, remember?" he said.

Samantha laughed. She dug into a pile of CDs squashed in the side pocket of the door. "What is this shit? Country? What's wrong with you?" She thumbed through them. "'Course, it fits you—lost dogs and broken-down love affairs."

Ted drove through downtown Minneapolis and got onto Minnehaha Boulevard, which led to the doctor's office.

Ted drove the Mercedes, but it was leased by the firm. The car made him ten years younger when he drove it. The Veteran's Administration Hospital sprawled over a bluff above the intersection of Minnehaha Creek and the Mississippi River. From the hospital, it was possible to see renovated Fort Snelling, one of the original white man's settlements in the Minnesota Territory.

"What're we looking for?" Sam asked.

Ted sighed. "I'm not sure. Dan Jensen suggested I should talk with his shrink, so I made an appointment. Right now, I'm just curious."

"And you have to tell Laurie something about why you're looking at a criminal case again, huh?"

12

"Right." He glanced at her. "My life is good now. I can't go back into this stuff, Sam. I still think about that little girl. Katie was her name. When I screwed up, it meant she didn't get justice."

Sam looked out the side window and said nothing. As they got near the VA Hospital, she turned back to him. "You think you got problems? Too painful? Shut up. I know your history. You felt like dying back then, right?"

"Yeah."

"When I was a cop, I killed a young boy in a basement. We thought he had a gun and wouldn't put it down. Got over to him and found out it was a bicycle tire pump. Now, you try living with that. Then, the next thing, my sister died."

Ted felt irritated with another lecture.

"You should listen to me, Teddy. I know what I'm talking about. You can't hide from the broken parts of your life. In fact, they become the building blocks for healing and new growth."

"Okay, okay. If that works for you, great. For me, this is the first time in my life I'm doing what I want to do. Not what my wife, or father, or anyone else wants. I'll take care of myself, thank you."

"We'll see." Samantha smiled. "But quit whining."

He turned the car into the grounds of the hospital. Ted parked the car, and they grabbed their folders and hurried into the main lobby. It was large, with big windows that allowed sunlight to flood the area. A receptionist directed them to the Psych Services area. They only waited five minutes before Dr. Jerome Strauss came out to greet them.

He was a tall, wiry man with gray thinning hair combed straight back from his forehead. It fell in a large cloud behind his ears to look like a Jewish Afro. Dr. Strauss removed a pair of tortoise-shell glasses and shook each of their hands. He motioned toward a hallway off the lobby. "We'll use one of our interview rooms."

Ted introduced Samantha Carter. "She's our investigator and the brains behind the whole operation." Sam smiled in response, although Ted had said this dozens of times before.

Strauss led them down a short hallway to turn into a room with a window next to the door. He settled them on soft chairs spread around a low table. He dropped a file on the table with a thump. The edges of the papers inside were curled from use.

Ted handed him the Release of Medical Information form. Dr. Strauss propped his glasses at the end of his nose, took the paper, and fitted it into the front of the file on the table. "An unfortunate case," he said and removed the glasses.

"Dr. Strauss, how long have you been seeing Dan Jensen?" Ted asked.

A rubbery smile curled Strauss' lips. "Call me Jerry. My father was a rabbi, and he always thought the Catholic Church was the only legitimate dictatorship in the history of the world. I was named after one of the popes. Can you imagine when I was in Hebrew school as a kid? All my friends were named David or Samuel. I should have gotten therapy myself." He laughed at his own joke.

"Okay, Jerry."

"I started treating him when he returned from Afghanistan the last time. Let's see. . ." Strauss hefted the file onto his lap and extracted a thinner folder. He paged through it. "Almost a year now."

"How often did you see him?"

"Every other week for a one-hour appointment."

"Did he benefit from your help?"

Strauss sighed and leaned back in the chair. "His IQ is average. Dan isn't capable of a lot of introspection, but he's a survivor and resourceful."

"You called him an 'unfortunate' case?" Sam said.

Strauss' eyebrows lifted. "The generals know all about how to win battles, but they forget about the human debris left behind—our own soldiers. You can't believe the psychological damage done to these young folks."

"He did four tours there."

"Yes. An unusually high number of times."

"He told me that he's been diagnosed with PTSD," Ted said.

"That's correct." He tilted his head. "As a matter of fact, Dan's case was worse than many others. It's common in battle zones. During World War I, soldiers came home from the trenches and displayed all the symptoms. It was known as 'shell shock' back then. In some

14

ways, we've become better at diagnosing it, but not much better at curing it."

"What would someone with post-traumatic stress disorder act like?" Ted crossed his legs at the ankles.

Strauss took a deep breath. "Want the Harvard lecture or plain English?"

"Let's try English," Sam said.

"Imagine you're driving with your two children in the car when you get a green light and start through an intersection. Some jerk ignores his red light and you see him roaring straight at the door where your child is strapped into the seat. It's happening so fast you can't stop it and can't avoid it. After the crash, you find that not only have you survived, but your kids have also. Post-traumatic stress is the result of a heart-stopping mixture of helplessness and terror from an event that overwhelms the body and mind at times. Later, when the victim senses a similar state of fear, the trauma kicks in again."

Samantha frowned. "Does the patient actually re-live the event?"

"Sort of. Some get flashbacks or nightmares. Sometimes it's just a feeling of constant anxiety, depression, shame or guilt that the person couldn't stop the initial event." Dr. Strauss leaned forward and chopped the air in front of him with a stiff finger to emphasize each point. "During their day-to-day activities, certain catalyzing events can trigger a re-living of the original terrifying event. Some become violent in their efforts to eradicate the trauma."

Samantha reminded him, "But you said Jensen's case was 'unfortunate'?"

Strauss rubbed his finger under his nose. "To start with, you need to understand a distinction. Many of the people returning from a war zone have 'post traumatic *brain injury*.' That is different from post-traumatic *stress disorder*. Traumatic brain injuries, which we call TBI, involve direct physical injury to the brain itself. Although both PTSD and TBI can happen to people in a war zone, their causes and symptoms are different."

"What causes post-traumatic stress in a war?" Ted said.

"The impact of psychological trauma, like the exposure of a threat to their own lives or their friends' lives. It can also be caused by a life-altering violation of the body, like rape."

"What's the point?" Ted leaned forward over the table.

"Dan's problem involved a *psychological* assault to the brain, but not a *physical* assault. Various traumatic stressors in war zones may not injure the brain, but they do change how the brain works."

"I don't understand," said Samantha.

Strauss smiled at her. "You seem normal to me," he laughed. "Let's look into your brain."

Sam glanced between Strauss and Ted. "Don't go there," she warned.

"Like any human, you have stressors in your life. Death of family members, loss of jobs, divorce perhaps, rejection. Neuroimaging studies suggest that your brain, when faced with stressors, operates in a learning mode. Although the stressors may cause discomfort, you learn from them and continue to explore and enjoy the world, using your experiences to create a healthy approach to future stressors."

"Well," Sam laughed, "I'm not sure anyone is *normal*, but keep going."

"PTSD involves a change in how key sections of the brain interact with one another. It's not an injury, but it's an altered way of operating which profoundly changes the way we think and feel. It changes the nature of the mind."

Ted said, "So how does this differ from a normal brain that learns a healthy approach to the world?" He remembered some of this information from the old case with Katie, the victim. He felt uncomfortable talking about it.

"The brain changes to operate in a survival mode. It's a brain that's on the defensive and demonstrates negative emotional, behavioral and cognitive reactions. In medical words, the shift can be observed in changes in the relationship between the emotional brain's limbic system—areas like the amygdala and hippocampus—and deep midbrain areas and the prefrontal and cingulate cortex."

Samantha swiped her hand in front of her like she was wiping a window clean. "Whoa, whoa, Doctor. What does that mean?"

"Sorry. I get carried away with this." He laughed and said, "I'll show you." He left the room and came back in a few minutes with a colored drawing, which he unfolded and spread on the table. Everyone leaned over the picture.

"Cross section of our brain. See the eye? That's the front of the brain and above the eye this curved darker section is the neocortex, or the 'thinking' part of the brain. In the middle of the brain is an organ called the thalamus. Here." He pointed with a wooden pencil that he'd pulled from his coat pocket.

Ted felt uneasy. So much of this information reminded him of the other case.

"Wrapped underneath the thalamus is the hippocampus. And this part, almost behind your eyes, is the amygdala. Got it?"

Ted and Sam nodded.

"Some people call the amygdala the 'reptilian' part of the brain. It's one of the oldest parts and was put there to keep us alive," said Dr. Strauss. "Let's suppose you see something threatening through your eyes. The stimulus goes to the thalamus and is split. Part of it goes directly to the amygdala while another part is sent to the neocortex. In a person suffering from PTSD, the amygdala may perceive a match to the stimulus."

"What does that mean?" Samantha asked.

"The war veteran has stored up in the hippocampus some fight or flight experiences. If the amygdala matches what the eyes see now to the historical record in the brain, it can trigger the hypothalamic-pituitary-adrenal axis and take over the rational brain. We call it the 'amygdala hijack.'" Strauss' face gleamed with pride.

"You're out there now," Samantha said.

"Here's the problem. The emotional brain activity from the amygdala processes information milliseconds earlier than the rational brain. So in the case of a match, the amygdala fires before any possible direction from the neocortex can be received."

"What does this have to do with Dan Jensen?" Ted asked.

"At times, the PTSD patient can even think he's in the middle of the original fearful event. It's a horrible nightmare, relived again and again."

Samantha stood up.

Dr. Strauss must have sensed the tension in the room. "Want something to drink?" He ordered two mineral waters and a Diet Coke for Samantha. A young man delivered them to the room in a few minutes.

Sam unscrewed the cap and drank for a long time. "Okay. Let's get back to it."

"I think Danny's case of PTSD is worse because he experienced more life-threatening events than the average soldier and that he probably feels guilty about."

"I've heard some of it," Ted said. He tipped the bottle of cold water up to his mouth.

"Oh, I'm sure he didn't reveal the worst parts."

Ted and Sam leaned forward.

"It took many weeks of therapy before he reluctantly told me the story. Toward the end of his last contract in Afghanistan, Dan Jensen was assigned to provide security for some engineers repairing a bridge that spanned a narrow valley. They were ambushed by several Taliban fighters. Although Dan's men were armed lightly, they were no match for the Taliban. Without much delay, they lined up all the Americans along the side of the bridge facing over the valley. As they moved down the line of men, the Taliban shot each one in the back of the head. Dan Jensen was on the end. The last one. He heard each shot, felt the bridge quiver as the body of his comrades fell forward, and waited for the shot to his own head."

Ted sat still.

"It never came. They told Dan they let him live so he could go back and tell the story as a deterrent to the Americans. He thought he'd screwed-up and was responsible for the disaster. Dan's never been the same since."

Ted heard Sam let out a big breath. She stood up and walked in a circle. "Feel sorry for that dude."

"That's why Dan's case is worse." Strauss picked up his glasses and turned them in his hand. "People with PTSD are preoccupied with threats. It's as if even something we'd consider a minor change is a threat to their survival. And they can't always react rationally to these threats."

"And that also means that if he witnessed his wife brutally killed in front of him, he could have been traumatized further?" Ted said.

"That's probably correct," Strauss answered.

Sam interrupted, "Or, if his wife did something to him to trigger the memory, could he kill her?"

Strauss shrugged. "Entirely possible."

"Could Dan stop this?"

"Absolutely not. Remember, his brain is often in survival mode."

Ted dropped his head and analyzed what that could mean for Danny's case.

"How did you counsel Danny, then?" Sam asked. "Meds?"

"Meds don't work well, but psychotherapy can be very effective with many patients. I felt like I was making some progress with Dan, but not much," Strauss said.

"Did you ever meet Mina, his wife?" Sam asked.

Strauss shook his head.

"Did he ever tell you anything about their relationship?"

"He said it was great and supportive," Strauss answered.

Back at the Mercedes, the doors were hot to touch from the sun. When they got inside, the rich smell of leather calmed Ted. They left the hospital grounds. He gave the car a little too much gas. The front end rocked upward while the tires squealed on the asphalt.

"Slow down, bro." Sam braced her arms against the dashboard. "What about Jensen's 'great' relationship with his wife?"

"He lied to Strauss."

"Why?"

Ted shrugged and quit talking. The car gained speed.

After a while, she said, "I know what you're thinking, and you're going to hit a dead end. PTSD and this 'amygdala hijack' aren't allowed as a defense in Minnesota or Outer Mongolia, for that matter. Don't even go there."

"Dan says he's innocent, and that might be true, but just in case the mental illness defense could be helpful. It may be all that he has in his defense."

She warned him, "That's bullshit. Doesn't mean a judge will even give it a moment's consideration."

"But I'd love to see the expression on Rogin's face when I hit him with this stuff."

"I know. Rogin's an easy guy to hate. But Teddy, listen to yourself."

"You don't know what I'm thinking."

"I know you better than the wrinkles on my mama's face. You're thinking you just found something to ride back with the cavalry and save the day. To prove all those things they said about you back then weren't true."

"Dammit, I told you, I'm not taking the case. Just a talk with Rogin about the doctor's evidence." His voice rose and became shrill. He didn't want her telling him what to do. Sam's shoulders dropped and she looked out the window.

They curved onto Highway 62 and headed west into the gauzy salmon and orange of the setting sun. The Richfield wetland pond glistened in golden sparkles. Ted turned north toward Minneapolis and folded the sun visor over to the side, hiding his face in a shadow. Neither of them talked. A moving truck cut in front of them and accelerated. A blast of acrid smoke puffed across them.

When she finally spoke, Sam's dry voice cracked. "And remember what Dr. Strauss said just before we left?"

"Huh?"

"Oh, you remember. You just don't *want* to remember. He said Danny told him he suffered from flashbacks, nightmares, a terrible temper, and the fear he'd wind up killing someone."

Chapter Three

The next day Ted sent an e-mail to the prosecuting attorney, Sandy Rogin. Ted asked for a meeting to talk about the Dan Jensen case before any charging decisions were made. He hesitated before tapping the *send* key and felt the pull of the case on him. Ted added to the email. "I'll be representing Mr. Jensen for now."

Ted had just started to list the reasons he could tell Laurie to justify getting involved in it when Rogin returned an e-mail to him: *I'll be straight with you, Teddy—it's going to be tough. Remember, you haven't handled a major case for a long, long time. When the investigation is done, your boy is going down so I can keep him off the streets forever.* Rogin agreed to meet and allow Ted to look at some of the investigation results up to this point. Ted hated Rogin for his arrogant attitude and, for a moment, considered how good it would feel to beat him.

He pulled out the oak drawer beside him. It rolled silently in spite of its weight. Inside, he picked up the card his father had sent him a year ago. It had reached Ted the day after the funeral. A letter "from the grave." The card felt rough and cool and had one corner crimped over from its home in the drawer. On the cover a boy ran through a wheat field bent to the side from an unseen wind. Above his head, he carried a model airplane. The sun lit up the wheat in gold and cast a shadow of the plane across the boy's excited face. Inside it read: *May you always fly!*

Below that, his father had scrawled: *Hope you finally get it together—*

The thoughts about his father and Laurie and their child Matt were all tied up in pain and regret. Before his father died, Ted had been a rising star in the prosecutor's office—until the big trial that turned into a disaster because of Ted. His father had stopped talking to him. The card summed up the disappointment his father had felt about Ted. He'd also failed to deliver justice to the young girl who was the victim. Six months later, Ted's father had died, leaving Ted with all the unresolved things he had wanted to get straight with his father. The guilt for both losses bothered Ted even now.

Starting the new practice was Ted's way of coming back. Now the last thing remaining was to keep his family together again. So far, things had gone as well as could be expected for a "second" marriage. Ted didn't want to jeopardize that.

He propped his father's card on his desk and stood up. Brushed aluminum window frames surrounded the glass in his office. Outside he saw circles of shallow water on the tar from the rain last night. He breathed deeply in the sealed office and realized he couldn't open a window to smell the dampness. But he was comfortable, for sure. And he didn't want to go back into the battle of a courtroom.

He felt the tug of the Jensen case as a rumble in his stomach. What about the ethical problem of the conflict of interest? He had known the victim. Could his client, Dan, waive that somehow? Would it be fair to him? And even if Ted worked the case to a successful conclusion, could he ever make his father happy?

His cell phone rang, and Ted answered. Sandy Rogin said, "Got your e-mail, Teddy. Time to talk about cutting a deal? If your guy will confess, maybe I'll see what I can do for him."

"I saw you in the TV news conference yesterday."

"It's only the third one, so far. Our plan is to announce each development as it occurs. And think about the poor family of the victim. Don't they deserve justice?"

"You're a true public servant, Sandy. Aren't you forgetting one of the *small* details?" Ted said.

"I prefer to be called Sanford. The body? I know—no *corpus delecti*, no proof of murder. Normally, that is a problem," he chuckled. "But not here."

"Oh?"

"You haven't seen the evidence yet, so I'll give you a couple teasers. Dr. Helen Wong, the medical examiner, was at the crime scene herself. She can testify to two things. The blood in the house matches the blood type of Mina Jensen. They took samples from several different spots and compared the DNA with a sample of her blood taken earlier by a blood bank—everything matched. Secondly, the quantity of blood found at the scene was enough that no one could have survived the loss of that much blood. *Ipso facto*, a death. A murder, in fact."

"Still, a pretty weak case."

"I admit it's circumstantial, but the law doesn't prefer direct evidence over circumstantial."

"Cut the law school crap."

"Teddy, I'm gonna make history with this case. I'll get the first murder conviction even without a body. Watch me. And don't forget to notify me under Rule 9.02."

"I've *read* the rules, Sandy. Don't fuckin' tell me about them." His irritation with Rogin caused Ted's back to stiffen. It felt good to yell at a guy like Rogin.

"Hey, Dude, no offense. None of us wants to screw up here."

Was he referring to Ted's past history? It made Ted even more determined to kick this guy's cocky ass. "I'll see you soon."

"Sure. We're still in the investigation stage. And if you happen to bring me some really strong evidence, I'm open to other scenarios. But the bottom line is, I think your boy did it." He hung up.

In his mind, Ted pictured Rogin. He was a tall man, and he used his deep tone of voice to get what he wanted. He wore heavy horn-rimmed glasses that matched the color of his beard—dirty blond. The glasses magnified Rogin's eyes so they looked larger than normal and suggested that he was able to see into everyone's secrets—good for a prosecutor.

Ted's desk phone buzzed softly. The receptionist told him his first clients of the day had arrived.

Ted tossed his gray suit coat around his shoulders and adjusted the cuffs. His new shoes were expensive and felt like a pair of leather gloves around his feet. A photo of Laurie and him still sat on the corner of his desk. It had been taken on their honeymoon in Rio de Janeiro. They were coming out of a bossa nova jazz club. It was on the second floor and tree branches grew in through the open windows, like the club was located in a tree house. Ted remembered he had finally flagged down a cab late at night. They'd had just enough money left to pay for the fare back to the hotel on Copacabana

Beach, a metaphor of their care free life at that time. The dreamy expression on Laurie's face always made Ted's heart lurch.

He walked into the quiet lobby. Two elderly people slumped on the couch drinking coffee. Hazel and Fred Gibson. It was their second meeting. Ted shot them a smile and led them into the conference room.

The room had green tinted windows that reminded Ted of working in an aquarium. The air was dry, and he took several sips of his water before starting the interview. He had a practiced speech that he gave to all clients, designed to assure them Ted Rohrbacher would do everything to help them preserve their assets and, at the same time, screw the government. People loved that part the best, and it always drew a chuckle from them.

Then Ted listened as they described what they wanted. Hazel did most of the talking. She waved her hands, but not a hair on her head moved. She smelled of floral perfume. Fred looked as if he might doze off but maintained an upright position and nodded at the appropriate times. Even though Ted already knew exactly what he'd do for them, he had to listen as Hazel droned on about the heavy burden of taxes and all the communists in Congress.

When Hazel paused to pat her hair, Ted jumped into the conversation. He told them how their trust would be structured. They nodded as if they understood. Ted could hear the air conditioning click on and smelled a puff of cool, dry air from the vents.

The receptionist burst into the conference room. Ted was about to complain, but she shouted, "Ted, get out here. Now."

He rushed to the lobby and found three people standing behind Dan Jensen. His face twisted, and he lurched toward Ted. The other people were from the media. Ted recognized Carolyn Bechter from Channel Six TV. She'd covered the courtrooms for years, and it showed in the lines on her face and the dry blond hair. "Teddy," she purred. "Aren't you lucky? Does this mean you're coming back into the arena? What's your defense going to be?"

"You all have to get out—"

The Gibsons edged out of the conference room. Fred slid close to Bechter. The senior partner of the firm, Lowell Minot, burst into the lobby also. "This is totally unacceptable," he said in a quivering voice that made his bow tie vibrate. "This is a respectable law firm." He glared at Ted.

"Is there a defense?" a reporter from the *Pioneer Press* asked, ignoring the senior partner. "The prosecutor has said they're very confident Jensen will be charged and convicted."

"We're still investigating." Ted resisted the urge to bad mouth Sandy Rogin.

"How can the prosecutor possibly go ahead without a body?" the reporter continued.

"It's never been done before in Minnesota. I've got the same question you do."

"You haven't been in a courtroom for years now," Carolyn Bechter interrupted. "Are you ready?"

"Get out of here." He waved his hand toward the front door.

Bechter said, "We'll be watching you, Ted." She paused and laughed, "When you get involved, it's always news for us."

Minot sputtered with outrage again. Fred Gibson stood closer to Bechter. He fluffed the thin gray hair on his head and said, "So, you're Carolyn Bechter. You don't look like you do on TV."

Dan had slipped into the conference room and now looked out at the lobby. Ted noticed that his shoulders twitched every once in a while. When the reporters realized they wouldn't get more out of Ted, they slowly left the lobby. He apologized to the Gibsons although there was a pink glow in Fred's lined cheeks. Ted rescheduled their meeting, and the Gibsons left. Ted walked into the conference room, shut the door, and sat down at an angle from Dan. "What the hell are you doing here?" Ted asked.

"I got scared. And the media's been following me all over."

"Well, you're going to ruin my practice. Don't ever come again without an appointment."

Danny looked away for a moment but wouldn't apologize.

"Where are you living?"

"Cops have got the house sealed. I'm at my sister's." His eyes searched around the room as if looking for something. He asked, "How's Laurie holding up?"

Ted paused. How should he answer that? "She's devastated."

"So, you talked to Dr. Strauss? I remembered that you handled a big case as a prosecutor involving mental illness. That's one reason I came to you. Figured if anyone knew this stuff, it was you."

"Yeah." Ted didn't want to talk about it. He changed the subject. "I've got some news for you." Ted squared himself toward Danny and set a legal pad on the table top. He told Dan about the scheduled meeting with Sandy Rogin. "Before I talk with him, I need to know as much as possible from you so I'm prepared."

Jensen nodded and waited.

"When they found your wife's car in a park at Lake Minnetonka, they ran tests on it and found some evidence of blood in the trunk. Not all the testing's finished yet, so let's talk about what happened in your house."

"Uh, yeah. Well, our marriage probably looked okay to you guys, but it was rocky, I guess. We hid it well. Trying to run your own company is twenty-four seven, you know. But it was the last deployment that really messed me up."

"Tell me everything, Dan. I need to know it or I can't defend you."

"Sure. You know I started my own company, Jensen's Total Security." His head bobbed up with a thin smile before dropping forward again. "Business has been great. Every time there's a terrorist attack anywhere in the world, my business doubles. People want their kids protected, their homes, their lives, and even their office Christmas parties."

"I always thought you were making a fortune."

"Sure. But lately, business has been tough, gotta admit it. I've been losing money. It should turn around, though."

Ted saw Dan's eyes follow everything. "I never asked why you enlisted to go to Afghanistan in the first place."

Dan's face blushed red for a moment. "I wanted some kick-ass fun. Oh, I got that all right. But I also wanted to do something for my country." He wore a black t-shirt with a large gold chain hanging from his neck.

26

Ted moved the interview back to the facts. "What about the night that Mina disappeared?"

"Well, I'll admit that we were drinking and started to fight."

"You two had been having trouble?"

Danny bounced his head down once. "Yeah. She'd even taken me to court to get an order for protection, but after listening to both of us, the judge dropped it. Fact is, she told me she wanted to start over."

"I remember you own some guns?"

"Yeah. Passed the little background check and started to buy them. Some I needed for work."

"Keep them in the house?"

"Right. There are lots of people who could come after me."

Ted glanced at Danny and saw a frown on his forehead. His shoulders twitched.

"Where are the guns now?"

"At home, I suppose. Cops found two missing."

"Oh?"

Danny said, "An old .38 police special. Almost a collector's item. And then there was a small nine millimeter. A Walthur P99. Oh, and the silencer for that is missing, too."

"How much did you drink?"

"I don't know what hit me that night. Normally, a few beers wouldn't knock me out, but that's what happened. I do remember some guy coming into the house. Didn't know who it was. I thought maybe it was the guy—well, I didn't know who the hell he was. Next thing I know, I'm fighting with him. Trying to protect her. Then everything's a blank until I woke up the next morning." The gold chain hanging from his neck clinked together against his chest. "What the hell do you think?"

"But you waited to call the police."

"I didn't know what to do. I panicked."

Ted sighed. "You're going to tell a jury that?"

"That's the truth. I thought the guy killed her. There were some things going on."

"What?"

"I think she was having sex with some other guy." He dropped his head down. "Like I said, we had a few problems." His face jerked up. "Not enough for me to kill her, though," he added.

Ted was surprised but didn't show it. Ted wrote notes on the pad. "What made you think that?"

"Little things. She was gone a lot. When I asked her, she'd ignore me."

"You know who she was seeing?"

"I think it was some guy she met at the gym. A Russian guy. I think the cops were able to find him. They probably questioned him already."

"So you fought with the guy?"

"Can't say for sure who it was. All I can think is the dude killed her while I was passed- out and had taken the body to cover it up. I don't know." His voice trailed off in a soft huff.

"And this guy's motive was what?"

Danny shrugged.

Ted leaned back. The more he talked with Danny, the worse the story sounded. If Rogin knew all this, Danny would be charged soon. Still, the other suspect should be checked out. The police had probably interviewed the Russian guy. Ted and Sam could follow up on that. "Any idea where the body might be?"

Dan shook his head.

"How about Mina's work?"

"Before that night, I checked with some of her friends at the bank. Remember, she worked in big data. She was a genius with details and planning. I tried to sniff around and see if anyone knew about Mina. Nobody would talk."

"Danny, look." Ted turned his body to buy some time. How could he convince Danny to try to get any deal he could? "I think I should talk to the prosecutor about working this out—"

"I'm not guilty." With a clenched hand, Dan slammed the top of the table so hard a bottle of mineral water shook from side to side.

"Then what the hell's the defense gonna be? 'Cause from what I've heard so far, it doesn't look good for you."

"The other guy?"

"Do you have any proof of that?"

Danny squinted at Ted. "Let's go back to my mental illness. How about insanity?"

"What?"

"Can't you say I'm insane? Isn't that a defense?"

Ted sighed. "Dr. Strauss can testify about your mental illness, but an insanity defense in Minnesota is almost impossible." Ted stood and walked to the far wall. A small bookshelf held a row of tan and brown law books. He selected the paperbound one called the *Minnesota Criminal Law Handbook*. He flipped through dozens of pages until he came to the part he wanted. "Here." Ted opened the book on the table before Danny.

Ted pointed his finger and read, "Statute 609.026. A person is not guilty if, at the time of committing the alleged criminal act, they were laboring under a defect of reason as not to know the nature of the act or that it was wrong." He looked at Danny's eyes. "It's called the 'M'Naghten Rule. Most states still use it."

"Can you qualify me?"

"Dan, you know it's wrong to kill someone, don't you?"

"Like, yeah." His head bobbed.

"You're clearly not insane." Ted could smell the sour odor of sweat on Dan. And fear.

Dan stared at the table top.

Ted walked around the corner of the table. He came back and, putting his palms on the table, leaned forward. He felt the warmth on the surface from the sun shining in through the window and let it relax him. The more they talked, the worse things sounded. He was about to tell Dan that until he looked up at Ted once again.

For an instant, Danny looked fragile—nothing like someone who'd been in a war zone. Four deployments. Ted couldn't imagine what that would be like. What had really happened to him? While Ted had been in Minneapolis, comfortable and safe, Danny had been risking his life. At the least, Ted owed him some effort. And maybe Danny's mental state was bad enough to help him. But how? There wasn't a defense for post-traumatic stress disorder. Could the 'amygdala hijack' that Dr. Strauss had talked about work? Would it be enough of a threat to Rogin's case that he'd consider some plea bargain with Dan? Or outright dismissal?

Ted's stomach rumbled when he thought of the case he'd been involved in with a mental illness defense. The big one he'd lost. He couldn't go there again.

Dan looked from the window to Ted. "So maybe we can use the amygdala hijack?"

"Let me think about it."

He jerked up to stand next to Ted. "Just 'think about it'?" he yelled and looked toward the door to the lobby as if to see if anyone was out there. "It's my fuckin' life."

"Dan, your story has some holes—"

"But you're the expert in this mental stuff. That's why I had you talk to Dr. Strauss." Danny circled around the end of the conference table.

"Danny, just because you say you're innocent doesn't mean a jury will agree."

"It's my life we're talkin' about. Can't you help me?"

"Uh . . ."

"This is bullshit," Danny yelled. His shoulders shook and he lurched toward the door.

Ted was worried the other lawyers in the office would get upset again. There'd already been more upheaval in one day than there had been in years.

Ten minutes later, Dan was gone and Ted leaned back into the comfort of the thick leather chair behind his desk. His domain. Organized and familiar. Sun shone in the window, and he could see particles of dust swimming aimlessly like fish in an aquarium. He could hear the faint whirr of air conditioning and it smelled metallic.

His secretary had e-mailed the Gibson file to his In Box for review. Ted spread it across the center of his computer screen and started to page through his notes again. He tried to concentrate. The forms for creation of a trust were lengthy and dull to read. Questions about the Jensen case tugged at his mind. He pushed them away and focused on the trust forms—but he left the office to go home early before finishing the work.

Ted came into the kitchen for a glass of Pellegrino mineral water. After remarrying Laurie, Ted had moved back into the home with her and Matt in Tangletown, an old section of Minneapolis. Its streets followed the twists in Minnehaha Creek, which flowed through the middle of the neighborhood. It was a great metaphor for their fragile relationship.

As he added a slice of lemon, Laurie walked into the kitchen. She gave him a quick hug, but pulled back to look at him, searching his face for clues about the case. He ignored her purposely and looked out across the back yard. It sloped down toward the creek in a large green bulge that looked like the yard was pregnant. Through the open window he could smell damp leaves and the neighbor's lilac bushes.

Laurie said, "You're going to help him, aren't you?"

He set down the glass and looked into her eyes. When Laurie wanted information, they shrunk into green dots that stared back at him. Husbands and young children were forced to tell the truth. "Yes. I'll look at some of the evidence, talk with the prosecutor, and see what I can find out." He sat down.

Matt bounded into the kitchen. "Hey, gotta run. See you dudes later."

Laurie frowned and looked at the clock on the counter. "Soccer practice doesn't start for another hour."

"Yeah, but there are some girls involved, and they're all waiting for me," he kidded. "Hey, old man, are you gonna take Uncle Dan's case? Gonna crack some ass?"

"This isn't the soccer field," Laurie said.

"I'm doing Dan a small favor. Then I'll be out of it. You won't see my name in the papers."

The expression on Matt's face looked, for a moment, like he was disappointed. He smiled, jumped through the back door, and let it slam on his way out. The wine glasses in the cupboard clinked precariously.

"Too bad they never had any kids. With all that money they made, the monstrous house—Mina always felt bad that she couldn't get pregnant." Laurie pulled out a tall glass from the cupboard for her own water. Two ice cubes clinked into it when she brought them from the fridge.

"You were so close to her. Did you ever know or suspect she was seeing another guy?"

"Mina? Having an affair?" Laurie sniffed and gave a thin laugh as if to dismiss the idea immediately. "I know she had some, uh, problems with Danny, but I can't imagine her having an affair." She spoke quickly.

"Well, if Dan is innocent and someone else really killed her, what would be the motive?"

"I don't know. Robbery?"

"Nothing valuable was taken from the house." Ted shifted in the chair, feeling the hard wood jab into his back. "But if there was a jealous boyfriend—"

Laurie blinked her eyes and turned away.

Chapter Four

The following morning in the Hennepin County attorney's office on the twenty-second floor of the Government Center in Minneapolis, Sanford Rogin III plotted his moves. If the investigation went as he thought it would, Rogin was going to charge and convict Dan Jensen. And he'd flick off Ted Rohrbacher like a fly.

Rogin's team leader, Zehra Hassan, and a paralegal met with him in his large office. Hassan had become a famous prosecutor after successfully winning dozens of high-profile cases and, more importantly, surviving a couple attempts on her life. She had finally agreed to get out of the line of fire and instead supervise a team of prosecutors in the office. No one was more qualified to do so than Zehra Hassan.

Not that Rogin wanted any supervision. In his mid-thirties, he craved the spotlight now. When he'd graduated from Northwestern University law school, he'd worked in private practice for a few years but grew tired of constantly reviewing construction contracts that were thicker than most books. When the opportunity arose for a job as an assistant county attorney, he'd jumped at it. The work was much more interesting, even if the pay was lower.

Rogin had developed a dream—someday he would become the first assistant to the elected county attorney. It was the first assistant who really ran the office and had the power. On its face, the plan was ludicrous. Rogin was an introvert, had few friends, and was more of a technician in the law than management material. But he knew that a good prosecutor had to be like a steel plow—once you charged a case, you dropped the heavy metal plow, ground forward without hesitation, and never missed any details. Rogin's tenacity would win out in the end. Now he'd been assigned one of the biggest murder cases to ever come through the office—the perfect vehicle to carry him into the new position.

And because of the gruesome details and the missing body, the press had picked up the case and had run it in the news almost every day. It couldn't be better for Sanford Rogin, except for the fact the investigation wasn't finished. But he was so certain of Jensen's guilt, Rogin had already drafted the complaint. As soon as he could, he'd file it and start the criminal process. He'd be the first prosecutor to ever win a murder case without a body. It would certainly be tough, but the evidence collected so far was just enough to prevail. Especially with the medical examiner's testimony about the quantity of blood found at the crime scene. Sandford Rogin III would be famous.

But for now, there was also the annoying presence of Zehra Hassan.

"You should at least give Rohrbacher the courtesy of sharing all the police reports. Let him know what the evidence is so far," Zehra warned Rogin.

"I'll give him some of it."

"Of course, but I was on the defense side years ago. I know what a tough job he's got."

"I don't give a shit. He's a schmuck. Grant bounced his ass out of this office years ago for good reason."

Zehra glared at him. "Don't underestimate Ted. He's a lot smarter than you think, and he's tenacious. The more evidence he can look at, the better he can advise his client. It may save everyone time and money."

"This isn't about money, Zehra. It's about justice for Mina Jensen. To put a guilty son of a bitch away, any way we can." He drew out the words like he was lecturing her. "But you forgot one thing about Teddy—he's over the hill. He's scared shitless to even come back into a courtroom with a major case." Rogin laughed and held a file up in the air. Gary Hill, a third year law student at Hamline University, scrambled out of the couch and came over to Rogin's desk. Hill took the file. Rogin said to him, "Don't forget to check on the Q and A for Chopsticks."

"Who?"

"Dr. Helen Wong. The medical examiner. Did it ever occur to you that I need her statement?" Sarcasm tinged the edges of his words.

"I'll check on it now." Hill stood, cradled the file under his arm, and started to leave.

"You're an ass," Zehra told Rogin as she held out her arm to stop the law clerk. "I'm not going to stand for your racism about Dr. Wong, or anyone, for that matter. Drop it, Rogin, or I bounce you off this case now. If you think that stuff will get you anywhere around here, you're wrong. I don't ever want to hear something like that again. Got it?" Her nostrils flared as color spread through her face.

"Whatever." He reached for a blue racquetball on his desk and squeezed it rapidly in his left hand—although he never played racquetball.

"And I don't want you treating Gary the way you do. Apologize."

"He doesn't mind. That's the way I was broken in when I started. You gotta be tough to take all the bruising of a trial lawyer."

"Under me, things are different." She stood in front of him and wouldn't move.

"Sorry," Rogin said to the law clerk and chuckled as if he were in a locker room. Then he turned to Zehra. "And you don't need to babysit me." Gary Hill left the office.

"Believe me, I don't want to be here anymore than you want me here. Bud Grant ordered me to make sure nothing goes wrong. And nothing will."

"Aww. This is almost a lay-up for me." Rogin waved his hand in front of him to dismiss her concerns. He took a deep breath that stretched the blue suspenders over his chest. He'd gained a few pounds that he intended to shed before he charged Jensen and had to go to court. He looked out the window. At the street level, wind scattered leaves and scraps of paper across the city.

Rogin's dirty blond hair made him look older than his real age. Dark smudges under each eye emphasized the fact. He'd grown a thick beard to further intimidate people.

Hill came back in. "I got it here." He held up a manila folder stuffed with papers.

"Good work. I'll share it with Rohrbacher when I meet him." Rogin pumped his fist in the air, then changed the ball to his right hand. When he squished it, muscles in his forearm bulged in response.

Zehra planted her hands on her hips. "Don't screw this up, Sandy," she warned him.

"Is there a legal requirement that you notify defense counsel about all the evidence?" Hill asked.

"Not this early," Rogin barked before Zehra could say anything more. "Not yet."

"Because it's still in the investigative stage?"

"No, but if you're working with an honest defense lawyer, it's the smart thing to do," Zehra added. "You don't have to reveal everything, but give him a good idea of what his client is facing."

Rogin pointed at her. "There's nothing in the Code of Ethics."

"Technically." Zehra waved her hand at him. "And what if we decide, after all the investigation, that Jensen is innocent? Or that we can't prove his guilt beyond a reasonable doubt?"

"This is bullshit. That's possible, but I'm not gonna hold my breath. I say the guy's guilty. And as far as proving it, I know I can get him convicted."

"I'll make the final call on the case. We'll analyze the evidence and make the decision. Don't forget it."

Rogin's phone rang. He answered his wife's call. She asked him to stop at the store on the way home and buy lettuce and salad makings. "Sure, honey," Rogin said. "What's that? Swiss chard? I'm sure I can find it and, yes I'll ask for help if I can't." He softened his voice. "How's our little mouse, MacKenzie?"

"Too bad she learned to walk," she kidded. "I can't keep up with her."

"I'm up to my ass with the Jensen case, but I'll get home as soon as I can. Give you a break. Take a walk or something."

"How about a Cosmopolitan instead?" She laughed and hung up.

Zehra walked to the door of his office and leaned on the frame. "When do you meet with Ted?"

"Tomorrow morning. Should be quick." Rogin leaned back into the leather chair behind his desk. "Besides, I've got a secret weapon I can use on Rohrbacher."

"Oh?"

"With his background of ethical complaints, we could file another one against him."

Zehra dropped her arms along her sides, and her eyes opened wide. "That's not going to happen under my supervision."

Without moving his head, Rogin swung his eyes to look at her. "We'll see about that."

Zehra shook her heavy hair back from her face and glared at him. "Be very careful with this case. From my own experience, I know these investigations have a way of coming unraveled, just when you think everything's sewed up. It could easily blow up on you and ruin everything."

He pointed his index finger at her with his thumb up in the air to look like a pistol. "I'm all over it."

The next morning, accompanied by Gary Hill, Rogin stood in the hallway outside the main door of the county attorney's office. A large encampment of the media swarmed around him. Rogin lifted his chin and smiled as broadly as he could. "Mornin', folks. I don't have a lot of time."

Carolyn Bechter from Channel Six TV started. "Are you going to charge Jensen?"

"Too early to say. But this gruesome crime warrants the maximum charge and penalty," Rogin said.

A print media reporter asked, "Do you have any new evidence?"

Rogin took his time answering. He nodded but waited to build the suspense. "We do, indeed. I just learned that the victim's cell phone will be analyzed as soon as possible."

There were loud murmurs that ran through the crowd.

Bechter interrupted, "But Sandy, you still don't have a body?"

Rogin dropped his eyebrows to appear serious. "We're working on that. Besides, we have enough evidence to still go forward even if we don't find Mina Jensen's body." He looked at his watch and realized that Rorhbacher would be there in a few minutes. He didn't want to divert the media attention from himself to Rohrbacher. "Sorry, folks. There'll be more for you soon. I promise." He waved like a minister tending his flock of parishioners and stepped through the double doors into the grand jury room. Gary Hill followed him with a metal cart that looked like one from a grocery store. It overflowed with files and two laptops. Rogin wrapped his arm around Hill's shoulder and directed him to assemble the case across the long table.

The room was the largest space on three floors. Around the outer edge, two rows of comfortable chairs ringed the walls. In the open center, two tables sat side by side. One had a silver coffee pot on it while the other held many objects stacked on it, each enclosed in plastic bags.

Rogin could have used a regular conference room for the meeting, but he wanted to impress Rorhbacher by reminding him of the power of the prosecutor's office. No expense had been spared to pay for the investigation, testing, forensic analysis, witnesses, law clerks, computer programs, and victim/witness advocates.

It was five minutes after nine o'clock when a clerk brought in hot coffee and water. The juror's seats that circled the edges of the room were vacant now. After a sip of hot water—he never drank coffee—Rogin looked around and smiled to himself.

"Do you know Ted?" Gary Hill asked.

Rogin snorted quickly. "He was in this office a few years ago. I thought he was a loser back then, and I was proved right when he screwed up a major murder case."

"But Zehra seems to think he's a really good lawyer."

"Her opinion. He's hiding out in the suburbs. Afraid to come back into battle in a courtroom."

The left door of the double set opened, and Ted Rohrbacher walked in. Rogin saw a tall, thin man who carried a thick leather briefcase. He moved quickly and shook Rogin's hand, then turned to Hill. Ted's grasp was firm and dry. He accepted coffee and sat down across the table from Rogin.

"Sandy," he said.

"I prefer Sanford. How's business?"

"It's great. I'm busy and making some good money for once."

Rogin waved his hand. "We got serious stuff to discuss here. What do you want to know?"

"I told you that I agreed to represent Dan Jensen only while the case was being investigated. I haven't seen any of the police or forensic reports."

"I've got the physical evidence seized at the house over on that table." He pointed at the pile of objects encased in plastic bags. "But let's start with the medical examiner's statement."

"Dr. Wong?"

"Right." Rogin glanced over at Hill, who handed the manila file to him. Rogin tossed it on the table in front of Ted. "Be my guest. We'll give you the lead detective's statement, too. Oh, I forgot. This is Gary Hill, one of my law clerks." Ted nodded toward Hill while Rogin stood up.

He started to leave. He stopped and turned to Hill. "You brought Father O'Brien's statement, didn't you?"

"Who?"

"The lead investigating detective," Rogin said and looked at Ted. "We call him 'Father' because he gets more confessions out of these thugs than anyone I know."

Hill dug through the metal cart beside the table and pulled out another manila folder. "Here it is." He set it on the table beside Ted.

Rogin clapped Hill on the shoulder to thank him and walked to the door. "Enjoy the light reading, Ted. I've got to work on getting your client charged." Rogin left the room.

Ted opened the manila file and removed a transcript-like document. It was a question and answer format taken by the chief investigator, Detective Sean O'Brien from the Minnetonka Police Department. He had interviewed Dr. Helen Wong. Ted pulled out his laptop, set it on the table, and booted it up. He'd take notes.

Interview with Dr. Helen Wong. MPD Case # 345-576773 Detective S. O'Brien. M. Carville reporting.

Q: State your name and title, please.

A: I am the chief medical examiner for Hennepin County, and I am a professor at the medical school at the University of Minnesota.

Q: You hold both positions?

A: Yes.

Q: Tell us what your educational background has been to qualify you as the medical examiner.

A: Medical degree from the University of Minnesota and a post graduate degree in forensic science from Columbia University. I also have a law degree from Hamline University.

Q: I'll refer you to the evening of May tenth of this year. Do you recall an investigation you went on?

A: Yes. I remember because it was unusually warm and humid weather at the scene. We opened some of the bedroom windows to cool off.

Q: Do you always go to the scene?

A: Not me, personally. Usually one of our newer physicians would do that. In this case, I was scheduled to be on duty anyway, and according to the police, they'd rarely seen anything like what they found.

Q: What did you bring with you?

A: Nothing high-tech like you see on TV. I bring my GPS to find the crime scene, a paper notebook, my iPad, a magnifying glass, a flashlight, and latex gloves. Depending on where I'm going, I may even take sunscreen or insect repellant. A lot of what I do at the crime scene is pretty low-tech.

Q: Sherlock Holmes-tech, huh? What are your responsibilities at a crime scene?

A: I could put it this way: all medical examiners subscribe to the Locard Exchange Principle.

Q: What's that?

A: Edmund Locard was a police officer and professor in France. He developed the principle that at a crime scene, wherever the criminal stepped, whatever he touched, or whatever he left serves as a witness against him. That can include fingerprints, footprints, hair, fibers from his clothing, glass he breaks, tool marks, blood, semen, any evidence like that can be used against him. As Professor Lo-card often said, "This is evidence that, unlike human wit-nesses, does not forget, is factual, and can't be wrong."

Q: Okay. What do you mean?

A: I look for any of this kind of evidence. Usually, the body itself will provide much of the evidence. Of course, in this case, that wasn't possible.

Q: We'll come back to that, Doctor.

Ted continued to read as Detective O'Brien led her through a series of questions that revealed the evidence she and the techs had accumulated: the mattress samples, the photos from every possible angle, samples of the blood from the wooden floor and from the wall, an estimate of the quantity of blood, a bloody footprint found outside the bedroom, the blood spatter analysis, and the work done to attempt retrieval of fingerprints. He kept reading.

Q: Did you test the blood?

A: At the scene we do a preliminary test with an instru-ment called a hemastix. It will identify the substance as blood, but it can't tell us if it's human, animal, or rat. More specific testing was done in the lab. We took samples from twenty different spots at the scene.

Q: And could you identify whose blood it was?

A: Through DNA testing, it was an identical match to the blood from Mina Jensen.

Q: Where did you get the match?

A: We were able to contact a blood bank that had drawn blood from her.

Q: Find any fingerprints?

A: Of course, the technicians found dozens of finger-prints all over the scene. But they were from both Mr. and Mrs. Jensen. An unusual one was a thumb and forefinger with faint blood stains, on the back door frame. I'm not sure the lab has identified the source yet.

Q: Did you find any others?

A: Yes. But most of them proved to be relatives and a person identified as Nicholas Korsokov. Apparently, he was a friend of the deceased. There were also many prints that couldn't be identified.

Q: Can you establish the cause of death?

A: No. Since there wasn't a body, I can't say that conclusively.

Q: Do you have an opinion as to whether a death even occurred?

A: I do think there was a death of a human being.

Q: And how can you say that?

A: We were able to estimate the quantity of blood that had been left at the scene in the bedroom and the spa downstairs. There was a significant amount of pooling of blood in both locations. The human body contains approximately five liters of blood. At the scene, we estimated there was about four quarts. Anyone who had bled out that much couldn't possibly survive and would have died. If not in the room, then later somewhere else. There's no doubt the victim would be dead.

Q: So, you can't say that death was caused by blows to the head or trauma to the body?

A: No. I can't speculate on the exact cause. However, the scene showed obvious violence on a massive scale. All I can say is that the loss of blood was of such a quantity, no human could have survived it or the probable trauma as shown by the bloodstains.

Ted placed the report on the table and reached for the other file folder, O'Brien's own report. Ted remembered him from the time Ted was a prosecutor. O'Brien was a small man with a permanent squint caused by too many years of holding a smoldering cigarette in his mouth.

Interview with Homicide Detective Sean O'Brien, Minnetonka Police Department. MPD Case #345-576773, Sergeant P. Larson. M. Carville reporting.

Q: Please give us your name.

A: Detective Sean O'Brien, Minnetonka Police—Homicide.

Q: How long have you been with the police department?

A: Twenty-eight years. Started right after I got out of the Marines. I made homicide detective eleven years ago.

Q: Were you assigned the case of Mina Jensen?

A: Roger that. I was assigned as the chief investigator and was at the scene of the crime within five minutes of the call.

Q: Did you find anything unusual about the crime scene?

A: The body was missing.

Q: Anything else unusual?

A: The smaller bedroom, the one they used as a media room, had a square mark left by a rug. The color of the carpeting inside the square was darker than the surrounding carpeting. Probably because the outside carpeting faded. Means someone took the rug out.

Q: And why is that important?

A: Well, assuming the murder occurred in the other bedroom, the body was gone when we got there, right? That means the killer had to dispose of it somehow without leaving any evidence. We did find a long streak of blood at the door to the hallway, but that was it.

Q: Did you find any other blood deposits in the house?

A: Yes, sir. The floor had several streaks of dried blood. There were spatters on the walls and ceiling, and a large quantity of blood on the side of the mattress. Along the edge where the floor met the wall was a blood stain that looked like someone had dabbed a mop. Probably the victim's hair. It suggested a violent fight where the body was thrown from one spot to another. The main bedroom has a circular staircase in the corner that leads to a lower-level spa underneath the bedroom. It appeared that at some point, the body rested next to the staircase for some time as the blood pooled both at the top of the stairs on the wooden floor and dripped down the stairs to pool in the lower level. The quantity was so large, some of that was still wet. The techs took samples from all over. So our working theory is the killer took the rug from the other room, dragged the body a short distance, then wrapped it in the rug to get it out of the house without leaving a trail of blood.

Q: Why do you think that?

A: A body that was bleeding as much as this one probably did would leave a trail a mile wide. But we found nothing outside the bedroom and the lower-level spa. It had to have been wrapped in something. The rug seems the most likely.

Q: Did you question Mr. Daniel Jensen about this incident?

A: We had several talks.

Q: Did he ever confess to a crime?

A: No. He denied killing his wife, although he did admit having a fight with her just prior to the murder.

Q: Is that unusual to deny it?

A: No. It's human nature. None of us wants to admit to doing something wrong. Everyone I've ever interrogated has minimized or evaded the truth—for a while.

Q: Did you investigate the family's cars?

A: Yes, sir. We did a thorough check of both cars, including the trunks.

Q: Did you find anything?

A: We found the victim's car parked near the beach on Lake Minnetonka. We checked the trunk and didn't see anything. However, the boys from the sheriff's crime lab did a Leucocrystal Violet test.

Q: And what's that?

A: It's a chemical that turns bright purple when put on a surface where blood is located—even if it's been washed off and can't be seen by the naked eye. They found some traces of blood in the trunk of the victim's car, which turned out to have been the same type of blood as Mina Jensen. Other than that, there wasn't any other evidence in the car. And no body.

Q: You find this unusual?

A: Yes. Maybe the rug was thick enough to soak up the excess blood, or maybe the victim was fitted into a sealed plastic bag. I don't know for sure. Our working theory at this point is the body was transported in her own car and disposed of at some point. A lake is a common place to dispose of a dead body.

Q: Are you still searching for the body?

A: Of course. We've also got the county sheriffs helping us since our jurisdiction ends at the borders of the city. Besides, they can use their water patrol to search the lake.

Ted closed the report and leaned back into the comfortable chair. He didn't feel comfortable at all. He glanced at his laptop but knew he didn't need to take any notes. Of course, there was more evidence that he would look at, but Rogin had purposely given him the most damaging evidence. Things looked bad for Danny Jensen.

As a former prosecutor, Ted understood why Rogin was so confident. Still, there were a few aspects that bothered Ted. The fact that Korsokov's fingerprints had been found. The man with whom Mina Jensen was having an affair? Then there was still the conflict of interest problem that Ted would have to figure out. In spite of Dr. Wong's opinion, the victim's body was still missing, and it would make it harder for Rogin to prove Dan guilty beyond a reasonable doubt. Then there was Dan himself. His "amygdala hijack" might provide some kind of defense, or at least give Ted bargaining power. Ted wasn't sure how he would present it, but the challenge tantalized him. But even if Rogin wouldn't listen to it, what if Ted could get a judge to agree to the defense? It had never been done before; therefore, the chances were slim. Only a really good lawyer could pull that off. That lawyer could be Ted Rohrbacher.

He thought of what Rogin would do next. Once the investigation was finished, if Rogin still believed Jensen was guilty, Rogin would sign and file the complaint accusing Jensen of second degree murder. But Rogin wouldn't stop at that. Within a few days, he would take the case before the grand jury. In Minnesota, only a grand jury could indict a suspect with first degree murder—which carried a much heavier penalty than the second degree murder. Rogin would present the evidence to the jury, without the public present as the rules allowed, and get the indictment. The statutory penalty would mean Dan Jensen could face life in prison without the possibility of parole—ever.

Chapter Five

When Sanford Rogin returned to the grand jury room, Ted had packed up his laptop and was ready to leave. Rogin talked to Ted but didn't look at him, as if Rogin were too busy. "Got everything you need, Teddy?"

"I'd like to follow up with the other reports you have."

"Sure, but see what I told you? Your boy's in a shit load of trouble."

"You've got a few problems with the case."

Rogin shrugged. "If a prosecutor waits for the perfect case, he'll never win anything."

"What if Jensen's innocent?"

"You defense lawyers all say that. If you can show me he's innocent, I'll do my ethical duty and drop the case. But unless the investigation turns up something weird, I'm betting on Jensen."

"Would you do me a favor?"

"For you, of course."

"If you do file the complaint, give me the courtesy of calling me first. I'd like to prepare my client."

"By all means. Have a great day, Teddy."

Ted left the room and turned to the right to go down the stairwell at the north end of the building to avoid the press. He exited two floors below and took the elevator to the Public Service level. He thought of calling Laurie to assure her that he was almost out of the case. Ted tried her cell phone. She didn't pick up. He dialed her direct line at work, even though she'd asked him never to call her there.

She answered. "Ted, what have I told you?"

"I . . . I was at the prosecutor's office just now. I looked at some of the evidence against Dan Jensen."

She spoke quickly. "It's all wrapped up?"

"Uh, not yet."

"Ted—" Her voice took on a sharp edge.

"Laurie, I owe him a little bit of help."

"Why? Why would someone who did that to my cousin—"

He didn't know how to respond. Finally, he told her, "Samantha's checking on a possible suspect."

"You know how I feel about all this."

"Of course."

"So why are you doing this to me?"

Ted could picture Laurie turning around in her chair, twisting the hair along the side of her face between her fingers. He could also see her face coloring red with anger. "Okay, there's more here than I thought originally. It shouldn't take long to check out things. You know I don't want to get back into court, and especially into a big media case like this. Sam will do most of the work."

Laurie didn't answer for a long time. "I'll see you tonight." She hung up.

He pocketed his cell phone and walked across Fourth Avenue to the parking ramp in long strides. He smelled the food trucks on the plaza selling hot dogs, hamburgers with onions, and Mexican fajitas. Blue and yellow umbrellas sheltered the vendors from the hot sun. He calmed down. His phone rang and he took Samantha's call.

"You still want to see the crime scene? I got clearance from the MPD and the prosecutor," she told him.

He didn't answer for a moment. He always dreaded going to crime scenes. The place of death retained bad odors, like the smell of smoke that stayed in clothing. And since he and Laurie had been there often, it made the journey even more difficult.

In ten minutes, he picked up Samantha at her house, drove through traffic to get out to the suburb of Minnetonka on the west side of Minneapolis, and thought the only good thing about the trip was that he'd been able to put the top down on the Mercedes. It was black like the color of the car and the leather interior.

They curved slowly around the streets leading to the house. A soft breeze, scented with lilacs, swirled into the open car. All the forensic work had been completed, which meant Ted and Sam wouldn't disturb any possible evidence, although they'd still be careful during their time inside.

Ted crawled along the street until he came to the long curving driveway. It was a huge house set among even bigger homes that all fronted on Lake Minnetonka. Some had iron fences with stone gates closed to the public. The Jensen house was sheathed in gray shakes with black trim and had dull red shutters on each window. Set up on a low mound of land, it looked even larger.

"They must've been raking it in." Samantha whistled as they turned into the curved drive.

"I hadn't seen Dan for years, so I've never been out here." When they stopped, Ted felt a flutter in his chest. The old case, the one he'd lost, had occurred at a home in the same suburb. It was also on the lake, and a young girl named Katie had been killed in that house. Today she'd be about his son Matt's age.

The neighbor's house had a stand of lilac bushes that leaned over from the weight of hundreds of purple flowers. The fragrance perfumed the still air around the Mercedes. Ted paused for a moment in the open car to breathe it all in. He felt better.

Beyond the house, the lake rippled in shiny waves, and gulls cawed sharply. Their white wings contrasted against the dense green trees behind them. A Meridian yacht cut through the dark water. At three stories tall, it looked like a floating wedding cake.

"Come on, Counselor." Sam reminded him of the job they had to do. She wore a black wig with straight hair and copper highlights. When he squinted at it, she explained, "Too busy this morning."

An American flag rippled in the wind on a pole in the front yard. Strips of yellow tape still covered the front door. They'd been given a key along with permission to enter the house. Samantha carried a digital camera, and Ted had brought a small hand-held tape recorder. Over the years, they'd found the combination worked the best. Sam hefted her large handbag from the back seat and strapped it over her shoulder.

"Let's get this over with," Ted urged her.

When they got closer to the house, the immensity of it stretched away on both sides. A path of black and gray slate led to the front door. Woodpeckers tapped at the corner of the house to dig into the cedar shakes. Birds called from the surrounding trees. Ted ducked under the tape and unlocked the front door. He paused for a moment before entering. Samantha gave him a shove from behind.

Inside, the house smelled stale—like he remembered his elderly grandmother's house, but without the mothball odor. It was silent. No sounds of air conditioners whirring, no water softeners running, and no televisions chattering in the background. It took several minutes to cross through the living room over soft carpeting to enter into the kitchen. It had a wooden floor and was large enough to accommodate a wooden table surrounded by eight chairs. An abandoned toaster rested on the counter with a trail of bread crumbs leading away from it. Like pieces of black rice, mouse turds circled the crumbs. A jar of blueberry jam sat next to the toaster along with a butter knife beside it. Two clean bowls were propped upside down in the sink. The faucet dripped, and the splat of water sounded loud.

The kitchen was expensively decorated, but it looked like it had been used mostly for making coffee and toast.

Ted hesitated to walk into the house further, especially because he had known Mina. But it was absolutely necessary to get a feel for the crime scene. As a prosecutor he'd been to several of them. After a while, they blurred into similar impressions. The lack of human life pervaded everything. He could never put his finger on what caused the feeling. Was it the silence? The stale smell? The absence of the normal groans and creaks of a living space? Or were there ghosts that had taken over now?

After Rogin e-mailed more of the police and forensic reports, Ted and Samantha had skimmed through them. Today their purpose was to simply absorb the scene and try to find something, anything that might be of use in Dan Jensen's defense. Maybe they'd discover a clue the police had overlooked.

They circled the main house first, leaving the bedroom and the death scene for last. Off of the living room was a large media room. A square pattern in the middle of the carpeting was brighter than the surrounding material. A rug had lain there while the rest of the carpeting was discolored from use. A large flat-screen TV hung from the far wall. Unlike in most homes, it was flanked by two floor-to-ceiling bookshelves that stretched to both corners of the room. Ted walked to the one on the right side. He read down through the titles. Mina must have been the reader. Her tastes were eclectic. A biography of Gloria Steinem, a history of the civil rights movement, a dog-eared copy of a book on how to grow hostas, an entire row of Patricia Cornwell's novels, a dictionary, several three-ring binders with titles about "big data" on them, and a book with a red cover about Buddhism.

A container of DVDs sat next to the TV. They were filed in a long row and in alphabetical order. Not one was out of place. Ted read through some of them: *The Best of Agatha Christie Mysteries, CSI Miami*, the *Daily Show, Downton Abbey, Homeland, Rizzoli and Isles, Saturday Night Live (The Best of)*, and more *CSI* episodes. On top of a plastic square a dog dish was tipped over in the corner.

He followed Samantha toward the back bedrooms. They passed through many other rooms. All of them were decorated and full of furniture, but unused. The hall was more narrow and claustrophobic than Ted recalled. Tan carpeting muffled their steps as they walked forward. Several photos hung along one side. Grandparents, parents, and what appeared to be siblings. By far, the majority of photos were of their pet dog, a Jack Russell. He had been photographed in every conceivable activity—eating, jumping, lying on the floor, wagging his tail, and cuddled on Mina's lap. Ted saw the color of the dog matched the color of Mina's hair.

The photos brought back a few memories of Mina, her infectious laugh and the killer smile that could cause a lot of men to melt. But there was something odd about the photos. Ted had never noticed before that of all the photos, there were none of Mina and Dan together.

At the end of the hall were two bedrooms. Before they reached either one, they encountered a long brown streak across the blond wooden floor at the edge of the bedroom. This must be the blood smear that the experts had identified as having been left by a body dragged out from the second bedroom.

Ted stepped around it carefully. He could see where the techs had cut several sections of the mattress and removed them for testing in order to identify it as human blood, in the first place, and try to match it with a person. With his back against the wall, Ted edged further along the hallway. When he reached the first bedroom, he glanced into it. A desk sat in the corner with a cooling pad for a laptop on it. The police had seized Mina's computer that had been there. A bookshelf crowned the top of the desk with various books and three-ring binders all lined up in neat order. There wasn't any evidence in the room, so Ted kept moving toward the second one.

He turned through a narrow door and stopped to catch his breath.

On the far wall, floor-to-ceiling French windows opened onto a stunning view of Lake Minnetonka. The windows made a turn at the corner of the house and continued to give him a view of the outdoors. He saw two Adirondack chairs set at an angle to each other on a stone path that led down toward the lake. A tanning cot flanked the chairs. Mature trees bunched over the yard, casting much of it in shadows.

The reports had all mentioned the quantity of blood in the room, but nothing prepared Ted for what he saw. There were more chocolate stains all over the room than he could imagine. It looked like half the floor was soaked in blood. Next to the door someone's bloody foot had left a print. About the only thing the forensic people had been able to identify was the size of it, judging it to be a male foot, size eleven. They had also identified the blood on the shoe as Mina's, the same throughout the bedroom. A brown splotch on the side of the mattress led down to a dried lake of blood on the floor below it.

It wasn't readily identifiable, but Ted could barely see the faint outline of a head and shoulders.

The blood stretched out in streaks around the room as if the body had been moved during the assault. A large pool surrounded the top of a circular stairwell that disappeared into the spa below the bedroom. Ted looked down into the dim light and saw another large pool of blood on the tile floor below. It puddled next to a Stairmaster.

On the arm a small white towel hung limply, one side of it drizzled with cinnamon stains.

Various objects were scattered around the room: pillows, some books in the corner on the floor, and a glass vase. Pieces of it lay along the opposite wall from the bed. It must have shattered when it hit the wall as there were faint remains of a water stain on the wall about three feet off the floor. Dead lilies, their stems now gray, lay among the shards of glass.

Ted stopped moving and tried to breathe deeply. All his thoughts of Mina in this house, alive, with Dan, came flooding back to him. Maybe he shouldn't have come out here after all.

Samantha tapped his arm. When he looked up, she pointed to the far wall. Several brown spatters of dried blood rose along the wall and over the ceiling. Some formed round globs, while many looked like spear points with a triangular head on top and a long, dripping tail that fell toward the floor. They both studied the wall for a long time.

Samantha said, "I'm not an expert, but it looks like someone stood about here." She inched her way along the side of the bed, careful not to step in the dried blood on the floor. She turned around the edge of the pool of blood until her back faced toward the far wall. Sam stopped and looked over her shoulder at the wall again. "Right here. Using a blunt instrument, the blood must have collected on it and, as it was swung, some of the blood spattered onto the wall."

Ted moved his head as if he were watching the arc of the weapon.

"We'll have to interview the analyst and see what she has to say. See if there's anything she may have left out of the official report," Sam said. "I think it was someone from the sheriff's lab named Mooney."

"Look at that." Ted pointed at another area of the wall to the left. The blood pattern there revealed several sizes of drops, some large, dripping, others smaller droplets. And some looked like they were propelled across the surface, stretching up toward the ceiling at about the same angle.

"Anyone find the murder weapon?" Sam asked.

Ted shook his head. "Not yet."

Samantha walked over to the wall and peered at it closely. "The velocity of the assault will cause different patterns. See here." She tipped her head toward the longer streaks. "Those probably came when the weapon was moving at the maximum arc and velocity."

"How do you know that?"

She grinned. "You can't be a homicide detective for as long as I was without picking up some of this stuff. I also studied a lot on my own." She looked back at the wall. "These are called cast-off patterns. I'm assuming the experts also determined the point of convergence."

"Where the murderer was standing?"

"Right. They can even tell the probable height of the killer and whether he was right or left handed."

"I've watched the crime scene analysts do it. I remember they used to stretch strings from each stain along its probable direction. Then they measured the angles of the strings to pinpoint where the blood originated from—where the body was when the killer used the instrument."

"We know enough to be dangerous." Sam laughed as if to counter the feeling of violent death all around them. "We could probably commit a crime and get away with it."

Next Ted walked to a spot on the wall where a bullet had penetrated. It left a large puncture in the sheetrock. He could see where the analysts had dug out the bullet itself. If it had left a deep enough hole, the angle could be measured and an estimation of the location from which the gun was fired could be determined. The analysts at the sheriff's crime lab had identified the caliber as a .38 and the striations left on the bullet from when it squeezed through the barrel of the gun. If the gun were ever found, they could compare the striations on the bullet to the gun itself for a match.

Ted noticed that he'd been sighing involuntarily. He couldn't help it. The thought of what must have happened in this space, the broken body, the pain, and the rage. He could almost hear Mina's screams and feel the violence to her. He swayed on his feet.

Samantha pulled on his arm and led the way out of the room. "Has Dan given any hints where the body is?" She must have had the same feelings Ted had had while thinking of Mina's body and the sacrilege of just dumping it somewhere without concern.

"Says he fought with a stranger who must've taken the body, so therefore, how could he know where it is?" It was hard to talk.

As he backed out of the room, Ted looked at the footprint again. He kneeled beside it. A sharp line ringed one edge while the middle faded into the color of the wooden floor. There were no tell-tale markings of tread type or defects in the sole of the shoe for identification purposes. Ted called to Samantha, "Do we know what size shoe Jensen wears?"

She had reached the kitchen already. From her large handbag, she pulled out her laptop and set it on a corner of the counter. In a few minutes, she had scrolled through the investigation reports and interviews done by the police. "Let's see. He's a size nine and a half," she called down the hallway. "That one is a size eleven."

Ted stood and came into the kitchen. "The police interviewed a guy named Korsokov. He's the guy they suspect of having an affair with Mina. We should talk to him also."

Samantha shrugged. "My guess is the cops probably concluded our friend Danny is the most obvious suspect. They would've questioned this other guy, but sometimes they miss things. I'll run down the mysterious man of the bedroom."

"Great."

"From when you were a prosecutor, Ted, you know how these cases work. There's unbelievable pressure to get a suspect identified and get a conviction as soon as possible."

"Maybe they're moving too quickly in this case." Ted looked at her. "After all, Korsokov's fingerprints were found all over in the kitchen."

She sniffed. "You're reaching for the clouds, T-man. He admitted that he'd been here before. Doesn't prove *when* he was here or that he killed her."

"Just trying to think of anything that may—"

"I know. You think like a defense lawyer. I'm the one to remind you of reality occasionally."

"Thanks," he said sarcastically.

"Hey, where's the Jack Russell?"

"Dan's got him where he's staying at his sister's house. Jon Stewart is the dog's name." Ted stopped to think. "Why didn't the dog bark?"

"Huh?"

"With all the violence going on in that bedroom, you'd think the dog would've gone wild. Tried to protect Mina. But none of the neighbors reported hearing any barking." Ted walked to the kitchen door and stood for a moment. "And what's the motive for the killing?"

"Rogin's going with domestic violence, plain and simple," Sam said.

"Dan told me they were trying to patch things up." His eyes caught Samantha's eyes. "Mina had asked him to try a new start."

Her head lolled forward. "And it's not Dan's fault he's got some mental problems. War does that to lots of people. I got an older friend who came back from Viet Nam hooked on drugs. Took him years to kick. Too late for the rest of his family." She blinked her eyes. Samantha straightened and folded the laptop closed. "Anything else here, T-man?"

"I have to get out." They hurried back through the living room. Ted's eyes searched for any other possible piece of evidence that might have been missed. He locked the front door, and they walked back to the Mercedes sitting in the sun with the top down.

Samantha tugged on the side of her wig to readjust it. "The prosecutor still has a major problem—no body." She leaned her hip against the side of the car. "Never seen a case like this in all my years."

Ted took several deep breaths of fresh air. He could smell the lake. "And there's no direct evidence in there to prove Dan was the killer. No murder weapon with his fingerprints on it, for instance. It's all circumstantial at this point." His voice carried a hopeful tone to it.

Sam frowned. "We still don't have a defense."

"The amygdala hijack?"

Sam waved her hand in front of her chest. "Forget it." Sam opened to door to the car, dropped her laptop on the back, and settled into the passenger seat. "We have to find Korsokov. Maybe he's the stranger Dan fought with."

When Ted turned the key in the ignition of the Mercedes, the engine was so quiet that he couldn't hear it start. He always left a crime scene with the same lonely, sad feeling. This one had been the worst. He knew where the feeling came from. Human life was large: the physiological miracle of a functioning body, the laughter, hard work, playing sports, and having sex to procreate even more life. But every crime scene seemed to shrink life. The spaces were confined. The distances from daily life shortened. Death reduced everyone to a small, sad ending.

Ted took a deep breath. He smelled the new buds on the lilac bushes and watched them bob in the faint breeze. They were alive and anxious to blossom in bright purple colors.

Chapter Six

After several days of fruitless pursuit of Nikolai Korsokov, Ted and Samantha decided to hunt him down at his workplace. The police had interviewed him after his fingerprints were discovered at the Jensen home. Korsokov worked as an ambulance driver and a hot yoga instructor at the All Fitness Center.

"So, if you're dumping the case, why are we doing all this?" Samantha asked Ted.

He frowned and said, "If I'm going to investigate the case, I need to do a thorough job. If we find anything incriminating about Korsokov that the police missed, it could mean Dan's case might be dismissed. Quick and easy. That's all."

Sam's brows dipped over her eyes. She didn't believe a word he said. "And the fact that Mina is your wife's cousin—that's not a conflict of interest for you?"

"Probably is. I'm not sure how to handle it right now. But I'll be out of the case before that issue blows up."

She scrolled through notes on her iPhone. "Looks like the cops talked to him initially, but let him go since they figured our boy is the killer."

"But the guy had an affair with the victim—he sure looks suspicious."

They drove in Ted's car north on Chicago Avenue toward the hospital where Korsokov often worked driving the ambulance. Along the street small buds opened on the trees, giving them light green halos. Ted swerved around a bus lumbering away from the curb. Turning onto 28th Street, he found the entrance to the inner courtyard of the hospital campus. He slowed down to enter the parking ramp on the right side. They came out into the sunshine, squinting at the change from the darkened ramp.

At the emergency entrance, Sam and Ted talked to the admissions nurse. She said Korsokov was on duty and had just gone across the campus to the cafeteria for his lunch break. "Can't miss him. He's big," the nurse told them.

They crossed the courtyard that stretched for almost two blocks between the wings of the hospital. In the center, shaded by new growth on the trees, several picnic tables and lounge chairs hid among the bushes. It looked like a quiet park on a college campus. Several people lounged at the tables or lay on the grass, eating and drinking. Most of them wore light blue smocks with matching pants. Hospital couture.

Samantha led the way. They walked through the park and went inside to ride an escalator down to the basement level cafeteria. They had both studied a photo of Korsokov from mug shots taken at the police precinct. He was a tall man with blond hair, broad shoulders, and blue eyes that were slightly crossed.

Luckily, Ted spotted their man in a back corner, finishing off a plate of spaghetti. Ted signaled Sam, and they both backed off by the entry to wait. Samantha bought a bottle of mineral water. The dining room resembled the United Nations with people from every part of the globe eating their lunch. They were all dressed in either light blue smocks or long white lab coats.

In ten minutes, Korsokov got up from the table and walked to the exit. He placed his tray on a moving belt and hitched his camouflage pants up around his waist. He wore a dark blue shirt with a logo on the chest that read Fischer Ambulance Service. He had a plastic ID card clipped to the upper pocket of the shirt. He was in good shape, and his chest stretched the fabric of the shirt tightly across his chest.

Samantha and Ted followed him out of the cafeteria to the escalator and up to the street level.

Korsokov walked toward the park in the middle of the complex. He stopped to look up at the clear sky before he started to walk to the left where his ambulance was parked. Sam and Ted surrounded him immediately. Sam pushed her private investigator badge into his face while Ted stood on the other side.

Korsokov blinked a few times, jerked his head back and forth, and stopped. "What? What you want?" He spoke with what sounded like a Russian accent.

"Just to talk for a while," Sam spoke softly. Between the tone of her voice and the way she used her body to crowd him a little, she was effective. It came from all that police training about interrogation, Ted figured. It always amazed him how she was able to not only get people to stop for her, but also to talk to her. Sometimes people even began crying as they confessed painful secrets to Samantha Carter. She could've been a successful minister, salesperson, or con man.

"I got nothing to say to anyone," he sneered.

"I think you've got a lot to say." She introduced herself and Ted.

Ted told him, "I'm representing Mina Jensen's husband in a criminal investigation. There's evidence that you knew the deceased . . . uh, Mina. That true?"

"What if I did?"

Samantha smiled up at him and looped her arm inside of his. He wore a heavy gold wrist band. They started to move off deeper into the park. Korsokov allowed her to walk him into a shaded spot at the end. Quiet and alone. She said, "We know you were seeing her and that she had a bad marriage." They both sat while Ted stood above them.

"I already talked to the police. Why should I talk to you?" Korsokov said.

"We could always get a subpoena to force you to talk. Want to do this the easy way?" Ted asked.

"See, we can do that in this country," Sam said. "Let's talk about you."

"Like you Americans always say—Whatever. Stay cool." He crossed thick arms over his chest. His expression looked passive on the surface, but underneath he seemed cocky and cunning.

"You married?"

Korsokov wouldn't answer.

"Where are you from originally?"

He frowned. "Moscow."

Samantha shook her head. "You're not Russian. I can tell by your accent."

"Yes, I am—"

"No, you aren't."

"Okay. Ukraine. Kiev. Hate those bastard Russians, but when I tell Americans I am from Ukraine, no one knows where it is. So I say Russian." He smiled briefly at his own cleverness.

"How long have you been here?"

"About four years."

"How long have you driven the ambulance?"

"Not long. A year, maybe." Korsokov looked out at the open spaces in the park, glanced over his shoulder, and turned back to face Samantha. He acted unperturbed.

She waited before asking the next question. "You're not legal, are you?"

Korsokov didn't respond.

"Don't worry." She pulled out her badge again and showed it to him. "See, I'm a *private* investigator. You work with us; we'll work with you. How are you licensed to drive the ambulance?"

"I got friends," he grinned.

"Why did you come here?"

Korsokov hesitated. "I like the lakes."

Samantha snorted with contempt for his answer. "Who are you kidding?"

"I . . . I do have—how do you say it—distant relatives here. An uncle."

"What does he do?"

"I don't know."

Samantha looked at Ted and rolled her eyes. "You did spend time with Mina Jensen, didn't you?"

"Yeah."

"Did she talk about her marriage?"

"Told me it was bad. She wanted out." Korsokov became a little more cooperative.

"Did she say anything about her husband?" Sam asked.

Korsokov's eyes narrowed. "He was violent to her. They argued a lot. That's what she said."

The sound of birds chirping was drowned out when a lawnmower roared from the far end of the complex. Ted could see a man start to push a red mower along the edges of the grass. He walked fast, and when he turned the first corner of the lawn, the sound was muffled by his body. Cut grass spewed from the side of the mower, and the fresh cut smell floated toward them.

"Did she want to leave him?" Sam asked.

"She told me yes."

"How often did you see Mina?"

"Couple times a week. At my hot yoga class."

"Ever at her house?"

"Never."

Samantha sighed. "Nick, the neighbors said—" She bluffed him. Korsokov shrugged.

"And your fingerprints were found inside the house."

"Okay, okay. Two, maybe three times I was there when husband was gone." His shoulders hunched and he raised his palms into the air. "Never had sex. Never."

"Just for the record, Nicky, at this point in time I don't believe you," Sam told him. "Let's cut to the chase."

Korsokov's chest swelled in pride, but he didn't take the bait from Samantha.

She leaned closer to him. "Did you love her?"

Korsokov stood up abruptly. Ted moved to cut him off, but Sam held Ted back with a light tap on his arm. Korsokov walked a few steps away, turned around, and came back. He said, "I felt sorry for her. I wanted to help her. Her husband is brutal man."

"And marry her?"

"Yeah. Mina wanted to dump her husband, marry me, she said."

Samantha stood up and moved closer to Korsokov. "Nick, let's cut the bullshit."

The shrill whine of an ambulance cut through the peaceful park. As the ambulance turned into the emergency entrance, the sound died suddenly as if it had drowned in a pool of water.

Korsokov's eyes opened and he tilted his head as if he was trying to focus his slightly crossed eyes on her. He looked angry.

"You wanted to get married to Mina Jensen to get a green card. Isn't that the real reason?" Sam said.

"No."

"And you saw that big house and all the money she had. That looked good, didn't it?"

He wagged his head from side to side.

"Shall we talk more about you being illegal?"

"Okay, yeah. It looked good and I wanted a green card. But I wanted to help, too."

Sure you did," Samantha said with sarcasm in her voice. "How'd you meet her?"

"She started talking to me one night at class. She told me about husband and about green card and how lonely she is."

"Stop it, Nick. I don't like it when you lie to us. You already knew about marrying an American citizen and green cards; you didn't need her to tell you that."

"Okay," he snapped. "You're right, but Mina reminded me. I thought it would be good for both of us to get married." He wiped a hand across his forehead. Muscles bunched down the length of his arm, causing a blue tattoo to twitch in response. It was a drawing of a curved knife, a scimitar.

"You hot? Want a drink?" Holding onto the cap, Sam withdrew the bottle of water she'd bought from her pocket. "Here. Haven't opened it yet."

He held the bottle, screwed off the cap, and drank about a third of it.

"Are you sure that *Mina* brought up the subject of marriage and the green card?"

"Yeah. She came after me. It was okay with me because she's real pretty."

Sam asked him, "How did you communicate with her?"

"We talk at the class and texts, mostly." He patted a cargo pocket on the side of his pants. Although he answered Sam's questions, Ted watched his eyes. They moved constantly and revealed intelligence. Survival intelligence.

"By the way, what size shoe do you wear?" Sam asked.

"Huh? Eleven."

"When was the last time you saw her?"

"One day before she was killed."

Ted noticed that Korsokov wore a big ring with a stone that looked like a diamond.

"Did you have a fight with her?" Sam asked.

"Never." Korsokov shook his head. His crossed eyes made him look slightly comical, but his expression was serious and deadly.

"You're lying again, Nick," said Ted.

"Maybe she changed her mind about leaving her husband to marry you and you wouldn't get a green card?" Samantha interrupted and drew out the words slowly. "So you got furious with her. Didn't mean to kill her, but you did?"

He wouldn't respond.

"What else did Mina say about leaving her husband?" Samantha asked.

"Nothing. Wait; there was something odd she asked me about all the time."

"What?"

"She always asked me to steal syringes from the ambulance. So I did."

"Why? Drugs?"

"Not with me. I don't think she used." He glanced back at the ambulance in the covered entry to the emergency room. "As you say in Minnesota—gotta run. Just because I'm immigrant, you all think we're bad." He hurried away from them.

"Hey, you're welcome for the water," she yelled after him. Samantha frowned. "Typical of a lot of these guys who are here illegally. And lots of the Russians are gangsters, probably that 'uncle' he mentioned."

"Ukrainian gangsters," Ted corrected her. They started to walk back into the parking ramp. "You think there's a gang connection? Were they going to burglarize the house?"

"It stinks like gangsters to me. Maybe they were in the house when Dan and Mina surprised them, forcing the killing of Mina." She shrugged. "Did you see the bling on that guy? Not cheap. I've learned over the years that the most obvious explanation is probably the correct one."

"Where'd you learn to be so good at interrogation?"

"I'm a parent, remember? You men don't know all the secrets moms use to extract information from the biggest liars in the world —kids to their parents."

Later in the afternoon, Ted sat on a tall stool looking out at the snarled traffic on Lyndale Avenue in south Minneapolis. He waited for Laurie in the Starbucks coffee shop where they'd spent so much time in the past, trying to heal their relationship. The smell of roasted coffee beans brought back many memories—some difficult ones, but now there was hope for the new beginning.

It seemed like another life when, because of him, Laurie's anger and disappointment had finally overwhelmed her and she'd said a divorce was the only option for her. He tried to talk her out of it, but most of the family supported her, and the divorce followed quickly. Then, with a lot of work on both their parts, they'd come back together and even remarried. Things were getting better although the relationship was still fragile.

What would happen today? He worried.

The coffee shop represented neutral territory. But the fact that Laurie had initiated the meeting bothered him. He knew what the subject of conversation was going to be.

When he saw her round the corner from Lyndale Avenue, he slid off the stool. She still looked beautiful to him. Coming from work, she was dressed in a short skirt and pressed blouse and had a yellow silk scarf looped around her neck. A breeze blew it across her face while she fumbled with the door handle.

The image slammed him back years earlier to a vacation they had taken along the Gunflint Trail in northern Minnesota. They stayed at a lodge buried deep in the forest next to a kidney-shaped lake. After a day of cross-country skiing, they'd trudged back to the lodge. Laurie's face shone bright red from the chill, and her scarf blew across her face while she unstrapped the skis.

They hurried to their private cabin, both aware of the need for each other. Ted had chilled wine while the staff had prepared a fire of oak and birch to warm the small room.

Sweaters, scarfs, boots, pants, and underwear fell off as if the material had disintegrated. Ted rolled back the down comforter and they jumped in. Legs and arms intertwined and they found each other's lips. He kissed her and felt the growing warmth, sensed her urgency, and responded with his own needs.

Afterward, they collapsed against each other and Ted pulled the sheets and comforter over them. Panting and kissing, they laughed with joy at the brief union they'd created in spite of all the distractions of life.

In the coffee shop, Ted hurried to open the door and pulled Laurie in by the forearm. "You look great," he said.

"Not bad for all this wind. I haven't got much time from work." She managed the recruiting for a large financial company in downtown Minneapolis. Recently, they had cut back on staff but expected the remaining people to still accomplish as much work as before the layoffs.

Ted got her a small latte and brought it back to the table. He climbed into the chair opposite from her. "Want anything to eat?"

She shook her head.

He waited for her to start the conversation.

"So, what are you doing about the case?"

What should he say to her? He knew what she thought. To stall for a little time, he took a long sip of his coffee. He drank it black and bitter. "Samantha says to say hi to you," he said finally.

"How is she doing?"

"Things are quiet with all her kids for now."

"What about the case?"

"We just interviewed a possible suspect this morning. A guy who was having an affair with Danny's wife."

Laurie's eyes bored into Ted. She was good at that. It could mean many things: anger, curiosity, or even intense interest. It had taken Ted many years to decipher the meaning behind different stares. They all reflected her passion about life. She lived intensely— her job, being a mother, her volunteer work, her intelligence, and for those that she loved. "I don't believe she was having an affair. She was my cousin, and I would've known about it."

"Laurie, there are some intriguing aspects to the case."

"Like what?" She knew he was stalling.

"Like there are some holes in the prosecutor's case. What if Dan is innocent?"

"Something happened to him in Afghanistan. Changed him. But I have a hard time believing what you just said."

"You're biased because of Mina."

"I'm biased because he looks guilty. And the prosecutor must think the same thing."

"All right. How about this? I ran into Joe Mollner. Remember him? College friends with Dan? Joe told me that when Dan came over to his house, he always played with Joe's kids. Wrestled with them on the floor. Does that sound like a gruesome killer to you?"

Laurie didn't respond.

"And you've worked at the company with some vets from the Iraq war who suffer from PTSD. You should think about that and how it might have affected Dan."

Laurie turned her head and looked out the big window. A city garbage truck roared along the street, scattering papers and leaves in its wake. Without turning back to him, she asked, "What are you going to do to defend Danny?" Her voice was flat, businesslike.

"I talked to Dr. Strauss, Danny's therapist, about it. No question that Danny had some problems with PTSD and probably suffered from something called an 'amygdala hijack.'" When she frowned, he explained it to her.

"That's a defense?"

"Technically, no. But I could use it to pressure the prosecutor into cutting a deal for Dan. Maybe he could plead guilty to a less serious offense."

"See what I mean?" She turned to look at him.

"What?"

Laurie leaned forward. "You're hooked, Ted. I can tell it, and I'm mad about it."

Ted could imagine the bright cogs in her brain whirling to fit the information together.

"What if the prosecutor doesn't give you the time of day?" she asked.

"Then we go to court, and maybe I create some new law."

She slammed the latte on the table top. Her forehead wrinkled into dark lines. "Wait a minute. Wasn't this PTSD defense used in the, uh, *old case?*"

Ted felt heat rising into his face. Dammit, she couldn't leave that crap alone. He fought back, "Yes. But this is different."

She flipped her hand in front of her face. "Oh?"

"It's not that—"

Laurie interrupted, "I don't believe it. Ted, you're trying to redeem yourself for that old case. You can't go back there." She gulped her latte. "There are a lot of things that are difficult about you, but you're a damn good lawyer. But now you're talking about going to trial. You told me—"

"Maybe this guy who had the affair with Mina could be the killer."

"Aahh." She blew out a lungful of air.

Ted shook his head. He wanted so badly to keep the relationship growing, but he wouldn't lie to her. The more he investigated it, the more he was pulled into the case. "This means a lot to me."

"I can understand how you want vindication for all the crap they threw at you, but I don't want you involved at all. You've got a conflict of interest problem, if nothing else."

He stood up from the chair and raised his voice. "Just give me a little time. I'm getting out of it as soon as possible."

"I know what's going to happen." She shook her head. "You're going to get so consumed with it that we'll never see you at home. Just like before. Our reunited family is still a fragile thing between all of us, Ted."

"I know."

"Okay, I'll give you a few days to keep working on the case. But don't blow what we've accomplished so far." She swung her head quickly, causing her hair to flip around under her chin.

Ted had seen that move thousands of times before. Although he was upset with her, a part of him melted inside. It was such a familiar gesture. "If I can't find anything in Danny's defense, I'll drop it right away. All right?"

She looked away from him and didn't say anything for a long time. She glanced at her watch and finished her latte. "I have to get back." Laurie swung her large purse from off the back of the chair onto her shoulder. She patted the side of the purse, and Ted could hear the jingle of car keys. Before slipping off the chair, Laurie cleared her throat. "You don't know how hard this is for me, too. We're doing so well now. I hope this case doesn't come between us."

Ted's stomach tightened. "Don't worry; it won't." He hoped that was true.

"And remember about your commitment to be a better father to Matt. You've consistently missed some of the most important things in his life. Things that are important to *him*, Ted, if not to you."

"I know."

"I'm just warning you: you don't have much more time with him. In a year, he'll be gone, off to college, and on his own. How do you want him to remember the times with his father? Oh, wait a minute, what times?" Her voice dropped lower as she accused him. "All you're thinking about right now is yourself." It hurt, and part of what she said was absolutely true. She stood up and adjusted the scarf around her neck.

"I haven't forgotten. He wants to see a movie at the Riverview. Tonight. We're going together."

She nodded and turned toward the door. With long, graceful steps she moved away. Suddenly, she turned back to Ted. "Here's the final reason I don't believe Danny's innocent." Laurie glanced to her left to make sure no one was standing nearby. "Mina texted me several times this winter that they weren't getting along. He was abusive to her. She was worried."

Ted jerked backward. "Danny admits they fought. Mina even went to court for a protection order. That doesn't mean he killed her."

"Then something's wrong, Ted. There's something you're missing about the case." She hurried through the door and left a faint whiff of her perfume, Paloma Picasso, which she still wore. He thought of the words to a Doors song: . . . *don't you love her madly, don't you need her badly, don't you love her as she's walking out the door?* A hollow feeling carved through his chest.

Chapter Seven

It had taken longer than Hennepin County Deputy Sheriff Kenny Seabloom had expected, but his commander had agreed to let Kenny handle the cell phone investigation. During the search of the Jensen home, Mina's phone had been found under the bed. It was the first time Kenny had been given the opportunity and he didn't want to blow it. Usually he was ordered to perform low-level investigative tasks—something Kenny felt he was beyond at this point in his career. The sheriff's department usually contracted for cell phone data extraction with a local expert named Dr. Charles Leonard.

Kenny had driven into downtown Minneapolis to the sheriff's crime lab located one block away from the deep hole in the ground where the new Minnesota Vikings team would play football once the stadium was finished. Most local police departments couldn't afford to staff and pay for a full crime lab, so they depended on the sheriff's lab. It was one of three labs in the state, including the Minneapolis Police ab and the Minnesota Bureau of Criminal Apprehension with locations in St. Paul and Bemidji. The sheriff's crime lab could handle several functions in their sections, including biology and DNA analysis, crime scene investigation, an evidence section including storage, firearm and tool mark exams, and the fingerprint section.

Seabloom stepped into the tiny lobby, signed in after showing his identification, and was buzzed through into the back hallway and labs. Each section had a separate room or lab. He walked down the hall until he came to the property room. It was the size of a warehouse and had floor-to-ceiling shelves that were all enclosed. Each shelf rested on steel tracks set into the floor so they could be moved easily.

When Kenny told the attendant the case number and what piece of evidence he wanted, the attendant moved to a control panel. She pressed two buttons, and the huge shelves began to separate from each other, rolling along the tracks in the floor. Seabloom could hear the grinding. In a few minutes, the shelves stood apart at intervals from each other. With the attendant, he walked down the aisle until they came to a stack with numbers written on the side. "This is it," she told Kenny.

He squeezed between the towering shelves. The attendant used a key to open a sealed compartment. She lifted out a box filled with items all hidden in plastic baggies. "Over here," she said.

He followed her to the end of the row and watched her set the heavy box on a stainless steel table. Pale light came through the tinted window above them. She dug into the contents of the box until she straightened and held up a tan mailing envelope. "Here you go," she said.

A red tamper-evident sealing strip crossed from one side to the other and held down the top flap. Below that, he saw handwriting that listed the agency name—Minnetonka Police Dept.—their case number, the agency inventory number, and a description of the phone. Written partly over the red sealing tape were the initials SKO. Probably Detective O'Brien.

Seabloom was about to take it when she stopped him. "Have to sign for it. Chain of custody, remember?"

"Sure. Of course." He recalled the training he'd received, taught by a lawyer from the county attorney's office. All evidence must be accounted for every step of the way from the seizure at the crime scene, to the transport to the lab, to the placement in storage, to any removal, and to the courtroom for a trial. If any of these steps were unaccounted for, a clever defense lawyer could create questions in the minds of a jury that the gap in the possession meant someone had tampered with the evidence.

The attendant held out a clipboard with a form attached to it. "Sign here and put the time out."

"You're not computerized?" he asked.

She shook her head. "Next year, they promised."

Seabloom took the envelope, split the end to open it, and saw the iPhone at the bottom. It had already been dusted for fingerprints that confirmed the presence of Mina Jensen's prints, so it wasn't in a plastic baggie anymore.

He left the lab and drove in the squad to an older area of Minneapolis called Prospect Park. The hilly oasis was hemmed in by a freeway to the south and a major, four-lane commuter artery to the north that connected Minneapolis and St. Paul. At the highest point in the park, an old stone water tower stood guard with a roof that resembled a witch's hat. New green grass and scrambled bushes tumbled down the sides of the hill to spread among the strange houses below. There was no uniform architectural style, which is what many of the residents liked about the neighborhood.

As Seabloom turned off University Avenue, he climbed a slight incline, curving to the right. The houses were painted different colors. He saw a bicycle with fat tires and wide handlebars leaning against a picket fence in the front yard. One of the white handle grips was missing. He turned at the Russian Orthodox Church topped with the onion-shaped cupola. A black wrought-iron fence surrounded the church. Kenny climbed even higher up the road in the neighborhood.

Following the numbers, Seabloom found the house and laboratory of Dr. Leonard. He stopped, reached across the seat for the envelope, and got out. The house next to Leonard's looked like it leaned to the left. Seabloom cocked his head in the opposite direction, but the structure still tilted away from him. A long garden ran along the side, in jeopardy of being crushed if the house fell over. He could see roses blooming in bright spots among the green leaves, red, yellow, and pink.

Dr. Leonard's house didn't have any landscaping. Seabloom stepped up two concrete steps and knocked on the wooden door. It opened and a small man with a protruding belly peered at Seabloom from behind round glasses. "Yes?"

"Dr. Leonard?"

"Oh, of course. You're from the sheriff's department. Come in." Leonard stepped aside, closed the door, and sipped from a sweating can of Coke. He talked fast. "Keeps me awake. Every man has his vices; this is mine." He smiled quickly. Seabloom followed him.

They walked through a small dining room with a table covered in reports, stacks of paper, and three laptop computers, two of which were open and booted up.

Dr. Leonard moved into the back of the house. It opened to a spacious lab with three more PCs in the corners. "My humble laboratory," he giggled. "What have you got for me?"

Seabloom opened the end of the envelope and pulled out the iPhone. "Can you retrieve any data off this?"

"Probably. Follow me, young man." Leonard skipped to the PC in the right corner. Next to it sat a black machine about the size of a shoebox. Across the top of it in blue letters all slanted to the right, it read "Cellebrite." Leonard crumpled the Coke can and bent down to a small refrigerator to get another one. He popped it open and took a long drink.

"How does this work?" Seabloom asked.

"This little baby here, the Cellebrite, is a miracle machine. The Universal Forensic Extraction Device. Made in Israel. They're not cheap, but they work. Best on the market."

Seabloom handed him the iPhone. Dr. Leonard turned it over and pried off the cover on the back, removed the battery, and studied the label beneath it. "Okay. Let's start the process." He set the Coke on the table next to the PC. He plugged a flash drive into the right side of the Cellebrite and from a rack on the wall he selected a wire cable about eight inches long. "Let's try number forty-seven."

"What's that?"

Leonard sighed as if he'd explained this a hundred times before. "Cell phones are incredibly complex because there are over 3,000 of them out there. There's a staggering variety of proprietary platforms out there, depending on the company manufacturing the phone. I've got eighty-five cables that I can choose from. Cable fifteen may be able to extract video but not address books. Then cable twenty-four may be able to get the addresses. Part of the 'art' to this process is learning which cables may work for me." He sniffed with pride.

Seabloom watched as the doctor plugged cable number forty-seven into the iPhone and then into the left side of the Cellebrite. He tapped in instructions on the machine's keyboard and waited.

74

Several light blue letters crossed the screen at the top of the machine. Ten minutes later, Leonard said, "It's not working. Let me try something else." He keyed in more instructions, and the Cellebrite flashed a message instructing him to use cable number thirty-three.

Dr. Leonard clicked the side of the Coke can against the machine and talked to it. "You sneaky trickster. I should've known." He blinked and looked up at Seabloom. "Sorry. I'm a geek, and I love this little guy." He focused on the Cellebrite and plugged a different cable into the side. "Okay. That's the one. I'll start the acquisition of the data now." He slid back in the rolling chair and took a long drink from the Coke can.

"What can you get off the phone?"

Leonard stifled a burp and said, "People think they've got privacy with their smart phones. They don't. I always say everyone is walking around naked. I can get almost everything off of a phone."

"Even if it's been deleted?"

Dr. Leonard waved the hand holding the Coke across his chest. "I can go back as long as two years. I can get phone book information, addresses, calendars, texts, missed calls, incoming calls, e-mail, photos, video, and even web browsing sites. I can peek into people's lives and learn things that even their spouses don't know." He smiled decadently.

They waited for twenty minutes. Leonard drank another can of Coke.

"Okay, Charles," Dr. Leonard spoke to himself. "I think we're ready for show time." He unplugged the flash drive from the right side of the Cellebrite and swiveled in his chair to face the PC. He slipped the drive into it and waited for the program to open.

A screen opened with several icons in different colors. "I'll prepare a full report for you, of course," Dr. Leonard said. "What are you interested in?"

"Can you check texts and phone calls?"

"With my eyes closed." He ran through a series of keystrokes and hit the print button. Across the room, the printer whirred to life, and in a few minutes, Dr. Leonard had pages of paper with a narrow column of numbers. They ran down the left side, web sites and names. He handed the pile to Seabloom.

The investigator blew out a big breath. "How the hell are we going to go through all this?"

Leonard leaned back in the swivel chair. "Don't mean to tell you how to do your job, but I can help."

"Huh?"

"See, people tend to do the same things over and over. Call the same people, go to the same web sites, things like that. Look for the patterns. That will reveal the day-to-day activities of the person."

"Makes sense."

"But we'll go to the outliers."

"I've heard of those." Since Seabloom really didn't know what that meant, he waited for the doctor to explain.

Dr. Leonard sighed and said, "Okay. The odd things. The uncommon numbers, sites, people. Those are clues to what they may be trying to hide by purposely not going there often. That's where their secrets are. Out of hundreds of photos, I may find one shot of a naked woman on a guy's phone. Guess who's having a secret affair?"

"Yeah, I guess so."

"I've got good news for you." Dr. Leonard stood and handed Seabloom a pen. "I have the software to search for us, of course. You can make some notes. You asked for texts and phone calls. I think you should also look at web sites. I included them, too." He walked to the opposite corner, sat before the PC, and keyed in instructions. In ten minutes, Dr. Leonard had narrowed down the long list to one page. He handed it to Seabloom.

The investigator read it:

1. Call to 612-345-5634 Daniel Jensen (Date included)
2. Text to 952-545-6001 Laurie Rohrbacher (Date included)
3. Web site for Anson BMW in Wayzata, MN
4. Two calls to 612-345-5634 Daniel Jensen

Seabloom looked up. "But you said these were unusual activities. Dan Jensen was her husband. Wouldn't she call him all the time?"

Dr. Leonard shrugged his shoulders. "The data doesn't lie. Is she calling him *too often?* Don't you see—that's unusual. It's a clue."

Seabloom continued to read:

5. Three calls to xxx-565-4500 River Bank
6. Five texts to xxx-345-6686 Nicholas Korsokov
7. Website for Discover Cards
8. Calls to 952-545-6001 Laurie Rohrbacher
9. Four visits to the Lynn Peavey web site
10. Two visits to web site for Chico's clothing
11. Two calls to 952-455-3444 Anson's Car Repair
12. Three texts to xxx-234-7896 Public Library
13. Text to Evergreen Lawn Service
14. Seven photos of a large man with blond hair, a thick neck, and eyes that looked slightly crossed.

The investigator finished reading and put all the papers into an accordion folder he'd carried with him.

"Doesn't make much sense. You sure you didn't find any calls to 911? We found the phone under the bed in the room where the murder occurred. Why wouldn't the victim call 911?"

"That's why it's called investigative analysis." Dr. Leonard drew out the words slowly.

Seabloom felt his face get hot. "I'll work on it." He was determined to do a good job on this case, even if the doctor didn't have much confidence in him. "You talked about outliers, but these calls all seem totally normal."

Leonard cocked his head to one side. "Maybe they're too normal. Each one of us has secrets. The tough part is finding them."

"Well, I've gotta get back to the prosecutor with this information." Kenny cleared his throat.

"Who are you working with?"

"Sandy Rogin."

Leonard whistled. "Watch your backside. I've handled a couple of cases with him. He's tough and he'll do anything to win."

Seabloom thanked him and left. Outside he stood by his car and did a quick fist pump. He was anxious to show the commander what he'd found. Kenny didn't know what it meant, but it certainly looked important. Whatever. He felt like this was finally his chance. A stiff breeze had blown up from the west. Although it was illegal in Minneapolis to burn anything outside, the wind carried the oily stench of burning trash.

Chapter Eight

When she stomped on Sanford Rogin's back for the third time, he heard something creak in his chest. He prayed that it wasn't a rib cracking. His daughter MacKenzie squealed with laughter and ran back toward the door to do it all over.

"Hop on Pop," she shouted and started for his back again. She could time her jump just right so that at maximum velocity, she'd launch herself into the air, raise her feet high, and slam them into his back as her full weight fell on him. She called it "fly-jumping."

Rogin, for his part, pretended to be in great pain and moaned every time she landed on him. It caused her to laugh even harder. He wondered how many more years they could play this game before it finally became dangerous for him.

After he'd been pounded for as long as he could stand, Sanford put a stop to the game. "Let's watch cartoons," he pleaded with his daughter. His wife came downstairs with a cup of coffee and smiled proudly at him. Then his iPhone belted-out the song "In-A-Gadda-Da-Vida," signaling a call.

It was his law clerk, Gary Hill, calling. "I'm waiting at the office. Are we still meeting?"

Rogin sat up straight. He took a deep breath to see if his chest still worked. "Yeah. I was playing with my kid and lost track of time. I'll be there in a little while." He was about to hang up when he ordered Hill, "If you see anyone, don't say a word." He'd thought of a sneaky way to slam Ted Rohrbacher early in the proceedings, and Rogin was anxious to put it into action.

In thirty minutes, Rogin ran his swipe card through the security checkpoint at the Hennepin County Government Center. It was deserted except for the contract security officers. Since Rogin was there often on Saturdays and Sundays, he knew most of them and nodded a greeting. He expected that the office would be equally as deserted as the atrium of the Government Center. Few of the prosecutors ever worked on weekends. That's why he did. The simple fact of working more and harder had paid off for Sanford Rogin. Preparation was his strength—even in law school, where he was able to study longer than anyone else.

On his floor, he hurried toward the double glass doors, used his swipe card again, and pushed through. The office smelled stale and closed. Even this early in the morning, it felt warm since the air conditioning was turned off on the weekends. He'd purposely worn shorts and a t-shirt. He found Gary Hill in the library and walked in, shutting the oak door behind him.

Bookshelves covered three of the walls and were crammed with hard-bound law books. The bindings were colored cordovan, tan, and dark green. In the corner, a small desk held a computer terminal with a printer underneath. In the center of the room was a long oak table, expensive and polished. Around all four corners of the table, law books, files, piles of paper, and the remains of someone's box lunch from Jimmy John's crowded the space. Rogin swept aside three of the books to get room for their work.

He asked Hill, "See anyone?"

"No."

"Okay. Let's get this sucker cranked out."

"Don't you think we should run this by Zehra?" Hill stood off to the side. Behind him, a wide window gave a view of the skyline of St. Paul on the far horizon. Dirty gray clouds hid the sun.

"Shit, no. You know what she'd say."

"That's my point."

"She's a great prosecutor, but she's not aggressive enough. We're gonna cut Rohrbacher off at the knees before he can even get started." Rogin pulled up a chair in front of the computer terminal and keyed in the web site for the Rules of Professional Conduct in Minnesota.

"But she's your supervisor."

"She'll find out, of course. But by then, it'll be too late for her to do anything. I'll get a lecture and that'll be it." He paused to look up at Hill. "Think of the stakes here. We're fighting crime, and the Jensen murder is one of the worst. When we convict this animal, our ultimate boss, Bud Grant, won't care how we did it, just so long as we get a win." He turned back to the screen.

"I don't know, Sanford."

Rogin slammed his palm on the small desk. "God dammit! Are you helping me or not? If you want off of the biggest case of the year, just say so. There's a dozen other law clerks begging to help on this one." He glared at Hill, who backed away toward the window and remained silent.

Rogin scrolled through the long list of ethical rules that regulated how lawyers worked in the state. Some of the rules applied to the relationship between lawyer and client. Others applied to the relationship of the lawyer to the courts and then, the relationship of the lawyer to the public in general. Rogin moved the cursor down through the rules regarding the courts. He finally found it.

"Here it is," he announced to Hill. "Rule 3.3b. *Candor Toward the Tribunal.* Here's what it says: 'A lawyer who represents a client and who knows that person intends to engage or has engaged in a crime or fraudulent conduct relating to the proceedings shall take remedial measures, including disclosure to the tribunal.'"

"So what?"

"So, Dan Jensen has engaged in a crime—hiding the body and not revealing its location. Rohrbacher is under a duty to disclose this and, if he knows where the body is, disclose that also." Rogin stood and paced in a circle. "He hasn't done either."

"I'm not sure, Sanford . . . we studied that in law school last year. I think it means if the lawyer knows his client intends to bribe or intimidate a witness or a juror, or intends to commit a new crime, then he has to tell the court. Maybe you're going too far with this."

"I don't give a shit what they told you in law school. This is the real world of hard-ass criminals. We've got a duty to do everything we can to stop a dangerous thug like Jensen." He stared at Hill. "And think about the family of the victim. Don't you think they deserve some justice?"

Hill collapsed into a leather chair and stretched out his legs. He wore red Converse basketball shoes and blue jeans. A black stocking cap covered his head. "Yeah, I guess. But I don't like this. We haven't even charged Jensen yet."

"You file the ethical complaint with the Lawyer's Board of Professional Responsibility. It would be improper, as the lead prosecutor, for me to file it."

Hill snorted a laugh. "Improper?"

"Yes." Rogin frowned and turned back to the computer. "Here's everything you need for the formal complaint."

Hill shifted to one side of the chair, then the other. But he didn't get up to prepare the documents.

"What're you waiting for?" Rogin stood and walked over to tower above Hill. "You want a job here after you graduate?"

"Of course I do," Hill said. "But you're trying to fit a round peg in a square hole."

"You help me nail this asshole Jensen and you're gold."

"But . . . what do you have against Ted Rohrbacher?"

"Nothing. This is strictly business," Rogin said. He circled the expansive space of the library. "I just don't respect Rohrbacher. When he worked here, he was lazy and arrogant. Selfish. But what I want to do is charge and convict the killer, and anything I can do to make it more difficult for a defense lawyer, I'll do it. That's my job."

Hill uncurled himself from the chair. He stood up and faced Rogin. "I have to call Zehra first."

"I'm warning you, don't throw away an opportunity."

"I really don't think we should do this." He pulled off his cap and ran a hand over his shaved head.

Rogin didn't respond. He walked out of the library and slammed the door.

On late Monday afternoon, Ted met with Samantha at his law firm. She came into the lobby wearing a t-shirt that said "Spelman College" in blue and white letters. She wore blue running shoes of the same shade. Today she had on the copper-colored wig.

An elderly woman sat in the corner reading a Conde Nast travel magazine. When Sam came in, she dropped the magazine in her lap and watched.

The firm's receptionist smiled and said, "May I assist you?"

"Sure. I'd like some of that free coffee and to see Teddy Rohrbacher, please."

"Free coffee?" The receptionist's eyes traveled up and down Sam's body; then she said, "Of course. Please wait right here." She edged out from behind the large desk and stood up while flattening her skirt along her legs. It was a beige skirt that matched the thin woolen sweater she wore draped around her shoulders. Adjusting the collar of her white blouse, the receptionist paused long enough to page Ted. She left for the back room.

Ted came out quickly. He said hello to the older client and took Samantha by the arm. "This way for *your type of people*," he kidded her in a quiet voice. He wanted to make sure Sam knew of his decision to take on the case. He needed her help.

"I'm just fightin' for my rights, Mr. Rohrbacher." Her eyes opened wide to show lots of white. "Can you help me, please?"

Ted gave her a soft push toward his office. Once they turned the corner into the wide hallway, they laughed. Thick carpeting muffled all the noise. He closed the door of his office behind them and offered Sam a seat on the couch. In her younger days, she'd been shapely, but she had gained some weight in recent years. The t-shirt stretched across her ample chest. Ted sat at the other end of the couch.

She took a deep breath and looked around. On the far wall, two Leroy Neiman paintings showed a quarterback about to throw a football and a golfer at the top of his swing. "Where'd you get that crap?" she asked.

Ted frowned. "You have any idea how expensive those are?"

"So what? Get rid of them."

"The decorator the firm hired recommended them. I like sports."

"I like champagne, but I wouldn't have paintings of champagne bottles on my walls."

"Okay." He was interrupted by the receptionist, who ghosted into the office with a wooden tray, two china coffee cups, and a pot of coffee. Silver servers held sugar and cream. She smiled briefly and backed out of the room.

Samantha fluttered her eyelids.

"Hey, I happen to like this life around here," Ted protested. "You could get used to it, too." He smelled freshly brewed coffee, which he poured into the two cups. The luxurious trappings made him feel successful.

"I'm sure I could." She shook two packets of sugar into her coffee, followed by cream, and stirred it with a spoon for a long time. "So where are we on Jensen's case?"

Ted pulled down the knot of his tie and opened his collar. "Okay, I have to admit that some aspects of it look intriguing. I owe it to Dan to talk to Rogin about the case. See if I can get it dismissed before Rogin charges anything." He opened both arms in front of him. "If that doesn't go anywhere, I'm in big trouble. It could jeopardize all of this," he nodded toward the expansive office, "and my family."

"Here in your cocoon?"

"Quit giving me shit about this."

"Okay." Sam took a long drink of her coffee, held the saucer in her hand, and set it on the serving tray. She stood up and adjusted her wig.

"Will I ever get to see your real hair again?"

"Not for a while. So I can fold up the tents on this one? My 'financial people' will send your 'financial people' a bill for what I've done to date." She laughed and turned back to him. "What about Laurie?"

"She doesn't want me involved in any way."

"But you're already involved, aren't you?" She looked closely at him. "And you're going to be even more involved."

Ted twisted to his side on the couch. "Dammit. You know me better than anyone. Okay, if I could win this impossible case, well, maybe it could even give me back my reputation."

"I'm not talking about *you*. I'm talking about is there any possibility you could help Dan Jensen? That's a question worth answering."

Ted's face colored red. "I don't need your lectures." His voice rose.

"You're the best lawyer for this case, but I'll shut up. My mouth's gotten me in trouble enough times before." Samantha started to leave.

Ted's phone rang. It was Zehra Hassan from the county attorney's office returning his call. Ted waved at Samantha to stay as he answered at his desk. "Thanks, Zehra."

"You're calling the wrong person, Ted."

"I thought you supervised Sandy Rogin."

"I do." Her tone of voice was dismissive.

"Come on, Zehra. We go back a long ways."

"Our boss, Ulysses Grant, is impressed with Rogin and has given him authority to handle the investigation and the case. He's also put a ton of resources behind him. They're going all out to get your suspect charged. At best, I have a veto power."

"I'm wondering what Rogin's agenda is."

She sighed. "I'm not sure, but knowing Sandy Rogin, he'll go all the way."

Samantha sat on the couch and poured more coffee.

"Things have changed for me," Ted said. "I'm out of criminal law and finally making some good money."

"Good for you. I have work to do."

"Wait. I get the sense that Rogin's particularly anxious to screw me."

There was a long pause, then Zehra said, "You don't know?"

"Know what?"

"About Rogin?"

"I know he's a jerk. What else could there be?"

"Um, I guess it's not important anyway."

"Zehra, what the hell are you talking about?"

"It's ancient history. And like you said, you've moved on and grown up." Without explaining any more, she hung up.

Chilly air wafted from the vent beside the couch. Ted rolled his chair back from the desk and stood up. He ran his hand through his hair. He said to Sam, "Zehra was sure hands-off. Something's wrong, but she won't say." He told Samantha what Zehra had hinted about Rogin.

"That's easy. I'll tell you." She set her cup on the desk.

"Dammit! Why is everyone so hush-hush about this?"

Samantha raised her eyebrows. "You really don't know? When you got into that trouble as a prosecutor, the person in the office who led the charge to get you fired was Sandy Rogin. I had just retired from the police force and heard the gossip. Grant agreed with him and canned your ass."

"And I was so stupid, I never even suspected him. This makes everything different."

He thought about the Jensen case. If he got totally involved, it would be grinding, gut-wrenching work—even now that his hatred for Sanford Rogin had taken a leap upward. Then he saw the folded card from his father on the corner of the desk. He lifted it and remembered what it said inside.

All his determination to avoid becoming involved in the case crashed in around him.

He walked to the window and watched people struggling through traffic along France Avenue, trying to find their way between shopping centers and restaurants. He was quiet for a long time. Then he turned back to face her. "I can count on you, Sam?"

"Got your back."

His face suddenly flattened and the wrinkles smoothed out as if a burden had been taken away. "'Cause we're going all the way with this. I'll beat that bastard."

"You know I'm with you."

"We've got to work fast."

Samantha adjusted her wig by pulling it down tighter on her head. She said, "You really know what you're taking on?"

Ted's eyes rose to meet hers.

"There's the conflict of interest issue—you knew the victim."

His stomach tightened. "I know, but it's too late to back out now. I'll take the risk and deal with it later. I think I can get Dan to waive the issue."

"You can't screw up this one, Ted. The stakes are too high for everyone this time."

Chapter Nine

Besides Samantha, there was one other person Ted needed to help him if he was going to defend Dan. He hoped that she was free. When he'd worked in the county attorney's office years ago, he'd met Jackie Nguyen. She'd matured from a silly new law graduate into a tough and savvy lawyer. Ted always knew that she was smart, but now with age and experience, Jackie was dangerous—if you were on the opposite side from her.

She had graduated at the top of her law school class, and unlike most lawyers, Jackie loved the technical aspects of practicing law. She memorized the arcane details of cases, rulings, and statutes— and remembered them all. That's what Ted needed now, especially if he was going to assert the new defense of the amygdala hijack. Jackie would love to sink her teeth into something so challenging.

Would he be able to convince her to help?

They'd offered her lunch at Jimmy's, a dining spot in a western suburb of Minneapolis. The walls were painted bright colors, with swirls and dots in corn yellow, blue, and hunter green. Sitting in a booth, Ted could smell grilled burgers as a waiter passed by him, balancing the food on an outstretched arm. As usual, the restaurant was packed with people. Samantha and Ted waved at Jackie when they spotted her in the bar. She slid into the booth on the opposite side from them.

She swirled a glass of dark red wine. "Spanish Rioja. My favorite." She sipped a tiny amount. "All I'll allow myself today. What do you want?" She wore a light camel blazer over a pink scoop-necked cotton blouse. She didn't wear a necklace or any jewelry and very little makeup.

Ted ordered a Diet Coke and Sam asked for coffee. Jackie ordered a Cobb salad.

"We need your help," he told Jackie. He noticed her shiny black hair that looked like curved parentheses around the pale, round face.

He hadn't seen her for a while, and Ted noticed new wrinkles spreading in faint spider webs from the corners of her eyes. Jackie removed her horn-rimmed glasses and set them next to the glass of wine.

"You've heard about the Jensen murder case and the missing wife?"

"Heard about it," Jackie said.

"That's my new client. Dan Jensen. The government's still investigating it, but they've focused on Jensen as the main suspect."

Jackie shrugged. "Hope he's paying you one hell of a lot of money. It sounds like he's toast already. Even without the body, the prosecutor's theory of the case will probably work. If successful, the prosecutor will make history."

"That's exactly why the case is tempting." He dangled a hook before her. Jackie certainly didn't need the money, but the legal challenge might be enough to get her help.

"Oh?"

"They still haven't found the body."

"Still, the defense lawyer would have to be damn good to win this one."

Ted hunched his shoulders forward. "That's the point. You said this case could make history in the state. But *who* is the one that'll be remembered? The prosecutor or us?" Then he leaned back, sipped on his Coke, and waited a few minutes. Jackie poked at her salad and stirred the romaine leaves around. "I need your help," he told her. "So far, it's just me and Samantha. I'll use a law clerk from the firm."

"I thought you were practicing estate planning," Jackie said.

"I am. This is the only criminal matter I have. I'm hoping we can put together enough of a defense to convince the prosecutor to drop the case. Or maybe offer the defendant a plea bargain. Then I'm out of it."

Jackie set down her fork. She studied Ted's face and glanced at Sam. "You in on this too?" she asked Samantha.

"He's paying me well," Sam answered. She smiled briefly.

Jackie nodded and turned back to Ted. "You sure you're up for this? I seem to remember you fell pretty hard when you left the office."

He felt his face heat up. "I'm okay. In fact, this is exactly what I need right now."

"Bored with tax planning?" Jackie chuckled.

"No." Ted lied and shifted in the booth. "It's just that this case has some fascinating aspects. If I could pull off a win here, it'd go a long way to helping my reputation."

Jackie waved her fork in the space over the table between them. "Forget it."

"Well, let's talk about the case, okay?"

"I'm too busy, Teddy," Jackie told him. "Don't go chasing this —it isn't worth the headaches."

"I'd certainly understand if you couldn't follow the case to a conclusion. I really need help in the research about something called the *amygdala hijack.*" He watched her eyes. He hoped that barb on the hook might be enough to snag Jackie.

Jackie looked up from the salad bowl. Her gaze jumped from Ted to Samantha. Jackie leaned back in the booth. "What did you say?"

"It's an aspect of PTSD that might give us something of a defense." Ted explained what Dr. Strauss had told them.

"That could be interesting. I've never heard of it." Jackie's black eyebrows lowered. "You got a solid expert opinion?"

Ted nodded. "Solid gold. He's the one who suggested it to me."

"What do you think about all this psych stuff?" Jackie asked Samantha.

She popped her hands open over the barbeque sandwich half-eaten on her plate. "I think it's hocus pocus, but since T-man insists on working the case, it's probably the best possible defense."

"And if we aren't allowed to use it in a trial, we could always appeal, get it reversed, and create new law in the state," he added.

Jackie finished chewing on the greens, washed it down with a gulp of wine, and said, "Pretty tough."

"That's why I need you."

Her face tightened and she nodded. "Any other suspects?"

Sam answered, "We've interviewed one, so far. And we're still investigating."

"I don't know, Ted," Jackie sighed. "What about that suspect? Can't you blame it on him?"

"He certainly stinks like he's guilty, but we don't have enough evidence yet to convince the prosecutor. And we've been assigned to Judge Edith Vang."

Jackie's eyes opened wider. She'd been a law clerk for the judge years ago and knew everything about how the judge worked and how she made decisions. Jackie's knowledge would be invaluable for Ted. He knew that would tempt her also. "And I need a favor," he tugged at her again. "I've got a personal reason to beat the shit out of this prosecutor."

"Huh?"

"Sandy Rogin."

A smile turned up the corners of Jackie's mouth. "Why didn't you say so in the first place? I've had a few cases with him. What a jerk. I'd be glad to help beat that guy and get the case tossed. Talk to my office manager about the financial arrangements. Where do we start?"

Several hours later, Samantha Carter shifted up into third gear in the old Mazda Miata she owned. Without a sound, it leaped forward. The car was one of her most treasured possessions, and she loved to drive it. "I don't want to miss meeting with this witness," she said.

"Thank God we've got Jackie's help." Ted ignored her comment. He sat in the passenger seat.

"I remember her from when I was a homicide detective and she was a new prosecutor. What a twit! She's sure changed. I'd trust her with any case now."

"And thanks for driving. How's the car running?"

"I haven't got many possessions in life, but this Miata is my baby," she reminded him. "It's vintage. Owned by a retired accountant who maintained it perfectly. I do the same."

Ted had his elbow balanced on the open window. He ran his hand over the leather covering under his arm. The car was banana yellow, and it felt light and responsive to Sam's every touch. "Where do you get the time to take care of it?" he asked.

"Gotta make time. When you own something so fine, it's a crime to let it deteriorate." She glanced over at him. "Like a lot of things in life, it's important to care about things other than yourself." Sam reached down between them to grasp the gearshift carefully, pushed in the clutch, and shifted into fourth gear. The steering wheel was wrapped in black leather, and walnut wood paneling crossed the length of the dashboard. She looked over at him and asked, "You've thought about what we're going to present to Rogin?"

"Keep it simple. The fact they don't have a body yet combined with the threat of raising the amygdala hijack. When Jackie's through researching the issues, we'll nail him with everything."

Samantha looked back and forth between the freeway and Ted. "That's it?"

Ted frowned at her. "And the fact Dan Jensen denies killing his wife, of course."

"That's not much, and you know it."

"Okay. So, we're talking to this person you found." His voice rose over the whine of the wind around them. "What I really want to do is kick Rogin's butt all around the courtroom."

"That's the plan? Kick some butt? Ted, we have to investigate and prepare a stronger defense than what you've got planned."

He shook his head. "Remember, the government has the burden of proof. *They* have to prove the murder, not us. We just sit back and poke holes into their case."

Sam turned back to watch the road. By the firm set of her face, Ted could tell that she disagreed with him. Ted asked about the woman they were driving to meet. "How'd you find her?"

"When I checked the name Nick Korsokov through the national criminal data base, an old case popped up. Just like Mina Jensen, the other woman was, apparently, a girlfriend of Mr. K. Katrina Albert's her name. And like Jensen, Albert disappeared. Her friends reported her missing and the police investigated. They questioned Korsokov immediately, but he wouldn't admit to anything. And then the woman showed up about three weeks later."

"What'd she say?"

Sam turned her head toward Ted. Today her hair was her own and straightened. It flipped across her face. "Nothing."

"What?"

"Oh, she said Korsokov had a business opportunity for her but wouldn't say anything more."

"How'd you get all this information?"

"I've still got solid contacts in the police departments around the Twin Cities. If I don't embarrass them or reveal sources, I can get pretty much whatever I want."

"So we're going to talk with this woman?"

Samantha's lips tightened as she thought. "Right. But I can just about guess what happened. For years, the girls have come pouring out of the Eastern bloc countries and into the U.S. sex trafficking rings. They get conned by guys who claim they're talent brokers from Hollywood. Everyone in the world wants to go to Hollywood. These guys promise the girls a shot at the big time. They even pay for the transportation. When the girls get here, they're kidnapped and put out to hustle for the talent brokers."

Sam eased the car into the far left lane and speeded up. It was late afternoon and the sun dipped low on the western horizon behind them. It lit up the road, the green trees, and the white marble of the St. Paul Cathedral until it glistened like it was wet. "No one can prove it. Since Katrina Albert wouldn't say anything more about him, the police dropped the case against Korsokov."

"Remember you thought there may have been a Russian gang that got into the Jensen home and killed Mina?"

"It's a theory at this point in time." Glancing down at the clock on the dashboard, Sam said, "That's what I want to ask Katrina." She crossed four lanes to exit from Interstate 94 onto Dale Street in St. Paul. Coming off the ramp too fast, she swerved to avoid a line of bicycles coasting down a slight incline toward the cross street. "The old Rondo neighborhood," she said.

"Gone now."

"My grandparents lived here for a while. It was a tight African-American community that got split in half when the freeway went through it. My grandpa worked at the box factory back on Cretin

Avenue. First black person to get in there. I remember the celebration in our family when he came home with the first paycheck." Samantha looked up in the rearview mirror as if she were looking back in history.

Ted waited a moment then said, "How were you able to find this woman?"

"Trina?" Sam grinned. "A lot of talking and charm. A couple of the Minneapolis cops have had a thing for me for years. I'm not too proud to say that I fan those flames every once in a while. One of 'em opened the closed file on the case for me. Then, with the help of Google, I tracked her down to an apartment in Ramsey Hill." She laughed. "Wish we'd had Google when I was still a detective in homicide. My life would've been a lot easier."

"So we've got an appointment?"

"Not if she's boogied already. She wasn't too happy to meet about this, but I got her to sit tight until we could get to her." She looked at the clock again and sighed.

Sam took a left onto Selby Avenue and pushed the Mazda over the speed limit. They raced past the St. Paul Curling Club and several new restaurants. The Ramsey Hill area was an old section of the city perched on bluffs overlooking St. Paul. In the late 1800s train and lumber barons had built huge stone mansions to take advantage of the view. Curving around the top edge of the bluff was a street appropriately named Summit Avenue. It resembled the rampart on a stone fort, hiding the royalty of St. Paul behind it. Today, however, most people couldn't afford to maintain the mansions. Many had been broken up into apartments that rented for almost as much as the original homes probably cost to build.

Samantha barely slowed for the stop sign on Western Avenue, turned right, and drove a few blocks more before rocking to a halt in front of a three-story red brick house. A small yard led to a wraparound wooden porch which held three pieces of white wicker furniture. A wooden swing hung from the ceiling of the porch at the far end. On the seat, a cat curled in the sun and didn't pay any attention to them as they walked up the sidewalk.

A corner of the house rose on the left side to peak at the roof in a turret that was sheathed in green copper. Hydrangea bushes, heavy with blue flowers, edged the sidewalk, so full they forced Ted to twist between them to reach the front door.

He peered through the stained glass window in the door and saw a row of mailboxes. The door was unlocked. He stepped into a small hallway and heard his shoes click against the tile floor. Samantha ran her finger along the row of mailboxes, found Katrina Albert's name, and pressed the button beside the box. A buzzer sounded.

Finally, a tinny voice from a speaker said, "Yeah?"

"Katrina? This is Samantha Carter. We're here in the lobby."

"Yeah. I'll be down. We'll talk in the back."

In five minutes a small woman opened the second door, stepped into the lobby, and pointed with her hand to the front porch. Sam stuck out her own hand and shook hands with Katrina who turned and then shook Ted's hand. She had long bleached hair that hid the real color revealed in a brown gash along the part on the top of her head. She had a prominent nose, big green eyes, and neglected teeth. Katrina was pretty and moved with energy.

She led them onto the front porch and said, "We'll go around the back. More privacy." Off the steps and onto the crowded sidewalk, Trina led them to the left and past the long outside wall of the house. Near the back corner, a wooden arbor channeled them into a back yard. A metal table and two chairs sat amongst boxes of potted plants shaded by several linden trees. All of it crowded the small space. Yellowed leaves were scattered over the stone pavement on the ground.

Ted couldn't hear any of the traffic noises from the street and instead heard the chirps of goldfinches as they darted among the branches, yellow bodies contrasting with the dark green of the leaves they hid behind.

Samantha looked around and gave a low whistle. "Pretty nice for an apartment building."

Katrina agreed. "Yeah. The house is registered as a Minnesota historical site, so the landlord keeps it up nice." She glanced back at the arbor as if watching to see that no one followed them into the secret garden. She took a seat in the closest iron chair and waited.

Samantha stepped in front of Ted and sat opposite Katrina. She also waited and watched.

"Thanks for meeting with us," Ted said finally.

A sharp glance from Sam told him to keep quiet. He took a step backward and trusted her to know how to handle this.

In the silence, Katrina fidgeted in the chair. She sniffed a few times and said, "So, like, what do you want to talk about?"

"Mostly, Nicholas Korsokov," Samantha answered.

Katrina's shoulders tightened. "I don't know much. . ."

"That's okay. Anything you tell us could be helpful."

"Is he in trouble?"

Sam chuckled. "No, he's not. But we are defending a client whose wife may have had an affair with him. The wife has disappeared. We would like to find her."

Katrina dropped her eyes to the ground, and they seemed to trace the shapes of each stone in the patio—gray and black and cracked in spots.

"So, you were involved with him at one time, right?" Sam asked.

"Not much." Katrina's eyes flicked up, then dropped again.

"Oh, I think you were involved a whole lot, right?"

Katrina shook her head.

Samantha cleared her throat and leaned forward in her chair. "Are you from Eastern Europe? I can hear something in your accent."

Katrina looked up at Sam. "Yeah."

"Where?"

"Prague."

"Albert's not your real name, is it?"

Her head cocked to the side, but she answered, "No. Novotsky's my real name."

"Now we're getting somewhere. How did you meet Korsokov?"

Ted noticed the setting sun blazing in the crowns of the trees, turning the greens to yellow and gold. Underneath, shadows drifted out from the edges of the garden, bringing a damp smell with them.

Katrina said, "A lot of the immigrants hang together. Nicky was, I don't know, just around. He was strong and seemed to know everyone. He helped a lot of us get started."

"Oh?"

"Yeah, like where to get help, where to buy food, find apartments, jobs."

Samantha lowered her voice. "Did you date him?"

For an instant, Katrina's eyes moistened and grew rounder. She nodded but didn't say anything.

"I bet he dated a lot of women, huh?"

"I found out later, yeah. Lots of them. He's a bastard."

"We really don't care about your relationship with him. What I'm interested in is what he was doing. Was he putting women on the street as prostitutes?"

"Yeah." She sniffed quietly.

Ted noticed the sound of more birds. They must have returned in anticipation of evening coming. He saw nuthatches flitting among the golden limbs and watched as wrens swooped gracefully into the small houses built along the back wall of the garden. Around his feet, he felt coolness rising from the stones. The corners of the garden disappeared in new shadows.

"So, how did he get women to cooperate?" Sam asked her.

She didn't respond but shifted her hips in the metal chair.

"You worried?"

"Kind of. I mean, I don't know you, and Nicky probably still knows where I live. Not that I see him anymore," she added quickly.

"I think I understand. I can tell you this: I also don't think we'll need your testimony in trial. Your secrets will be safe with us." Sam's face softened. She looked so sincere.

Ted marveled at her skills. Not only her expression, but the tone of her voice and her body language all conveyed a sense of openness, of trust. She should've been an actress.

"So, Katrina, he treated you badly?" Sam asked.

"Yeah. He's a bastard. He said he had connections to some local film people. They had connections in Hollywood. When I look back on it, I'm embarrassed that I ever even believed him, but like, at the time it sounded real."

"But how'd he get you on the street?"

"Oh, I never did that. Nicky would text me and say he had a connection, some dude, who might be able to open doors for me. All I had to do was go to his hotel and have sex with him. Nicky would handle the rest."

"How long did you do that?"

"He had me out on the road for three weeks before I could escape and get back here. Never again."

"He ever bother you again?"

A smile split Katrina's face. "No, because I finally decided to go to the St. Paul police. Nicky always threatened to turn me in for deportation, but then I decided to risk it by going to the police. A nice woman helped me."

Sam nodded. Ted came closer and leaned on one leg.

"I also helped one other girl get away from him." She dropped her head and wiped a finger under her nose. "Yeah, but another one never came back."

"Unfortunately, some missing victims are never found. Happens more than people think." Samantha waited without saying anything. When Katrina lifted her head, Sam said, "So, do you know any of the other women who were involved with him?"

Katrina's head hung forward. She said, "Only one. That I helped."

Sam's voice softened to the point Ted could hardly hear the words. "Did he have any partners?" Sam asked.

"Yeah, but I never met any. He kept things pretty secret." Trina lifted her head. Her eyes opened wider. "I think he called them 'investors,' and some of those women could have been his partners, too."

"Did he ever mention the name Mina Jensen?"

"No."

"Did you go out for the three weeks because you loved him?"

"Partly, yeah."

"What else?"

"He threatened to kill me."

Chapter Ten

The Hennepin County sheriff's water patrol boat cut across the choppy waves of Lake Minnetonka. Deputy Sheriff Kenny Seabloom had worked in the patrol and had been promoted to an investigator. But he still loved to drive the boats. Today he was in command of one boat and was also training in his partner, Deputy Jane Johnson. Two divers sat on the transom in the stern of the boat. They were all determined that today the team would find the body of Mina Jensen. A second boat worked the opposite side of the bay from Kenny.

He felt good since he'd finally been given another responsible duty to perform. It would give him a chance to prove his competence. One of the divers on the transom smoked a cigarette. Every puff he took blew past his head in a long white stream.

A small flotilla of private boats followed in the wake of the sheriff's boat. Some boats had been hired by the news media, but most were gawkers and retired people who lived on the edges of the lake. Because of the large number of boats, the atmosphere was almost party-like in spite of the grim work of the sheriffs and members of Mina Jensen's family who rode in one of the boats.

Lake Minnetonka was the largest lake in the metropolitan area west of Minneapolis. It wasn't a circular lake. From above, it looked like someone had taken big bites out of the edges to create dozens of inlets, bays, islands, and harbors. Built along the shoreline were some of the most expensive homes in the Twin Cities area. In fact, the lake was so popular that boat traffic in the summer had to be monitored by several sheriff patrol boats to avoid collisions and to break up rowdy parties.

Deputy Seabloom felt the chilly wind that penetrated the jacket of his uniform. The temperature would rise into the seventies by the afternoon, but it was still cool this early in the morning, especially out on the open water. He felt sorry for the divers although they were dressed in wet suits and dove throughout the entire year, even in the winter. And they were paid very well.

Over the roar of the engine, Seabloom shouted to Johnson, "We'll continue the search from over there." He stretched out his arm and pointed at a large bay to their right. He turned the wheel, and the boat leaned over on its side as it curved into the bay. A high wall of white water shot up from along the stern.

Ahead of the boat, he could see the wood ducks and mallards scattering and the loons watching until, at the last minute, they curled their black heads and dove underwater. But the gulls weren't afraid. They circled overhead, curious or more likely hoping for some kind of a meal to satisfy their constant hunger. As he eased back on the throttle, Seabloom could hear their caws.

The wind couldn't reach the boat sheltered inside the bay. It became still and quiet. The sheriff's boat slowed, and Seabloom felt the wake from behind him lift the stern momentarily until the boat settled down into a wallowing path toward the shoreline. The engine's exhaust gurgled in the dark water.

"At least we're searching in a lake, not a river," Seabloom said to Johnson. "The currents in a river make it almost impossible to find anything, and it's really hard to see under there."

"How do you know the body is here?" she asked.

Seabloom tugged the bill of his deputy's cap lower on his face to shade his eyes from the rising sun. "The victim's car was found in that small park in the bay behind us." He nodded toward the bay from which they had left a half hour earlier from their mooring at a steel dock. "Of course, we searched that bay first. No body. So we decided to start here since the road into the park parallels this bay." On the shore, ash trees crowned a green space that included picnic tables and permanent brick grills for cooking. Across a gravel road, a small pond was surrounded by buckthorn bushes and thick woods. He turned forward to look across the bay they were entering.

The divers had strapped on their air tanks and were adjusting face masks. Black wetsuits with bright blue striping down the arms and legs hugged each of their bodies. The older one tossed his cigarette butt into the churning water behind him. He reached into the bottom of the boat to grab a long length of rope. He tugged on one end that had a large loop tied into it. He wrapped the rope between his palm and elbow into a tight circle.

Behind the sheriff's boat, the remaining private boats also slowed down. By an unwritten rule, they remained at a distance away. Seabloom noticed clouds pushed before the wind from the west. The clouds might bring rain, and he wished they could work faster.

He maneuvered the boat along the shoreline, checking on his GPS to position them on the same spot where they'd left off yesterday. Satisfied, Seabloom shifted the engine into neutral. He climbed up over the deck onto the bow and released a claw anchor. The chain attached to it clattered across the gunwale for a long time until the anchor hit the bottom. When he returned to the cockpit, Seabloom reversed the engine and tapped on the throttle to engage the anchor below them. When he felt it grab, Seabloom shut off the engine.

Without the noise of the boat, the silence seemed eerie. It matched the grim mission they were about to resume.

Seabloom knew that just because Mina Jensen's car had been found on the shore of the lake, there was no guarantee the body would be here. Investigators speculated that the body had been wrapped in something that minimized blood loss. Without further clues, however, it was logical to at least start the search here. Besides, the press, the public, and the extended family were all anxious to find the body and bring closure to this difficult part of the case.

So far, the sheriffs had been searching for days. They had started in the previous bay, moved out into the deeper parts of the lake, tried other inlets and points along the shore, and returned to try this bay again. This time they would expand their work using the jackstay search method.

"You guys need any help?" Seabloom asked the divers. "Remember, you're looking for a body, but it could also be wrapped in a rug or carpeting, maybe even plastic, according to the homicide boys."

They looked up and shook their heads. The older man assembled a series of bright orange buoys that looked like small dumbbells. Wrapped around the narrow middle section was a bulge of rope.

Next, he checked some black weights that had metal loops on the top of each one. He grunted as he set the weights on the transom.

Seabloom leaned against the plastic steering wheel. Johnson stood next to him. He said, "The orange things are the surface buoys. They'll be attached by rope to those down weights, which will rest on the bottom of the lake."

"Have you already searched off the shoreline?" she asked.

"Two days ago. We used the arc search method. See, we figured if the body were dumped off the shore, it probably would be pretty close. For that kind of search, the arc is the easiest and most effective."

"How does it work?"

"Two guys. One on shore is the line tender, who's actually in command and holds one end of the line. The diver goes into the water with the other end. He'll start right next to the shore with his hands on the line at about fifty feet from the tender. At the line tender's signal—two pulls—the diver begins to swim in an arc from the shoreline. When he's gone through the arc and come back to the shore, he signals the tender with one pull and turns in the other direction. The diver moves along the line another fifty feet. Then he makes an arc in the opposite direction. Once he's gone out to the end of the line, the diver comes in, and they move everything down the shoreline to start over."

"What are they doing today?" Johnson said.

"They're going into the deeper water today. So they'll use the jackstay search method. It's better because it resembles a grid pattern search. Trouble is, it takes a lot more time."

"What do we do if we have to go to the middle of the lake?" she asked.

"We use the new ROV."

"What's that?"

"Remote Operated Vehicle. It cost a fortune, but the funding came through and we bought one. It's like a remote toy with a camera on it. We can get to the deepest parts of the lake with it, if we need it."

Seabloom looked behind him at the group of boats bobbing in the water. He could see binoculars and video cams trained on his

101

boat and the divers. It used to make him feel uncomfortable, but he also realized the community and the victim's family needed information, and they needed something to do, something that made them feel like they were contributing to the effort.

The two divers hooked the ends of lines to C-clamps on their waist belts, grabbed two underwater lights, adjusted their masks, and flopped backward off the stern. As they descended into the water, several lines of rope hissed over the transom after them. In a short time, one orange buoy popped up near the boat.

Seabloom pointed at it. "That's the first surface buoy. It's attached to an up and down line that is tied to the down weight. In a few minutes, you'll see the second buoy." He waited until the buoy bobbed in the green water several yards from the boat. "In between the two buoys, the divers lay another line on the bottom of the lake called a search line."

"It's a guide for them?" she asked.

"Right. The lead diver will take the line in his hand, and on the other side of the line, the backup diver will swim right next to him. Together, they'll search the area on either side of the line. Once they've gone the entire distance of the search line, they'll adjust their angle, move the rope and buoys, and do it all over again."

"It sounds tedious."

Seabloom nodded. "I couldn't do it." He stepped around the seat and balanced his walk to match the heave of the boat in the waves as he moved toward the stern. He lifted a heavy black object with bright yellow edges. "Body recovery bag," he told Johnson. "When we work in deep water, we use this kind. See, it's really a mesh bag. It allows the water to flow out so we can lift it off the bottom yet retains the forensic evidence inside. These handles are reinforced so they won't break, and it's even got one on the end if we need to winch the body out of the water."

Johnson's face twisted. "Will the body be visible in there?"

"Sort of. You can see it through the mesh, and we can seal the bag." He noticed her expression. "I know. You won't find me digging around down there." He pointed over the gunwale. "Every day that passes when we don't recover the body, decomposition occurs.

I've had divers tell me that when they go to lift the body into the recovery bag, it can literally fall apart. Arms come off, feet, you know."

Johnson braced herself on the back of the chair and swayed with the movement of the boat. "No thanks."

He pressed the subject, as if this were some kind of a test for new trainees. "After a few days, the skin will start to come off, marine animals may feed on it, and then it's really hard to get the whole mess into the recovery bag."

Johnson's eyes dipped toward the bottom of the boat.

Seabloom said, "Some of my friends in the medical examiner's office tell me about these 'floaters.' One time they recovered a body that popped up from a stream bed. Ten days underwater. When they put the body on the autopsy table, the guy's t-shirt moved from the things crawling out of him—"

"Okay. I think I get the idea."

Seabloom laughed to relieve the tension. "Yeah. Takes a special person to dive. But it's such an important mission for everyone. At least this lake is pretty clear. Should make the search easier."

By noon, the divers were cold and exhausted. They climbed into the boat and wrapped themselves in thick blankets. The older one lit a cigarette and watched the slight breeze draw the smoke away from him. Seabloom could see the frustration that pinched his face.

"Lots of junk down there, but no bodies," the diver said. "Take a break. We'll come back."

Seabloom started the engine and turned sharply toward the open lake. They'd head back to the dock, get some food and hot coffee, and rest. Then the divers would start all over again.

In twenty minutes, Seabloom tied off the lines that held the boat next to the rubber tenders on the dock. They were in a small marina, of which there were dozens around the lake. He held Johnson's hand as she took a high step off the boat and stretched her foot onto the steadiness of the dock. Together, they walked up to a sheriff's SUV. It was dark brown with yellow and blue trim and had the official logo of the Hennepin County Water Patrol painted on both sides of the vehicle. At the back end, another deputy handed out paper cups of hot coffee and wrapped sandwiches.

"Starbucks?" Johnson asked.

The deputy laughed while he handed a cup to her. "Budget cuts. You get my coffee today."

She made a face but took a deep drink of the hot liquid.

While they waited, the other boats that had followed them all morning came into the dock and tied up one at a time. A reporter from the local TV station, Channel Seven, came over first, trailed by the camera man who hefted his equipment.

"Aren't you worried about that falling overboard?" Seabloom joked with the team.

"It's insured." Calista Freeman, a reporter from the station, laughed. "Find anything?"

Seabloom took a long drink of his coffee and shook his head.

Even the hardened reporter frowned with frustration. Any time there was a search for a victim like this, it tended to draw people together even though they all had different interests in finding the body. "What's next?" Freeman inched closer to Seabloom.

He could smell her cologne and noticed that under her light jacket, she wore a tight-fitting sweater. "Back out this afternoon. We'll finish that bay." He swept his hand toward the area they'd just left. "Depends on how the guys hold up. They'll probably keep going since we all want to find her." He felt the increasing power of the sun as warmth across his back. Maybe the rain would pass by without stopping. Shadows grew under the ash trees. Two squirrels chased each other over the ground, chattering as they crossed the gravel road, and ran into the dark tangle of buckthorn bushes.

"Can't you use something like sonar?"

"We can always use our new ROV. But with a lake this popular, you can't believe how much junk there is on the bottom. So it's pretty tough to distinguish a body. The divers found a 1954 Oldsmobile yesterday. Probably someone ice fishing back then, broke through, and decided to leave it."

Freeman laughed. "Reminds me of the small town where I grew up in northern Minnesota. It was so boring the city would tow an old wreck of a car onto a frozen pond at the edge of town. They'd sell raffle tickets to guess what date it would finally fall through the ice in the spring."

"Sounds exciting."

"Most of us got out—with just our lives." Freeman frowned as if she were serious, then laughed again. She leaned closer to Seabloom.

Jane Johnson came over with a sandwich. She offered it to Seabloom. "Is ham okay?"

"You really think this is edible? Do you know who made it?" Seabloom nodded toward the deputy who still handed out coffee and food to people.

"I'm starved."

"I'll trust your recommendation, Jane," Seabloom said.

The older diver walked by. He dropped his cigarette onto the damp earth and rubbed his boot into it. "Let's get back out there, Sea." The diver cocked his hips to one side. "I promised the family we'd find their daughter."

Reminded of their mission, the others all started to separate and drift off in different directions. As Seabloom looked up, he saw a group of people walking toward him, including the parents of Mina Jensen.

When they reached him, a blond woman introduced herself as Laurie Rohrbacher, the cousin of Mina. "I've been with them constantly." She pointed to the parents.

"Hello, Kenny," the father said. "I know you're busy, but could we have a minute?"

Seabloom stopped. He'd become close to the family and was on a first-name basis with them. "Of course, Harry."

"Any news?" Harry asked. His wife, Jessie, stood beside and a little behind him.

Seabloom sighed. "Nothing yet. We're going back out as soon as possible."

Harry wore khaki pants and Finnish walking shoes—soft tops with water proof rubber soles. He had a Twins baseball cap on that covered his thin gray hair. His wife wore a black and gold University of Iowa sweatshirt with a hood, which hung limply over her back. "Anything?"

"We're trying."

"You go too slow," Jessie said in a loud voice. Harry patted her shoulder, but she kept talking. "At this rate, we'll be here forever. Meanwhile, we aren't looking in other places."

"It's standard procedure so we don't miss any possible clues," Seabloom said.

"Well, I'm not happy with this." Her voice became shrill.

Seabloom was tempted to say something to shut her down, but after years of these situations, he understood what grief and fear did to everyone, especially the family. The other five people congregated around the edges of the conversation. They were strangers who had been moved by the news reports and had volunteered to help in the search. While Seabloom and the divers covered the water, two other deputies had led this group on a coordinated search of the thick woods behind the picnic area. So far, they hadn't found anything either.

One of that group insisted to Seabloom, "There must be something else we could be doing."

"All of us are working hard. Sometimes patience is the best thing," Seabloom said.

"Well, I can take as much time off work as it takes to find her. I'm not giving up."

"It's that monster she married," Jessie shouted. "Why isn't anyone forcing him to tell us where our little girl is?" She looked around the small group as if they could answer her. They nodded, but when no one said anything, Jessie placed her fingers in front of her mouth, her face quivered, and she started to cry.

Harry reached over to wrap his arm around her shoulders. "We just want her home." He looked from the volunteer to Seabloom. Harry pulled off his cap and held it over his chest. His eyes were red-rimmed and circled in deep gray smudges. His face looked as thin and tired as his hair. "It's like this hollow space in my chest. I can still see her as a child when I used to push her up on a swing and her hair would float across my face and I could—"

Laurie stepped forward. "What's your success rate at finding missing people?"

Seabloom wiped his hand across his mouth while he thought about how to answer her. He didn't want to get in trouble with the commander, but he also wanted to be honest. "Usually, we find the victims, but there are always cases where we never find them. But we're doing all we can."

"I'm sure you are," Laurie said. She stepped back to put her arm around Jessie. Their heads tilted together.

Seabloom wanted to say something, anything that might comfort them or give them hope. He didn't have the words or facts. Even after years of this work, he still couldn't entirely insulate himself from a family's grief. He was supposed to be detached and professional. But this case tugged at him more than others. Maybe it was the brutality of the murder or the wanton disregard by the killer for the family's suffering. Why wouldn't he simply tell where the body was? Of course, he had lawyered up and been told to shut up. Seabloom understood all that, but he also had to face the family and see their pain every day.

It motivated him and the entire team to work harder. He watched as the volunteers spaced themselves apart from each other and formed a line at the edge of some buckthorn bushes. At a signal, they all moved forward, heads lowered as they scanned the ground before them. They soon disappeared amongst the thick cover of the bushes.

One of the counselors hired by the county attorney's office through the victim/witness advocate team got out of her parked car and walked over to them. Amanda Cahill was her name, and Seabloom had met her before since she was a contract therapist who worked often with crime victims.

After saying hello to everyone, she asked, "Anything yet?"

Seabloom shook his head. "We're about to go back out, but the divers needed a break. It's tough work."

Harry looked out across the choppy water. Wind blew strands of thin hair that poked out from under his cap. He didn't respond. His wife patted her lips with her hand, her eyes moistened, and she fought for control. Beside her, Laurie's face was pinched with grief.

Cahill moved closer and touched Laurie Rothbacher's forearm. "That's okay. Let the grief out. After a while, you'll find something

107

to hang onto, something that will carry you forward and help you survive this."

"I don't know," Laurie whispered. "We were so close, and now—"

Cahill said, "I lost my husband to a drunk driver. He died at thirty-six. My life broke into a million pieces, but out of that, some of those broken pieces gave me a message that carries me even today." She paused and said, "It taught me to appreciate every day and to use those same broken pieces to heal and grow. It's ironic that things should work that way. In time, I think you'll find the same thing."

Jessie nodded and leaned against Harry. He said, "Thanks. I know that's your job, but right now I'm so damn mad I could kill Dan Jensen right here." His face blossomed red and his eyes grew in size.

Seabloom's commander walked over from the food truck. "Deputy, I need you to take your boat to Smith's Bay. Reports of a couple drunk fishermen over there."

Seabloom protested, "But I'm in the middle of the search."

"This shouldn't take you long. We'll use the other boat if you're not back." The commander started to turn away, finished with his orders. "Look for an eighteen-foot Lund. Two guys are trying to troll but they have a small problem—they forgot they're still anchored. Give 'em a ticket or get them off the lake. I'll depend on your judgment." He walked away.

Seabloom finished his coffee and crushed the Styrofoam cup in his hand. Another low level waste of his time. When would they figure out that he was capable of much more sophisticated investigations? He sighed and headed for his boat. He would race over there, ticket the damn drunks, and get back in time to go out again on the search.

In twenty minutes, he had returned. The fishermen were not legally drunk, so he had to let them go. That was okay with Seabloom since he got back more quickly. After securing his boat, he started up the dock toward the landing on shore. The divers walked past him along the footpath to reach the boat. They carried fresh tanks. The younger one looked up into the pewter sky, then stepped into the boat. If the weather changed to rain, they'd have to stop soon and come back tomorrow morning.

Seabloom waved his hand at Johnson and started back to the dock. Then he heard a shout from the woods. Several more people yelled something, and Seabloom stopped walking. He ran across the gravel road that paralleled the lake and entered the woods. He found two of the searchers bent over underneath a large, tangled buckthorn bush. The deputy in charge of the ground search party had his arms out wide, trying to hold the group back. "It's a potential crime scene. Get back, please," he yelled at them.

Seabloom gave assistance and helped pull back the more excited searchers from under the bush. In five minutes, the area was clear and the group stood around in a semi-circle before the bush. Seabloom inched forward. His breath caught in his throat.

Under the bush was a small, oblong mound of fresh dirt that looked as if it had been turned over recently. The soil was clear of the sticks and leaves that covered the surrounding area, and there was a faint footprint at the corner of the mound, like someone had stomped down the dirt. The mound rested in shadows and was almost hidden underneath the bush. Surrounded by heavy woods, the wind died out leaving the scene in silence. The setting sun lengthened the shadows from the trees.

Seabloom tried to control his breathing. Had they finally found her? He was about to turn and run for his radio when he noticed something on the ground. At the north end of the mound, a piece of cloth lay partly buried in the dirt. With weathering, it looked gray and reminded Seabloom of the color of gravestones.

Chapter Eleven

The next morning, Ted stopped home on his way from the office to talk with Laurie. He'd finished an early meeting with a ninety-year-old widow whose good health probably meant she'd live another ninety years. She was concerned about the rising level of taxes in Minnesota. She threatened to move to Florida, where there wasn't any income tax. All her friends were in Naples. Ted worked through the morning to shelter her immense income from as much of the tax bite as he could. Complaining that it was still too much, she left and Ted was free to spend time with Laurie.

He and Dan were scheduled to meet for lunch. Ted was anxious to get the truth from Dan, once and for all.

Ted parked in the drive. The exterior of the house was stucco, and green shutters flanked all the windows in the front. The back yard sloped down until it ran into Minnehaha Creek as it made a lazy turn on its way to the Mississippi River. The area was called Tangletown because of the tangled streets that had been constructed around the meanderings of the creek. The style of the homes there reminded Ted of the 1940s and of old cars with big fenders that had once occupied the single-car garages. He hurried inside.

Laurie was working from home and met him in the kitchen—the neutral area reserved for all serious conversations. She waited in front of the microwave for a cup of water to boil. She had two tea bags laid out on the counter. "How was your meeting?"

"Whew. Another rich discontented client. They pay well, but it's tough to put up with them sometimes."

The microwave binged and she removed the first mug. She placed a bag of green tea into it and heated the second cup. She turned to face him. "Are you really happy in your new practice?"

"What? Sure, and I like the pace—predictable and slow."

Laurie shifted her back to him and took a long time dunking the tea bag up and down in her cup. When she turned around and handed the cup to him, Ted could see her eyes were red. She blinked them several times. "I miss her so much," Laurie whispered.

He reached for her with his arms and cradled her shoulders. "I remember all the time you spent with Mina when Dan was in Afghanistan."

Laurie nodded and played with the seeping tea bag, bobbing it up and down in the cup. "We were really close. Of course, when Danny got back and he started the company, she got busier and we kind of drifted apart, but we remained best friends." Frown lines crowded above her eyes, and she told Ted about the search the day before at Lake Minnetonka. "They found something buried, but it got too late to finish so they were going to start again this morning. I was with Jessie and Harry all the time yesterday. I had some work to finish, so I couldn't go back today."

Ted glanced at her. "I'm guessing it would be tough for you if they found Mina."

"You're right. Pulling her out of the ground—I couldn't stand to see that."

The microwave beeped again. Laurie withdrew the second cup and put a fresh tea bag into it. She took a deep breath. "I think about her all the time. Can't get her out of my mind. She was funny and such a tomboy. She'd do anything, always pushing the edge. She was smart, too. Really good at math and organizing things." She grinned at Ted and continued, "Mina was so analytical. I bet she did more than Dan to get the company going."

"I think you're right. But she must have bowed out; he's going broke." He lifted his cup and smelled the grassy scent of the tea. "What about the allegations of her having an affair?"

"At first I didn't believe the stories. But as I thought about her, I don't know. Maybe it could be true. I know their marriage was really strained. And she was concerned about him."

"Dan said they had patched things up and were planning to start a family." Ted decided to add a little sugar. When he opened the cupboard next to the sink, he found it—in the same place they had kept it before the divorce. It made him feel good. Some things about their past lives hadn't changed.

Laurie sipped from her own cup of tea. "So you're going to talk with the prosecutor tomorrow?"

Ted let a lungful of air escape as he set the cup on the counter. He told her about Katrina Albert and how Korsokov looked more suspicious as they investigated.

"Then you're going to be out of the case?" Her eyes bored into him.

"We've interviewed witnesses. I'll hit Rogin with everything I've got and try to get the case dumped."

"Didn't the police talk to all the witnesses? Why do you need to spend any more time on that?"

"They decided early in the case that Danny was guilty. I don't think they went far enough in their investigation."

The lines in Laurie's face creased, and she frowned. "But you're getting out, right?" She lifted the cup to her mouth, and Ted watched her lips tighten over the edge of the rim.

He didn't tell her about hiring Jackie to do the legal research for a possible defense of the amygdala hijack—if they needed it. But he also didn't want to lie to Laurie. "Soon."

Laurie said, "Ted, I don't know how to say this . . . you can't feel okay about this."

"Okay about what?"

"Getting back into a case like this. Besides the fact that it's my cousin who is dead, you promised that you'd never go back into a courtroom again."

To cover up the flutter he felt in his chest, Ted drank from his tea. "I'm not," he assured her. "We'll wrap up our investigation. I've already e-mailed Rogin the new evidence we've found. I'll talk to him and that should do it." His words came out fast as if he were also trying to convince himself that he could slip out of the case easily. After all, he recognized that now he really wanted to see it through to the end.

"And you've got Samantha helping you."

"Yes, I've got Samantha."

"When you were at your best, you were always so inventive. And I have to admit that your charm could win over any jury." She set down the cup so hard that it clattered on the granite countertop. "Listen, I'll put it bluntly, Ted. I'm warning you to get out of this soon, real soon. Matt is very proud of you for the changes you've made, but he wants a father at home, not in the courtroom. I've committed to you in marriage again, but my patience won't last forever."

Ted nodded but didn't reply.

He left the house and, at noon, drove his Mercedes into the parking lot of a sprawling restaurant in northeast Minneapolis on Marshall Avenue. It was called Psycho Suzie's. He planned to take Dan for lunch and have a "come-to-Jesus" meeting with him. Normally, that would occur in the office, but he wanted Dan to be slightly off guard. Ted wanted to keep the surroundings light. That way, he could drill into Dan with his questions.

As usual, pickup trucks and a few cars filled the lot. Ted climbed out of his car and left his briefcase behind. He crunched across the gravel on his way to the front door. Over the embankment in front of him, the Mississippi River flowed by in a twisting, powerful current. It glistened in the sun, but as he looked closer, Ted saw the water looked bluish-brown. Still, it smelled fresh and damp and reminded him that summer was coming.

Pyscho Suzie's was one of the most popular bars, with a restaurant attached, in northeast Minneapolis. It had started a few blocks away in an abandoned 1950s A&W drive in, which the owners converted into a tiki bar with a big outdoor patio. Since the weather in Minnesota kept people inside for months at a time, when spring came the patio overflowed with patrons. Even if the temperature was only 50 degrees, Minnesotans starved for sun insisted on occupying the patio, where they shivered in shorts and t-shirts. The restaurant soon outgrew that location and moved down the street to the larger space.

Every time Ted entered the door, he smelled frying burgers and beer. The entire place retained a tiki bar atmosphere while fake palm trees leaned forward from the corners and the bar looked like it had been constructed of bamboo.

He wound his way among the tables and patrons. Dozens of long-necked beer bottles stood on the tables before people who were eating lunch, laughing, and watching the big screen TVs hanging from the ceiling. Sports analysts were commenting on the beginning of the Minnesota Twins baseball season. Ted spotted Danny in the back corner, cocktail nestled between his hands. He glanced around and looked uncomfortable—just what Ted wanted. When he saw Ted, he brightened. Ted flashed a fake grin at him.

"Yo, Counselor. How's my case look?"

"Uh, we gotta talk." Ted sat next to him. When the waitress came over, he ordered lemonade. She set two plastic-covered menus on the edge of the table.

Danny sensed that something was wrong. His small eyes narrowed as he studied Ted for a clue. He wore a loose blue cotton sweater that opened in a "V" at the neck to expose a golf shirt underneath. The collar was frayed on the edges so that it looked like white fuzz.

The waitress interrupted when she placed a cold glass of lemonade next to Ted. He took a sip before he launched into his client. "I'll be meeting with the prosecutor, but before I do, there are some things about your story that don't make any sense. I want to know the truth once and for all."

"Told you."

"I don't think you've told me *everything*." Ted blew out a big lungful of air. "Let's start with this," he said sarcastically. "You told me you and Mina were going to start a family, but Mina was having an affair? With this Ukrainian guy? Doesn't make any sense."

"It's complicated." Danny glanced over his shoulder to the side. Around his neck, the gold necklace swayed in the same direction.

"Quit playing games with me."

The noise of bottles clinking, plates clattering on tables, laughter, and the noise from the TV enveloped both of them. It created a bubble of privacy. Ted thought about how difficult it was for any suspect of a crime to tell the truth. It was human nature to mitigate responsibility, to avoid it, and to minimize guilt.

He said, "Samantha got all the records from domestic abuse court. Mina filed two orders for protection petitions against you."

"We had our problems. But she dropped them all," he added quickly.

"What the hell am I supposed to do to defend you?" Ted shouted. Two tables of people next to them looked up from their hamburgers.

"Mina was unhappy, okay? Maybe she had the affair to make me jealous." Danny lifted the cocktail, a margarita, to his mouth and chugged half of it. Ice cubes clinked when he dropped it back on the table. Catching the eye of the waitress, he ordered another.

Ted couldn't believe it. "Make you jealous?" he repeated. "Don't you see how that also gives you a motive to kill her?"

"Yeah, but I didn't." He opened his hands in front of his chest and shrugged. He glanced over his shoulder again.

Ted propped his head on an uplifted palm. Then he asked, "Where was your dog the night Mina was killed?"

"Jon Stewart? At home with us."

Ted frowned. "Was he friendly to strangers?"

"Usually not."

"Wouldn't he bark like hell if someone else came in and killed Mina?"

Danny shook his head. "Don't know. I was passed out. Those beers hit me unusually hard."

The waitress returned with Danny's drink and took their lunch orders. In spite of trying to have a more healthy diet, Ted ordered a cheddar cheeseburger. They were especially greasy here and delicious. A loud cheer erupted from the crowd in front of the TV by the bar, then died down into slaps on each other's backs.

Ted pointed his finger in Danny's face. "I'm done fuckin' around with you. You either tell me everything you've 'forgotten,' or I'm out of here. You can defend yourself. I understand that my clients lie to me at one time or another, but I can't represent you like that."

"But what about our history? Doesn't that count for anything?"

"Of course it does. That's why I've done as much work as I have already."

"What about the amygdala hijack?"

Ted sighed. "I can't guarantee that will work."

115

"Dr. Strauss?"

"In addition to him, we'd need to get a second expert to bolster what Strauss has to say. Even so, Rogin may not bite on it." Ted pointed his finger at Danny again. "In Rogin's opinion, just because you've got PTSD doesn't relieve you from culpability for murder."

"Yeah, because I didn't kill her."

Ted waved his hands in the air in front of Dan to stop him from talking any more. Both of them leaned back in their chairs and fell silent. Ted's phone buzzed. He noticed it was Samantha calling. "What's up?"

"You still having lunch with our boy?"

"Yeah."

"I just found some dynamite."

"I'd like to use some right here."

"You know I still get access to the national criminal data bases? I did a lot of checking on Nick Korsokov and found that, three years ago, he was a suspect in a similar situation to our case."

"Oh?"

"He was allegedly involved with another woman, not Katrina, who disappeared under unexplained circumstances. She's never been found as far as I can tell from the police records. Sound familiar?"

Ted sat up in the chair. "Was Korsokov charged with anything?"

"No. He was questioned and released. Not enough evidence, apparently."

Ted hung up and turned back to Jensen. "By the way, what size shoe do you wear?" Ted asked him.

"Nine and a half."

The waitress had set two plates on the table. On each plate there was a slab of beef squeezed between a bun, surrounded by a mountain of fries that smelled hot and greasy. Both of them stopped talking to concentrate on the serious business of eating an enormous burger that was difficult to hold in two hands. After several eager bites, Ted spoke softly. "Dan, I know you don't want to hear this, but there may be a chance to minimize any prison time for you."

"Oh?" He wiped some grease off his chin with a paper napkin.

"*If* you happen to know the location of Mina's body and would tell me, I could take that to the prosecutor."

Dan's face flushed red. "You still don't fucking believe me, do you?" He shoved the plate away from him. Through clenched lips, he said, "I don't know where she is. Simple."

"I know, it's just that—"

Danny's eyes burrowed into Ted's. "No, you don't know. You've never come back from some of the scariest shit in your life to re-enter your country." His anger built. "And then you try to fit back into the civilian life. Sometimes it's just impossible."

Ted realized there was nothing to do except to let him run out of steam. Everyone had secret rooms in the back of their minds and hidden actions that were never revealed to the public. But Dan seemed to have more secrets than most. Sometimes, when Ted looked deeply into his eyes, it was unsettling. Could his client be capable of murder?

Dan kept talking, faster now. "Oh sure, I've made a truck load of money, but the dreams still come to me at night. I can still see every detail of the bridge. I can't shake it." He looked off toward the crowd in front of the TV. The afternoon game shows had started, and fake laughter carried across the room. Jensen's eyes drifted away to the ceiling.

"I'm sorry, Dan."

"You can't imagine how hard all this is on a marriage, too." He blinked a few times and focused on Ted.

Ted sighed. "Okay. What else can you tell me?"

"I'll do anything to help." Danny drained the last of his marga-rita. With his fingers, he lifted the slice of lime out of the glass. He squeezed it and played with it. His shoulders jerked. "There might be something else." He spoke slowly.

Ted looked at Danny. He could smell the tart lime juice. He waited.

"Somebody wanted to mess with me."

"What?"

"Well, back in the war zone, in Afghanistan, I was in charge of security for a small engineer team. They were assigned to pretend to inspect a bridge. But the true mission was to gather intelligence for a bigger assault." Danny looked up at the waitress to order another drink.

"I heard about this from Dr. Strauss."

"Okay, so we didn't get much information, but on our way out, things were cool. We'd booby-trapped the bridge, and then we got hit."

"Taliban?"

"Right. Ambushed us. We walked right into it. Well, *I* walked us right into it. My fault. They lined us up and shot everyone except me." His eyes rose to meet Ted's, and his shoulders shook. "The command kind of covered it up and didn't assign any blame, thank God."

"What does this have to do with anything?"

"About six months ago, a brother of one of the team who was killed on the bridge contacted me, mad as hell and blaming me. It was his only brother. I tried to explain, but the dude was an ex- Navy SEAL who'd been deployed in Iraq, so I couldn't bullshit him." He squeezed a puddle of ketchup next to his fries.

"Did he threaten you?"

"Well, he never said 'I'm gonna kill you' or anything like that. But I felt scared and figured he'd be capable of doing something if he wanted. I told him I was sorry."

"So you think maybe he killed Mina as revenge for his brother?"

Danny shrugged and twirled his margarita glass between his fingers. He twisted around and looked into the far corner of the restaurant, then turned back to face Ted. "Don't know, but these Special Forces guys are elite fighters, and a lot of them are really fucked up. I mean, even *before* they go into a hot zone. And I fucked up the mission. I was in charge of security and I blew it by not doing the prep work on the terrain that I should've. The bogies were hiding right under our noses before they struck us."

"You didn't tell the police about this guy who threatened you?"

"No. They were convinced from the start I was guilty. I thought I'd better shut up until I talked to you before I said anything more."

"Got a name for him? Phone number from caller ID?"

"Yeah. Guy's named Demontre Harrison. Lives in the Twin Cities. Small world, huh?" Dan reached into his pocket for his smart phone. He keyed in some data and found the number for Harrison. "Be careful."

"Samantha knows what she's doing. She'll win him over with charm." Ted looked at the work he'd done on the burger. Comfort food, which he needed at this moment. He squirted more ketchup on it and took another bite. Moisture from it trickled down the outside of his hand. While chewing the last of it, Ted said, "This guy, Harrison, ever meet with you? Ever come over to the house?"

Danny shook his head. "I never met him in person. Didn't want to have anything to do with him."

"But he threatened you?"

"Yeah. Because he said, 'We'll *deal* with this, man. I promise.'" Danny lifted his own hamburger and bit off a big chunk of it. The cuffs of his sweater were in danger of catching the run-off from the hamburger. "And then, later, there was something strange at the house."

Ted wiped his hands. "What?"

"I came home one day and noticed pry marks on the back door. I don't think anyone else would have seen them, but I'd just had the doorknobs and locks on both the doors replaced. I saw fresh marks."

"I didn't see anything in the police reports about pry marks."

"Like I said, no one would notice them."

"Do you think someone had been in the house?"

"Oh, yeah. There were things changed around and a faint smell of cologne. Not mine. I asked Mina. She said she didn't know anything about it. At the time, I figured she was lying, but now, after all this—"

Ted leaned back in his chair. This information could change everything. Why hadn't Dan told him earlier? It also meant the case would stretch out longer than Ted had anticipated. This meant a lot more work for everyone.

He watched Danny chomp on the last of his hamburger and swallow it. All that remained on his plate were a few squashed fries and a smear of ketchup. The fries looked like they were dead, lying in their own blood.

Chapter Twelve

"Woo-ee," Sandy Rogin yelled at the screen of his laptop while he sat in his office. "Everything's set." Rogin pumped his fist into the air. "I've got to get the case charged and finally moving."

Zehra Hassan got up from the leather couch in Rogin's office. "Hold onto your pants, Sandy. Haven't you seen the new evidence that Rohrbacher sent us?"

"Of course. He's trying to make Korsokov look like the killer. But the cops interviewed him twice. He's suspicious, but not guilty."

"You should go back and review the new information. Then all of us will make a charging decision."

Rogin batted the air in front of him with his hand. "Aww, you worry too much. We got this in the bag. Right, Maureen?" Rogin turned to the young woman who stood at the end of the desk, Maureen Hanrahan.

She was the newest hire in the office. She'd graduated from law school a year earlier. After clerking in the county attorney's office, she'd been hired as a lawyer and assigned to Zehra Hassan's trial team but was supervised directly by Sanford Rogin. Since Gary Hill wouldn't do what Rogin ordered him to do, he had told Hill to hit the bricks. Instead, he recruited Maureen, who'd been anxious to help in any way.

She was a small woman, shapely, and had light skin and dark red hair. "From my grandmother. One hundred percent Irish," she had told Rogin.

"I like it," he'd said while he smiled at her.

Maureen shook her head. "When my grandma came from County Mayo, she wanted to put it all behind her and get American citizenship. We never even celebrated St. Patrick's Day, though my grandma loved to drink brandy. By the way, you can call me Mo."

Maureen was grateful to have any job as a lawyer since the market was so glutted for new graduates. Consequently, when Rogin had approached her to help in the Mina Jensen murder case, she'd readily agreed. After all, Maureen wanted to make the best impression she could on the powerful boss who now looked at her. But now, she responded to Rogin's boasting by cautioning him, "I think Zehra's got a point, Sanford."

Zehra nodded and turned to him. "Sandy, stop celebrating and think this through. What if we charge the wrong guy? Not only is it morally wrong, but think of the fallout in the press. Think about how our boss will react."

Rogin tilted his head and continued to squeeze the blue ball.

"How much do you really know about Korsokov's background? We should at least check out the info that Ted gave us." Zehra circled around the end of Rogin's desk opposite from where Mo stood.

"Uh, we're working on it." Rogin's phone rang. He answered his wife. "Hey, sweetie. Did you see the morning news? Your husband's on a roll." He listened for a while. "Sure. I'll be late tonight, but I can take over if you're going for a run. No prob. Kiss MacKenzie for me." He hung up and turned back to Zehra. "What were you saying?"

Zehra sighed. "I'm warning you to be careful with this case. Ted's a lot smarter than people give him credit for."

"It's just typical defense bullshit. Try and throw up a smoke screen and blame someone else." Rogin stood up and stretched to his full height. He wiggled his shoulders to relieve the tension and set the ball on his crowded desk. "I've looked at everything, and I'm still convinced that Jensen's our man." He ran his hand over his thick beard. White teeth peeked out when he smiled at Zehra.

She walked over to the large window that looked out to the east, over the turn in the Mississippi River that flowed by the University of Minnesota campus. "This case is odd."

"There you go again."

She turned back to face Rogin. "You keep ignoring the fact that we still don't have a body."

Rogin blew out a lungful of air. "We've been over this a hundred times. We don't need one. We got the guy." He turned to Maureen. "And I got the best second-chair in the office."

Mo's face brightened and she moved closer to them. "I'll do everything you need. We're going to win this case." With a closed fist, she pumped her arm once in a short arc.

Zehra shook her head. "You've both got the right attitude, but it takes more than that to win a tough trial. What else are you doing?"

Rogin walked to the far side of his office. He passed several chairs, a conference table, and two couches. When he reached a white board, he turned it toward the middle of the room. "Mo?"

She put on a pair of oval glasses. The left frame was held together with tape. Maureen searched through the drawer in a small desk by the window. "Here." She handed him a red felt marker.

He drew the number one on the board and circled it. "I've convinced the sheriff to double the number of deputies searching for the body." He wrote it on the board. "Of course, he likes the attention anyway and would love to be the one to find the body." He wrote a two on the board. "I leaned on the police chief to add more detectives to the investigation. We now have four of them—four, Zehra—combing the neighborhood in Minnetonka around the crime scene."

Zehra crossed her arms in front of her chest. She leaned to one side and waited as Rogin continued.

"We've tripled the amount of money devoted to this case. Our boss was even willing to go higher, but I thought I'd save that money in the bank until later if we really need it." He drew the number three on the board and circled it. "The sheriff's crime lab is working overtime at our request to process all the forensic evidence. They're way over budget, but they think this case is worth it."

Zehra's eyes opened wider. "I've never heard of that."

Rogin sniffed and said, "I told you this is special. All I know is they've pulled out all the stops for this case. They're doing DNA testing on every God damn thing the investigators found anywhere near the crime scene. You got any idea how expensive all that is?"

"And it takes a lot of time," Maureen reminded them.

Zehra stepped up to the board. "Okay. It all sounds great, but you still have only a circumstantial case, Sandy."

"Sanford," he corrected her. "So what?" He turned to Mo for confirmation. "Last I learned in law school, a case can be proven

122

with either direct evidence like an eyewitness or circumstantial evidence."

Maureen nodded, and her face flushed with their shared excitement.

Rogin followed Zehra around the board and stood next to her. He towered above her and poked his finger into her shoulder. "You're just too careful. We've got to be aggressive with a crime like this."

Zehra's face reddened and she shouted at Rogin, "I've tried a hell of a lot more cases than you have, *Sandy*. You're forgetting one small thing—the jury. We can never predict what a jury will do, no matter how much money and effort we put into the prosecution." They backed away from each other. She said, "Once again, what do you really know about the defendant? Or this guy, Korsokov? Have you investigated their backgrounds?"

No one answered her, each of them busy with his or her own thoughts and motivations.

The silence made the beeping of Rogin's cell phone particularly loud. He hurried all the way back to his desk and answered it. Detective Sean O'Brien was calling.

"Listen, Rogin, I got something for you," the detective said.

Rogin could hear the rasp in his voice from the thousands of cigarettes he'd smoked over the years. "What's up? I'm really busy here, Sean."

"Hold on to your pecker. The sheriff's water patrol just called. Seems they found something buried next to the lake. Don't know if it's our victim, but I'll keep in touch."

"Good, but I've been extremely busy getting this case ready for charging."

"What're you waiting for? I got a lot of my men anxious for you to get your ass moving."

"Then find me a body," Rogin yelled.

O'Brien hung up.

"Maybe Zehra's got a point," Maureen said. She came over to Rogin and reached up to put her hand on his shoulder. It rested there for a few minutes.

Rogin blinked his eyes and thought for a moment. "All right. I'll get all our investigators out to assist the police, and we'll turn out everything thing this animal has done in his life. We've got to convict him and get some justice for this family."

"You can get Grant to pay for all that overtime?"

Rogin's face creased into a smile, and he nodded with confidence. "I got more than that."

Zehra frowned. "What are you talking about?"

"While you've been taking your time and agonizing over this case, Grant and I have been talking." Rogin paused and walked behind his desk. He turned and announced, "Grant's given me the go-ahead to charge Dan Jensen with second degree murder. But I'm going to raise the potential penalty by taking it to the grand jury right away for the first degree indictment."

Zehra stood still. "Did you tell him about this new evidence the defense turned up?"

"Not yet. He's anxious to get this case going."

"Sanford, this is irresponsible."

"He's the boss; it's his call ultimately."

"I'll talk to him right now," Zehra insisted.

"Too late. He's made up his mind." Rogin turned to Maureen. "You ready for the ride of your life?"

Maureen's voice was crisp. "I'll do whatever I can. I've cleared off my schedule for the next month."

Rogin looked from one woman to the other. He leaned closer to Maureen. He could smell her musky perfume and admired the creamy color of her skin. She was a lot better to look at and work with than Gary Hill. He smiled at the thought of all the hours they'd be forced to spend together.

"All right. We'll attack this with an atomic bomb. Nothing, I mean nothing, will be left to chance," he assured both of them. He barked out orders to Mo to activate an even larger team of help: victim/witness advocates for all the potential witnesses, a larger cadre of law clerks to do the tedious but critical legal research to fight all the objections they anticipated Rohrbacher would make, added investigators from the office to be pulled from ongoing investigations, and a dedicated group of support people to handle the voluminous paperwork he anticipated.

Maureen tapped all the directives into her laptop. "I assume you want me to file the ethics complaint against Rohrbacher? I've prepared it already."

Rogin gave one nod of his head but didn't look at Zehra.

"What ethics complaint?" Zehra shouted.

"It's nothing. I'm just going to give Teddy a headache," Rogin said.

"I haven't agreed to this. What the hell do you think you're doing? There aren't any grounds to file a complaint. You'll commit prosecutorial misconduct, which can jeopardize any guilty verdict in the future. Are you thinking through all this, Sandy?"

"You're just not aggressive enough."

"No," Zehra said. "I'm not on board with this decision." She hurried to the door. "I'm going to see Grant right now." She shot out of the office and hurried up to the floor above to the head of the office, Ulysses Grant.

She pushed through the double oak doors into his spacious office. A large Persian rug covered the parquet wooden floor. Zehra could smell the faint odor of a cigar—even though it was a non-smoking building. Grant sat behind his desk and looked up. Against his black skin, the whites of his wide-open eyes stood out prominently.

"Bud," she used his nickname, "we've got to talk."

Rogin and Maureen burst into the office and stood on the opposite side of the room from Zehra.

Grant stood. His shirt stretched across his chunky body. "Slow down. What's the problem?" He came around his desk and offered all of them seats in the couches set at an angle to the desk. No one sat down.

Zehra started first. She complained about Rogin's renegade approach to the case. Her voice rose when she got to the ethics complaint. "We've never done anything like that. It's immoral."

Rogin responded by stressing the need for an aggressive approach to the case. "You told me yourself that you want this animal convicted and sent to jail. The public demands it, and so does justice." His face colored pink with his passion.

Grant took a deep breath. His eyebrows lowered and his face turned even darker to the point the freckles across his nose disappeared. "I don't like this, Sandy. I told you I'd open the bank to pay for a full investigation and prosecution of the case, but that doesn't mean doing anything improper. The press could kill me with this." He turned toward the large window that covered the entire wall. "I agree with Zehra. I'm ordering you to drop the idea of an ethics complaint." He turned back to face Rogin. "Any questions?" It was obvious that Grant really didn't want any.

Rogin breathed deeply but straightened his shoulders when he said, "I got it. But I think you're both wimping out on this. We've got to hit the defense with everything we possibly can. I'm not going to lose this case."

"You better not lose it," Grant said. He paused, puffed on his cigar, and added, "If you do find some solid reason for filing an ethics complaint, that's okay by me. But it's got to be legally solid."

Rogin winked at Maureen as they filed out of the office.

Ten minutes later, Rogin sat alone behind his desk. He slumped into his large leather chair and swiveled so that he could look out the window. He felt the tension drain from his body and realized that he'd have to pace himself. It would be a long and tough fight. The defense lawyer didn't worry him. Instead, it was the jury. Because he had to admit that Zehra was right—no one could predict what a jury would decide. Even the strongest prosecution case could be tipped over if a stupid jury believed a defendant, felt sorry for him, or just simply went off track. There wasn't much Sanford Rogin and all the money and power he could assemble could do to prevent that. He stood up and felt a sharp pain in his chest that disappeared quickly. He hoped it was from MacKenzie jumping on him and not something worse.

He resolved to prepare so thoroughly that he'd be the first prosecutor to actually control a jury. He'd make history. He wouldn't need to use an ethics complaint.

Rogin sat behind his computer and scrolled down to the template for a second degree murder complaint. The one he'd previously drafted with Daniel Jensen's name was still in the computer. He opened the new software from the court system that allowed him to e-file the complaint. With a few key strokes, he formally filed the complaint and set the case in motion. He asked for one million dollars in bail. Jensen would have to appear in court in less than thirty-six hours to either go into custody or post the bail amount.

That done, he e-mailed a copy to Ted Rohrbacher and also sent seven copies to all the major news media in the Twin Cities. He felt a tingling in his stomach. He'd never admit it to anyone, but even after all the years of experience, he still felt nervous about this one. That was good since it would keep him sharp all the way to the end.

Chapter Thirteen

As Ted crossed over the skyway from the parking lot to the Government Center at nine o'clock two days later, he felt nervous about the upcoming court appearance. He'd yelled at his secretary in the office earlier and now regretted it. Dampness formed under his arms, and the sun slanting through the windows of the skyway seemed too bright. Nervousness gave way to anger. Rogin hadn't even warned Ted the complaint would be filed. Ted had planned to bring up the amygdala hijack and try to negotiate a way out for Dan before he was charged. Too late for that now.

It also meant that Ted would be drawn deeper into the case—something that made him the most nervous, although he knew he was fully committed by now.

Painful memories of battles in the courtrooms from past years flooded his mind. He passed a musician playing a guitar with his case opened on the floor for tips. He sang Bob Dylan's song, "Positively Fourth Street." ". . . when I was down, you just stood there grinning."

He knew his fear was ridiculous. How could a simple courtroom cause so much pain? But it wasn't the room itself; it was the thoughts of embarrassment and humiliation that had started from a courtroom disaster. And guilt for an innocent victim—never to receive the justice she was due.

Ted was here to fight against Rogin's request for one million dollars in bail. Jensen faced two choices: he could deposit the full amount of bail, as cash, with the clerk of court or he could pay for a bail bond. Dan had contacted one of the oldest bail bond companies in the county.

Stein Bonding was a second generation company which provided jobs for even the third generation of the family. The patriarch had died years ago, leaving the business in the hands of his son, Humphrey "Bogey" Stein. Most people assumed the nickname came from the actor. Actually he'd picked it up in college betting on a golf game. Humphrey had won the match and the money with a bogey. With the explosion of crime rates in the eighties and nineties, Bogey had also made a fortune helping people get out of jail—legally.

He was a friendly man, impeccably dressed, always smiling, and loved to be in court. Five days a week—Stein seldom took vacations from his business—he visited the courtrooms. He carried a large Styrofoam cup of coffee with him all the time and sipped from it throughout the day.

A bail bondsman worked like a bank. If bail was set at one million dollars, Dan Jensen could contact Humphrey Stein. He would agree to put up a "bond," which was a guarantee to the court that if Jensen skipped town, Stein Bonding would pay the bail amount in cash to the court. For his services, Humphrey charged ten percent of the bail amount as a non-refundable fee.

It was rumored that Bogey had never lost a bond. There was a simple reason for this. Stein was connected to a national network of bondsmen and thugs who could find anyone, anywhere in the country if they really needed to do so. The families of the defendants also hunted them down and talked them into returning to the jurisdiction, especially if it meant one of the families losing the house that had been used as collateral for the bond.

When Ted entered the Government Center, he turned left to read the huge electronic board on the wall. In blue letters it listed all the cases to be heard for the day and which courtrooms they were assigned. It resembled the departure/arrival boards at airports. As assignments changed, the board clicked over with new information. He scanned the board and discovered Jensen's case would be heard across the street at the Public Service Facility, the PSF.

He had a little time before the Jensen case would be called. One of Ted's old mentors, Judge Anthony Beardon, still served on the bench. Since he hadn't seen the judge for years, Ted decided to say hello.

He rode the elevator to the seventeenth floor and turned right into the hallway that fronted the courtrooms. The opposite wall was constructed of floor-to-ceiling glass. It overlooked an open atrium, enclosed between the two towers of the Government Center. Across the atrium, Ted could look into dozens of offices since they also had glass walls. Each office looked identical—beige walls, dark gray carpeting, and desks covered in tan plastic laminate. Most people sat in front of computer screens with flickering colors reflected off their expressionless faces.

Ted walked through Courtroom 1798 and opened the huge oak door that led into a narrow hallway behind the judge's bench. He turned left and found Judge Beardon's chambers, or office, still in the same place.

In a small anteroom, Ted met the judge's law clerks. Hearing Ted's voice, the judge bounded out from his chair to greet him. "Ted, how the hell are you?" Beardon pumped Ted's hand and smiled widely.

"I'm great." He put his left hand on the judge's shoulder. "I think."

The judge pulled him into the chambers, and they sat in two green leather chairs before the judge's desk. Oak bookshelves filled with heavy law books lined one long wall. A silver putter leaned against one corner of the shelf. "Haven't seen you in years. How's your new practice going?" Although the entire building was non-smoking, the judge shut his door and lit a cigarette.

"Great. I'm finally making some good money, and the work is easy. What more could I ask for?"

"You were always one of the smartest lawyers I knew. I often thought I should've left the bench to go back to private practice and make a pile of dough, like you." White smoke swirled around the bald crown of the judge's head like the twist of an ice cream cone. His face was so wrinkled that it looked impossible for any more to have room to form, although Ted thought he saw some new lines through the cloud of smoke.

He assured the judge, "But you've done something good with your life. You've served the cause of justice all these years and have helped so many people, me included."

Beardon waved his hand in front of his chest. "I did what I could." His blue eyes focused on Ted. "What brings you back in here to the jungle?" His voice carried a hint of concern.

"I'm taking the murder case of Dan Jensen. The one where his wife's body is still missing? It's been all over the media."

The judge nodded his head while he thought. He looked up past Ted and through the big window of his chambers. "How long has it been since you did battle in a courtroom, Ted?"

"Quite a few years."

"Don't get me wrong now, but how sharp do you feel? Are you up to date on the new laws?"

"I think so."

Beardon stood and rubbed his lower back. "I know you like a son. And I'm not telling you what to do, just like I'd never give my own son a lecture. But I'm concerned, Ted."

Ted bristled at his words. This wasn't what he'd expected from the judge. Ted had expected to be supported and encouraged. "What do you mean?" Thoughts of his own father flashed through his mind. The judge's words sounded similar to those lectures.

Turning to face Ted, he said, "You left a boatload of wreckage around here. For the courts, your employer, the victims, and yourself. I don't want to see it happen again."

"I don't think it will," Ted insisted.

"Because if this case blows up, your career is dead—even your estate-planning practice, maybe forever."

Ted felt heat building in his lower body. What the hell was this? "That was a long time ago. I've changed."

"I'm sure you have. Can you still get out of the case?"

"No." Ted started for the door.

Hidden behind a swirl of smoke, Beardon called after him. "I'm only trying to help."

Ted walked fast to the PSF. A breeze came up from the Mississippi River, seven blocks to the north, and cooled him off. It smelled damp. The judge's words had stung badly. But Ted didn't have time to dwell on them now.

The façade of the PSF building curved outward and had windows across the front. Though it led into the courtrooms and, eventually, the jail, the PSF still looked inviting. Ted pulled open a door.

When he stepped into the lobby, reporters swirled toward him like he was a drain in a sink.

"Mr. Rohrbacher," someone shouted.

"Ted, Ted," called a print reporter and jogged over to him.

Ted tried to edge around the security desk and get into the weapons screening line. He couldn't make it. Bright lights clicked on and he blinked. The people in front of him became dark silhouettes. He worried that Dan Jensen wasn't there yet—a bad sign when you want the bail reduced.

Two microphones jammed into his face. A person behind one said, "Are you worried your client might be taken into custody?" More microphones probed at him like the proboscis of an insect.

"In my opinion, bail should be reduced. Mr. Jensen hasn't become a flight risk overnight," Ted replied. The mob squeezed closer to him. He could feel the heat from some of the bodies closest to him.

"What's your defense going to be?"

"Do you have a defense?"

"Why isn't Mr. Jensen here?"

"Will you hire experts to try and get him off?"

"Do you have information about where the body is?"

Ted managed to back his way along the control counter toward the weapons screening. If he could just make it that far, he could shake off most of the reporters. Two steel stands held a rope between them to direct people toward the machines. Ted rounded the first stand and felt it give way from the pressure of the crowd. He hurried to the machine, flopped his briefcase on the moving belt, dropped the metal items in his pockets into a gray plastic box, and walked through.

The alarm bell rang, and Ted stopped before going into the courtroom area. The deputy picked up a hand wand and swept it down the front side of Ted as he held his arms out to the sides. Then the deputy wanded him on the back side down to his shoes. Finally, he nodded for Ted to proceed. He put his possessions back together again and entered.

Ted walked into a second lobby that curved around several courtrooms. He reached the double doors of the last courtroom.

These were used for initial first appearances and pre-trial confer-ences between the lawyers. More than ninety percent of all criminal cases were settled at the pre-trials with a plea of guilty to some level of criminal responsibility.

Thankfully, Ted saw Dan standing next to an open counter on the opposite side of the lobby from the courtroom. He smiled and chatted with a female clerk who leaned over the countertop. When Ted approached, Jensen said goodbye to her. He turned to Ted and frowned. "What the hell's going to happen here?" He was dressed in an expensive blue suit which hid his paunchy stomach and an open collar white shirt.

"We hope to get your bail reduced."

"Hope?" Jensen shook his head from side to side. "That's all we've got?"

"No, of course not," Ted snapped. He picked up a piece of paper that had been filled out in triplicate. It was labeled Bail Evaluation Risk Assessment. Typical government-speak. On the pre-printed form were several boxes that had been checked by the clerk when she had interviewed Danny earlier.

Jensen looked over Ted's shoulder and tried to read it. "What the hell is this?"

Ted ignored him and scanned the list, which, among other cat-egories, included:

Prior convictions—
    Felonies __ Misdemeanors__
Gun involved—
        Yes__ No__
Drugs involved—
        Yes__ No__
Number of years at home address— ___
Married— Yes__ No__

Depending on which box was checked, each one was assigned a different number. At the bottom of the form, the interviewer had added up all the numbers for a final score. Dan Jensen had scored under ten, which was low. The judge would decide bail based on many factors, but the bail evaluation would be a strong part. Ted felt better after having seen the score.

He took a deep breath and shepherded his client into the small courtroom. Two thirds of the benches were crammed with media people. At least inside the courtroom, they couldn't ask any questions and had to remain quiet. Instructing Dan to sit in the front row, Ted slipped through the wooden door in the railing and walked up to the clerk. He sat next to the raised bench from which the judge, Edith Vang, listened to other cases. Ted whispered that his case was ready to be heard. When he turned, he saw Sandy Rogin sitting in the corner at the prosecutor's table. Ted felt like going over and smacking him in the face. Instead, Ted forced himself to remain calm. He set his briefcase on the defense table, said hello to a public defender, Jeremy Webster, and sat down.

Then the public defender's case was called. Webster looked back toward the audience area and nodded at his client. A young girl came forward. She wore a pink dress, had bare legs with a tattoo of a yellow flower on her calf, and wore pink, high-heeled shoes that were too large for her. She steadied herself and walked to the front to stand beside Webster. She balanced on the podium and waited for the clerk to formally call the case.

A plea negotiation had been agreed to by the prosecutor and the defense. The girl would plead guilty in return for no jail time and probation. Restitution would be investigated and become part of her probation contract.

"Ms. Chupinski, how do you plead to theft of property over $1,000?" the clerk said.

"Guilty."

Webster began to question her and advised her about the right to trial and the presumption of innocence that she was giving up by pleading guilty. After he was finished, he asked her what had happened.

"Well, I was really broke, so I thought I could rob the jewelry store at the Mall of America. I got out there and found a store. The saleslady had laid out some nice stuff on the counter, and when she got distracted, I grabbed as much as I could hold and ran. I got outside and hid under the bushes on the north side, you know, by IKEA?"

"Did security catch you there?" Webster asked her.

"No way. I was hiding in the bushes waiting for my getaway ride."

"Your *getaway* ride?"

She paused, "Yeah. The city bus. Guess it was a dumb idea 'cause while I was waiting the Bloomington cops found me." She gave a weak smile to the judge and tilted her head to the side.

Ted and Dan Jensen were called next. They stepped aside to allow Webster and his client to leave then stood behind the same podium. The clerk read the name of the case. The court had installed a sophisticated sound system that recorded everything said in the courtroom, eliminating the need for a court reporter. A thin black pole with the knob of a microphone at the end arched up from the podium.

Rogin waited for the judge to open the file folder that the clerk handed up to her. Judge Edith Vang pushed up the square glasses perched at the end of her small nose. She was the first Hmong judge to be appointed to the bench by the governor. When she looked up, Rogin began, "Your Honor, the State of Minnesota is requesting the court to set one million dollars bail on Mr. Jensen. As you can see, he's been charged with second degree murder. In our opinion, that warrants bail at one million."

"Just because of the complaint?" the judge asked Rogin.

"Because, Your Honor, the penalty carries a maximum imprisonment of forty years. That by itself will cause the defendant to think about fleeing."

"I'd refer the court to the bail evaluation checklist," Ted added. "My client scores very low. I ask the court to reduce the bail under five hundred thousand." He could feel his breathing come back to normal. The setting began to seem familiar. Old instincts came back to Ted, and he shook off the dust on his skills from lack of use.

"Your Honor, I object," Rogin called out in a harsh voice.

"You don't need to shout, Mr. Rogin," the judge said.

"Also, we have the bigger issue of public safety, which is the primary purpose of setting bail."

"I know the law, Mr. Rogin."

"Of course, but this defendant is a dangerous man and we fear for public safety. Actually, the county attorney's office would prefer him to be in custody, but we're willing to compromise with this bail and we urge the Court to agree."

Ted responded, "Speaking of public safety, Mr. Jensen doesn't have any criminal record, has been a life-long resident of this county, and runs his own business. That doesn't sound like a person who's a threat to public safety." He paused. "Frankly, he's had some business setbacks recently, and the $500,000 bail is all he can afford. To him, that amount is the same as one million to others."

"I've looked at this carefully and will set bail at five hundred thousand." The judge closed the file to indicate that she was finished with the issue.

"But, Your Honor." Rogin tried again.

"I've made my decision," Judge Vang told him and studied a computer screen planted next to her on the bench. "Looks like I'll draw this case for trial. Any chance of settling, gentlemen?" The judge stared at the two lawyers.

"I'm not sure. I'll talk it over with my office," Rogin said. He looked at Ted.

Ted saw Rogin's enormous eyes behind his glasses. Ted sniffed in contempt. "So far, Mr. Rogin hasn't talked to me at all."

Judge Vang spent another five minutes trying to get the lawyers to work out a settlement. "Okay. Let's see." She peered at the computer screen. "I'm setting this for further hearings in three weeks."

Rogin interrupted, "I don't think the government can be ready—"

"Oh, you'll be ready, Mr. Rogin," the judge said. She glanced up. Her shiny black hair flipped from one side to the other as she looked between the computer screen and the lawyers.

"My client maintains his innocence," Ted said. "I will file a motion to challenge his statement to the police."

"Fine," Judge Vang said.

"Anything else you'd like to let me in on?" Rogin's voice had an edge to it.

Ignoring him, Ted thumbed through the purple *Criminal Law Handbook* that he had carried to the podium. It was two inches thick, and when he opened it, it smelled of new paper. He said, "I also filed the proper documents under Rule 9.02 to notify everyone that we will assert a mental illness defense."

"You don't mean that he's mentally incompetent?" Rogin shouted.

"No. But he suffers from something called the amygdala hijack."

"What are you talking about, Mr. Rohrbacher?" the judge asked. Her face pinched around her eyes.

"It's new mental health research that I will demonstrate for the Court."

Rogin interrupted, "This request is the only crazy thing about the case."

Judge Vang considered Ted's words for a moment. "I'll direct you to file a brief, and I will listen to arguments at the Omnibus hearing. We are way behind on our numbers in this county, and I want your case moved along. Is that clear?"

Both lawyers nodded and marked their calendars. The judge checked to see if the clerk had recorded her ruling on the bail motion. Satisfied, she folded the Jensen file and grabbed for the next one on a tall stack next to her.

Rogin sputtered as he backed away from the podium. From the audience, a small woman stood to meet him. She had bright red hair. Rogin introduced her as Maureen Hanrahan. She stepped up to Ted and offered her hand. He shook it and felt her strong grip.

"Nice to meet you, Mr. Rohrbacher."

"Call me Ted. You're going to second chair Sandy?"

"Right. It's a big break for me, and I'm really excited to help in any way I can." She had eyes with a slight tilt, like those of a cat, and that were unafraid to be open all the time.

"It should be interesting." They chatted for a few minutes. Although Maureen seemed pleasant, Ted felt apprehensive. Not only was she working for Sanford Rogin, but Ted could sense her ambition. She tried a little too hard to be friendly.

Rogin picked up his briefcase. He jerked his head toward the door to tell Maureen to leave, and he followed behind her. When Rogin passed by Ted, he leaned close and whispered, "This will be your last victory in the case. I promise it." Rogin slammed through the wooden doors in the railing and glanced at the media lined up in the back rows. He paused long enough for them to scramble out of their seats and follow him outside.

Ted delayed leaving and held Dan back by the arm. When the media had cleared out, Ted lifted his briefcase off the table and walked Dan through the double doors of the courtroom.

The inner lobby was crowded with dozens of people. The ones wearing suits or nice sweaters and slacks were lawyers—for both the prosecution and defense. Several wooden benches overflowed with people. Some sat and played with smart phones, others sprawled out and slept. It smelled like too many bodies crammed into too small a space.

"You never fuckin' call me," one angry man yelled at his lawyer.

Another pleaded with her boyfriend's lawyer, "You gotta get him out. He's the father of my baby, and her birthday's comin' up next week."

"But this is a domestic filed by you," the lawyer reminded her. "He beat you up and stabbed you."

"I still love him. It was jus' a misunderstanding."

Ted maneuvered Dan through the crowd and pushed through the glass door to the outer lobby. In the far corner, Rogin held court before a large group from the media. Hanrahan stood next to him, dressed in a tailored jacket, pants, and a cinnamon-colored scarf fluffed around her neck. She had her hip cocked to the side and looked confident with the media. When the mob spotted Ted and Dan, they rushed over to them. Several of the men hefted cameras to their shoulders and started filming. Others poked microphones at Ted.

"Congratulations Ted. You won that round," a reporter from the *Star Tribune* said.

A young woman from *City Pages* said, "Can we get an interview with you two? It's important our readers understand your defense."

"Hey, I'm Jason. I write a blog called *Courting Crime,* and I want to do a post on your case that exposes the truth. What do you say?"

Ted tried to brush them back with his free arm. Using his briefcase, he guided Danny toward the front door. "I can't talk about much right now. We're happy with the judge's ruling, of course," he said.

The clump of reporters trailed them across the lobby. Questions fired from all around. It was impossible to answer any of them. "You may as well talk with us," Carolyn Bechter shouted. "It'll all come out anyway. This is your chance to set the record straight."

Ted glanced back at Dan and saw a tense expression on his face. He flicked a brief smile at one person but kept trudging ahead. His shoulders thrust forward. Ted had counseled him earlier to ignore the questions. Ted would do the talking. When Dan noticed Ted looking at him, he grinned, but his eyes bounced around at the crowd behind them.

They had almost reached the door. Ted stopped long enough to switch the briefcase to his other hand and pull on the door handle. Behind him, people crushed closer. They must have sensed Ted and Dan were about to get away. Ted turned around.

It happened quickly.

One of the TV reporters managed to muscle her way next to Jensen. "Where's the body?" she yelled. "Where's the body?"

Dan stopped. A red flush grew from his throat and crossed his face. He shouted, "Get the fuck away from me, lady. You're talkin' about my wife."

"The sheriffs are searching for the body but haven't found it yet. Can you add anything to that?"

"I'm innocent," Jensen screamed. He lifted his arms and grabbed for the reporter. In her defense, the cameraman slammed his equipment into Dan's shoulder. Immediately, four other cameramen converged around the fight and kept their cameras running behind blazing lights.

Dan shook off the first camera from his shoulder and, with the other arm, took a swing at the cameraman, who ducked. Bracing himself, Dan took another swing and missed again. Ted dropped his briefcase to wrap his arms around Jensen's chest. Cameras danced around them from all angles. Ted felt like he was back on the ice during a hockey game, fighting again and trying to calm down a team-mate.

Dan screamed in a shrill voice that Ted had never heard before. His eyes bulged from his face. He almost broke out of Ted's grasp, but Ted got him closer to the door and pushed his body through it. After they spilled outside, Ted went back for his briefcase, then jumped outside again.

"Get the hell out of here," Ted yelled at his client.

Swarming in a cluster behind them, the media followed. As Ted jogged along the sidewalk, he put distance between them and the mob stretched out in a long line behind.

After they crossed the street, Ted and Dan climbed the stairs in the ramp. At the car, they paused and looked back. No one had followed them. Ted breathed heavily. "What the hell was that all about?"

Dan shook his head and dropped it forward onto his chest. "Don't know. What happened?"

"You don't remember? That was one hell of a performance. And every TV station in the Twin Cities will have film of you on the news tonight." Ted walked in a circle to calm down. "How do you think that'll look? A nice, quiet, peaceful client, who would never be capable of killing his wife," he said sarcastically.

"I don't know, Teddy. It happens every once in a while." Dan raised his head from his chest and looked at Ted. His eyes had retreated deeply into his head, and for an instant Ted couldn't see any sign of life behind them.

"I guess I just snapped," Danny whispered.

Chapter Fourteen

Deputy Kenny Seabloom watched as a crowd of crime scene experts bunched around the mound of dirt under the buckthorn bush. They were all dressed in light blue smocks and blue latex gloves, and many had soft white masks over their faces—Smurfs, he thought.

The chief medical examiner, Dr. Helen Wong, had even come out to the scene. Usually an assistant would do the preliminary work. The notoriety of the case drew out all the big guns.

By now, police from the cities of Minnetonka, Shorewood, Mound, and Deephaven had all responded. Squad cars crowded the narrow gravel road, making it difficult for the ME to drive up to the crime scene. Seabloom had seen this before. The big cases always attracted everyone—both the curious and the creepy. At this point, Seabloom's main job was simply crowd control.

He watched as a second large van worked its way between the parked cars on the gravel road. It was brown with yellow and blue detailing and had a large logo on both sides that read Hennepin County Sheriff and under that, Crime Lab. It was the sheriff's mobile van. Since the city of Minnetonka didn't have a crime lab, they had called in the county experts.

Behind the van came another official car. Seabloom saw the elected sheriff himself get out and put on his billed cap. He wore a white shirt with brown striping and dark brown pants. Over that, his jacket had epaulets with four stars on each shoulder. Across the bill of his cap was a twist of gold braid—something he had designed for himself once he took office. Kenny didn't like the "spit and polish" the new boss brought to the department. But he liked the fact the sheriff could always squeeze money out of the politicians for guys like Seabloom—including his first cost of living increase in five years.

He'd only met the sheriff once, and he ignored Kenny now as he hurried to the crime scene. When the press noticed the sheriff, they converged in a knot around him.

"Sea, get over on the flank," Seabloom's sergeant yelled at him.

"Okay, Top." Seabloom moved to the left side of the crime scene area. Yellow tape stretched from one tree to another. Still, people pushed against the tape, threatening to snap it. Kenny worked his way along the edge, reminding people to step back. Another deputy joined him at the far end of the tape. Although Seabloom had been trained for this, it always bothered him. The job was like the arcade game of "Whack a Mole." As soon as he pushed back one group of curious onlookers, another blob of people surged forward in a different spot. Both deputies patrolled back and forth along the line.

Kenny glanced at the team under the bush and the mound of dirt. Several blue-smocked people kneeled around it. At a hand signal, two of them began to dig in a slow, careful manner. The dirt they removed was packaged in large plastic bags and carried away by rotating assistants.

Every few minutes, the work stopped as the photographers stepped in to take pictures. On the far side of the mound, a video camera had been mounted on a tripod and was filming everything.

The experts used small hand trowels as if they were on an archeological dig. One scoop at a time. Then they'd sift the dirt looking for any evidence or clues. When the dirt filtered down through the square screens, it was retrieved, bagged, and carried away to the van. The work was tedious for everyone.

His sergeant returned and shook his head. "Hate to tell you this, Sea."

"Now what?"

"Got the orders from the home office. They want you to get out to Bloomington to a landfill and pick up a wig."

"What the hell?" Seabloom yelled.

The sergeant sighed. "I know. I really need you here. Seems some worker at a landfill found a wig with blood on it that had fallen out of a garbage bag when it ripped open. They got concerned and called us."

"That's a waste of my time."

"I know. But you gotta do it. Probably nothing, but if we don't check it out and it leads to some serial killer, well, we're fucked. See what I mean?"

"Of course. But why me?" When the sergeant shrugged, Kenny stomped off to a squad car, radioed in for the location, and threw gravel all over the shrubs as he raced out of the park. He was so mad he could hardly slow down. Why did they keep fucking with him? The department received hundreds of calls from civilians—ninety-nine percent that were a waste of time. Why not give him something important to do? Maybe he'd transfer to a police department where he might be appreciated. He worried that he might miss all the action here.

He was back in an hour with the blood-stained wig. He had sealed it in a plastic bag that had red tape across the end that said *Evidence.* When he had the time, Kenny would log it into the crime lab. The techs would rank it a low priority but would do an analysis of the blood and try to match it with their database, hoping to get a hit. He hurried to the dig site. The sergeant waved at him with relief and motioned for Kenny to resume his position on the line again.

As the technicians dug deeper into the mound, Seabloom could feel the tension rise in the entire crowd. Mina Jensen's parents, Harry and Jessie, had been allowed to come closer and stand behind the crew. Jessie stood for a short time, her eyes misted over, and she turned to walk away. Harry looked after her, started to turn himself, and then decided to wait by the mound. He turned back to watch the progress.

One of the assistants from the crime lab shouted, "I've got something."

Seabloom felt the crowd surge forward before he actually saw the movement. He turned to hold them back and moved along the line. People bobbed up and down trying to get a better view around those in front of them.

"It's something long," the assistant said. "Here, under here." He asked for help.

The crowd went silent. The only sound was the swish of wind high among the tops of the pine trees. Kenny looked back at the dig. He could smell moist dirt as it was turned over. Now three people hovered over the site, their arms moving quickly.

One of them announced, "Here's the other end."

"Pretty small."

"It's wrapped in something furry, like a rug. I can't tell yet." The female tech scraped more dirt away from the mound with her hand trowel.

The gray piece of cloth Seabloom had first seen had been retrieved, bagged, and removed. He heard from the crime lab people that it looked like it might be from a pillow or a section of a sheet that had been torn. There were no special markings. By the weathering on it, the experts estimated that it had been outdoors for at least as long as Mina Jensen's body had disappeared. It gave Kenny hope they had finally found the body.

"I'm close," shouted one of the crime lab people. "Get me the brush." He took a soft brush from an assistant and started to flick off dirt from the top of the object.

No one spoke. Even the media people, held back by three deputies, remained silent. They had cameras balanced on shoulders with red lights blinking on each one as they recorded every movement. The reporters stood on tiptoes with silent microphones in their hands.

"Close now," a digger said.

Seabloom held his breath. He watched as two assistants squatted on either end of the object and gently lifted it from the mound. He couldn't see what they'd found.

Then he heard a collective moan from those people closest to the scene. Several people stood abruptly and stepped back. "Maybe there's something underneath. Keep digging," someone ordered.

"It's a damn dog," the person holding the object said. "Somebody buried their dog."

The crowd fell back all around Kenny. He could hear sighs of disappointment from everyone. People started to walk away in small groups. The media shut off their cameras and packed them in hard shell cases. Kenny could hear all the snaps shutting on the cases. He saw Jessie with her head down and saw her shoulders shaking. He waited for the order to clear the scene and removed the yellow plastic tape.

A tall, broad-shouldered man approached him. He had blue eyes that looked slightly crossed. The man stood next to a pine tree and gazed at the eviscerated mound of dirt. When he wouldn't leave, Seabloom asked him, "Help you, sir?"

"What they find?"

"Uh, I think it was the corpse of a dog. Someone must've buried their pet."

"No body?" He sounded like he was Russian.

"No." Kenny was about to get back to his boat when something about the man intrigued him. "You have an interest in this case?" he asked the stranger.

He shrugged and tilted his head to one side. "I knew the victim, Mina Jensen."

"Oh?"

"Not too well." He waved his hand and started to move back away from the scene. He wore a thick gold wrist band and had a big ring with an expensive-looking stone mounted in it.

"Maybe you could provide some information to our investigators."

"No. Don't think so."

"Then why are you here?" Seabloom tried to stall the man until he could get some help.

The Russian shifted his gaze from the overturned mound to Kenny's eyes. "I'm worried," the man said and walked away.

Chapter Fifteen

When Ted got back to his office at five-thirty, Laurie was waiting in the lobby for him. Dan Jensen had gone home. Laurie sat in one of the leather chairs and didn't move when Ted entered.

"Hey," he said to her.

"We should talk," Laurie answered as she uncoiled from the chair. The receptionist pretended to pat her blond hair into place while she peeked at them. Laurie followed him down the hallway and into his office.

Ted dropped his heavy briefcase beside the desk. Late afternoon sun streamed through the glass, giving a green glow to the soft corners of the overstuffed furniture. Such a peaceful contrast to the courtroom with its white glare, no green plants, and hard surfaces. He could guess what was coming from Laurie. He wanted to get this over with as quickly as possible; he and Sam were going to try and catch the new suspect, Demontre Harrison.

She wore tight blue jeans and a blue sweatshirt with the Minnesota Twins logo on the front. She sat on the edge of the couch. "I worked remotely today." Her face twisted in an unusual way.

He took a deep breath. "What?"

"Oh, you know *what*. Like who was that creature next to you on the five o'clock TV news? You think he looks innocent? My God, Ted, you've hooked yourself to a psycho. Did you watch it?" Her voice cracked as it rose in volume.

"No."

"Take my non-legal advice: before you go one more step, watch the news."

"But don't you see? When he snapped, that's what an amygdala hijack looks like. It almost proves it right there."

"What's an amygdala hijack?"

Ted explained it briefly to her.

"All it proves is that he's a dangerous nut who could and did kill Mina."

Ted didn't respond.

"When the hell will you get out of it?"

"I don't think I can now. Every defendant deserves a—"

"Dammit. He can get dozens of other lawyers."

"He doesn't have any money, and he looks guilty. No one will take his case."

"I don't care. Mina was my cousin. How can you keep going with this?" The skin stretched so tightly over her forehead that he could see blue veins. "You should spend time with her family like I have. See how much they're suffering."

"I know, but I'm also doing this for me, Laurie. I need to finish this."

"Why? Just to redeem your reputation? You don't need that."

He didn't answer. He didn't know what to say to convince her anyway.

Laurie stood and came close to Ted. She looked up at him. He recognized the wrinkles around her eyes and on the bridge of her nose. Intimate details that few other people knew existed. But now her eyes moistened. He could feel the warmth of her breath on his face. "I can't imagine her gone," her voice trailed off as she sniffed back more tears. "I miss her so much."

His throat tightened and he said, "I know."

"When Danny spent so much time out of the country, Mina was lonely. As cousins, we'd always been close, but that really brought us together."

"I remember that."

Laurie looked up at him and blinked. "Then how can you—?" Her voice trailed off. "Mina would do anything. I envied her guts. Even in little things. Like when we were shopping and a discount had run out the day before. Mina was always able to talk the sales clerks into still giving her the discount."

Ted moved beside her and cradled her shoulders in his arms. "You going to be okay?"

Tears ran down her cheek, and she swiped at them and sniffed back more tears. "I miss her so much I even thought I heard her voice the other day."

"Oh?"

"For just a moment. At Byerly's, in the deli section when I was picking up some potato salad. I heard someone talk, and the voice reminded me of Mina. I almost came around the counter but didn't. I didn't want to embarrass myself."

"Of course not." He let go of her and backed away. Laurie calmed down.

"There was a time, Ted, when I could recognize you walking from a block away. You moved so easily and quickly. The most handsome man I'd ever met. I would've followed you anywhere. But—" She blinked her eyes. "But I can't follow you this time."

"I told you there are a few small things to wrap up, then it's going to be over."

"I think you should move out of the house. I don't know what else to do right now."

"Just give me a week or so. We'll be in court soon and some major issues will be decided—like the amygdala hijack. Once that's finished, I'm out of the case." He vowed to get the case wrapped up as quickly as possible.

Her lips squeezed together. "All right. But I can't take it much longer."

He looked at his watch and remembered that he and Samantha were going to interview Demontre Harrison. He hesitated and wanted to try one last time to explain to her.

Ted shifted his shoulders and realized there was nothing more to say. "I've got to run. Meeting Samantha for more investigation. There was some guy who threatened Danny."

Laurie's eyes opened wide. "Didn't the police interview him?"

"No. Danny never told them about it. He just told me."

Reluctantly, he left Laurie and drove to Samantha's house. They used her car because they didn't want to look too successful in front of Harrison.

Sam pushed the Mazda fast up to Interstate 694, turned east and looked for the Central Avenue exit. Today, her hair was real and shiny black with gray roots. Her hair flapped around her face in the wind until she put on a blue baseball cap with "Spelman" lettered on the front.

"How'd you find this guy?" Ted asked.

She glanced at him and grinned. "We have our ways," she said in a low voice, then grinned. "The phone number Danny gave you worked. Imagine that."

"So we're going to an auto parts place?"

"Right. North of the city. Used to be dozens of 'em up there. Now people just order stuff off the Internet. We're going to one of the last of a dying business called Ace Auto Parts. Largest in the upper Midwest, they said."

They drove north on Central Avenue past one-story buildings that housed small businesses. Most were thriving. Plumbing stores, Korean grocery stores, auto repair shops, gas stations, a VFW, and a Dairy Queen that did not have a drive-through window.

Ted reminded Samantha what Dan Jensen had told him about Harrison breaking into the house.

"He thinks this dude was in the house? That he might've fought with him the night of the murder?" Sam turned back to watch the traffic and shook her head. "That's some powerful mojo. Doubt this guy will admit to anything."

"You can get anyone to admit to something," he laughed.

She turned her head forward to watch the traffic. For a long time, Sam didn't say anything.

"What's wrong?" Ted asked.

"How can you tell?"

"I know you."

Samantha sighed. "All right. I've got a gig coming up at the Dakota in Minneapolis in a couple weeks."

"You've played plenty of gigs. So what?"

"This is only a trio. Bass, piano, and yours truly. I've never been the lead before." She glanced at him. "Not only do I have to play solos, but I've got to make sure we start together, end at the same time, and the song is played correctly. I don't know if I've got the *chutzpah* to pull it off." She looked over at him.

"You? Not enough *chutzpah*?" Ted laughed. "So what's the problem?"

"This is different. There'll be lots of jazz fans in the audience. They'll know if I screw it up. And except for the clothes on my bod, I'll be up there on the stage naked." She turned her head back to watch the road.

They passed a huge sporting goods store that boasted the freshest bait in the Twin Cities. Behind the store stood colored shacks about the size of a large outhouse. Red and banana and celery green fish houses rested in the heat of the sun, waiting for their winter move onto frozen lakes.

Ten minutes later, Samantha turned right into the Ace Auto Parts parking lot. It was crowded and Sam drove around to the side of the building to find a place to stop. When they got out of the car, she pulled out a file folder from the back seat and checked inside.

"I got two photos of Mina Jensen from Dan and taped them back-to-back." She gripped the corners and pulled them out far enough to show Ted. Both sides were glossy with a different pose of Mina on each side.

The pleasant smell of fresh-cut grass came on the slight wind as they walked up to a double front door flanked by large windows. They stepped inside. To the right were racks with auto accessories, and to the left a row of high desks stretched around to the back corner. At each desk a person talked on a phone. Ted heard shouting, people calling across the room, and phones ringing. Each person wore a dark blue shirt with the Ace Auto Parts logo stitched above the pocket and a bright patch on the left shoulder that read "Pennzoil."

When one of the salespeople hung up the phone, Ted approached her quickly. "Does Demontre Harrison work here?" he asked.

She wore heavy glasses that had amber-colored lenses. "Tre? Yeah, out back. He's the manager of the yard." She jerked her head to the side to indicate the direction. Her phone rang again; she picked it up and ignored Ted.

As they moved toward a narrow door behind the woman's desk, another employee stopped them. "Gotta get a ticket."

"Huh?" Ted said.

"Two bucks each. What're ya lookin' for?"

"Mr. Harrison."

"Oh. You don't need a part out there?"

"No," Ted replied.

The man tugged on his earlobe. "Guess I still gotta charge you."

Ted paid and signed a form with his driver's license number on it. The man handed him a ticket. "Show it to anyone stops you out there. You're good to go." He stepped aside as Ted and Samantha walked down a narrow hall with grease stains on the concrete floor. Broken auto parts were stacked along the walls. As they reached the open end of the hall, dozens of wheel covers hung just outside the door, glistening in the sun like medieval shields.

They came out into the slanting light from the low sun. Ted shaded his eyes and looked up. For as far as he could see, there were hundreds of junked cars lined up in dusty rows. It looked like a graveyard of dead cars. Each car was parked at an angle facing the dirt roads that ran between the rows.

All the engines and hoods had been cannibalized, and the empty front ends were propped up in the air. Doors were open, hatchbacks up, the insides of the cars strewn around in the dirt, seats out, windshields smashed, and piles of broken parts stuffed inside the cars. Ted saw the words "row 7, spot 93" spray-painted on a window. Many of the cars had crumpled roofs and doors—obvious accidents. He thought of when those cars had been new and how excited the owners must have been. How they had smelled. Now they were all dead and smelled of dust.

They started to walk along the road. The sun still felt hot, and Sam pulled out a pair of sunglasses. They'd been told that Harrison was probably near row eighty-five. As they walked through soft dirt, Ted felt dampness collecting under his shirt. Neither of them spoke.

A man in a beat-up golf cart came up beside them. "Want a lift?" he asked. Ted and Sam climbed onto the back end. "We got the biggest yard in the state. What're you looking for?" Dark grease stains covered the steering wheel.

When they told him Demontre Harrison, the man said, "Sure. Saw him over on the SUV row. Here we go." He pressed the pedal and the golf cart hummed at top speed, followed by a rolling trail of dust.

In a few minutes, they saw a large man standing in the road. He wore jeans and work boots that were gray with dirt. His head was covered with a tan pith helmet, and he had a silver beard that contrasted with his black skin. Aviator sunglasses hid his eyes. When the golf cart came up to him, he turned and saluted the driver. Sam and Ted got off to meet Harrison. He wore a shirt that said Ace Auto Parts above the chest pocket.

The driver said, "Hey, Whiskey. These two wanna talk with you."

When they introduced themselves, Harrison backed up a step. "How'd you find me?"

Samantha smiled. "I can find anyone. Want to talk about Dan Jensen?"

"Got nothing to say."

"I would think that you'd want to talk with us here instead of answering a subpoena to come to court and testify," she suggested.

He looked out at the carcasses of the SUVs next to them. "Over there." He turned to walk toward a small shack with an overhanging roof on the front end. Two folding chairs sat underneath. He offered one to Sam. She declined, so they all stood beside the shack.

"You run this place, huh?" she asked.

"I'm the manager of the outside yard, yeah." He pulled off the sunglasses from his face and twirled them in his hand.

"Good job?"

"Pays the bills."

"You know who Dan Jensen is, don't you?" Samantha got to the point of their meeting.

Harrison nodded but didn't say anything.

"He tells us you made contact with him. That right?"

Harrison's eyes shifted from side to side. "Yeah. I did speak to the dude a couple times."

"Why did you contact him?"

152

"Had a little beef with him."

"What was that?"

"Nothin' important."

Ted interrupted, "Your brother isn't important to you? That's not what Jensen told us."

Harrison shifted his weight from one leg to the other. "Okay. So we had a connection about my brother. So what?" On the left shoulder of his work shirt was a yellow oval patch. In the middle, in rising letters, it read "Pennzoil."

"So what was the beef?"

Harrison wouldn't answer.

Everyone waited in the heat. The golf cart hummed from somewhere off to the left. A light breeze puffed across Ted's skin, and it smelled dry.

"Okay." Samantha moved closer to Harrison. Although she was six inches shorter, she pushed her face close to him. "We're talking about the death of an innocent woman here and the trial of an accused dude who may go to prison for the rest of his life. I'm like a smoke truck: I'll keep coming back to you, and you won't like the results."

Harrison's face darkened. He didn't move. Then he finally said, "What do you want?"

"Now we're getting somewhere," she replied. "Mr. Jensen says you called him, mad about your brother's death, and you blamed Jensen."

"Yeah. Something like that. My brother would be here today if it weren't for that cracker."

"Why do you say that?"

"Jensen was in command and he fucked it all up."

"But he couldn't possibly have known the enemy would be there," Ted said.

"Don't matter." The muscles along Harrison's neck bunched in knots, and he spoke slowly. "He was in charge, and he got 'em trapped like a bunch of coons up a tree."

"Ever meet with Jensen? In person?"

"No."

"He says you threatened him."

"Not true."

"You ever go into the Jensen home?"

"You crazy? No way." Harrison pushed the pith helmet back on his head to expose a shining bald forehead. Sweat glistened across it.

"You telling me the truth?" Samantha looked closely at him. "What would your mama say?"

Harrison laughed and his entire chest moved. "Hey, what you doing to me?"

"Easy question: were you ever at the Jensen house?"

"Okay. Maybe I was."

"Why did you go out there?"

"I was so upset about my brother. Didn't really know what to do."

"What did you intend to do when you got there?"

"Nothing. I don't know." He said quickly, "I never went inside the crib. Never."

"What did you do there?" Samantha moved further under the shade of the overhanging roof. A dribble of sweat ran down underneath her ear. It looked shiny against her brown skin.

"Just walked around it. Tryin' to figure out how to ease the pain of my brother's death. At this point in time, I still feel Dan Jensen is responsible for the loss. He should pay for that." His voice dropped to a whisper.

"Did you meet him there?"

"No way, man. I saw the guy's woman, though. The chick was sunbathing down by the lake."

"Did you make contact?" Sam asked.

"No. Just looked. Nice eyeful."

Samantha took the file folder from under her arm and removed the taped-together photos. She pulled it out by the corner and pushed it toward Harrison. He took in in his hand and turned it over twice. She asked him, "That who you saw?"

"Yeah. I remember her. Yeah, this is her."

"But you say you never talked with her or made contact with her? Ever?"

"No way." He handed the photos back to Samantha.

She held them by the corner and placed them carefully back into the file folder.

Ted raised his voice. "You think we should believe that you were sneaking around the Jensen house, were mad at him for getting your brother killed, and you never did anything?"

Harrison turned toward him. "You can believe what you want."

"But you just said that Dan Jensen should pay for your brother's death. Did you do anything to make Jensen pay for that?"

Harrison squinted as if the sun had shifted into his face. "I know what you're tryin' to do to me. Lots of dudes a lot better than you have tried to make me say things I don't want to say. All I can tell you is I've been mad at him from jump street. My only brother. I never knew my ol' man, my momma died of diabetes, and now I got nothing left for family. How would you feel?"

"I suppose I'd be mad. Which says to me you've got a lot of motive to do something to this guy," Ted said. He realized that his upper body tensed as he talked.

Harrison's breath came more slowly and his stomach drove in and out through a few breaths. He said, "I got nothing more to say."

In ten minutes, Ted and Sam had walked all the way back to the shop, left through the front door, and arrived at her car. She had closed the top to keep the seats from baking under the sun. Still, it was hot inside. Sam punched the air conditioning button after she started the car.

"By the way, what's a smoke truck?" Ted asked.

"When I was growing up down south, in the summer there was always an old truck that came through the neighborhood once a week to spray for bugs. It left big clouds of insecticide all over everything. We called 'em smoke trucks. Can you imagine what that did to our health?" Sam leaned forward and let the cool air blow against her face. She chuckled, "We got him."

"Got what? We didn't get a damn thing out of him. He looks guilty to me, but he won't admit anything."

"No, I mean we got his prints." She held up the file folder. "Glossy photos should show his prints beautifully. We'll compare

155

them with all the prints found at the crime scene. And if we find a match with his prints, we know that he's been lying. We'll be back to confront him—just like a smoke truck."

Chapter Sixteen

The following morning, after trying to meet with the bloodstain expert at the Hennepin County sheriff's lab for several days, Ted received a text from Deputy Sarah Mooney. She had a one-hour window between homicide cases to review her report with him. Ted drove into downtown and turned up Sixth Street. The lab was in a one-story tan building that looked like a warehouse for used computers.

Ted and Samantha had studied Mooney's report many times. Sam had some experience with bloodstain analysis but certainly wasn't an expert. So Ted had many questions for the deputy. As he got out of his Mercedes, he felt the absence of Sam—both her help and her presence. She was conducting more background checks on both Korsokov and Harrison.

He looked down the canyon created by the buildings along Sixth Street and saw horizontal rows of clouds, changing from salmon to turquoise as his eyes followed them up into the sky. Behind him, he heard the scream of an ambulance as it leaned around the corner and gained speed after leaving the Hennepin County Medical Center.

Ted entered a narrow hall at the sheriff's lab. He could see a small office at the far end divided into low cubicles and separated from him by a large bulletproof glass. A woman stood up from behind a divider and came to the window. She had Ted show an ID, and sign in, and she called for Deputy Mooney.

In a few minutes, a door behind Ted buzzed and a tall woman came into the hall. In one step, she met Ted, shook his hand, and led him through the same door. He followed.

Mooney wore a tan and dark brown sheriff's uniform that was unwrinkled and fitted like it had been tailored for her. On the left sleeve were two patches shaped like yellow slashes. Each one represented five years of service with the sheriff's department. Ted could tell by the boxy look of her chest that she wore a bulletproof vest, even in the lab. Dark hair was wrapped in a tight bun on the back of her head.

"Thanks for meeting with me; I've wanted to ask you several questions," Ted said.

"Sure. I'm working on three homicides simultaneously but caught a break. Sorry this took so long. We've very proud of the fact we are a resource for both the prosecution and the defense. Has the trial started yet?"

"No. Mr. Jensen's just been charged." Ted explained how he and Sam had read the bloodstain reports but still needed to talk with the deputy.

"Let's hurry." Mooney led him to a small office of tan sheetrock and a desk with a plastic laminated top. "Where do you want to start?" She offered him a chair that crowded next to a second one in front of the desk. "Water?" She gave him a sealed bottle.

"I used to be a prosecutor, but I never handled a bloodstain case before. Besides, I was never good at math. So, here on page seven of your report . . ." Ted flipped through the paper pages. He found the section. "So, you've written, 'to calculate the angle of impact, I used the trigonometric function: Angle of Impact $=$ arc sin W/L.'" Ted looked up at Mooney. She didn't wear any make-up. "What's that mean in English?"

She nodded her head. "Frankly, I don't think you need to understand that, and I'll explain why in a minute." She shifted her weight in the chair, and it creaked. "Bloodstain analysis is part science but also part art, based on experience and training. Do you know the background of the science?"

"My investigator is a former Minneapolis detective, so she's taught me a few things." He noticed several photos of two children propped on the shelf behind her.

Mooney glanced down at her metal wristwatch. "I'll give you the short version. The first published work of bloodstain pattern recognition actually occurred in 1895 by a Polish scientist. In more recent times, in the murder case where Dr. Sam Sheppard was accused of killing his wife, bloodstain analysis was critical to the investigation and conviction. The case led to a TV series and a Hollywood movie called *The Fugitive.* "

"Tommy Lee Jones."

"Right."

"In our case there aren't any witnesses to the murder, so I'm hoping you can tell me what really happened."

Mooney sucked in a deep breath. "No pressure on me, huh?"

Ted swept his hand through the air between them. "I didn't mean it like that."

"I'm impressed. Very few defense lawyers have asked me to tell them the truth. Usually, they're looking for any sliver of evidence they can use to get their client out of trouble."

"I'll do that later, but right now let's talk about the crime scene." He looked at her dark eyes and held them for a moment. "As the analyst, what kinds of conclusions can you tell me about the murder?"

"Here are the usual types of conclusions I can tell you. The origin of the bloodstains, the type of weapon used, the direction the weapon was used, the positions of the victim and the assailant, and the location and movements of both of them."

"It sounds like you may as well have been there in person."

"Sort of. I can come close. The scientific evidence never lies." She put her hands on the chair's armrests and pushed herself up. "Why don't you come with me?"

Ted waited until she walked into the hall since the office was too small for both of them to get through the door. Mooney turned the corner into a wide hallway and moved past a lab on the right side. The top half the wall was glass, and Ted could see people dressed in light blue smocks. Each one wore a face mask.

"DNA testing," Mooney explained and kept walking. "In your case, I didn't have a body, as you know. Unfortunately, that made it difficult. But I still obtained a lot of information."

"And you prepared a lengthy report."

"Yes, based on the techniques I'll show you. Blood leaves the body by two mechanisms, passive and projected. Passive includes drips and oozes. Projected occurs from arterial spurts, castoff blood, and impact spatters. I found all of these at this crime scene."

"So, the passive is all the blood found on the floor and down in the spa?"

Mooney stopped. "Right. And by measuring the quantity of passive blood evidence, the ME was able to determine the victim had died, that the human body couldn't lose that much blood and survive. Dr. Wong concluded that 'the continuous loss of blood, unchecked and exacerbated by the trauma, led to death from exsanguination.'" She quoted the doctor's report from memory.

"She really talks like that?"

"It means bleeding to death."

"But without the body, what could you do?"

"When blood leaves the body in the projected form, it becomes spherical until it strikes something which we call the target. When it does, it splashes in different patterns, and it's the shape of those patterns that 'talk to me'—even without a body."

"Sure. A drop falls on the floor and splatters in a circular pattern."

"Right. Let's go a little further. If the angle of the impact changes from straight up and down, the shape of the bloodstain will change." Halfway down the hall Mooney planted her forward foot and made a sharp turn on the ball of it. She led him to a closed door. She keyed in a code on the box next to it, and the door buzzed. She pushed it open to enter a conference room. "Just had a training session," she said. "Sorry about the mess. I left my laptop in here."

Ted followed her to the end of a long table and saw a laptop sitting on the edge. Mooney booted it up and tapped the keys to open a file. On the screen some blobs appeared. They were dark brown and had a variety of shapes.

"You're giving me a Rorschach test?" he kidded.

Mooney didn't laugh. "Here's an example. The first roughly circular drip stain has fallen straight down at a 90-degree angle to the floor." Then she pointed to a second blob. "This one is a back spatter pattern at a 45-degree angle from the surface, and the third was at a ten-degree angle."

The last stain looked like a long, thick comet with three tails stretching out below it.

"That formula you quoted me before?" Mooney reminded Ted. "We measure the length of the solid part against the width to tell us the angle from which the blood sample came. That may not mean anything to you, but I'm trying to help you understand."

"And that tells you what?"

"I'll get to that. So far, we've talked about passive stains. They were important at the Jensen crime scene to identify the points where the body had been located, but projected blood spatters told me much more."

Ted stepped back from the screen. "Projected means they flew off the murder weapon? I saw brown splatters on the wall in the Jensen bedroom."

She nodded. "Let's suppose the assailant struck the victim in the head with a hammer. At first, the weapon would only strike hair and skin, leaving no blood stains. But as the cranium was compromised, there would be impact spatters from the hammer striking it. They're considered low velocity spatters which come from an object moving at less than five feet per second. In turn, this results in larger spatters, which are typically four millimeters or greater in diameter."

"What can you tell me about those?"

The deputy clicked through several more screens until she came to one that showed the wall at the crime scene. A series of strings were attached to the stains on the wall, ran to the middle of the room, and converged at a single point—a black stick, planted in a pool of blood on the floor.

"This picture shows how I can determine something called the 'point of convergence' and the 'point of origin' of the blood stains."

"What are those?"

"The point of convergence shows me the location of the blood source—that is, where the victim was when she was killed, and that leads to the point of origin. That tells me the positions of both the assailant and the victim." She smiled and showed a full mouth of straight teeth. When it was obvious Ted didn't understand her,

Mooney continued, "Think of it this way. Point of convergence gives me the two-dimensional view and point of origin gives me 3-D."

"How do you measure it?"

"We use these lines, stretched along the axis of each stain, and key the angles into a software program." She pointed at the spot where the lines came together on a black stick. There were several sticks on the floor, each one holding strings that met at a white marker on the stick. "That large bloodstain on the floor represents where the victim was. As the assailant struck her, the blood created impact patterns but also castoff patterns along the trajectories traced by the strings. We analyze the angle at which they struck the walls and ceiling."

"It's almost like you were there. Kind of creepy."

She grinned. "There's more."

"Oh?"

"By determining the point of origin, I can conclude that the victim was probably standing when first struck." Mooney clicked to a new screen on the computer. "See these stains lower on the wall?"

Ted leaned forward to see the screen.

"Then, see how the stains go up higher on the wall and even reach the ceiling? That shows me the victim fell to the floor where the attack continued until she died."

"When the killer was swinging the weapon, it would pick up some of the blood and throw it off onto the walls and ceiling, right?"

"Correct. I also found stains from expired blood."

Ted frowned.

"Those come from blood that's blown out of the mouth, most often. Blood with air bubbles in it. See here." She clicked through more photos until she came to the desk in the bedroom. "I found them underneath the desk. That suggests the victim, at one point, may have tried to seek shelter under the desk, blew out some blood from her mouth, and was moved back into the room."

Mooney opened a new file and scrolled down. "I can also identify the probable murder weapon. It's an Eastwing claw hammer. It shows up clearly here." She leaned closer to the screen and gestured Ted to follow her. "This demonstrates the classic fan pattern when a hammer hits the surface of the skull."

"Is it difficult to collect the evidence?" Ted asked.

Mooney sighed and leaned back in the chair. "I often have to crawl over the floor to get close enough to the stains. I use a jeweler's loupe for the close-up work. Actually, the worst part is that it gets hot. And I can't wear my vest, for instance, which makes me nervous at any crime scene."

"Wouldn't it be cooler to take it off?"

"Remember, this is a murder scene. Even though the cops try to clear it of suspects, what if the murderer was hidden and popped out just as I'm sprawled over the floor?"

"See what you mean."

"I don't think there's much more to show you here."

"Okay." Ted followed the deputy out of the conference room and back to her office. As they sat, he said, "Pretty amazing." When he looked at her, Ted saw her eyes grow small. Her lips tightened. A single strand of hair fell across her face, and she used a finger to tuck it behind her ear.

"Coffee?" she offered. When he agreed, she reached behind her to get two Styrofoam cups and a battered metal thermos. On the side in faded colors, it said Hennepin County Sheriff. She unscrewed the top and poured tepid coffee into the two cups. "Sorry, but it's the best I've got. Better than what the department provides."

He sipped it. It was bad, but he didn't want to slow her down in any way by commenting on it. "Something's wrong?" he asked in response to the troubled look on her face.

"Well, I do have some questions about the crime scene. Things that don't make sense to me. That aren't logical."

"What do you mean?" He set down the cup.

She leaned forward, and the Kevlar vest bunched up under her chin. It looked uncomfortable. For a moment, she didn't say anything. "My report is thorough and complete." She sat back and let her breath out.

Ted could tell that she wanted to say more. "This is important to many people. We need to know the truth. What else can you tell me?" he prodded.

Her eyes flared for a moment. "Okay. First, I always put the truth in my reports."

"Of course, sorry. Wrong word."

"Remember, the valuable aspect of scientific evidence is that, unlike human witnesses, it doesn't lie and isn't mistaken. I told you that one of the patterns we find is called an 'arterial spurt.'"

"Like when an artery opens up and shoots blood out?"

"Right. Wounds directly to the heart, arteries in the neck, arms. I found an arterial spurt on the wall by the bed. But it's not logical."

"What do you mean?" His stomach rumbled quietly.

Mooney's voice dropped. "The victim was small at five feet, four inches. The arterial spurt was too high on the wall for someone of that size."

"So what does that mean?"

"I don't know except to say it's not logical. Maybe it doesn't mean anything. I'd like to be more helpful, but I don't have an answer for you. That bothers me when I can't explain the evidence I find." She looked at Ted. "We can also estimate the height of the assailant by the directionality of the stains which we determine from their angles. Sometimes I can even tell if the killer was right or left-handed. Remember?"

He didn't remember but said, "Of course."

"This evidence suggests a killer who was taller than the defendant, Mr. Jensen."

Ted thought of the size of Korsokov and Harrison. Their heights fit what Mooney was telling him.

"Then the stains drop lower, which may suggest that the victim was already unconscious, lying on her stomach. Usually, the initial blows fall on the face as the victim faces the attacker and tries to fight him off. I did show you the strings to the sticks that indicated the victim went down during the attack." She chewed on her lip. "That might explain it."

"But you said the victim was first stuck when she was upright and then fell to the floor."

"I know. Again, I can't explain everything."

"Any other concerns you have?" He had already pulled out his legal pad and scribbled notes as quickly as she talked. His stomach rumbled louder.

"Well, yes. I didn't find a drip trail on the killer's escape route."

Ted paused and thought about it.

"We didn't find a murder weapon—the Eastwing claw hammer —at the scene. That means the assailant carried it away with him. Normally, there would be blood stains from the weapon dripping the last of the blood off of it. Or the hands of the killer would be covered in blood and would also drip as he left. Think about it: most killers leave quickly after they're done. That means they swing their arms in wide arcs with the weapon still in a hand. That motion causes projected blood stains in a drip trail on the floor as they leave. I expected to find them in the hallway, the floor outside the bedroom, and maybe even further from the crime scene. But I didn't find *any* at the Jensen home."

"Maybe the killer wrapped it up with the body?"

"Possible."

"Wait a minute. How about the bloody footprint?"

She nodded once. "That could represent an escape route. But the edge characteristics are not good." Mooney stopped talking. "Between you and me, can I make a guess? Something that I would never be able to testify about?"

"What?"

"Could there have been a second person involved in the murder? That might explain some of the discrepancies I found. I don't know, since I can't say with scientific certainty anything more about it." Her cell phone buzzed. She looked at it and stood up. "Sorry. I have to leave. There's an alleged homicide in South Minneapolis, and I'm on duty."

"A homicide in the morning?"

"Hey, people don't stop to have scrambled eggs with bacon before they kill someone."

Ted felt stupid for asking. "Okay. Can I talk to you again if we need more information?"

"You *should* talk to me."

165

"Huh?"

Mooney took a deep breath and let it out in a burst. "My report indicates this is a typical crime scene, and that's what I believe. I beat out three men for this position, and I don't like to be uncertain about my conclusions. But I can't find all the answers for this case."

"But you can't say *why*?"

"No." She frowned with frustration.

Ted slid into the depth of the metal chair. The backrest dug into his lower back uncomfortably. He waited for a moment. "I didn't see these questions in your report."

"I report conclusions, not questions." Her eyes flicked up to him. "Besides, you're the first one who ever asked."

Chapter Seventeen

Two weeks later, Ted met with Arvid Johnson, the son of a wealthy family whose business empire had just spun off a start-up company that marketed low-budget programming for television stations. Arvid stood to make eleven million dollars for the hard work of being born into the family. He had come to Ted for help avoiding the one million dollar tax bill that he didn't want to pay. Ted and Arvid sat in the conference room drinking coffee from white china cups with faint blue designs that looked like human veins. Through the use of several loopholes and legal tax credits, Ted had managed to reduce Arvid's tax bill to forty-seven thousand dollars.

"It's still a damn crime," Arvid complained. "It's those left-wing nuts who try to tax the wealthy. We get screwed every time we turn around simply because we believe in capitalism." He drank the last bit of coffee since he never let anything free go to waste.

Ted nodded but cut short the meeting. He had to get downtown to meet Jackie. They would argue the request to Judge Vang to allow the use of the amygdala hijack in Jensen's defense. "You should be happy, Arvid."

"I would be, but we're turning into a communist country and going to hell on top of it."

Ted ushered him out to the lobby and sent him on his privileged way. Back in the conference room, Ted paused for a moment. He'd done a great job helping Arvid Johnson, but Ted felt hollow. He looked down at the two cups on the table and saw they were both empty.

An hour later at the Government Center he crossed the second floor atrium. He had two hours before the hearing. He'd try to convince Judge Vang to allow the amygdala hijack as a defense. He had twenty minutes before he met with Jackie to put the final preparations on their argument to prevail.

From a fountain in the middle of the floor, three streams of water arced into a large pool. Lawyers, clients, clerks, and homeless people sat on the edges. Ted walked around the corner of it on his way toward the skyway. The noise of dozens of voices echoed around the atrium. As he passed an escalator coming up from the ground floor, he saw the head of Maureen Hanrahan rising with the escalator. When she noticed Ted, she smiled and stepped off the moving steel belt. He stopped and said hello.

"We met at the bail hearing. Share a coffee with me?" she asked. "There are some things I'd like to talk to you about."

Ted agreed but said, "It has to be quick."

Five minutes later, they stood before the counter, and Maureen looked up at the menu. She brought out a pair of oval plastic glasses and propped them on her small nose. "Never needed these when I was younger," she admitted with a grin.

Once they received their order, they sat at a small circular table and watched people stream by in the crowded skyway. Baristas shouted orders, and Ted could hear the coffee grinding from behind the counter. He looked at Mo as she sipped her latte. She wasn't beautiful, but her hair, make-up, and confidence created a combined effect that was impressive. "So, what did you want to talk about?" he said.

She wiped foam from her upper lip. "We're prepared for the mental illness argument today. Are you still pursuing that?"

"You know that I have to bring up every defense I possibly can for Jensen's case. My partner has found some persuasive law in our support. Would it make any difference to Rogin about cutting a deal?"

"Probably not. It's not every day a husband is found in a blood-soaked room and his wife is dead and missing."

"That's my point. There must be something mentally wrong with him."

Mo frowned at him. Green eyes held his for a moment. "We will never agree."

"I don't expect you to." He wondered what she was really after. Why was she talking to him? She must have authority from Rogin. Maureen was much younger than Ted and still had that casual, comfortable, and slouching confidence of youth.

"I'm not supposed to say this, but there may be a tiny opportunity to settle the case." Mo sat back in her chair.

"Oh? I don't think Jensen will agree to anything. But what've you got?"

Maureen leaned forward again. "I think—don't ever tell anyone or I'll lie and deny everything—that Bud Grant would be willing to bend a little if we could find the body. Rogin's a different matter, but in the end Grant is his boss and makes the final decision."

Ted drank from his coffee. He could smell the cinnamon that he'd shaken in earlier. He sighed. "Don't think that's going to happen. Jensen says he's innocent and has no idea where the body is."

Mo laughed and said, "From your experience, you know they all say they're innocent."

"You're right—until the deal becomes good enough for them, and then damn if they don't suddenly remember that they just might be guilty after all."

"Look, Ted, I'll be straight with you. If I could 'find' the body, it'd be a big deal for me. So can you help? Can your client help himself?"

Why was she offering this? Did she want to make an end-run around Rogin? If she were successful, it might catapult her career far ahead of the usual long climb up the bureaucratic ladder. He scraped his chair back from the table. "I appreciate you telling me this, Mo. And I won't say anything, but it's not going to work."

She shrugged. "Guess we'll just have to beat you in court."

Her efforts to maneuver the case around Rogin impressed Ted. "I don't plan to lose."

"You defense lawyers never do."

He stood up to leave.

She started to say something but stopped. Did she know about his history? "Things could get a whole lot worse for you and your case."

"What's that supposed to mean?"

Maureen didn't respond. She lifted her briefcase from the floor and absentmindedly checked through her purse. "I have to prepare for court. Thanks for the latte." She spun around, and her green silk scarf floated over her shoulder. In a minute she was gone.

Ted hurried back to the Government Center to reach Judge Vang's courtroom. He had a little more than an hour to review the argument with Jackie Nguyen. He was thankful she'd agreed to back him up and help.

He walked across the skyway. Through the floor-to-ceiling glass, he could see on the north side of the courthouse various food vendors with their carts spread across the sprawling plaza. Veggie sandwiches, hot dogs, and pizza all warmed in the carts. Dozens of people still lounged around the circular waterfall over which water cascaded from street level down one story below. Several young women had pulled their skirts high on their thighs to let the sun tan their legs.

Ted went through the security checkpoint and took an elevator up to Judge Vang's courtroom. As he worked his way deeper into the building, it became increasingly quiet. The air temperature dropped to chilly, and there were no smells inside the courtrooms.

He would meet Jackie in the small conference room next to the judge's courtroom. His law clerk, Joe Kopp, had prepared the briefs that Ted would use for his request to allow the use of the amygdala hijack. Joe had wanted to sit down and talk it over with Ted the day before, but Ted didn't have time. He'd grabbed all of Joe's work, stuffed it into his briefcase, and left the office.

Ted found Jackie already in the conference room. "I've got a good feeling about this," she said as Ted dropped his bundle of papers and files on the round table between them. In the corner, a sagging leather couch had arms that were worn bare and rough from years of clients waiting with sweating hands for their trials.

He tilted his head to the side and raised his eyebrows. "We've got solid law behind us. But we're on new ground here. Have you got any reading on Vang?"

"When I worked as a law clerk for her, we never got a motion like this, but she tries very hard to be fair. If there's any way we can convince her of the injustice of not letting us try this defense, she should go for it." Jackie put her hand on Ted's shoulder. "And

170

remember: no funny stuff. She won't appreciate your sense of humor. In fact, I don't think she has a sense of humor."

"I'll play it straight."

"If you can." Jackie shook her head. "I've never seen you play anything by the book."

Joe Kopp entered the room and took a seat beside Ted. "Jackie's awesome. She thinks about the big picture, and I do the grunt work." He smiled and his eyes glistened with anticipation.

"You can see in our brief," Jackie said, "that the hijack theory isn't completely new. It's been offered in seven other jurisdictions. No court has allowed its use, but the language is helpful for us. Remember, Vang likes to think of herself as a progressive judge. You've got to constantly remind her of the chance for her to create a new precedent. She may go for that."

"I know this is a long shot, but I think we've got a chance," Ted said. He turned to Joe. "Is Dr. Strauss here yet?"

"He's waiting in the hall." He opened his laptop.

Jackie said, "It'll be a long shot to win this. But Vang likes to be on the cutting edge of new law."

The team spent another half hour reviewing the argument that Ted would make before the judge. As they stood to walk into the courtroom, Joe said, "Uh, Ted, there are a couple cases you should really look at. Here." Joe held out his opened laptop.

Ted glanced at his watch and brushed past him. "Later, Joe." They all turned out of the conference room and pushed through the double wooden doors into the courtroom.

"Here he comes." Ted turned to see Sanford Rogin and Maureen charge into the courtroom right behind. They were followed by two law clerks that pushed what looked like a large metal grocery cart. It was filled with laptops, law books, three-ring binders, cords, and four bottles of mineral water.

Rogin came over to stand beside them. He towered over Jackie and said, "You've gone over to the dark side, I see."

"You mean the side of the oppressed," she responded.

His blond hair was messed and looked thicker than usual. "We're all after justice."

"You are? Since when?" she asked.

"Funny." Rogin forced a fake laugh. "You won't be so cocky by the time you get out of here."

"We'll see."

"You're making a big mistake tying your career to this case," he warned. "Thought you only defended innocent people."

"Shove it, Rogin." Jackie turned away from him and sat down in the padded chair behind the polished wood of the counsel table. It stretched out to give both her and Ted plenty of room.

Rogin ambled away, rocking from side to side as he made his way to the prosecutor's table.

"Always a pleasure," Ted said. He noticed Maureen Hanrahan sitting on the far side of the counsel table. She refused to make eye contact with him.

He and Jackie spread out their material. Except for the constant low rumble of talk from the audience area behind him, the center of the courtroom was silent. To his right, the jury box with its wooden railing and padded black chairs stood empty. One of the chairs held a crumpled notebook and a short pencil, probably forgotten by a juror from a previous case.

Today there wouldn't be a jury for Ted's case. The argument was a legal one that only the judge could decide.

After years of practice, he forced himself to look calm and even disinterested. Inside, his stomach churned. Although it was beginning to feel more comfortable, he still didn't want to be in the courtroom. Some lawyers never got over the butterflies before a hearing. Some even threw up. It must be how performers felt before a show.

Ted looked up at the clock on the wall. Where was Dan?

Judge Vang's clerk entered the courtroom through the floor-to-ceiling wooden door beside the raised bench. She asked Ted, "Are you ready, Counsel?"

"I'm waiting for my client. He should be here any minute." He felt a sharp pain in his stomach.

The clerk frowned. "The judge will be out in four minutes."

Ted turned around to see Dan pushing his way through the crowd at the outside door of the courtroom. He wore a tan cotton suit, and his face was damp with sweat. He thumped through the swinging doors and collapsed in the chair between Ted and Jackie. He wiped his forehead with a dry hand. "Sorry, guys. Business details on a major contract."

"This doesn't look good to a judge, Dan." Ted leaned over and spoke in a sharp whisper.

"Yeah, sorry."

The clerk announced the judge's entrance and she came around the corner, stepped up the two steps to the bench, and sat behind it. The audience in the courtroom quieted. The judge adjusted her glasses on her nose, peered at the computer screen beside her, and raised her head. She looked out at the people sitting in the courtroom. "Ready everyone?"

When both Rogin and Ted stood to say yes, the judge ordered Ted to begin.

Ted took a deep breath. The room was silent except for the hissing of the air conditioning fans from the ceiling. "I've filed a motion with the court and provided a copy to counsel. The Minnesota Rules of Criminal Procedure, Rule 9.02, requires that I give notice to all parties. I've done that." He paused to allow the judge to flip through his written brief. "We're asking that scientific evidence of the amygdala hijack be allowed in our defense of Mr. Jensen, and we have testimony to support it."

"Get to the point, Mr. Rohrbacher," the judge said. If she recognized Jackie, the judge didn't show it.

"Of course. I can offer the testimony of our experts on the subject. I plan to call Dr. Jerome Strauss to testify about his research." He heard a loud, exaggerated sigh from Rogin, but Ted ignored it.

"I'll allow the testimony," the judge said. It was a good sign that she didn't deny his request immediately and was willing to listen.

Ted announced, "The defense calls Dr. Jerome Strauss." Joe Kopp left the courtroom to go into the hall, find Dr. Strauss, and escort him back. In a few minutes they both came through the large double doors. Strauss laid several large charts on the table by Ted. After being sworn in by the clerk, Dr. Strauss climbed up the few steps to the witness stand. He sat and looked around the courtroom.

Ted began by asking about his professional qualifications, awards, education, and publications. Then Ted focused on the amygdala hijack.

Strauss' eyebrows arched over his face. "I think our law should be changed to allow it in court. I've written extensively about the issue. I'm proud to say that this area is my specialty, and I'm known as a national expert."

Ted looked up at the judge and back to the doctor. "Let's assume that Mr. Jensen insists that he didn't kill his wife. But he also admits that he passed out somehow, and when he woke up she was missing, probably dead." Ted paused to make sure the words he chose were correct. "So, what if Dan Jensen was wrong and really killed his wife?"

"Okay." Strauss looked at Ted.

"But what if he did it under the handicap of a mental deficiency? Can you tell the court about the amygdala hijack?"

Dr. Strauss smiled. "Sure. Would you hand me the charts I left with you?"

Ted picked up each one and stuck a small square form on them to identify them as official exhibits. He wrote numbers on the forms, carried them over to Rogin and Maureen to look at, and then took them up to Strauss.

"Let's review the medical school lessons, briefly." Strauss spread the charts across the flat space before him. He lifted one and held it upright. Ted recognized the cross-section of the human brain with various parts marked in different colors. Everyone shifted their chairs to get a better look.

Strauss pulled a wooden pencil from his lab coat pocket and pointed with it. "See, here behind the eye, in the deepest part of the brain, is the hippocampus, the thalamus, and the amygdala right here under the frontal lobe. At the back of the head is the occipital lobe. That's this one in light blue."

The judge curled her body to the left to get a better look.

Strauss said, "Here's the process our brain goes through. First, we see something that might be threatening in our environment. The stimulus—what we perceive—goes to the occipital lobe and then to the thalamus. From there, the stimulus is routed to both the amygdala and neocortex. That's the one here in rose. The neocortex is the 'thinking' part of our brain. The rational part. The amygdala, on the other hand, is the older, reptilian part of our brain that controls our emotional and 'fight or flight' responses."

Ted leaned back in his chair. He thought of the old case and how this material came back to him stronger and more upsetting than he had imagined it would. He leaned forward, and Dr. Strauss continued talking.

"This part, in green, is the hippocampus, which stores our past experiences as memory. It can be accessed instantaneously. Under normal circumstances, the neocortex analyzes the stimulus and directs us to react—in a rational, normal manner." Strauss looked up at the courtroom. "Let's say your boss is yelling at you. Instead of punching him—which we may want to do—you remain rational and fight back by telling him the reasons why you didn't make the mistake he's accusing you of making." He looked from the judge to Ted. "Understand?"

They both nodded.

Strauss continued, "But in people who suffer from post-traumatic stress disorder, the brain can operate much differently. Because of the traumatic events it's experienced, the reaction of the brain changes. It can 'short-circuit', so to speak. We have to look at the amygdala now." He pointed with his pencil. "The key to understanding this is to know that the amygdala processes the stimulus milliseconds *earlier* than the rational part of the brain. So here's what can happen."

He used his pencil to trace an imaginary event entering the eye, traveling across the brain and splitting between the neocortex and the amygdala. "If the amygdala perceives a match to the stimulus from an experience stored in the hippocampus that tells the amygdala it's a fight or flight situation, then the amygdala triggers the hypothalamic-pituitary-adrenal axis and hijacks the rational brain." He leaned back with a glow on his face. "It overrides the rational part and shuts it down. Can't be controlled."

Ted interrupted, "Would you explain that more clearly?"

Strauss cocked his head to the side, waited a minute and then said, "In the case of a match between a frightening, deadly memory and the new stimulus, the amygdala will act before any possible direction from the neocortex can be received."

"What does that mean?" Ted asked.

"Neuroimaging studies suggest that people with PTSD are preoccupied with anticipating and dealing with threats. It's as if every problem, even if it's a small one, becomes a threat to their survival."

"Can the reactions be violent?" Ted said.

"Yes. No one can make you do something against your better judgment, but the amygdala always can. Someone whose brain is hijacked will react irrationally and destructively."

"Out of control?"

"Out of control. They could easily be violent, especially if the match reminds them of a life-threatening memory from their past that has already disabled them day to day, like post-traumatic stress disorder. With people like Dan Jensen, the emotional response to perceived danger can be an immediate and overwhelming one that is out of proportion to the actual stimulus because it has triggered a much more significant emotional threat. It could lead people to do all kinds of violent acts."

Ted led the doctor through Dan Jensen's experience on the bridge in Afghanistan and the resulting mental illness. Then he asked the doctor for his expert opinion.

"For Dan Jensen, it's even worse than for many other people who suffer from PTSD because of the severe trauma he experienced."

"This isn't 'new' science, is it?" Ted looked at the judge to see her reaction.

Strauss laughed. "No. It's solid science. The research and concept has been around for years. The term 'amygdala hijack' was first used in research dating back to 1996." He smiled with pride and said, "My own research has also been published extensively."

"Can you say with reasonable scientific certainty that the amygdala hijack could take over Dan Jensen's brain and cause him to be unable to keep from committing a violent act, like killing someone?" Ted asked him directly.

Dr. Strauss looked from Ted to the judge. "Of course he could. The human brain hasn't had a hardware update in the last 100,000 years." Straus turned his head back and forth like he was performing on a stage. He lectured them. "You can understand why this emotional aspect developed quite early. When our ancestors saw a stranger approaching they wondered: am I going to eat him or is he going to eat me? They didn't have time to Google it, so to speak, and analyze the threat. The problem is exacerbated with PTSD patients because, like all of us, they're still dealing with the 'flight or fight' response. But unlike us, their brain paths are now wired differently." He blinked a few times and said, "Of course, my family thinks my brain is wired differently." Strauss giggled at his joke until he noticed the judge glaring at him.

Ted felt good. Dr. Strauss' testimony had gone well, and Ted thought that there might be a slim chance the defense could work after all.

Rogin cleared his throat. "I have a few questions for you, Doctor," Rogin said. "I understand your testimony to mean a person who goes through the amygdala hijack can do some violent acts. Maybe even kill someone else. But the hijack doesn't last for long, does it?"

"That depends on the person. It's impossible to say how long the episode would last," Strauss answered.

"Well, it wouldn't go on for days, would it?" Rogin sneered.

"No, of course not."

"So, we're talking about something that would last for only minutes?" Rogin said.

"Probably, but I can't say for certain."

"You can say for certain that even if Dan Jensen experienced an amygdala hijack it wouldn't last long enough to wrap a body in a rug, drag it out of the house, hide the body, wait several hours, and then call the police. Am I right?" Rogin's voice got louder.

Strauss blinked his eyes and said, "No."

Ted asked the doctor to remain on the witness stand and said to the judge, "I've marked some additional exhibits as one through twenty-one. These are copies of several scientific studies that have been conducted over the years about the amygdala hijack." Jackie handed him the packet that Joe had prepared. Ted walked around the table to the bench and offered the stack to the judge's clerk. "Opposing counsel has already received a copy." He glanced at the audience and saw his son Matt and two friends sitting in the corner. Ted felt proud.

"Any objection to the admission of these exhibits, Mr. Rogin?"

"No," Rogin said. His burly body dwarfed the chair that he leaned back against. His voice rumbled across the room. "But the Government objects to *everything* Mr. Rohrbacher has offered as proof."

Ted walked back to the counsel table. He reached into his briefcase and pulled out a DVD. He put a small white sticker on it with a number. When he was finished, he stood and walked to the clerk. "I've marked this DVD as exhibit twenty-two. It's the TV video of Mr. Jensen reacting to the harassment of the news media. It clearly shows him capable of experiencing an amygdala hijack." He waved his hand across his chest to summarize. "So, as you can see, this defense is rooted in solid, extensive research that's proven the existence of the hijack. We should be allowed to at least present it to the jury. It's an opportunity to push the edge of the state of criminal law in this jurisdiction."

Vang's expression didn't change.

"It's a chance to bring the law into the twenty-first century with the latest psychological understanding and research."

Judge Vang turned in her chair and bent her head down to review the exhibits. After five minutes, she swiveled back to face the courtroom. "Anything else?"

For a moment, he felt deflated. "In our brief we cite the Minnesota case law and federal law on the subject. You'll notice in the *Ballou* case from the state of Wisconsin, the court considered the use of the amygdala hijack under some restricted conditions. We're asking that you allow us to do the same here in—"

"That's absolutely wrong." Rogin stood to interrupt Ted. "That case isn't similar at all. Counsel is stretching things here, and I object."

"I can make up my own mind, Mr. Rogin." The judge looked at Ted again. "Why should I follow anything coming out of Wisconsin except the Green Bay Packers?"

A ripple of laughter crossed the audience behind Ted. "Of course, you're not required to do what a court there has done, but it's precedent that the hijack *can be allowed in a trial.*"

The judge took a deep breath. "What's the Government's response?"

Rogin took a long time to stand. He cleared his throat. "We object to all of this. I'll cite case law in just a moment, but let's face the truth: every horrendous crime involves someone who has an unnatural mental makeup. Otherwise, they wouldn't commit the crime. This supposed 'defense' is an excuse to avoid legal responsibility," he grunted. "It's just hocus-pocus psychology." His voice trailed off as if his point was so obvious he didn't need to say anything more. But he did. "And as for the DVD, It doesn't prove anything except the defendant is a violent and dangerous man. Counsel can't tie this behavior to any psychological theory. I object."

Judge Vang turned back to Ted and smiled. Jackie had told him if that happened, it was a good sign for their case. It meant the judge was listening to his arguments. Maybe she'd agree.

He felt more confident. "And the court will note the case of *State vs. Willoughby.* That case should be dispositive of the issue."

"*Willoughby?*" Rogin jumped up. "You're relying on *Willoughby?*" His eyes behind the glasses looked larger than ever.

Ted felt a jolt go through his gut. Rogin seemed way too sure of himself. "That's right," Ted replied. He turned to Jackie, who shrugged.

Rogin scratched at his beard, and his words came out quickly. "If counsel is quoting that case, this decision can be made right now."

"Oh?" The judge sat up straight.

"Right." Rogin turned back to Maureen, who handed him a copy of another case. "Here is the newer case, *State vs. Johnson,* which overruled *Willoughby.* Just came out last week."

Ted sucked the air to catch his breath. He didn't have any idea what Rogin was talking about. Joe must have missed it, or maybe that's what Joe had wanted to talk to him about in the conference room. Ted had ignored him. As any good lawyer did at times, he'd have to fake it. "It can be distinguished easily."

Judge Vang looked at him. She asked, "How?"

"Uh . . ." His chest pounded and he felt like a fool. A failure. Memories of the old case and his collapse crashed in around him. Ted fought to stand still. He had screwed up badly, and it showed to everyone in the courtroom. "The facts aren't exactly the same."

"In what way?" Judge Vang said.

Ted felt faint. He realized it was time to shut up before things got worse. "If the court will give me a minute to review the *Johnson* case, I can answer that."

"No. I've heard enough. Let me read the *Johnson* case." Her clerk handed the copy to the judge, who settled into the high-backed chair and flipped through the pages. In a few minutes, she pulled her chair forward toward the desk and said, "This is a close question, and it's highly unusual. However, I agree that the state of law in Minnesota is archaic on the issue of mental illness." Noise broke out from the audience. The judge rapped her gavel. "I'm reluctant to do this, but I will at least allow the defense to present the evidence of an amygdala hijack to the jury." She glared at one lawyer, then the other. "I want this case set for trial immediately. It's been delayed far too long already. The clock's ticking, and I want a date certain for the trial to begin in less than three weeks." As her robes swirled around her ankles, she left the courtroom.

Ted dropped into his chair. From behind, he heard the thud of the large courtroom doors opening as people burst out.

An hour later, Ted came back to his office alone. He found Samantha sitting quietly in the lobby.

"Tough day at the factory, huh?" she said and stood up. She followed him into his office, where he shut the door and collapsed onto the couch. He didn't speak and fought-off the memories threatening to overwhelm him.

"You okay?" Samantha sat next to him and put her arm around his shoulders. "Slow down. Take a deep breath."

"I don't know," Ted muttered. "I totally screwed this up, like before. But this time, I won."

"She ruled for justice. She's a good judge."

"Jackie was right. It worked." He dropped his head back against the cool leather.

Samantha removed her arm and whispered, "Now the pressure's on. You can't screw up anymore. This may be Jensen's only chance."

He leaned forward. "And my only chance."

The receptionist knocked on Ted's door and entered. "Special delivery for you, Mr. Rohrbacher. It arrived earlier and it looks important." She handed him a long envelope.

He turned it over and saw that it was from the Lawyer's Professional Responsibility Board. "What the hell is this?" He tore open the envelope and scanned the complaint. Samantha must have sensed trouble as she got up and stood beside Ted to read over his shoulder.

His breath came hard. Years ago, when he'd lost the big case, he'd been reprimanded for his unethical conduct. He'd come close to losing his license to practice law. The complaint read:

Violation of the Minnesota Rules of Professional Conduct Rule 1.7 Conflict of Interest: Current Clients

(1) A lawyer shall not represent a client if the representation involves a concurrent conflict of interest. A concurrent conflict of interest exists if:

(2) There is a significant risk that the representation of one client will be materially limited by the lawyer's relationship to a third person or by the personal interest of the lawyer.

The letter that accompanied the formal complaint alleged that since Ted was related by marriage to the victim, there was a conflict of interest with his current client, Daniel Jensen. An investigator would be assigned to the case, and a hearing before the Board would be scheduled within eight weeks.

Ted collapsed into his chair. Memories threatened to overwhelm him.

"Slow down," Samantha cautioned him. "Take a deep breath."

He picked up the complaint again. Rage started to replace his fear. "Rogin's trying to fuck with me," he shouted and threw the papers to Sam.

She read them also. When Samantha handed them back to Ted, she said, "Not Rogin. Look at the signature at the bottom. Maureen Hanrahan filed this."

Chapter Eighteen

The day after the court ruling, Kenny Seabloom attended a small retirement party for an older deputy. He noticed Samantha Carter across the room in the basement of the old court house. Although weak coffee and tasteless cake had been served, it had all been eaten in five minutes. After making his formal appearance, Seabloom was anxious to get back to the investigation. He sensed it was the opportunity for him to break out of the ranks and be noticed.

Like many former law enforcement people, Carter had come to congratulate and support the other officer. Kenny knew her because shortly before she retired, they had worked on a joint task force. Carter had been helpful to him when he was a rookie. After she gave him a quick glance and nod at the party, she separated and worked her way to the coffee. When Samantha found the pot was almost dry, she looked around for more.

Kenny moved toward her. "I'll help," he said and raised his hand to the deputy tasked for refreshments and food.

"Hey, Seaweed." Samantha grinned at him. "How the hell are you? Still suited up, I see." She looked up and down at his uniform and gave him a quick hug.

"They're finally letting me serve the coffee," he joked.

"Trust you that much, huh? Hang in there, man. It gets better. You should try being a female cop."

"Hey, you hear the one about the lawyer who was accused of ethical violations because he not only had sex with a client but also charged her his regular hourly rate?"

"Naw." Samantha looked up at him, waiting for the punchline.

"True story. Of course, the ethical rules allow a lawyer to charge more for a skill in which he has a special expertise."

Sam chuckled and shook her head. "The lawyers I've met—I can believe they'd do anything."

"You used to play jazz, didn't you?"

"Still do. In fact, I'm rehearsing for a gig at the Dakota, and it's got me nervous."

"Can't ever imagine you nervous about anything." Seabloom laughed.

"I'm the lead. And when you think of all the really great musicians who've played on that stage—well, it makes the hair on the back of my neck stand up."

"Let me know when. I'll come to cheer you on." He changed the subject. "How's retirement?"

"Good news—I get to play a lot more jazz. Bad news—I'm still working. Hired on the Jensen murder case."

Kenny's eyes opened. "You are? I'm working it also. Just got off Lake Minnetonka the other day. Tough work."

"Was the victim's family there?" When he nodded to her question, Sam added, "That's the hardest part of the job—talking to the victim's family. I remember. But the case is the strangest one I've been involved with in years. Any idea if you'll find the body?"

Kenny shrugged his shoulders. "You know that sometimes we never find the body. If we don't find it in the lake, we'll expand our search. That's when things get tough."

Samantha frowned.

"We may have to go to the Mississippi River."

"Oh, yeah."

"Everyone hates working there. The current, the crappy water, and the danger it poses for our divers. In fact, many of the bodies are found with drag lines."

"Drag lines?"

"See, in a lake the divers can spot the body and retrieve it themselves. In the river, the current's so strong and the water's so cloudy, they often can't see anything. Even the sonar doesn't work. So they use a drag line with hooks. Something like a fisherman would use. They hope to snag a body. Sometimes it works pretty well."

"Hope you don't have to go." Samantha accepted a Styrofoam cup of warm coffee from another deputy.

"I know, but this is a big break for me. Instead of having me run shitty little errands, I get to do something important on the biggest case in the department right now."

Sam sipped the coffee.

He ran his hand through thick hair. "Well, there's something else you may be interested in."

"Oh?" Someone bumped her from the side and apologized, then broke into a smile to say hello. Samantha turned back to Kenny.

"In your investigation, ever come across a guy named Nick Korsokov?"

Sam bounced her eyebrows up and down and glanced to the side. "Cops found him originally. Then we interviewed him. I think he's dirty."

"Well, he showed up at the site of a possible body recovery. Media was there, of course. We found someone's favorite dog instead. But Korsokov was there. And he told me he was 'worried.'"

"What'd you do?"

"Wait a minute. This is a fair trade, right? I tell you; you tell me?"

"Who do you think you're talking to? I'm gonna take you downtown and turn you around. Of course."

"Okay. Uh, kinda on my own, I did some checking on him. I'm not officially authorized to do this, so don't say shit to anyone." He frowned to make his point. "But I interviewed some of the people at the ambulance port at the hospital where Korsokov usually works."

"Oh?"

"Seems that he and Mina Jensen were close, very close. Several people suspected they were having an affair because even though she didn't work there, she met him often."

"That's what we think."

"I got another idea." Seabloom gripped her elbow and steered her into a quiet corner. "You gotta keep this to yourself. I could get busted for it."

"I remember what it was like in the police department. I could tell you some stories about my own escapades. Not all of 'em were totally legal, either."

"Okay." He lowered his voice. "Well, I'm convinced he was involved in a prostitution ring."

"We think so, too."

He tilted backward. "How the hell did you know?"

"We found a witness who worked for him briefly. I know about it."

"What you don't know is that he and Mina Jensen were probably working together."

Sam shook her head in dismissal. "Never saw any evidence of that."

"That's 'cause you probably never talked to the people Mina worked with."

"You're right. Uh, I haven't gotten to that yet."

"I did." He looked over her shoulder, and his body stiffened. The sheriff himself was coming toward them. He wore his official jacket with five decorative gold bands wrapped around each arm. The badge on his chest had been enlarged at his request. A captain walked beside him and carried a briefcase.

When he arrived, Samantha turned around to say hello. "Thanks to me, Mark, you got elected sheriff." When he frowned at her, she added, "I voted for you three times. That was your margin of victory, wasn't it?"

It took him a moment, but then the sheriff bent backward in a loud laugh. "You cops never respect us."

"That's because we're better."

They chatted for a few minutes. Finally, the sheriff noticed Kenny standing beside them. He looked at Kenny's nametag and said, "Carry on, Deputy Seabloom." He turned and walked away while the captain followed in his wake.

"Close personal friends, huh?" Samantha kidded him.

Kenny scowled. "He's all politician. I've wanted to be in law enforcement since I was in high school. But the way they treat me, I've really had it up to here." His palm flattened and he flicked it over his head.

Samantha shrugged.

Kenny's phone buzzed. He grabbed it off his belt and answered. It was dispatch.

"Deputy Seabloom, you're assigned to retrieve a gun from a civilian. Called in five minutes ago. It's a .38 caliber found hidden under a bush. Get out there ASAP. We're getting heat from downtown about this, and they don't want it screwed up." Seabloom listened to more instructions and the address. When he hung up, he told Sam the details.

"Kenny, that's a block from the Jensen house. It's the same caliber as the missing gun. Get your butt out there now," she said.

"I don't know. We've been getting hundreds of calls from the public to tell us they've found something or solved the Jensen murder case, or even found the body."

"Shut up and get moving. This one assignment could make your career—finally."

Seabloom dropped his coffee cup in a round basket lined with a plastic bag. It was full of pink paper plates smeared with chocolate frosting that had cake crumbs stuck on them. "Gotta boogie." His phone rang again. The dispatcher gave him another assignment.

"Commander says that after you retrieve the weapon get out to a landfill in Eagan. Someone found a bloody wig." The dispatcher gave him the directions.

"So what?" Kenny said.

"Commander wants every, and I mean every lead followed-up."

Kenny sighed and hung up. He turned from Samantha to leave.

"Hey. What about Korsokov and Mina Jensen?"

"I'll get back to you."

"So you think they were in business together?"

A pained look crossed Seabloom's face. "I don't have any evidence I can point to, but I think they were really close. Maybe he owed her money? Maybe they worked together. There are lots of reasons for him to want to kill her, though."

"Why do you say that?"

He started to move away from her but said, "Several of the nurses who worked in the emergency area at the hospital overheard the two of them arguing. Korsokov complained to the nurses about his girlfriend, Mina."

"Hmm."

"Sometimes they were violent arguments, apparently. Combined with his showing up at the dig, makes him seem pretty suspicious in my book."

"I agree, but he's covered up pretty well."

Kenny dropped his eyes to the floor. "No one in the department will give me the time of day, but I know there's something odd about this case. They may have gotten the wrong dude."

Chapter Nineteen

Ted assembled the team in his office. A small space around them glowed in soft light from two lamps on the desk while the smudge of shadows hung from up in the corners. Samantha and Jackie hovered around his desk, and Joe Kopp sat on the couch with a laptop opened and balanced on his upraised legs. His scuffed shoes contrasted with the polished leather of the furniture. Ted had considered firing Joe until he calmed down and realized the mistake in court was his own fault, not Joe's. Joe had even tried to warn him.

"It's a whole new ball game, guys." Ted raised his voice to get their attention. "And I want things to change, starting right now." He felt energized by his win, and it propelled him forward. The steps in the preparation of a criminal case felt familiar again.

"So we're going ahead with the hijack?" Sam asked.

"Of course, but we can't depend on that alone. We have the other suspects. If we can show they *might* have killed Mina that will go a long way to creating reasonable doubt in the minds of the jurors."

"Like I said, from jump street," Samantha added.

Joe said, "But we can't prove they killed Mina Jensen."

"The government has to prove the case. All we have to do is create a reasonable doubt in the jury that Rogin's got the right guy," Ted said. He looked at Jackie. "You think we should focus on the mental illness stuff?"

She bobbed her head up and down. Shiny black hair patted her cheeks. "I'll work on the hijack; you get the suspects nailed down."

Ted remembered the ethics complaint. He asked Jackie, "Can you represent me during the investigation and the hearing before the board?"

"Of course. From what you told me, it's crap. For starters, we'll get Jensen's waiver of any conflict on the record in court."

"Thanks," Ted said. "But everything's coming up fast. Can you pull a defense together by then?"

"Gladly. I may even handle the ethics complaint for free just to stick it to that jerk Rogin."

"Great." Ted started to sip from a china cup full of hot coffee but was too excited to take the time. He set it on his desk. He looked up and called over to Joe. "You'll be in charge of all the research, including whatever Jackie needs. And don't bill this out on the regular firm software. I don't want my law partners shitting bricks over your extra work."

He turned to Samantha. "You got the Harrison print comparisons yet?"

She wore a red running suit the color of a stop sign and had a tangle of her own hair in cornrows across her head. "Working on it. The techs at the lab owe me some favors from years ago. So we should have an answer soon." She stirred three packets of sugar into her coffee, lifted the cup to her mouth and sipped it to test the formula.

"We've got to change the whole plan."

Silence blanketed the room.

"We'll work on both defenses," Ted said.

"Teddy." Sam set down the coffee cup and saucer on the desk with a clink. "Just because you won the motion and we can present evidence of the amygdala hijack to a jury, that doesn't mean they'll really agree with it. The case is still a loser."

He swept his hand in front of them. "That's why we're also going to focus on Korsokov and Harrison," he insisted.

"We've had this conversation before . . ." Samantha said.

"I told you it's a new ball game." Ted stepped out from behind his desk and paced in a circle. "I know the amygdala hijack is a long shot, but we're still Dan's lawyers. We need to be more aggressive."

"That's great, Ted, but even with Dr. Strauss' testimony, it'll be a tough sell to the jury," Jackie reminded him.

He stopped and yelled, "And that's exactly why we'll also build a case against both of the suspects, too. Besides, this is different. It's personal now. Maybe none of you can understand that." His breath came hard, and he felt his face flush.

"I know it's personal," Jackie yelled back at him. "I also know how crazy your thinking can get at times. It's a dangerous thing when a defense lawyer starts to believe in his client's innocence. Be reasonable."

His shoulders hunched forward and he walked back to his desk. He tried to pick up his coffee cup, but it shook in his hand, and he dropped it back on the desk. "I've been *reasonable* since I left the courtroom. I've been quiet and reasonable for years. Now it's time to go all out and defend Dan Jensen like he deserves to be defended."

"Even if he could be guilty?" Jackie said quietly.

"I don't think he is. And besides, we have a duty to zealously represent him."

No one spoke for several minutes. Then the tension in the room dissipated like the steam from the hot coffee. Samantha walked over to the large window. Outside the wind bent the trees to one side, but the branches and leaves fought back, resisting the onslaught. Joe remained on the couch, pretending to be busy with his computer.

Ted looked around, stretched his arms, and sat down. His saw the card from his father, and the entire memory of the old trial and the defendant's case of mental deficiency that was used against Ted came back to hit him.

He stopped for a moment and took several deep breaths. Ted stood up straight and put the card from his father into the right hand drawer of the desk and pushed it closed on silent rollers. "Okay. We're going to turn both Harrison and Korsokov inside out. What size shoe does Harrison wear? Were his fingerprints in the Jensen home? Where were both of them on the night of the murder?"

Jackie took off her glasses and twirled them in her hand. "Why didn't the cops investigate Harris

"Never knew about him until Danny told us. I forwarded the information to Rogin. I'm sure the cops are all over Harrison by now."

Samantha walked to the middle of the office. "With all the drama here, I forgot to tell you—the sheriffs may have found the gun that was shot in the house." She explained that her friend, Deputy Seabloom, had retrieved a weapon located one block from the Jensen home. "They'll check for prints and bullet comparisons."

"How do they do that?" Joe asked.

"They extracted the spent bullet from the wall of the Jensen home. When a bullet is fired from a gun, the barrel leaves distinctive markings on it called *striations*. When they get the gun found near the house back to the lab, they fire a bullet through it. Under a microscope, the lab techs can compare the markings on one bullet to the other. If the striations on the test bullet match those on the bullet found at the crime scene, it's the same gun." She watched Joe to make sure he understood. "And if they're really lucky, they'll lift some prints off the gun that could tell us who fired it in the house—maybe the killer."

Ted interrupted, "And if the prints are Korsokov's or Harrison's, that proves they were in the house during the murder. We've got to lean harder on them. For instance, your deputy friend said Korsokov was at the dig. Why?"

"And how did he know about it?" Jackie asked.

"The media had been covering the body search at the lake. They reported it on the news."

"Sure." Jackie shifted in her seat. "And how about the beer bottles that Dan drank from?"

"What?" Ted asked.

"Were they ever tested for the existence of drugs?"

Ted and Sam looked at each other. "They were never found."

"Jensen says he normally doesn't react the way he did to two beers, but he passed out. Tells me there was something in those beers besides beer."

Ted walked over to the window. Gray clouds stretched across the sky. On the horizon, a yellow streak peeked out from underneath the dark bank. The silhouettes of birds beat across the sky on their way to the west. Wind hissed around the top of the office building.

From behind him, Sam raised her voice. "You don't want to hear this, but just listen." She hesitated. When Ted didn't respond, she said, "I understand the new plan, but I'm worried you're losing your objectivity. You can't get personally involved with Dan Jensen's case," Sam pleaded with him.

"I'm not."

"You know that all defendants lie to some degree. What if Jensen is really guilty of murder?"

He turned to face her. "He still deserves the best defense we can possibly give him."

"Come on, Ted. That's the speech you make in law school or to a reporter. This isn't a high school hockey game. Focus on what you should do, not on beating the brains out of the goalie—even if we'd all like to beat the hell out of Rogin."

He felt his face flush. "Okay, you're right, but I don't care. I'm in this to win. Period." Ted's phone rang. He answered the receptionist.

"Ted, the partners have convened a meeting in the conference room tomorrow at noon." Her voice was smooth and dry.

"Why?"

"I don't know."

It didn't make any sense to Ted. "What's on the agenda?"

"You." The receptionist hung up.

At the same moment, Sam's phone played a Motown hit. Ted heard the vocals: *Jimmy, oh Jimmy Max, when are ya comin' back?* She looked at the screen. She looked up at Ted. "That's the sheriff's crime lab. The print analysis is done."

"What does that mean?"

"I'll call now." She dialed and waited. Sam left a voicemail to call her back immediately.

Ted wondered why the partners wanted to talk with him. In law partnerships it was almost always about money. They were probably still concerned about the cost overruns from Joe Kopp's research billed to a criminal case. Ted would take care of that easily.

Sam's phone rang again. She answered and talked with the lab expert who'd done the comparisons on Demontre Harrison's fingerprints. Sam listened for a long time and asked, "Did you compare his prints with all the prints that were found at the crime scene?" She grunted at the end of the call. Sam dropped the phone in her lap and took a deep breath before turning to face the others. "They're a match," she whispered.

"What?"

"I knew it."

"Huh?"

"He lied to us. Demontre Harrison's prints matched prints found inside the Jensen house."

Chapter Twenty

Late afternoon when Sanford Rogin got back to his office, he high-fived Maureen. "We're really going after Jensen now," Rogin shouted as he danced over to the window. He tried to make a few Michael Jackson moves but only looked awkward. He was anxious to get Jensen charged with first degree murder.

Maureen watched him gyrate and ignored the dance. She said, "But we lost the damn motion."

"Right, but it shows that he will rely on the amygdala hijack for a defense. The case is as good as over." He came back toward her while his head bopped up and down to some internal beat. At his desk, he stopped and slapped the top. "Teddy has gone absolutely crazy himself. He's the one who should be pleading mental deficiency!" He laughed alone at his joke. "Hey, how about some victory music?" He slipped behind his computer, tapped on the keys, and stepped back with a glow on his face. The guitars rang with a metallic buzz and the song, "Born to be Wild," thumped from the speakers. Rogin shouted along with the lead singer for Steppenwolf, "I like smoke and thunder. . ."

Zehra Hassan came into the room. "I find it difficult to offer you support, but too bad about Judge Vang's ruling," she yelled over the noise.

"And I hate to say thanks to you, but thanks." His hair had grown longer than usual and looked like a yellow helmet on his head. He turned down the sound.

"What're you going to do now?" Zehra asked.

"We're not going to worry about this hocus-pocus amygdala hijack. We'll put the full-court press on Jensen. Right, Mo?"

"You haven't even started the trial," Zehra said.

"And if things work out the way I've planned, there won't be a trial. He'll plead guilty. 'Course, if he's stupid enough to want a trial —that's even better for me. Can't wait to take that win to the media."

Maureen said, "We're going to the grand jury first thing tomorrow morning."

Zehra's eyebrows rose. "Already?"

"You gotta hit 'em when they're down," Sanford said. "This should be the knockout punch."

"Okay, enough of the sports metaphors. What are you really looking at?" Zehra asked.

Rogin sighed like he was lecturing his child. "Okay, Rohrbacher's also got a couple of lowlife suspects. They look a little dirty, but there's not much in the way of facts to tie them to the murder. I'm sure Ted will push it for all it's worth. Doesn't mean we have to agree."

"What about the new suspect?" Zehra circled the two as they stood before Rogin's desk.

"Some guy named Harrison. We're all over him like flies on shit. Don't worry."

"I do worry. Don't screw this up, Sandy."

"Yeah, yeah. I'm meeting with Ben right now."

Zehra nodded and walked to the door. "I don't want any major decision made without my final approval."

"Yes, sir." Rogin snapped off a quick salute as she left. He grinned at Maureen. "And thanks for the *extra* work you've done on the case. It'll take your career a long ways in this office. I'll back you for whatever you want from Grant."

"Aren't you going to tell Zehra about the ethics complaint?"

"Later. Grant okayed it. That's all we need."

"I feel uncomfortable hiding anything from her," Mo said.

Rogin waved his hand in the air. "Let me do the worrying. You're doing great." He walked to the far corner of the office and tapped the side of a coffee maker. "Want some?" he called back to her.

"No thanks. I'm already too wound up." She shifted her weight to the left leg. "I had a cup of coffee with Ted a few days ago." Then she walked behind his desk and turned off the music.

"What the fuck? I never authorized that."

"I may have followed your orders about trial procedure, but I'm co-counsel in this case, and I can meet with defense counsel any time I want." She glared at him.

"You didn't give away anything?"

"Of course not!"

"Sure, he's smart enough, but he's out of shape. He hasn't been in a courtroom for years. Look how he got slammed. He was damn lucky that Vang got the law wrong and ruled for him. He'll slink back to his boring work of estate planning, and that'll be the end of him. He should leave the courtroom for those of us with the balls to handle it."

She sighed. "Anatomy hardly plays a part in this."

"Whatever." He poured a large amount of coffee into a mug that said Hennepin County Attorney on the side of it. "And I don't want you ever talking to him again without me present. That's an order, or you're bounced off this case." When she didn't answer, which Rogin assumed was her agreement, he said, "We gotta be prepared to meet with the media after our win."

"Don't you think we should prepare for the evidence about Jensen's mental state first?"

Rogin shrugged. "I don't think any jury will buy it. Rohrbacher's stretching for anything. He's got nothing left in the tank."

"But Dr. Strauss sounded pretty convincing. What if the jury agrees?"

Rogin's face softened and he smiled like he did at his daughter. "Don't worry. Watch me knock that one out of the park."

"And what about this new suspect, Harrison?"

Rogin jerked his head to the side as if to dismiss her concern. "The cops talked to him. And so did our investigator, Ben Clark. We're going to meet with him right now for his report."

"Okay, but Harrison seemed to have a motive to kill Mina to get revenge on Dan."

"You're starting to sound like a defense lawyer. Drop it," he ordered.

Maureen followed him out into the hallway of tan sheetrock walls. They walked the length of the hall toward the conference room. They passed secretaries, victim/witness advocates, other prosecutors, various cops from multiple jurisdictions who hovered in the hall waiting to present their investigations for charging, and two new law clerks.

When they reached the conference room, Rogin entered followed by Maureen. It was a long room which had a new rosewood table in the middle. Comfortable chairs circled it, and at the end was a coffee maker, a white board fastened to the wall, and the leftover donuts from an earlier meeting. Sugary white crumbs traced patterns across the dark carpeting.

Ben Clark finished the last of a donut and licked purple filling off his fingers. He had been a Minneapolis homicide cop for over twenty years and had retired to collect his pension. Then he'd gone to work with the county attorney's office as an investigator for extra pay and a second pension—along with collecting some extra weight. He had a large, beef-fed body and was red-faced. His breath came in short spurts. He wore a tan sport coat and baggy brown pants that were belted underneath the bulge of his waist.

When he saw Sanford and Maureen, he smiled a purple grin. He'd been eating the left over pastries on the corner table.

"Ben, what's shakin'?" Rogin said and shook Clark's hand while twisting his palm around in a power grip.

Clark's tongue worked around inside his lips and he smiled again, this time with off-white teeth. "Was reading about the sting the FBI just did to catch some sex traffickers. Back in my day, the feds couldn't care less. Things have sure changed." He shifted his bulk to the other side of the chair.

"You used to bust pimps all the time, didn't you?"

Clark laughed and his cheeks quivered. "We had our own way of 'discouraging' those scum." When no one responded, Clark continued, "I remember me and my partner found a black pimp on the avenue one night. We'd been trying to get rid of him for months. He smiled real pretty at us and showed a whole mouthful of gold. We grabbed his ass and took him over to the Washington Avenue Bridge above the Mississippi."

"You told me this one before," Rogin protested.

Clark didn't stop. "Me and Wally got the dude out and hung him over the bridge by his heels. He was almost pissin' on himself.

We told him to get the fuck . . . er, sorry." Clark glanced at Maureen standing behind Rogin. When she waved her hand to indicate that it didn't offend her, Clark continued, "We told him to get the fuck out of town or next time, we'd drop his sorry ass." Clark tipped back in the chair and laughed harder. "Know what? Never saw that puke again." His face flushed a brighter red.

"Sure, Ben. About the Jensen case. You talked to this guy Demontre Harrison? Maureen has already prepared a subpoena *duces tecum* for you to serve on him for his work records."

"Roger that." He chewed on the last of his donut.

"You get enough to eat this morning?" Rogin kidded Clark.

"Your funding from the county board must be up this year. Those were the best I've ever eaten here."

Maureen said, "I sent the data extracted from Mina Jensen's cell phone to Rohrbacher as we're required under the rules."

"Anything we can use?" Rogin asked.

"It doesn't look like it. Which makes me wonder."

"Oh?"

"All of us have some parts of our lives that are secret but could be revealed by the data on our phones. But not her. Why not?"

Rogin sneered to expose a thin white line at his mouth. "Does it help me convict her guilty husband?"

"No, but—"

"Then don't waste your time on that shit."

"We should be prepared."

Rogin stared at her for a long moment. Finally, he said, "Let me handle this, okay? I've got some experience."

"I'm just saying—"

"You've said it." Rogin sat in the chair next to Clark. "How about this guy, Harrison? Is it just a typical defense smokescreen?"

"These defense lawyers are all as crooked as the scum they represent," Clark growled.

Maureen remained standing at the end of the table. She interrupted them. "Do either of you know if Mina's body has been found yet?"

Clark looked at Rogin, who shrugged his shoulders.

"Nope," Clark answered. "Unfortunately, that happens more than the public thinks. We don't always find missing people."

Maureen walked along the side of the room and took a seat across the table from the other two.

"We've been over this a thousand times." Rogin's voice sounded tired. "We don't need a body to convict Jensen."

Maureen frowned at him.

"We don't have a body, but we got a hell of a lot of blood." Clark snorted a short laugh. He stood up with a grunt and walked over to the table with the donuts. He lifted a Bismarck from the tray, took a large bite, and returned to his chair. The cuffs on the back of his pants hung over his shoes and dragged on the floor.

Rogin continued, "This is classic domestic abuse. Jensen is a thug who beats his wife all the time. Nothing happens until one day he goes too far and kills her. Nothing unusual or mysterious about it, unfortunately. Remember his performance with the media when he went crazy?"

"Can't we think outside the box here?" Maureen suggested.

Rogin took two deep breaths. "I'll think about the medical examiner who said there was so much blood at the scene that no one could have survived that beating. I'll think about the forensic experts at the sheriff's department who used a test mattress and poured blood on it to estimate the quantity of blood at the crime scene. They report the quantity is over one half the amount contained in a human body." He whirled his upraised finger in the air and concluded by saying, "I'll think about how no one, I mean no one, could have survived that bloodletting and left that room in any condition except d-e-a-d." He spelled out the word.

Maureen sighed and slouched back in her chair.

Rogin's cell phone rang and he answered. "Oh, hi darling. Sure, I can pick her up." He listened for a while. "Of course I'm busy. It's getting worse as we get closer to trial. But I've got time to get her from school. Anything else? Stop to pick up a movie at the Redbox? Sure. Bye. I love you, sweetie." He clicked off his phone.

Clark plopped a tan file folder to the middle of the table. "Everything I got on Harrison so far," he said. "He's got some problems."

"Oh?" Maureen reached for the file and pulled it across the table. She opened it and read Clark's reports. "He's a former Navy SEAL?"

"Honorably discharged. Deployed to Iraq for several tours," Clark said. "He was wounded and got the Purple Heart."

"Dan Jensen was in Afghanistan at about the same time. Is there a connection there?" Maureen asked. She turned over the page. "And I see Harrison picked up a criminal charge after he left the military."

"Lots of people do," said Rogin.

Clark added, "It's an old one, but he was charged with murder in Gary five years ago. He pled guilty to manslaughter and did a year in prison. Just got off parole when he moved up here. He's also got a few misdemeanors. See the one for driving while intoxicated?"

Maureen read through the rap sheet and nodded.

"He told me it was for 'driving while black.' I couldn't follow up on what happened to that. But the murder charge is a hell of lot more troubling to me," Ben said. A drop of purple jelly lodged in the corner of his lips.

When the other two looked at Rogin, he shrugged.

"Come on, Sanford. This is awfully suspicious," Mo said.

"Okay, I agree. But it doesn't automatically prove that he killed Mina Jensen. We need more than what you've told me."

"Uh, there is a little more." Ben coughed. "When I cornered the dude, I asked him where he was the night of the murder. He told me he was with his woman, a young girl named—" He reached across the table, retrieved the file, and read through his notes. "Uh, girl named Shanika Portiss. He said he brought her some fried chicken and a bottle of wine. They watched a movie at her place and he stayed the night with her. So I talked to Portiss, and the alibi didn't check out. She admitted seeing Harrison on occasion, but on the night of the murder, he definitely wasn't with her. And she got mad when I told her Harrison said he slept with her. In her words, she said, 'I'd never give it to a nap-head like him.'"

No one spoke around the table.

"And how is she so sure of that?" Rogin demanded.

"'Cause she always goes to see her mother in the nursing home on Monday nights."

Rogin pushed back from the table and stood up. "Okay, it looks suspicious. But we don't work with suspicions; we work with facts. And so far, Ben, you haven't shown me anything that definitely ties Harrison to the murder." He lowered his voice. "Of course, I want you to keep investigating this guy. I'm just not going to lose our focus. And if Rohrbacher tries to throw a phony defense at us, we can handle it."

Maureen stood also and moved around the table to face Rogin. "But—"

"We're done talking about it," he ordered. "You just keep doing a great job for me and your career is golden. Got it?" He stared at Maureen. She held his eyes with her own for a few minutes. Rogin knew if he stared hard enough and showed unwavering resolve, most people blinked and turned away. Eventually, so did Maureen.

The next morning, Rogin and Maureen waited in the cavernous grand jury room. Two rows of chairs hugged the outer walls to surround an open space in the middle of the room. One table sat in that space, covered with files and many clear plastic bags filled with evidence. A metal cart stood next to the table, and it was filled with evidence also. Maureen had made certain that all the subpoenas had been served to the witnesses. They were scheduled in one hour blocks of time.

Earlier in the week, the county attorney himself had called for the grand jury to be seated in order to review the evidence against Daniel Jensen. They would decide if the charges should be raised from second degree murder to first degree.

By court order, a maximum of twenty-three people, but no fewer than sixteen, were selected using a variety of techniques: voter's lists, driver's licenses, property ownership rolls, and state-issued ID cards. An effort had been underway for over twenty years to make sure that people of color and different economic means were adequately represented on the jury. In Minnesota, only a grand jury could indict someone for first degree murder. Rogin would seek such an indictment.

Unlike trials seen on TV, the grand jury deliberated in secret. Only the jurors, a court reporter, and the presenting prosecutors were allowed into the room. Rogin would call all the witnesses and question them. Occasionally, the jurors could ask questions also.

The targeted defendant, Dan Jensen, and his lawyer were not allowed into the room.

For this hearing, Rogin had organized the case, brought in the physical and forensic evidence, and lined up all the witnesses that he needed to get the indictment. No expense had been spared to pay for the investigation, testing, forensic analysis, witnesses, law clerks, computer programs, and victim/witness advocates. All the power of the government was focused on this process.

The outcome was never in doubt.

The rules of evidence used in trial were relaxed for this hearing. It meant that Rogin and Maureen could present statements of witnesses who might be limited in their testimony in a trial because of hearsay objections, for instance. Unless a prosecutor was totally incompetent, the hearing would be easy.

At five minutes past nine, the first of the jurors started to filter into the room. Most looked like they were going shopping at the Mall of America. Two men wore suits, and one woman was Muslim and covered her head. Some drank the government coffee and munched on pastries. Several of them carried small notebooks and pens they'd been offered at the door when they entered.

Slowly, they settled into the seats around the edge of the room, and after some shifting, the noise quieted. They looked at Rogin and Maureen.

After a sip of chilled water—he never drank coffee—Sanford looked along the line of jurors. He smiled quickly and explained the purpose of the proceedings to them. He asked for questions and received none. Next, the members of the jury were sworn in as a group to do their duty.

Maureen nodded at the victim/witness advocate, Georgia, who left the room for a moment. In the silence, Rogin could hear the fans from the air conditioners whirring in the ceiling. Georgia returned with a small Asian woman. She wore an expensive skirt and under a matching peach colored jacket, a pressed blouse. Four inch heels boosted her to average height.

"The State of Minnesota calls Dr. Helen Wong," Rogin said and pitched his voice lower to sound authoritative.

Dr. Wong walked to the witness stand carefully, as if she wasn't completely confident on the tall heels. She turned to take her own oath from the court reporter, who sat off to the side. When finished, Dr. Wong sat in the witness chair. She had thin legs that she crossed, and she spent a moment tugging at the hem of her skirt to pull it toward her knees. Shiny black hair surrounded a pale face that accentuated her dark eyes. She turned to face Rogin.

He had her identify herself. "Where are you employed?"

"I am the chief medical examiner for Hennepin County, and I am a professor at the medical school at the University of Minnesota."

"You hold both positions?"

Dr. Wong smiled briefly. "Yes."

"Tell us your educational background that qualifies you to be the Chief Medical Examiner."

After she recited her lengthy resume, Rogin paused for a moment. He leaned over the desk and pulled a thick file toward himself. Opening it, he said, "I'll refer you to the evening of May tenth of this year. Do you recall an investigation you participated in at the home of Daniel and Mina Jensen?"

"Yes. It was unusually humid that night—"

Rogin questioned her directly from her written statement about the crime scene and her opinion that the victim must have died from the quantity of blood found at the scene.

Rogin and Maureen called several other witnesses throughout the day and showed sealed bags of evidence to the jurors. They introduced the forensic testing results. By five o'clock in the afternoon, they had finished, and the jury had deliberated and returned with an indictment against Daniel J. Jensen for murder in the first degree. Rogin was able to get home in time to play with MacKenzie.

Chapter Twenty-one

Ted and Laurie had decided to meet outside the house, away from Matt. Things could get heated. They met at Lucia's Restaurant in Uptown and sat on black metal chairs along the sidewalk on 31st street. A blue awning hung over them, but the morning sun slanted in from low in the east. Ted felt it warm his bare arms and face. At this time of the year the nights still cooled off quickly, reminding him of the harsh winter they'd just passed through.

He wanted to get the meeting with his partners, scheduled for later, over with and get back to the case. Ted looked across the small table at his wife. The sight of her still caused his breath to catch in his throat. He didn't tell Laurie about the text Matt had sent earlier, supporting Ted and wishing him good luck with the case. Matt had encouraged him to "beat the hell out of the government."

They both ordered an omelet with pesto and Parmesan cheese with a side of slim French fries. Dark coffee sat in two mugs between them. Steam rose to hide Laurie's face momentarily.

She reached across the small table to cover Ted's hand with her own. "With this new ruling, can you finally get out of the case now?" she asked him. Her hand felt slightly damp, and her eyes softened.

"Uh, there are still a few details to wrap up."

Laurie hesitated, then said, "What? Won't the judge's ruling end the case?"

"Only Rogin has the power to dismiss the case. And right now he doesn't want to do that," he said. "What did Matt say?"

"He said he's proud of you." Laurie sighed. "So now what?"

He explained the suspects and the hijack defense. He kept it short.

She looked directly at him. "I haven't allowed myself to think of the possibility that Danny is innocent. Do you think he is?"

Ted wanted to assure her that it was true. He was torn between the challenge of the case, his need to win it, and remaining with her. "I think he is."

He didn't tell her that the new mental illness defense wasn't airtight. The suspects remained only that—suspects. The prosecution was still plowing ahead with the case against Dan. He planned to explain that to her later. Nevertheless, he'd committed himself. There was no turning back. She must be able to sense his determination.

The sun shifted through the trees across Hennepin Avenue and flooded the small space around the table. When she lifted her face, the light made her look tanned and revealed small cracks spreading from the corners of her eyes. The heat on Ted's arms reminded him of a trip to the Florida Keys years ago.

He had urged her from the hot beach where they lay in lazy indolence into the small cottage twenty feet up from the water. It was a gray clapboard house with no air conditioning. The wind off the water cooled it even on the hottest days. There was one bedroom with faded Venetian blinds in the windows and a small sheltered deck that overlooked the Gulf. Two plastic beach chairs angled toward each other under the roof. One had cracked slats in the back. It was all as simple as that.

The lovemaking was intense, and every physical sensation was magnified by the heat and sound of the wind and the smell of salt and the isolation of the small house.

Later, they had walked two blocks to Florida's Best Fish House. They stepped up from the beach onto a bruised boardwalk. A painted wooden sailfish leapt over the door. Ted remembered it was colored red that had faded into pink so bleached out it made the fish look dirty. A broken surfboard leaned against the wall by the door.

They sat with their shoulders touching but without talking and cracked crab shells open to eat fast. They tore apart several pounds of claws until the aluminum bucket at the edge of the table overflowed with exhausted shells.

Now at Lucia's, Ted watched Laurie sitting in the black iron chair, trying to shield her eyes from the morning sun. Could they regain what they'd shared in Florida? Ted moved to give her shade. When she looked at him, her face went blank, but her eyes stared at him.

Although she sat within a few feet of him, there were parts of her that were breaking off to float miles away. The growing distance between them made the Florida memory even more painful until something stitched across Ted's chest. He'd have to be careful and walk the tightrope between winning the case and keeping the relationship together.

The waitress came out of the narrow door to the restaurant, set two plates in front of them, and returned with more coffee. Ted crunched fresh pepper over the eggs. He cut a bite out of the end, ate it, and sighed with pleasure.

Laurie ate silently.

When they'd both finished, Ted said in a soft voice, "This is nice." He meant the entire moment.

"No, it isn't." Her voice pitched lower. "You know how mad I am?"

"I've got an idea, but I can't talk much longer. I'm meeting Samantha, and then at noon, my partners have a meeting scheduled for me."

Laurie frowned. "What's that about?"

"Probably money, as usual." The chair scraped over the sidewalk as he pushed it back from the table. "I'll get rid of it as soon as I can and finish up the case." He smelled the stink of exhaust from an SUV that accelerated around the corner behind them.

"Here's what I still don't understand: in spite of the fact I'm about to kick you out of the house again, why the hell do you risk everything?" She stood and moved on the other side of him to put the sun at her back. "What is it that draws you back into the courtroom?"

He took a deep breath. "It's the challenge of a chess game."

Laurie nodded her head. "You're really good at it, Ted. But you've promised me that you'd get out of this case. You've lied to me repeatedly. I've given you some time to wrap this up. You're still wallowing in it. I don't understand your stubbornness or your dishonesty with me. I think you should move out of the house right now."

The change in her voice surprised him, but she was always brutally honest. She could intellectually understand what drove him but still hate what he was doing. Maybe he could still charm her.

He reached for her arms and pulled her closer. He wanted to hug her, but she pushed away. "You make the choice, Ted. You're really in this to prove something. You don't have to. I'd love you the way you are now. You could be a better person than you were back then."

"It's more complicated than that. I feel like my father's watching, and I've got to prove to him that I'm not a total failure."

Her expression hardened and she stepped back from him. Laurie turned and started toward Hennepin Avenue. From over her shoulder, she glanced at him but kept walking. The sun cast her back in a shadow, and the bottoms of her feet looked dark blue.

Ted hurried in the opposite direction to reach his Mercedes a block from the restaurant. He cornered it onto Hennepin Avenue and worked his way through the morning traffic around Loring Park. Dodging between cars through downtown, he finally made it to Northeast thirty minutes later. Ted rocked to a stop in front of Samantha's house.

When he stood at the front door, he could hear her shouting inside. "You better not be disrespecting me," Sam warned someone. "Don't talk back like that. Even if I'm not your mother, you can listen to me." Sam must have finally heard his knocking because in a short time, she came to the door.

"Hey, Teddy. Come on in," she said with a tired voice. She wore tight blue jeans and a tan blazer. Today her hair was her own, and it looked beautiful.

He didn't want to pry into her business, so he remained silent, watching her face contort as thoughts must have wrestled with each other in her head. She sighed. "That child. What she needs is a good whoopin', but she's too old." Her shoulders drooped and she lifted the gold chains from around her neck and let them slip between her fingers one at a time.

"You okay?"

"I'm always okay. This parenting gig never ends, you know?" She looked up at him.

Ted felt awkward because he hadn't done such a great job of parenting. But he nodded in agreement.

"Hey, I've been looking at the new reports you got from the prosecutor. Mina Jensen's phone data." Sam jerked her head toward the back of the house for him to follow. They wound around the dining room table that was piled with music charts and two empty coffee cups. She turned a corner into a small bedroom office. It had floor-to-ceiling bookshelves that were stuffed with hundreds of books. In the corner a desk groaned under the weight of more books, piles of paper, and a laptop.

Samantha put her hand on top of one stack of papers to steady it as she ran her fingers down the side until she found a yellow tab. She pulled on it and removed a file without disrupting the pile. "Have you looked at the forensic results from the data extracted from Mina Jensen's phone? Here it is." She handed him a copy.

"No. I haven't had the time." Ted flipped through it until he came to the end summary. He read it carefully. He looked up at Sam and said, "Doesn't make much sense."

"No, and that's what intrigues me."

"Huh?"

"Wouldn't you normally expect someone to be calling for their hair appointments, facials, maybe something about the dog, her friends, or her job? There's not much of that."

"Yeah." Ted read the material again. "So, these entries were deleted by Mina, but the expert was still able to retrieve them?"

"Right."

Ted whistled. "I'd better be more careful with my stuff."

"Shut up. This is serious."

"I still don't see what's so intriguing to you."

"Here's something for you." She carried two sheets of phone records out to the living room table. Pushing aside a stack of music, Samantha flattened the papers on the table. Her finger traced down the list of dozens of calls. "Here." Her finger stopped. "See, before this there are lots of calls and texts to Korsokov. Then, on May eighth, the calls stop. Dead. Not even a text from either one."

"Two days before the murder."

"Right. What the hell happened? It must be a fight. Why else would she suddenly stop communicating with him?"

"Danny found out and stopped her from contacting Korsokov?"

Sam shook her head. "It seems like he knew about it for a long time before May eighth."

Ted's stomach rumbled like he was hungry. He looked out the window and saw a weeping willow that hung over the corner of Sam's house. The tree needed trimming as the tips of the branches scratched against the window. "Let's talk to Korsokov again," he said.

"Yeah—" Sam turned and led him out to the living room again. She told him about meeting Deputy Seabloom at the retirement party and how Korsokov might have been in the prostitution business with Mina.

"Come on, Sam. That's so out there, I can't believe it."

She nodded. "Maybe so."

Ted felt the weight of her words churn through his mind. "We still need to talk with the Russian."

"Ukrainian," she corrected him. "We need to confront both Korsokov and Mr. Harrison. Both of them are lying."

He looked at his watch. "Let me know when you want to catch those two. I have a meeting with my law partners, and I don't want to be late."

"Those rusty old cash registers? What do you care?"

"They're my partners, and if I ignore them, they can make my life difficult."

Ted drove back to his office, parked, and walked across the tar lot. Warmth radiated up around his legs from the black surface. When he got up to the firm's lobby, the receptionist noticed him but didn't say a word. She twisted a strand of blond hair behind her ear. Ted said hello. She mumbled something and nodded toward the conference room. He opened the door and walked in.

Sun came through the window onto the white shirts of his partners to tint them pale green. All five of them sat in the cool shadows at the far corner of the room. When he entered, they shifted in their chairs. They had left the chair at the head of the conference table for Ted. He grabbed its back, spun it around, and sat in the soft seat. It smelled like new leather.

The partners had called the meeting, so Ted waited for them to talk. Two of the partners couldn't stand each other, so normally there were few partnership meetings. When they were forced to attend, everyone almost always argued about money. Each partner thought he should get a larger share of the profits because of the extra work they did for the firm. Of course, if everyone actually took a larger share, there wouldn't be any profits left to go around.

Ted heard the air conditioner hum and smelled the dry air coming from the vents. He felt the armrest that reminded him of velvet. In the middle of the table, a silver coffee pot sat surrounded by six china cups and saucers. There were never any pastries provided at these meetings. Someone was always on a diet.

Lowell Minot, the most senior partner by eleven years, cleared his throat. "Thanks for coming, Ted." Two others nodded in agreement.

"Sure," Ted said.

"We appreciate you taking time off to make this meeting," said Cameron, the newest partner. He had a master's degree in tax law and was a CPA.

Minot swiveled his chair to face Ted, although he was still angled to the side. "We're all happy with the work you've done here since you arrived. As the oldest member of this firm, I can tell you that you've brought in a tremendous amount of estate business. Your billings are always up to date, and you keep your personal costs low. Commendable." When he spoke, his teeth barely opened so that many of the words had a "shh" sound to them.

"Get to the point," Cameron urged Lowell.

Ted agreed. He steeled himself to defend the hours he had used up on Joe Kopp.

"Yes." Minot snaked his neck forward. "We understand that you are more than casually involved in this horrendous murder case. Is it true the murderer, er, accused murderer, has retained you?" His eyes climbed up over the half-frames perched on his nose. They found Ted and stared at him.

"That's true, but—"

"And has a hearing of any sort been scheduled? Will you represent him through a public trial?" Lowell continued. "Because no one has ever been in such a position in the history of this firm."

Ted felt warmth rising from his lower body. The meeting wasn't about money, after all. "He's an old friend of mine. It will go to trial, but I'm trying to get it dismissed as soon as—"

"And even worse," Minot said, "we just learned of an ethics complaint filed against you." There was a collective hush around the table.

"That was filed by the prosecutor. It's bullshit," Ted tried to explain.

"You know that the practice of law has changed over the years. When clients are shopping for a law firm, they research each one of us. The law schools we attended, our awards, our activities, the type of cases we handle, and if any ethical complaints have been filed." Minot had turned and was facing Ted directly. The volume of his voice increased as he warmed up, and it sounded like the rush of storm waves on a beach.

"Of course, but Dan Jensen is a client like any other client that a lawyer would represent."

"That may be what you think, but a messy, highly publicized *criminal* case reflects badly on all the rest of us," Cameron added. "How will the ethics complaint be handled?"

"I'm getting rid of it as soon as I can."

"Very well, but you don't seem to grasp the gravity of our concern about this," Minot said.

Ted sighed. "Give me some time on this. I'll take care of everything."

"Our accountants have warned us that billings could drop quickly. You know that we recently leased new cars for each one of us. You wouldn't want to lose your Mercedes, would you?"

Ted shook his head and stood up. He walked around to the back of the chair. "Nothing's going to happen." His voice rose. "Don't worry. I can't believe you're doing this after all the money I've brought into this firm."

Without looking at Ted, Cameron added, "Some of us warned you about getting into the dirty practice of criminal law. And you insist on pursuing it. It's the last thing we will tolerate, and yet you took on this case with all the publicity. It's hurting our billings already, which means my share of the profits is in jeopardy. I'm not happy." He shook his index finger at Ted.

Lowell stood up and pushed back his chair. He looked down the table at Ted. "I think I've made our concerns very clear. We've been recording this, and I will simply warn you—if you continue to pursue this case with all the bad publicity it will bring to the firm, you are going to be removed from the partnership."

Ted shouted, "You can't do that. The bylaws won't let you."

"Our outside counsel has already reviewed the docs. We can do it, I assure you. You will be given a sizable severance package, of course, but you're out. And I'm sure you're also aware that, under the bylaws, the firm will retain all your clients because you've signed the no-compete clause."

The partners had obviously practiced this entire show because as soon as Minot's words faded, they all stood and filed out of the conference room, leaving Ted standing alone.

Chapter Twenty-two

Sanford Rogin had filed the Notice by Prosecutor of Omnibus Issues with the court and had given a copy to Ted. In the Notice, Rogin quoted from the rule, which read:

Rule 7.01 Notice of Omnibus Issues

a. In any case where a right to a jury trial exists, the prosecutor must notify the defendant or defense counsel of:

(1) Any evidence against the defendant obtained as a result of a search, search and seizure, wiretapping, or any form of electronic or mechanical eavesdropping.

(2) Any confessions, admissions, or statements in the nature of confessions made by the defendant.

Under the Minnesota Supreme Court case of *State ex rel. Rasmussen vs. Tahash*, Ted had responded by demanding a "Rasmussen" hearing. The judge would decide what evidence would be admitted in the trial and presented to the jury.

Specifically, when Dan Jensen was first arrested he'd been questioned by police and had admitted that he'd fought with his wife just prior to her disappearance. It made Dan look quite culpable and gave him a motive for her death. However, when Ted interviewed Dan, he said that he'd asked the police for time to talk with a lawyer. The police had promised to do that but continued questioning Dan without a lawyer.

Dan had asked Ted earlier, "I saw this on TV. Cops didn't read the *Miranda* rights so the case was tossed out."

"What it really means is your 'confession' may be thrown out, not necessarily the entire case. The prosecutor will be prevented from using any of your words in the trial with a jury. That's what I'll try to accomplish."

"But I didn't *confess* 'cause I didn't kill Mina."

"Sorry. I meant your statement," Ted had told him.

Two days after the partners meeting, Ted had would appear before Judge Edith Vang to argue his motion to suppress Dan's statements. He needed badly to win this fight.

Once again, Joe Kopp prepared an excellent brief, although it wasn't brief. It started by listing the facts about the interrogation of Dan Jensen by the police. The second part contained a long legal argument for preventing the prosecutor from using the statement. Kopp had listed dozens of previous Supreme Court decisions that supported their position. The brief ended with a formal request to follow the Rules of Criminal Procedure and case law.

Of course, Sanford Rogin had filed his own responsive brief, largely written by Maureen Hanrahan.

Ted had ordered Jensen to show up early. Joe Kopp came with Ted.

Ted wanted to blast Rogin for not warning him about the Grand Jury indictment. Normally, prosecutors, as a courtesy, would let the defense lawyer know ahead of time. The lawyer could prepare his client for the shock. Rogin didn't do that until after the indictment.

When Ted, Dan, and Joe reached the courthouse, the press clung to them like a hungry dog with a bone. They fired questions at Jensen, hoping to get another violent reaction that would be strong enough to carry the lead story on the evening news. This time, Dan remained calm and pushed his way carefully through the crowd.

Joe Kopp followed Ted and Dan Jensen through the doors into the courtroom. They approached a swinging section of the low railing that separated the jury box, counsel tables, and the bench from the public area. Ted led the way through it and into the "inner sanctum" of the courtroom where he'd do battle with Sanford Rogin.

Ted dropped his expensive briefcase on the defense table. The luxury of it and the weight gave him confidence. Behind him Joe rolled in a box-like briefcase containing all the legal material that may be required to win. They weren't sure exactly what questions Judge Vang may ask, so they came prepared for anything.

The air was dry. Noise swirled around the back of the courtroom, leaving the middle silent. Ted ignored most of the sounds and concentrated on the argument he would make. He could feel moisture under his arms. This was still an uncomfortable place for him.

He looked over at the prosecutor's table and saw Rogin had arrived. Maureen moved around the table, plugging in laptops and assembling paper files across the table. Rogin grunted something to Maureen, and left to walk over to the clerk who worked on a stack of files beside the judge's bench. High above, the ceiling rose in sections like the steps of a pyramid and glowed with intense white light.

Mo walked over to Ted.

"What do you want?" He could smell her perfume.

Maureen pointed at the legal pad and pen that Ted held in his hand. "Kind of high tech, aren't you?" She tried to smile.

He looked into her eyes. "That was a shitty thing to do to me."

"I certainly understand. Can I at least tell you that I've disagreed with Rogin on many things about this case? But I was forced to do it. Rogin would have fired me." She glanced toward the clerk's desk.

Ted shrugged.

Rogin was coming back toward them and she left. Part of Ted wanted to believe her, but he was so angry with both of them, that he didn't trust anyone. Ted intercepted Rogin in the middle of the room. "Why the hell didn't you tell me?"

"What?" Rogin acted surprised, but a creeping grin gave him away.

"The indictment. You know how hard it was to explain it to my client? Or how about the ethics complaint? You are really a piece of shit, you know it?"

"You're an experienced lawyer. You knew this was a possibility —in fact, a probability. I've got a responsibility to the citizens."

"What sentence are you asking for in the first degree murder charge?"

"Life—without parole. You go tell that to Jensen. Maybe he'll suddenly 'remember' where the body is and admit what he did."

Ted felt like slugging him right on the spot but turned away to walk back to the counsel table.

Joe had laid out research material for Ted to use in case he needed them. Ted opened the Minnesota Criminal Law Handbook. It was two inches thick. He paged through to the Rules of Criminal Procedure section.

He told the judge's clerk they were ready and sat down.

In his mind, Ted reviewed what he knew about the judge's history.

Judge Edith Vang had been born in St. Paul to parents who had fled from Laos after the Vietnam War. They had worked for the U.S. military and, as a consequence, were targeted by the new government that wanted to punish them for aiding the U.S. Her parents had been able to learn some English but preferred to maintain the Hmong language, which had only been written down for the people about forty years earlier. The community in St. Paul was populated with enough Hmong that the parents could survive on their old language with just a smattering of English.

The Hmong community was divided into several clans. Edith's clan was a more progressive one and adapted quickly to the American culture. As a result, Edith was encouraged by her clan to pursue education and, eventually, law school.

She was an attractive woman with large black eyes and straight black hair. A little taller than most Hmong, she was still short by American standards. She always dressed formally in American designer clothing. Usually a dark suit.

Because she had worked so hard herself, the judge expected the lawyers practicing before her to work equally hard. Jackie had warned Ted that meant to be on time and to be prepared.

Jackie had also advised, "She's very formal. Wear a tie, always stand when addressing the court, and don't leave anything on the counsel table except a cup of water—if her clerk has remembered to set out Styrofoam cups and a pitcher. And never, never bring in a cup of coffee. She'll hit the ceiling."

"Okay. Got it," Ted had agreed.

"She likes to rule for the underdog, so you may even have a chance. I've seen her bend the law to help someone who's fallen on tough times. Have your client there with you and tell him not to act arrogant or disrespectful under any circumstances."

"Yes, boss."

"And Ted," Jackie looked closely at Ted. "You can't bullshit her with your charm. It's meaningless to her and may even offend her. Keep it formal and stick to the law you have on your side. Somehow, you've got to let her know that your client is also a victim. Get her to see him as a human, not just another defendant in a line of hundreds of cases that she will—"

"Okay, I got it."

"—handle throughout the year. And don't ever interrupt her." Jackie sighed, "Good luck."

Ted's thoughts were interrupted when Judge Vang entered the courtroom. She took a few skipping steps up to the large bench and sat in a tall leather chair behind it. She almost disappeared behind the expanse of granite and oak that stretched before her. Two flagpoles stood behind her. One had the U.S. flag and the other the Minnesota state flag. Otherwise, no ornamentation broke up the stretch of tan wall that reached to the corners of the courtroom.

The judge leaned forward to pull a microphone closer. When she said good morning, her voice was amplified too much and she sounded like Darth Vader. The clerk adjusted the volume and the judge continued. "I believe this motion is yours, Mr. Rohrbacher. Are you prepared to present it today?"

Ted stood and thought she had emphasized the word *prepared* as a warning to him this time. He said, "Yes I am, Your Honor."

"Proceed." She leaned forward in her chair and folded her arms in front of her.

"As Your Honor is aware, the Rules of Criminal Procedure and the *Rasmussen* case give us the opportunity to challenge the way in which my client's statement was taken by the police." He paused to try and read the judge's reactions. Ted couldn't see any change in her expression. He continued, "We are moving the court to suppress Mr. Jensen's statement in its entirety."

"What evidence do you propose to show me?"

"We will call Mr. Dan Jensen to testify for the limited purpose of how he was interrogated."

"Proceed."

Ted nodded at Dan who stood up and walked forward. He reached the raised bench and looked up at the judge. To Dan's right, the clerk cleared her throat and read the oath to Dan who agreed to tell the truth. He walked around the clerk to take two steps up into the witness box next to the judge, who still sat higher. He looked good. A tailored tan suit and white shirt contrasted with a new tan from the weekend. He smiled slightly.

Ted started by asking him to identify himself for the record. Once finished with the preliminary questions, Ted got right to the point. "Do you remember being at home when the police arrived?"

"Yes."

"How would you describe the state you were in?"

"Totally messed up. I had passed out, woken up, and found the bedroom covered with blood and my wife gone. I was shocked to say the least."

"You called 911?"

Dan nodded. "Yes."

"And the police arrived?"

"Yeah. Quick. I was in a daze even when they got there."

"What happened?"

"Well, they asked me what happened. I told them all that I knew, which wasn't much."

"Anyone else arrive at your home?"

Dan's eyebrows popped up and he said, "You bet. Dozens of people. Must've been the entire Minnetonka police department. I can't remember much about who was who." He sounded confident and intelligent.

"Did the police continue to question you?"

"Right. I was still pretty out of it. And the house got so crowded with other cops that the first ones took me out to the squad car. I'll tell you that was embarrassing to have my neighbors see me getting into a police car."

"Did they get into the car with you?"

"They both did. I think it was a guy named O'Brien. Small guy, older. Smoked all the time so I could hardly breathe in the car. I think he did it purposely."

"Why do you say that?"

"Objection," Rogin shouted. "Irrelevant."

"I'll let the witness answer," the judge responded. "We don't have a jury here." She turned back to Dan and rotated her hand for him to continue.

"I think he kept smoking to make it uncomfortable for me, to get me to confess quicker."

Ted pretended to look through his notes to allow the statement to sink into the judge's mind. Then he asked, "Could you leave the car?"

"No. There aren't any handles on the inside of the back seat. One of 'em sat next to me, and the guy I think was O'Brien sat in the front seat, turned around toward me."

"Did they read you your *Miranda* rights?"

"I think so. I was still in shock so I couldn't understand much of what was going on."

"Did you understand your rights?"

"More or less. I mean, I'm not a lawyer."

"Did you realize that you could have a lawyer before you said one word?"

"Of course, but they kept telling me they were just trying to figure out what happened and find my wife. That the interview was a 'preliminary' one."

"Did you ask to have a lawyer?"

"Right. I felt kinda funny talking to them, 'cause it sure seemed to me they suspected I was the killer. So I told them I thought I should talk to my lawyer first."

"What did they say?"

"They promised me they'd let me contact a lawyer after they'd finished with some 'routine' questions, they called them."

Ted looked over at Rogin and Hanrahan. Rogin scowled. Ted asked Dan, "So, you told them about the fight you and Mina had earlier in the day?"

"Yes."

"Did they ever let you call a lawyer?"

"A few hours later. After they'd talked to me for a long time."

Ted told the judge he was finished questioning Mr. Jensen.

Rogin started by asking Dan, "You have a college degree, right?"

"Yes."

"You started and run your own successful business?"

"Right."

"Do you hire lawyers sometimes in your business?"

"Of course."

"So, you know the importance of legal counsel when you need it?"

"Sure."

"In spite of that knowledge, you went ahead without a lawyer and voluntarily talked with Detective O'Brien. Is that what you want us to believe?" Rogin's voice rose to mock Jensen, who didn't respond.

When Rogin announced that he didn't have any more questions, Dan left the box and returned to sit next to Ted.

Rogin stood and told the judge he had some evidence for the hearing. "We have the so-called *Scales* tape required by the Supreme Court when police question anyone. I'd like to play it for the court. I'll call Detective Sean O'Brien to lay the foundation for admission of the tape."

The judge agreed and Maureen left the courtroom. She returned with Detective O'Brien following her. He walked up to the witness box and sat down.

Rogin began questioning him. "You are aware that the Minnesota Supreme Court requires that all law enforcement, when questioning a suspect, record the interview and make it available for defense counsel and the court?"

O'Brien squinted and said, "Yes, Sir."

"Did you make such a recording when you interviewed the defendant?"

"We did."

"Do you have it with you?" Rogin started forward to the witness box. He was bent slightly forward, as if he were charging at the box.

"Yes, Sir. Picked it up from the property room right before I came to this courtroom." O'Brien handed the CD to Rogin. Rogin made sure the CD was authenticated and asked permission of the judge to play the tape. With large hands, he fitted it into the player.

The CD hissed for a short time and there were shuffling sounds until the voice of Detective O'Brien came on to identify the people at the interview, that they were in a squad car, and that the *Miranda* warnings had been given to Mr. Jensen. O'Brien asked, "Do you understand all of this?"

Jensen's voice was weak. "Yeah, guess so."

The rest of the CD played for a long time, but in the end Dan Jensen confessed that he'd had a big fight with his wife.

Although Ted had listened to the CD several times and knew what was coming, the damage those words did to the case still worried him. He forced himself to keep a straight face. There was nothing on the CD about Dan asking for a lawyer. He never made that request, contrary to his testimony.

After the CD had finished, Rogin excused Detective O'Brien and stood behind the prosecutor's table. In a ringing voice full of confidence, he told the judge, "The Government rests its case." With both hands, he smoothed his thick hair and sat down. Maureen leaned close to him, probably to congratulate Rogin.

Judge Vang raised her eyebrows and turned to Ted. "Anything more, Counselor?"

"We'll recall Mr. Jensen."

Dan took the witness stand again.

"Do you remember the police recording your interview?" Ted started.

"Yeah. They had trouble getting the machine to work. Detective O'Brien swore about the budget cuts in the police department."

"You still maintain that you asked to stop the interview to talk with a lawyer?"

"Yes."

Ted paused. "Then why didn't we hear you ask for that on the CD?"

Judge Vang leaned forward from the bench.

Jensen said, "Because they started the recording only *after* I'd asked for a lawyer several times. By then, I figured it was too late."

Both lawyers made closing arguments to the court. Forty minutes later, Judge Vang ruled that the defendant's incriminating statement would be suppressed and not allowed to be used in a trial. She also noted the case was already set for trial in one week—a date that would not be delayed.

Chapter Twenty-three

Deputy Kenny Seabloom cut a sharp turn with the sheriff's boat. He was on Lake Minnetonka again. The media coverage had thinned over the past few weeks. Only one boat followed them today. Seabloom shouted to Deputy Jane Johnson above the roar of the wind. "I can't wait to see how the ROV works. This should make a big difference. And finally, those dinks at the top have given me the responsibility to use it."

She nodded and scrunched her head down between her shoulders and faced the stern of the boat. Spray from the outside edge of the boat arced over the bow and showered her back. Another deputy, Clyde Webster, sat in the stern, shivering. He had his baseball cap with the sheriff department's logo turned backward on his head. He was an older man who had received special training on the new equipment—a remote operated vehicle, or ROV.

Unlike during the previous searches for Mina Jensen's body, this time Seabloom would be able to search in the deeper parts of the lake. On previous missions, they had been confined to areas closer to shore for two reasons. Their theory was the killer would probably have dumped the body close to shore because it was quicker. Also, the ability of the divers to go deep for long periods was limited. With the new ROV, Kenny could venture farther out in the lake and go down to depths of 1,000 feet.

Seabloom pounded over the wake of a crossing cruiser that looked to be the size of a small house. A young man in the back of the boat flipped an empty beer can into the water while he drew on a cigarette. For a moment, Kenny considered giving chase to ticket the offender. He hated the partying that went on across the lake, especially by young people driving their parents' big yachts. But the mission to find the body took precedence over tagging violators right now. The sheriff's boat stopped bucking up and down as they drove farther across the wake and out into the calm of the lake. Seabloom

checked his GPS and throttled back until the boat settled in a slosh-
ing motion from side to side.

He looked around to see if there were any boats that might interfere with the search. Two hundred yards away, a red Lund fishing
boat bobbed in the waves. Two men, one at each end of the boat,
sat with rods angled over the water. The lake contained many species
of fish, and in spite of all the boat traffic, it was productive.

He cut the engine and threw out the claw anchor. It splashed
into the water, and the chain rattled over the bow as it descended
into the depths.

Johnson said, "I've never seen an ROV before. It's smaller than
I thought."

"Pretty remarkable gadget," Seabloom said. He nodded at Webster, who stood up to prepare the remote operated vehicle. It was
about the size of a remotely controlled toy car and carried an underwater camera. On the top was a yellow air tank to control buoyancy.
Two lights hung underneath on either side of a large camera lens.
They all were attached to the top of a small motor, which read "Blue-
View" in bright letters on the front of the machine. A claw with two
pincers extended in front of the motor. On the back side, a black
propeller with three blades would provide the thrust for the vehicle.
Below that was a steel hook. Webster prepared the ROV by attaching
a 500-foot rope to the hook. He tested the remote control device in
his hand by triggering several switches. Everything worked.

"We just got this a few months ago. Wish I could've used it
earlier," Seabloom said. "But it takes 400 hours of training to be
qualified to run the vehicle. Web's our oldest deputy and was a diver
for years. He scored the highest in training, so they didn't kick him
into retirement." In response, Webster bobbed his head once at them.

Johnson adjusted her sheriff's baseball cap on her head and tugged
on her ponytail to make it fit tighter. "They must be expensive."

Webster chuckled. "Probably why we didn't get a raise last year.
This vehicle alone cost $151,000."

"Wow. Do you think it's worth it?"

"No question. Not only will it save us time, but it reduces the
risk to our divers. Remember, we're limited to the air in our tanks.

As we go deeper, it gets even harder. Sometimes we get snagged down there, which also adds to the risk and the lost time."

"I get it. The ROV can operate for a longer time."

"It moves about one and a half miles an hour, and you're right—it doesn't get tired."

Kenny stepped aside to give the other deputy room to deploy the vehicle. Webster made sure it was tethered to the stern of the boat, set it into the water, and turned it on. The vehicle hummed as it disappeared from the surface and pulled the tether rope behind itself. After a short time, all that remained were a few bubbles on the surface. He sat back and adjusted the controls on the monitor mounted on a seat in the boat. He waited for a few minutes for the vehicle to reach the bottom and then he switched on the lights and camera. Webster worked with the joystick like he was playing a video game.

"They say us old guys don't have the skills to run these things. Bullshit. I love this, and I'm better than the kids who trained with me." He grinned as he jiggled the stick back and forth to test response effects. At first, the image on the monitor looked murky and filled with bubbles.

"We're going a lot deeper this time," Seabloom told Jane. "Our first theory was the body close to shore because most killers are anxious to get rid of the body as quickly as they can. Since we haven't found anything yet, we decided that maybe the killer had a boat. To really dispose of a body, it's better to leave it in deep water." He nodded toward the stern of the sheriff's boat. "And until we had the ROV that would be the best way to prevent us from finding a body. This vehicle gives us an advantage we didn't have before."

"Sure," she said.

They crowded around Webster, who twisted a dial on the monitor. "Here we go," he said at last.

The image on the screen looked gray and slightly blurred, but they could make out the soft mounds at the bottom of the lake. Several objects came into view as the ROV cruised over them: a rusted beer can, a lawn chair, a metal cooler with a hole punched in the side, and a stick that had a long string waving from the end of it in slow motion that looked like white hair.

"Fishing rod," Webster explained.

They continued to watch. The bottom curved down into a shallow bowl. The ROV threaded between tall stands of waving plants. Bass and small northern pike darted in quick flashes from the exposure of the light to disappear behind the leaves. At this depth, unlike the commotion on the surface, it looked calm and peaceful.

"We got lots of invasive species in the lake now, unfortunately," Webster said.

"Gotten worse in the past few years," added Kenny. "Eurasian watermilfoil, flowering rush, and purple loosestrife. Most of it comes in on boats when they're launched. There are regs about cleaning off the boats, but lots of people don't pay attention."

"I thought our department enforced those regs," Johnson said.

"Sure. But we don't have enough manpower to populate every boat launch every day of the week. You should see this place on summer weekends. It's crazy busy. Besides that, we respond to drunk boat drivers, noisy parties, and of course, drownings. Last year alone, there were six near-drownings here and two fatalities. We don't have time to stop milfoil."

"Hey, guys. Look at this." Webster turned a dial to zoom in on a pile of crusty gray objects that slid underneath the ROV. "Zebra mussels. Hate those suckers. They're the worst thing to happen to the lake." He pounded his hand on the gunwale for emphasis.

"Lakes," Seabloom corrected him. "They're invading dozens of lakes all over Minnesota."

"How about those Asian carp that can jump into boats and knock over people?" Jane asked. "That's the grossest thing I can think of. Imagine a slimy carp knocking you down."

"Hate those, too. Nothing good ever came out of Asia except cheap transistor radios when I was a kid. All these are environmental problems that will cripple the economy of this state soon." Webster's face twisted like the dials on his monitor. "Nobody seems to get it."

"Question is: are *you* getting anything there?" Kenny changed the subject.

"Uh . . . nothing yet. Lots of junk. You'd be amazed at what things I find down here. Weirdest thing I ever saw was an entire car. Someone probably drove it onto the ice when it was too thin and fell through. Probably too embarrassed to ask for help getting it out. Nice vehicle, too. Brand new Lexus SUV."

"Reminds me of when I was a kid—"

"Jane, we've got work to do." Seabloom turned back to Webster. "Keep watching."

"Of course, now that people know we have the ROV," Webster continued, "we get calls all the time from people who've lost things. Lady called about her bracelet over the side of their yacht. Can we help them find it? 'Priceless,' they tell me. Bullshit."

After the ROV had covered the area around the boat, Seabloom raised anchor and they moved off by several hundred yards. Webster dropped the vehicle into the water again and began another search pattern. The monitor flickered and the image faded out for a moment. Webster swore and reached into his pocket. He pulled out a penknife, and two aspirin dropped onto the deck of the boat. He picked up the aspirin and said, "Ah, I'm gettin' old. I remember when I was in college and I carried two condoms with me. Now I carry two aspirin for possible heart attacks." After he put the tabs back into his pocket, he used the knife to twist a control on the back side of the monitor. The image came back into sharp focus.

Kenny looked up at the shoreline. He could see bright green leaves at the edges of the trees. They looked happy, as if they anticipated the warmth of summer. But he could also feel a bite in the early morning wind. Even the color of the water had changed from gray to a deep blue. It reminded him of the ocean. Deep and cold and impersonal.

They moved three more times, each time working their way parallel to the shore but remaining far out into the lake. Webster lit up a cigar and gripped it between his teeth. When he'd smoked it down to a stub, he tossed it over the stern into the water.

"Thought you were an environmentalist?" Seabloom said.

"It's biodegradable."

"So what?"

"Forget it."

Seabloom raised his eyebrows toward Johnson and dropped his complaint. He needed Web's help more than he needed to be correct about trashing the lake.

Jane asked him, "We going in soon?"

"Not unless we find something. Why?"

She looked at Webster in the stern and back toward Kenny. She lowered her voice. "I've gotta pee."

Seabloom laughed. "Being a deputy sheriff is rigorous. You'll have to tough it out."

She scowled at him. "Easy for you to say. Just hang your dog over the side."

"I'm kidding." He looked at his watch. "Yeah, we'll go inshore in a few minutes. I lose track of time with the ROV. It never has to piss or come up for air and a rest."

In five minutes, they were about to pull up and head for shore. Webster shouted, "Got something." He leaned forward and peered at the screen. He adjusted the dials. "Definitely. Look at this." His voice pitched higher and he talked faster.

They crowded around the monitor.

Webster rotated the joystick to bring the ROV back over the same section of lake bottom. At first, all they could see was a gray lump that resembled a long stretch of mud. As the ROV got closer, the lump changed into something that looked vaguely human. The tip-off was on the far side, where they saw an arm raised out of the mound with a hand attached to the end. Three of the fingers were missing, and it looked as if the body had tried to signal to someone in the last minutes of life—*here I am*. The skin glowed waxy yellow in the light of the ROV.

"That's a human body," Webster announced. "I'll come back over and get the readings for you Sea." He curved the joystick in a circle as the vehicle swerved around and came back over the body. "Got it?" Webster looked up at Kenny, who nodded that he'd marked the GPS coordinates. "Great. Let's get the dive boys down there right away."

"Can you tell if it's a female?" Jane asked.

"No. It's been down there for a long time. Almost totally hidden. I don't know that a diver could've picked it out unless he had his headlamp on full power." Webster coughed a smoker's hack. "Damn lucky we got the ROV."

Seabloom called to the backup boat at the marina in the bay around the closest point of land. Within twenty minutes, the second boat came roaring up to them with two suited divers in the stern. They pulled alongside of Kenny's boat, and they rocked together as the wake from the second boat dissipated outward.

One of the divers called over, "Got something?"

"Definitely a body."

"Stay above us. We're going in," the diver said. He and his partner strapped tanks on their backs, adjusted their masks, and fell backward over the gunwale. In ten minutes, they were up and bobbing in the water next to the boat.

"We need the bag," the diver shouted. "Body's too far gone."

Seabloom and Johnson removed the yellow and black body bag from a locker on the port side of the sheriff's boat. They unrolled it and made sure the lines of rope attached to the ends weren't tangled. Starting with the top end, they lowered it into the lake next to the divers, who each grabbed a side and slid beneath the surface, pulling it behind them. Kenny watched the yellow color turn green as it descended into the depths.

The divers remained submerged for a long time. A half hour later, Seabloom felt a tug on the line—a signal to pull up the bag. He and Jane each took hold of a line and struggled to pull the heavy load to the surface. The web design of the bag allowed a lot of water to flow out to make it lighter, but it was still heavy with a waterlogged human body.

When it broke the surface, Seabloom could see the muddy contours of a human body. They both grasped the handles along the sides of the bag and heaved it over the gunwale onto the boat. Water slopped across the deck. The bag felt cold from the deep water.

The divers popped up next to the boat. One removed his mask and said, "We put as many parts as we could find into the bag. It's been down there a while."

Seabloom dipped a plastic bucket over the side, filled it with lake water, and sloshed it over the bag to remove some of the mud and debris from the bottom. He zipped open the front of the bag and saw what appeared to be the chest of a human. It was covered with some kind of a shirt that suddenly moved in irregular bumps under the cloth. Several small white crabs scuttled out to zig-zag over the slippery deck. Johnson screamed and jumped backward. Kenny was startled also, and he used the edge of the bucket to scoop up the crabs and toss them overboard. One ran toward Webster, who raised his boot and stomped on it before throwing it over.

As the body in the bag warmed up, Seabloom could smell a brackish, rotten odor. It would only get worse if they didn't get it sealed and into the lab. He and Jane removed a solid plastic bag from the storage locker on the starboard side.

Webster lit another cigar and sat far back in the stern, watching the other two. "Sure feel sorry for those doctors who'll have to do the autopsy on this one. Bet they'll draw straws to see who gets stuck with it." He laughed and took a long pull from his cigar. "Helps cover the smell," he added.

Taking a deep breath, Seabloom peeled back the top of the bag. Sections of the skin were gone, exposing bone which was covered with green fuzz that looked like velvet. The face was missing, and he saw various marine creatures hurry back into the crevices where the eyes and nose had been as they hid from the sunlight. Johnson had moved to the bow. Kenny told her to come over and help. Together they lifted the handles on the web bag and set everything into the second body bag that could be sealed.

"Any ideas, Sea?" Jane asked.

Even though he'd observed many dead bodies over the years, this one was in the later stages of decomposition. Kenny fought the urge to throw up. ID would probably have to be dental—if even that could be accomplished. Before he zipped up the new bag, his eyes searched over what was left of the head of the victim. Would he find any clues there?

The lower half of the jaw was gone which gave the impression of a person with a terrible overbite. He turned and made a joke about it to Jane. When working with such awful aspects of death, gallows humor helped everyone to cope.

Webster had spent some time with the ROV reconnoitering the site after the divers had come up to the boat. Now he drove the vehicle to the surface and retrieved it with the rope. He watched Seabloom study the body and Webster dared him. "Go ahead. Touch it." He laughed and pulled the ROV out of the water.

A wave hit the boat on the side. It rocked back and forth so that the body rolled with the movement. That's when Kenny saw it.

The back of the skull was missing. He saw a hole with jagged edges about the size of a softball where the skull had once been. Although he wasn't a medical expert, he'd seen plenty of trauma on bodies to know that something had hit the bone hard enough to punch a hole through it. Seabloom talked fast in his excitement. "I can't tell if the body is male or female, but it's clearly been hit in the back of the head. The body is the correct size. I think we're looking at Mina Jensen." Sadness overwhelmed him, and he sat on the thwart of the boat. At the same time, he felt proud and was anxious to get her back to the ME for a confirmed identification. Maybe now the top brass would finally trust him to handle the tough cases.

He finished zipping up the bag carefully, secured it along the side of the boat, and started the engine. When he pushed the throttle forward, the stern dug down into the water as it gained speed. Kenny spun the wheel and headed for shore. Jane called in the information and requested transport for the body to the Hennepin County medical examiner's lab in Minneapolis.

Seabloom looked from Jane to Webster. "Thank God. We finally found her."

Chapter Twenty-four

Ted and Sam hurried north on Highway 65 to reach the auto parts store and catch Demontre Harrison. Samantha leaned toward him and rested her hand on his arm. She said, "Nice work in that courtroom, Counselor. Looks like you're getting your mojo back again."

"Hey, thanks. It's not as bad as I remembered it."

"Also, I heard on the news that the sheriffs found a body in Lake Minnetonka yesterday." Sam told Ted the details, including the speculation among everyone that it was Mina Jensen.

Ted sighed and looked at the road ahead for a long time but didn't say anything. He called Dan immediately, although Dan had heard about it on the news as well.

"Sure hope it's her," Dan mumbled and hung up.

They reached the Ace Auto Parts yard just as it was closing. Sun came over the fence on the west end of the yard, casting the carcasses of all the autos into deep shadows. With the engines removed from most of the cars and the hoods propped open, it looked more like a graveyard now. They paid for the ticket and hurried through the dusk to catch Harrison before he left.

"How do you think you'll get him to talk?" Ted asked Sam.

"I got my own mojo working now."

"The prints?"

"That's the start. Watch me." She led the way as the gray dust colored her feet and hid the red and gold sandals she wore.

They saw Harrison walking slowly toward the parts barn and recognized his pith helmet. They changed the angle of their charge to cut him off before he reached the sanctuary of the building and could disappear out the back. He looked up at the last minute, saw them, and stopped.

"What the hell?"

"Hey, Tre. We gotta talk, man," Sam called to him.

"Nothing to say," he shouted back.

"We got your prints. Inside the house. You lied. Can't believe you'd do that to sweet Samantha." She came up beside him and purposely crowded him. He backed up and looked down at her and then over at Ted. She explained the identification of his prints in the kitchen.

"I still got nothing to say to no one." Harrison crossed his arms over his chest.

"You got nothing to say? Then I'm the Hootchie-cootchie man myself. How about we start with that problem from Gary?"

Harrison's eyes opened wide and showed gold around the edges. He tilted his head but didn't give away any sign of understanding.

"The murder rap. Pled it down to manslaughter. And then the drug dealing charge on top of that. That one doesn't even seem too serious. So you did some time and skipped that hellhole of a prison to move to the land of ten thousand lakes. That ring any bells with you?"

Harrison lifted his head and turned his face to the setting sun. He sniffed the air. He looked down at Samantha. "Okay. Tha's right. But what the fuck? At this point in time, I'm past that shit. Tha's over. For now, I'm moving forward. Can't do nothing about the past, but I can make myself into a new man now. Right here. Too many people grinding me about that old shit."

"Fair enough. All I want to know is what the hell were you doing in the Jensen house?"

"Didn't kill no one."

"Never said you did." Samantha waited without saying anything more.

Finally, Harrison said, "Okay, I was in there. Once. I tol' you—I didn't like that dude on account of what he did to my brother. Through some friends in the military, I had access to the records of the mission my brother was on. Jensen was commanding. He had a responsibility for security and the preparation. He failed at both. I'm a former SEAL and that kind of shit is totally unacceptable. I'd just a' soon seen him dead, but I didn't kill no one."

"I got that. And I know why you lied to us before. Now, let's go this way: why were you in the house?" Sam asked again.

Harrison squinted his eyes, and Ted could tell he was wrestling with a response. Ted had learned from Sam that the best interrogation technique was silence.

Finally, Harrison cleared his throat and spat into the dirt. "Sheeit. Like I told you before—I hated that cracker. He shoulda been the one killed."

"I get your anger." Samantha sounded more like a social worker than an investigator. "But why did you have to go into the house? Were you looking for something?"

"Checkin' it out."

"Oh?"

"I found the crib and saw the dude's wife down by the lake. So I went into the house. Those white people out there don't think that crime happens in their 'hood."

Ted interrupted. "How do you know that?"

A wide white smile opened in Harrison's face. "Hey, man, I got contacts with the young gangsters—not that I'm a gangster. Too old. But those gangbangers target houses out there if they see a flag in the front yard."

"A flag?"

"Yeah. An American flag. Ever see one?"

"No, I never have. Describe one." Ted's voice took on an edge. He didn't like Harrison and didn't believe much of what he said.

Sam asked, "Why target a house with an American flag?"

Harrison chuckled. "'Cause those people almost always have guns. And that's what the gangbangers want to score. See, some of the homies get together and put a girl out front. She goes up to the door and knocks. If someone's home, she plays it off to asking for money for charity. 'Course, if no one's in the crib, they do the house to get the guns."

"Okay, but you went into the Jensen house?" Sam continued.

"Yeah." His eyes dropped for a moment. "Just curious, I guess."

"Did you plan to meet Dan Jensen inside?"

"Actually, never thought about it. I assumed the dude was gone to work."

"Anyone else in the house?" Sam said.

"Just before I went in, I saw a cleaning service van and someone got into it and left."

"Door open?"

Harrison shook his head. "Cleaning people locked it on their way out. I had to jimmy the lock on the back door and force it. I went into a mud room, through other rooms, and got to the kitchen. Never saw anything so big except on TV."

"What did you do?"

"Looked around."

Ted exploded. "You mean to tell us you burglarized a home and just stood there? You wanted to kill Dan Jensen and you 'looked around.' That's bullshit, and you're still lyin' to us."

Samantha waved her hand between the two men who had gradually leaned toward one another until their faces almost touched. "Back off, you two bucks. Let's give Mr. Harrison a chance to explain."

He rolled his shoulders a few times. "I don't take disrespect from any man. So I'm in the crib and I'm just curious how the guy who got my brother killed lives. And I find out the dude lives pretty damn well. I get more pissed off every minute I'm there. He's livin' like a king."

"Did you find anything?"

"Nothing that I needed. I didn't want any trouble, so I didn't lift anything. Only problem was the damn dog. Little shit that barked all the time. I got worried the wife might hear and come on back."

Sam took a deep breath and leaned back on her left leg. She looked up at the glow from the sun that had just fallen behind the wooden fence on the far side of the lot. A golden color curved over the top for a moment until it popped out of view. Three crows, silhouetted by the glow, beat their wings twice and lifted off the fence toward the light. A long shadow stretched out from the fence across the dead cars to finally surround the three people.

"That about it?" she asked.

"Oh, no. The best part's comin'."

"Oh?"

"Yeah. I went to the back bedrooms, and I found another dude there. Not the husband. I figured the old lady's fucking the dude and she took a break. I laughed when I saw him."

"Was he in the bed?" Samantha asked.

"Naw. He was in the second bedroom. Looked like an office. He was sittin' at a desk."

"What'd he look like?"

"White dude. Short hair and built up like he could take on Mike Tyson—in his good days. Like he'd spent all his time in gyms pumping it all up."

Ted looked at Samantha. Korsokov? he wondered. "Did you say anything?"

"Didn't have to. He looked at me like he was a tough guy. I played it off and really didn't give a shit. I laughed at how that dude was gettin' it right in Jensen's own house with his old lady. Fact, I figured that was some justice for Jensen after he got my brother killed."

"Say anything?"

Harrison shook his head. "Like I say, he was comin' on like a thug. The damn dog was barking, so I boogied."

"How many times were you in that house?" Ted asked.

Harrison pulled his helmet low over his face and said, "Once."

Ted watched the man's body language and didn't believe him. Cool shadows grabbed at their lower legs as Ted and Samantha left the parts lot. They hurried through the showroom in time to get outside before the door was locked. At the car, Samantha said, "The dude just can't seem to come straight with us."

"How can we get him to tell us what he was really doing there? Think he killed Mina?"

"We've gotten as much out of him as we can unless we come up with a lot of leverage, which we ain't got. Maybe he thought he could threaten Dan for some money. Or I could believe he killed Mina to get even with Jensen. But we got a big problem with that."

Ted sighed and opened the car door. "Right—we don't have any evidence."

In the Mercedes, Ted turned south on Highway 65 and sped to Minneapolis.

"We'll have to trap Korsokov again," Sam said.

"The emergency room at the hospital?"

"No. I did something old-fashioned." She glanced to the side at Ted and grinned. "I called the ambulance service he works for. I didn't ask if he worked there, but I simply asked if he was on duty today."

"High-tech investigation, huh?"

"That's the trouble with younger investigators. They think everything's on a computer and they forget the phone or even worse, the tedious work of face-to-face interviews with real people. That's where you score some gold."

"Can we still catch him?" Ted asked.

"Hope so. He's off his shift in a half hour." She peered at the digital clock on the dashboard. "We might just make it."

Downtown Minneapolis had cleared out most of the after-work commuters, so Ted made it to the south side in twenty minutes—with a little illegal speeding added. North of Lake Street they bumped up over the bridge that spanned the Greenway—a long bike path that had been made from converted rail tracks.

Ted turned into the parking lot of a two-story warehouse. A small sign next to a faded red door read Fischer Ambulance Services. There were no windows on either side of the door. As the tires crunched over gravel and dirt, he stopped the car. "Come on," Sam called to Ted as she ran toward the red door. Beside it, a two-story roll-up garage door was closed. Samantha pushed her way through the red door.

Inside, Ted saw a small office with a low counter. An older woman sat behind a computer screen. She was reading a *People* magazine. She looked up in surprise. "What . . ?"

"We have an appointment to see Nick Korsokov," Samantha said.

"Uh, le' see." The woman tapped her keyboard, squinted at the screen, and said, "He's just getting off a shift now. In fact, if you go into the bay, you might still catch him." She waved them off and seemed anxious to get back to the magazine. Her face disappeared behind the cover to be replaced by the face of the Duchess of Cambridge.

Ted led Samantha through a wooden door that opened into a large warehouse space. It was two stories tall and looked a block long. Facing toward them, a row of various types of ambulances were parked next to one another. As they hurried forward, the roll-up garage door squealed as it started to rise. It opened and an ambulance drove through, turned to the left, and searched for a parking spot.

Ted moved to the far right corner, where they saw an office. It looked like a temporary cubicle with glass sides that covered the top half of the walls. Inside, he could see two men in uniforms. One was talking on a phone while the other stared at a computer screen. Samantha followed Ted as they approached the office. The back door to the office opened, and Nick Korsokov stepped in. When he saw them coming, he looked back at the door but must have realized he couldn't get away.

Ted and Samantha reached the office. "Hello, Nick. Got some time to talk?" he asked.

Korsokov looked at the two men in the office and said, "Uh, friends of mine. Can you check me out, Bill?" He pushed his large body past Ted and Samantha. "Over here," he grunted.

They followed him to a far wall of the warehouse. There was a small table that held a square metal coffee machine. Packaged instant coffee, creamer, and sugar were lined up in a rack. Korsokov took a Styrofoam cup from a dispenser, drained coffee out of the machine and shook in dried cream. He used a thin straw to stir it. "Now what the hell do you guys want? I told you everything." He lifted the cup to his mouth, blew on it, and tested it with a sip.

"No, I don't think you've told us everything, Nicky," Sam said. She moved to stand on the opposite side of him from Ted. "For instance, we've learned about your 'business' ventures."

Korsokov took a longer drink from the cup. "Oh?"

"We've got evidence of the sex trafficking business you've been involved with."

He didn't change expression and continued to sip on his coffee, but Korsokov's body shifted backward to rest on his heels. "You got nothing."

"I think we do, and we just may go to the police with it. After all, I know lots of 'em." Sam smiled at Korsokov. "For now, that's not what we're interested in. We want to know about Mina Jensen."

Korsokov snorted and started to move to the left. Samantha cut him off. "I told you everything," he said.

"Okay, let's go through this the long way," she said. "You have been running a prostitution ring and probably other illegal scams."

"I don't know what you're talkin' about." He glanced to the side in the direction of the cubicle office.

"Let's get back to Mina Jensen," Ted said. "Did she work with you?" He saw flashing blue and red lights cross the wall in front of him. Someone must be testing the lights on an ambulance.

"Never."

"Cut the shit, Nicky," Sam said. "She was in business with you, right?"

Korsokov wouldn't answer.

Samantha sighed. "Have it your way. I'm gonna boogie out of here to the prosecutors. They'd be interested . . ."

"She don't work with me," yelled Korsokov. "We were going to marry."

"Is that why your prints were found all over her house?"

"Yeah. I was out there."

Samantha stepped back. "You were having sex, right?"

"Yeah, but it was more than that. But then she told me it was over. She quit calling, texting. So I go out there to talk it over. I mighta got a little rough with her, but I never killed her."

"How about Dan Jensen?" asked Ted. "Did you see him kill her?"

Korsokov snorted again and said, "How do you say it in America? Their marriage was 'house of cards.'"

"Were you out there on May tenth?" Samantha said.

Korsokov's eyes narrowed as he thought.

"Come on, Nicky. The night of the murder," Sam reminded him.

"Yeah. I wanted to talk to her about us breaking up. She told me husband wouldn't be there."

"And you saw that green card slipping from between your fingers. That made you so mad that things got out of hand and you killed her," Samantha said.

"Never. I thought—at one time—that we could maybe get together and she'd get away from that load she'd married." He pushed his face forward toward Samantha. "But you think I admit to killing her?" He tilted back his head and laughed.

Samantha frowned, and it was obvious she didn't believe Nick's story of love. "What about the Jensens?"

"What about them?"

"How'd they get along?"

"Bad. That's what surprised me about her, since she told me she was leaving that loser. Then she change her mind."

"Any idea what might have happened? Do you think Dan Jensen killed her?" Ted said.

Korsokov shrugged. "Don't know, don't care now. I'm just pissed off she stayed with him. Look at what happened to her." His head jerked up. "Hey, there was stranger out there once. Maybe he kill her."

"Who?"

"Don't know. Big black guy. Gray hair. Older guy, but I wouldn't want to take him on."

"What did he do?"

"Nothing. But one time when I was in Mina's office, he just showed up. I stared him down and that was all. He left. Saw him one more time, though. Maybe he killed her instead of husband. He looked like he could."

"Was he there the same day she was killed?"

"Yeah. But I can't remember for sure."

Samantha continued, "Why did you happen to be there the exact day she died?"

Korsokov opened his hands. "She hadn't called for two days. I was worried."

"Worried?"

"Yeah. But then I got a text from her on somebody else's phone. She wanted to see me right away that morning at the house. Told me Jensen would be gone. I told her I was workin', but she really want to talk to me that exact day." His shoulders bunched into big clots of muscle.

"But you found the husband there." Samantha took a step backward.

He finished his coffee, crushed the cup in his hand, and tossed it into a gray metal wastebasket with a dented side. "No. I had argument with Mina then left. Never came back that night." He took a deep breath and started to move toward the front door. He walked between the other two. Then he stopped and turned around. "There's something weird one time." Korsokov's eyes opened and he said, "One day, I come in through the garage and I find her carrying a thing that looks like a head from a fashion mannequin in a store."

"What?" Samantha said.

"It was white. Not too heavy. I ask her what the hell is that, and she got mad. Put it in a box and went into the house."

"Ever find out what it was?"

He shrugged and walked away.

Chapter Twenty-five

Sanford Rogin rushed through the skyway that led from the Government Center to the Pillsbury building. Maureen kept pace with him along his left side. They were going to find a quick lunch in one of the skyway restaurants.

"You don't seem upset by Vang's ruling about Jensen's statement," Maureen said. "We're going to need a break to counteract that."

From over his shoulder he said, "No problem. Jensen never admitted anything, anyway. We'll still nail his ass with all the other evidence."

"Ted did a good job."

"He *used* to be a great lawyer."

"He's good enough to win that motion."

Rogin stopped and pushed his face close to hers. "You got something for him? If so, you can get the hell off the ship right now." He felt heat rise into his face.

"Hey, chill. I'm just learning about trial work." She scowled at him. "Besides, who filed the ethics complaint against Rohrbacher?"

He wriggled his shoulders, backed off, and said, "Come on, I'm starving."

"What about the wig that deputy found in a landfill? The blood on it matched the blood type of Mina Jensen. Shouldn't we order a search?"

"In a landfill?" Rogin frowned. "Possible, but I'd guess the killer just threw it away. I doubt there's a body there. Besides, can you imagine the expense and time to dig up an entire landfill?" He resumed his march for food. From over his shoulder, he told her, "Don't forget to give notice of the wig and blood type to Rohrbacher."

"Of course." She hurried to catch up with him. "Wouldn't you rather go to the food trucks on Marquette?" she asked him.

Head forward, shoulders bunched, he replied, "No way. Don't have the time. We'll go to my favorite place. Manny's Authentic Tacos."

"Oh, come on. We've been there three times this week. There's nothing 'authentic' about it. The food's crap."

"What's wrong with a taco?"

"Should I start with the greasy, salty beef? The fake lettuce? The processed cheese? Which one?"

"So what? It's filler and it's cheap."

Maureen yanked on his arm to stop his express run to the restaurant. "All right. Here's the deal. I'll stop at Manny's with you, but then we go to the food trucks for me. I want something that's at least marginally healthy."

Rogin grumbled something unintelligible but agreed. He stepped back into the river of people plowing through the skyway in search of a cheap, quick lunch. Maureen followed him. Just then, Rogin's phone rang. He answered his wife. "Sure, honey. That's right, I almost forgot her birthday. Stop at Toys-R-Us? Of course I will. The case against Jensen is getting busy, and I'll be swamped for a long time. Yeah, don't worry; I'll get it done. A list?" He yanked the phone away from his ear and frowned at it. Resuming his conversation, Rogin said, "No, I don't need a list. I never forget anything." He listened for a few minutes. "Of course I'm watching what I eat. Maureen and I are going to the health trucks."

He closed his phone and led Maureen into Manny's. The smell of fried beef felt comforting to him. Once he'd gotten his pile of soggy tacos, they marched down the stairs to get outdoors. His phone rang again. He handed the pile to Maureen, who held it between her fingers with her arms held out in front of her. Rogin talked for a while until he burst into a wide smile. "God damn! Great work, Deputy. I'll check in with the ME right now."

"What?"

"They found Mina Jensen's body."

Where?" She almost dropped the tacos.

"Lake Minnetonka. This time they used the new ROV. Deputy sheriffs have moved it to the ME's lab."

"So the autopsy has been done?"

"Not finished yet. They've given it top priority, so we should have an answer soon. There's a damn big hole in the back of the head." He shouted so loud a few people stopped beside him on the sidewalk and stared for a moment. Rogin glanced around and smiled briefly. He grabbed his tacos and turned to walk over to Marquette Avenue.

Maureen said, "Think of how the family will react. It will give them some closure, finally."

"And it'll close our case for good, too. This will be even easier than I imagined. And what did I tell you—we don't need Jensen's statement after all. I'll let Rohrbacher know right away. I expect he'll come back with a request for a plea negotiation to settle the case short of going to trial." He stopped to tilt his head to the side and take a large bite out of the end of a taco. It crunched and he chewed quickly.

"I don't know . . . positive self-help talk won't change the facts, Sandy."

"Sanford. Assume the autopsy identifies the body as that of Mina Jensen. Beyond that, these docs can figure out amazing things. They may be able to testify for us at the trial what instrument caused the injury and other things that will nail Dan Jensen to the wall. Ever think about that?"

"Of course." Her face twisted when she watched him eat the taco. "But what about this new suspect, Harrison?"

Rogin crunched another bite from the taco. This time, grease ran out from the other end of it and dribbled over his hand. "We're meeting Ben after lunch. He's been checking out Harrison. In the end: trial won for the A-team, once again," he mumbled.

"Before you celebrate the victory by eating another taco, let's see what Ben's got."

A half hour later, they assembled around the long wooden table in the county attorney's conference room. Ben Clark looked at the table in the corner for left over pastries. He pulled open the edge of a white box and spied a donut. He smiled and lifted it to his mouth. "Mmm."

"Get the hell over here, Ben. We haven't got time for you to eat —again," Rogin ordered him.

Clark ambled back toward the other two, who sat at the table. He slumped into a swivel chair with a grunt and finished the donut. "These are the best. Glad I work here."

Rogin was impatient. "Ben, what did you find on Harrison?"

"Huh? Well, I told you about the murder rap in Gary that he plea-bargained down to manslaughter, right?"

"Yes."

"And how he took off from there after he served some prison time to come up here?"

"Right."

"You gotta understand that Gary is a shithole and the records there are equally bad. I had a lot of trouble just getting the dirt on him as it was. I kept e-mailing the county court records department, and they kept telling me they were still looking. So I finally called the city police and identified myself. They gave me the help I needed and they got the records."

"We know all this," Rogin said. He pushed back his chair and stood up.

"Yeah, well, after I got the information about Harrison, you wanted more. So I called my guys in Gary again. They went back to the well, but this time they hit a brick wall."

"What happened?" Maureen asked.

Ben licked a glob of yellow lemon filling off his finger. "They couldn't find anything earlier than 2006. It means that at some point, Harrison's records disappeared. I think he changed his identity."

"How could he get in the military?" said Mo.

Clark shrugged. "He probably had just enough supporting data. Fake Social Security ID, fake driver's license. I'm not saying I know for sure that he changed his identity, but that might explain why his records are missing."

"Or it could mean he had a way to make them disappear. It wouldn't surprise me coming from a place like Gary, Indiana," Rogin said.

"Right," Clark agreed. "When I e-mailed the clerk of court, they told me the records aren't even digitized yet. We did that here many years ago. They're probably still working with paper records."

Maureen said, "What does all this prove?"

Clark shifted his bulk to face her. "I think it means our boy is a born liar. Whatever happened, he's succeeded in obscuring his past for some reason. Obviously, he's trying to hide something bad. Personally, I wouldn't trust one word he says now."

Chapter Twenty-six

Two days later, Ted had scheduled a meeting with Dan Jensen and Samantha. Since the trial was scheduled to start the following day, Ted wanted a final meeting with him—a confrontation, really, to decide which defense would give him the best chance.

It wasn't unusual for criminal defendants to minimize or even lie about their involvement in an alleged crime, but Dan's story had never made sense to Ted. He wanted to pin down Jensen to the truth —or something close to it. After all, Ted was the one who would have to stand before a jury and try to sell the defense to them. He would either have to blame the death on Korsokov or Harrison or use the amygdala hijack—which would mean admitting that Dan had killed her but wasn't legally responsible.

Because of his law partners' concerns about the case, Ted told Dan to meet at Samantha's house in northeast Minneapolis. They arrived separately. Ted got there first. When he walked up to the door, the front windows were open, and through the screens, he could hear Sam practicing on her sax. The music sounded Latin, with heavy drums and a strong offbeat. When there was a break in the music, he knocked on the door. Samantha came to open it in a few minutes.

Today she wore blue jeans, and a pink hoodie sweatshirt, and her hair looked like a black halo around her head. "Just in time for the concert, T-Man." She stepped back as Ted walked through the door.

"I like that music, too." He smiled at her.

"It's called bossa nova. From Brazil. Combination of samba and American jazz." Sam walked over to the Bose sound system and turned it off. She looked closely at him. "Okay, what's wrong?"

"Huh?"

"You're clothing's all wrinkled. Not like you."

His chest stiffened and he said, "Laurie kicked me out of the house. No fighting, but a few tears. I thought this case would be something I could get out of quickly. Didn't turn out that way. She warned me, and now I'm in a hotel." He was comforted by Matt's call after Ted moved out. Matt still supported his involvement in the case, and Matt assured him that he could win everything.

Samantha shook her head. "You sure are dumb sometimes. Can't you see what you're risking here?"

"Of course," he shouted, "but I can't stop now." Ted stepped back from her and took a deep breath.

"It's the old case, isn't it?"

"I don't want to talk about it."

"Teddy, you don't have to prove anything."

"It sure as hell feels like it." He felt a pounding in his chest. The memories came back to him. There had been a brutal slaying of a young girl in a neighborhood close to Dan and Mina's. Ted, the best lawyer in the office, had been assigned to prosecute the murderer. The defense lawyer had raised a mental illness defense, but Ted had studied hard and become an expert about the subject in preparation for the trial.

During the trial, a combination of Ted's drinking and his arrogance had led him into an affair with the prosecution's expert witness on mental illness. When that became known, the case was thrown out, the murderer walked free, Ted was fired, and the victim, Katie, had been denied justice.

Ted's father hadn't talked to him for a year, and Laurie had insisted on a divorce. Although they had tried counseling, she remained adamant and pushed for the divorce.

Since then, Ted had severed the relationship with the witness, stopped drinking, and started his estate planning practice. He had even convinced Laurie to remarry and try it again. Ted had thought his world was improving—until Mina Jensen was killed. Now, he was back in the world he'd fled from and never wanted to experience again.

Samantha interrupted his memories. "Well, for both you and Laurie, I hope it's not too late and you can repair the relationship." She cradled the sax on its stand in the corner. "Where's our boy?"

"Should be here . . ." He heard the squeal of tires on pavement and looked out the window. Dan Jensen slammed the door of his Ford F-150 truck and looked to both sides as he hurried across the sidewalk to Samantha's house. Ted let him in.

"God damn, traffic's bad," Jensen said.

"You're not used to the inner city." Sam laughed out loud. "We're still using Model T's in the hood."

"Why do we have to meet again? We've been over this a hundred times before," Dan said. "Let's get this over with and get me acquitted."

"Sit down there," Sam ordered him. "I'll get something to drink. Coffee for everyone?"

"Got a beer?" Jensen sat in the blue leather couch that faced the small fireplace. He wore gray slacks and a faded blue t-shirt. He crossed one leg over the other at the ankle. His fingers tapped on the armrest.

"Look, Dan, we've got to get the facts straight so we can pick the defense that will give you the best chance for an acquittal. Got it?"

Jensen leaned forward. "Got it? What the hell? You don't think I 'got it'? This is my fuckin' life on the line. Of course, I 'got it.'" His voice was loud and bounced off the close walls in Samantha's living room.

"Okay, I'm sorry. We've all put a lot into this."

Jensen inched back, and Ted could see him swallow carefully, like he was digesting the weight of what Ted had just warned him about. "Yeah," he whispered.

Samantha came into the room with three mugs of coffee. "No beer for you," she told Dan. She set the mugs on top of a recent issue of *Downbeat* magazine on the low table in front of the couch. She went into her office and came back carrying an accordion file. When Sam sat beside Jensen on the couch, she opened the file and removed a thick pile of reports. Ted reached into his briefcase and pulled out a blue legal pad with notes written on it. Dan looked back and forth between the two.

"First of all, what the hell was Mina doing with Korsokov?" Ted asked.

Jensen sighed. "We've been over this . . . like I told you, I don't know for sure."

"You suspected them of having an affair, but could they have been in business together?"

Dan frowned. "What kind of business?"

"Prostitution," Ted said.

Jensen laughed and his chest shook. "No way. That's too crazy."

"We've got evidence that Korsokov was in it," Samantha said. "Did you have any hint Mina might have been involved in some way?"

"Nope."

"You told us that even though you fought with her in the past, just before the murder she had come to you to try and start over with your relationship?" Ted said.

Jensen's face shaded red around his cheeks and eyes. "That's true."

"All right." Samantha shifted her position to turn toward Dan. "We think it's possible Mina told Korsokov the affair was over and to get out of her life. When he became upset about that, he killed her."

Jensen didn't respond.

"Dan, do you know anything that can support that defense?" Ted said.

His eyes flashed at Ted. "Uh, maybe that's the guy I fought with."

"All right. That's not going to fly very far." Ted stood up and walked back and forth in front of the fireplace. "Let's go back to what happened to you. You said you drank a couple beers."

"Right."

"But Dr. Strauss said you weren't using anymore."

"I wasn't, but sometimes I just have a couple. That's probably why they hit me so hard."

"Dan, is there any chance those beers could've been drugged?" Samantha said.

He blinked while he thought about it. "Maybe, but who would've done that? I didn't have 'em in my hands all the time I was drinking. You know, I set them in the kitchen, the bedroom."

"Where did the beer bottles go afterward?" Ted asked.

"I don't know. A lot of things are kind of fuzzy for me."

"Well, if the beers hit you hard, that could have helped trigger the hijack," Ted said.

"I'm not sure about that."

"What's the last thing you remember happening?" Samantha asked.

"Let's see. Drinking the beers, me and Mina arguing about something, the fight with a stranger, and then I passed out. Don't remember anything 'til I woke up hours later."

"And—"

"The body was gone."

Ted let out a long sigh. "You've said this before. Can you remember anything else about the stranger in the house?"

Jensen shook his head.

"Was the guy black or white? Tall or short?"

"Can't remember. Big guy. Think he was a black guy."

"You think?" Ted raised his voice. "You're going to have to be more specific when you testify in front of the jury. Try to remember what happened."

"You're the lawyer. All I know is that I passed out, and she was dead and gone when I woke up," Jensen shouted.

"How can I argue that one of these other suspects killed your wife? We need more evidence about that. You've got to remember."

Jensen blinked but didn't say anything.

"Okay. Here's what I think happened, Dan." Ted stopped to face him. "I think you lapsed into an amygdala hijack and, unfortunately, killed your wife."

"What the fuck you talkin' about?" He slapped the arm of the couch with his open palm. "And if I did what about her body?"

Ted recognized that problem with the defense. Did Dan have help? Did he kill his wife and, in a panic, realize what he'd done and dispose of the body? But now lied about remembering anything? Ted walked to the front window with his back toward the other two.

Jensen's face turned red and he yelled at them. "I thought you were my defense team, not the prosecutors."

Ted looked out the window and saw green leaves dancing on a slight breeze. Two black kids came by wearing shorts that came below their knees, and one bounced a basketball. They both wore baseball caps too large for their heads so that the caps covered the tops of their ears.

From behind him, Ted heard Jensen clear his throat. "Hey, I'm sorry, man. I got carried away."

Ted didn't respond. Everyone shifted into their own thoughts for several minutes. Finally, Ted turned around. "One of the biggest issues the prosecutor will ram down our throats is the gap in time between when this happened and when you called 911."

"Yeah?" Jensen sat down.

"So what happened?"

"What is this, an interrogation?" Jensen started to stand and then sat back on the couch. "I'm sick of this. Okay. I told you: when I woke up, I didn't know what to do. I mean, how many times does a guy wake up to something like this? What would you do?" He looked from Sam to Ted.

Ted's shoulders slumped. "I don't know if a jury will believe you."

"The prosecutor's gonna drill into you about this like a dentist's drill, Danny," Samantha said. "He's going to accuse you—or someone—of disposing of the body after you killed her. This guy Rogin is no one to fool around with. He's an asshole, but unfortunately for us, a really smart and mean asshole."

"How many times do I—it sounds like a broken record."

"He's going to nail you with this point."

"Like our great president said, 'bring it on.' Check that off." He motioned with his index finger in the air.

Ted remembered the wig found in a landfill. "Did Mina have any wigs?"

Dan frowned. "Wigs? No. She had beautiful hair. I never saw any wigs around the house."

Ted told him about the landfill. Dan didn't have a comment so Ted said, "That's why we have to use the amygdala hijack. It's the best defense we've got," Ted said. "And I think that's what happened."

Ted knew that regardless of what he thought, it was still his job to defend his client zealously and try to get him acquitted.

"That means I'm admitting that I killed Mina?"

Ted nodded.

"No. No way. I mean, I couldn't have done that."

Ted looked at Samantha and with his eyes he communicated his concern: if Jensen had this same attitude during his testimony before the jury, the case was already sunk. They'd all lose. He sat down again in the chair at the corner of the couch. Ted picked up a mug of coffee and took a sip. It tasted strong and bitter.

"All right. Let's go back to the suspects," Sam said. "We have evidence that this guy who threatened you, Demontre Harrison, was in your home."

"Doesn't surprise me. I told you there were pry marks on the back door. How come the cops never came up with this stuff?"

Samantha shrugged. "I was a cop once. We're good, but we're not perfect. Sometimes it's 'group think.' The investigation team gets a theory of what happened, and before any other ideas can be aired, everyone's off and running with the first theory. Besides, the first anyone knew about him is when you told us. But this also can work for us."

"Oh?" Jensen refused the offer of a mug when Ted held it out to him.

Sam glanced at Ted. "What if Harrison was in your home and killed Mina to get revenge?"

Jensen had a blank look on his face.

"What I mean, Dan, is can you give us any evidence of that possibility?" Sam said.

"I never saw him in there. But, like I told you, he threatened me on the phone. Guy got a record?"

"Yeah. Serious."

"I saw some things out of place."

"What?"

"Stuff was moved in the kitchen. I smelled someone else's cologne."

"When?"

"The morning of the murder."

"How about after you woke up and she was gone? Did you smell anything then?" Ted said.

"Can't remember."

Ted raised his arms in the air and let them flop along his sides. "This is hopeless," he shouted. "You're no help in your own defense."

"Hey, you're the lawyers. What the hell am I paying you for?"

"Uh, you're not actually paying us anything right now," Ted said.

"Stop it." Samantha stepped between them. "This isn't getting us anywhere. What the hell is wrong with you, Ted?"

His frustration turned on her. "What is wrong? Let's start with the fact I may lose my partnership and my job. And the fact I've probably lost my wife again over this damn case."

"So it's all about you." Dan's jaw jutted out.

Ted didn't answer him.

"All right. We're done here," Sam said. She grabbed her mug and took a long drink of coffee.

Ted asked, "Another thing, Dan. What about Jon Stewart? Where was he?"

"In the house. What the hell?"

"Wasn't he especially close to Mina?"

"Best of friends."

"So why didn't he go nuts when she was attacked? The neighbors didn't hear any barking."

Jensen cocked his head to the side. "Don't know. Maybe 'cause the houses out there are pretty big and they sit far apart from each other."

Ted said. "What about you? Didn't you hear him barking?"

"Nope. I was out, man."

Samantha slammed her mug on the table. "'*I was out, man.*' That's your answer to everything. How convenient."

"You too? Whose side are you guys on?" Jensen jerked out of the couch and pushed his bulk up to her face. "Sounds like you're still a God damn cop."

Samantha shook her head and walked to the far side of the room.

"Don't attack her," Ted shouted. "That's not fair."

"I can take care of myself," Sam yelled.

Jensen's body twitched, and his head tipped to one side as it rotated from Ted to Samantha. "Okay, I get it. You're fuckin' ganging up on me. You told me that you were defending me all the way. Now you're lining me up like a firing squad." His eyes became small.

"The focus is not on us; it's on Dan Jensen." Sam planted a hand on each hip. "You haven't come clean with us since jump street. I'm not backing down until you tell us what happened."

"And I'm not talking to you anymore." Jensen started for the front door. "You don't know how tough this is on me. My wife is dead, my business is falling apart 'cause of the bad publicity, money's tight. I'm going to prison—"

Ted stepped in behind him and reached for his back. His hand touched Dan high on his neck. "Danny," Ted called after him.

Jensen's face turned bright red. He slipped to the side, swung wide with his hand, and caught Ted in the upper shoulder. Ted fell back two steps but regained his balance. Jensen came at him, arms stabbing through the air between them. He pleaded, "Don't kill them—" His eyes glazed over while his mouth opened like he was chewing on something, but no more sounds came out. Ted tried to block the punches. Jensen landed one on Ted's upper shoulder, and it glanced off.

Ted moved to the center of the room. He pushed against Dan to keep him away, but Ted bumped up against the couch.

A low grumble came from deep in Jensen's chest and he rushed at Ted, who fell down onto the couch. He tried to protect himself by raising his feet to kick at Jensen. Dan's voice finally came out in a long, high-pitched scream. "Don't kill me—"

Ted looked into his eyes and saw a dark, blank depth. There was nothing inside, and at that moment, Ted knew Dan Jensen was capable of killing.

Samantha stepped between them and grabbed Jensen's throat between her hands. With her thumbs, she dug into the sides of his neck to hit the sensitive nerves. Almost instantly, Jensen reacted. He dropped his arms, screamed in pain, and stumbled backward toward the fireplace. Samantha let go and followed him to make sure he was done.

He staggered to the side, holding his throat while coughing.

Ted could smell a dank, sweaty odor come off of Jensen. Ted breathed hard and stood up. "Thanks," he told Samantha.

"Always works."

"That settles it."

"Settles what?"

Ted paused. "We're going with the amygdala hijack defense. This proves it right here."

Chapter Twenty-seven

Deputy Seabloom had caught a break in the case. While the medical examiner investigated the recent body he'd found in Lake Minnetonka, he took some vacation time to watch the Dan Jensen trial. He'd come early to get a front row seat. He could feel the tension ripple throughout the room. This was the biggest case to ever be tried in the state.

He thought of the parents of Mina Jensen. With all the suffering they'd been through and all the work law enforcement had done, Seabloom wanted the jury to find Jensen guilty. The courtroom bulged with people, reporters, lawyers, law enforcement officers, and the extended family of Mina Jensen. Kenny felt chilled from the air conditioning, and it smelled dry.

The wig Kenny had found in the plastic bag at the landfill had been analyzed at the sheriff's lab. The blood on it matched Mina Jensen's blood type. That set off a new storm of investigation. Seabloom had taken the information to the prosecution team immediately. Would they argue for a delay in the trial?

Kenny studied the lawyers as they sat behind the long tables in the middle of the room. Rogin was a big guy, burly, with blond hair that looked like it needed a comb. He'd never pass an inspection in the sheriff's department. His assistant was a small, thin woman. Pretty in an old-fashioned way, Kenny thought. Across from them, Ted Rohrbacher circled behind the desk. Obviously nervous, he had the moves of an athlete. An Asian woman sat next to him, and a young guy with a sport coat that was too small for him kept lifting laptops out of a metal cart to place them on the table. Between them sat the defendant, Dan Jensen.

He seemed sick. Pale skin and a shiny forehead. Still, the guy looked like he could handle himself in a fight. Rough around the edges. Kenny let his thoughts run to imagine what it must have been like when Jensen was killing his wife. The amount of blood alone would have been horrendous. If Kenny were in his place, he didn't think he could sit as still as Jensen did now.

Judge Vang sat behind the bench, a small head covered with shiny black hair. She looked up when Rogin spoke in a loud voice. "As you can see, Your Honor, we may have found the missing body of the deceased."

"In the lake?" the judge asked.

"We don't know for sure yet. The Government asks for a continuance to investigate further."

"But this isn't the first body suspected of being the victim in this case, right?"

"Yes. We should have the results at any time."

The judge dipped her head forward, and it disappeared from Kenny's view. When she raised it, she said, "I don't like this. The trial date has been set for some time now. I don't want any further delays."

"But what if we've found the body?"

"You don't have to shout at me, Mr. Rogin. You're the one who charged this case and got the indictment for first degree murder *without* a body. Why should I delay the trial any longer?"

Rogin opened his mouth but no words came out.

"Call the jury in," the judge told her clerk.

Fourteen people filed in from the tall doors that led to the back hallway. They looked like a group of people Kenny might see at the state fair looking for food. Dressed in different ways, different colors, men, women, young and old. Twelve people would decide the case, but there were two alternate jurors in case someone got sick.

While he waited, he reflected on his own satisfaction. As he sat there, the medical examiner should be completing the investigation of the lake body. They had to call for a forensic dentist named Dr. Hanson to try and identify the teeth. Unfortunately, he'd been on vacation, so the authorities had to go with their second dentist. It all added up to a further delay. Kenny felt in his gut that the body was that of Mina Jensen. His commander would finally appreciate what Kenny could do.

He looked up to see the jury seated and quiet.

Sanford Rogin began by making an opening statement. He stood behind the counsel table and fastened the middle button on his suit. Heavy glasses made him look intimidating, but when he smiled, Kenny could see the jurors relax. Rogin stood at the corner of the table. His assistant assembled several stacks of paper next to him.

He spoke with a loud voice and seemed to have all the confidence in the world. His hands chopped at the air as he argued each point. He listed, in great detail, all the pieces of evidence the government would present to the jury in order to convince them beyond a reasonable doubt of Dan Jensen's guilt.

When he finished, Rogin took a deep breath and sat down. The woman next to him patted him once on the shoulder.

Seabloom was impressed and felt good that the prosecution was in such capable hands. From Rogin's argument alone, Kenny was convinced of Jensen's guilt. How would the defense fight all that evidence?

Ted Rohrbacher followed and also stood. He left his coat open and moved his lanky body from around the table to stand in front of the jury box. He didn't have any notes. For a long time, he remained silent and then, in a low voice, began to speak. He talked about Jensen's background, his service in Afghanistan, his mental health problems, and the difficult relationship with his wife, and something called the amygdala hijack.

Kenny hadn't been impressed with Rohrbacher at first. Of course, most defense lawyers didn't impress him anyway. But as this one kept talking, Kenny found himself admiring the man. His voice was lower and, combined with the words he spoke, made his points seem reasonable. Logical. Believable. Kenny felt hollowness in his stomach. Had he and law enforcement done enough? Was there any chance the defendant could get off? After such a violent crime, how cold Jensen walk away? Kenny felt sick at the possibility.

Rohrbacher continued, and now he was starting to show the strain. His voice rose and the muscles in his neck constricted. Passionate. The guy meant what he said, and it looked like the defense lawyer was giving everything he had to his case.

"I ask you to keep an open mind until you hear both sides before deciding. But you'll come to the conclusion that the government has failed to prove Dan Jensen guilty beyond a reasonable doubt because of a mental deficiency called the amygdala hijack. We will present evidence about it so that you understand how it works and why Dan Jensen is not legally responsible for his wife's death," Rohrbacher finished. He paused for a moment, walked back to the counsel table, and sat down. Silence blanketed the courtroom.

According to the rules, the prosecution started with their witnesses. Rogin called dozens of them over the next couple of days. Kenny was able to attend most of the court sessions. Detective Sean O'Brien took the stand for the entire morning. Cops, deputies, and investigators who had participated in smaller parts of the investigation all testified. Several people from the lab came in and told how they had taken custody of physical evidence, tested it, and then gave the results. Dr. Helen Wong took time out from the unidentified lake body autopsy to testify about the crime scene and her conclusions. Deputy Sarah Mooney, the crime lab expert on bloodstains, testified well, as she always did.

Rogin's assistant, a woman named Hanrahan, shuttled constantly from the counsel table to the back of the courtroom, where she met different people from the county attorney's office. They carried files, evidence, plastic bags with objects inside, notes, and sometimes simply whispered messages in Hanrahan's ear. She was younger than Rogin and had energy. Occasionally, Kenny would notice the two of them disagree about something. Rogin almost always won, but the woman stood up to him, and Kenny gave her credit for that because he knew Rogin was tough.

On the fifth day of the trial, the prosecution paused to have two tech assistants wheel in a large- screen TV on a cart. In five minutes, they slipped in a DVD and cued it to play. Kenny was back again and had to shift his body to the side to see the screen from where he sat. But he watched as the camera covered the crime scene. He knew one of his colleagues had taken the film with a new camera called a Panascan. It had super high-def and resembled a fisheye lens in that it could capture images from anywhere in the room.

While Rogin had the technician prepare the film, one of the cops who had been on the scene described to the jury what they would see on the film. Kenny smiled to himself when Rogin paused before starting the DVD. Kenny knew what was coming. Rogin was so good at this.

The lights in the courtroom dimmed and the film began.

As the camera "walked" down the long hallway in the Jensen mansion, Kenny could sense the reaction of the jurors. There were small yellow tents that marked the spots where evidence had been found at the scene. Murmurs started, a few throats cleared, and then, when the camera came into the bedroom and the carnage was revealed under bright lights, the jurors gasped out loud. Some turned their heads momentarily but couldn't resist watching. The witness was good also. He spoke in a flat, matter-of-fact voice that contrasted with the horror the jurors saw in colored detail on the high-def screen. Rogin drew out this part of the trial for as long as he could.

Throughout the trial, the lawyers had been courteous to each other, objecting in measured voices and reasonable tones. As expected, Rohrbacher objected to much of the state's evidence. The judge seemed to be ruling in his favor more than Rogin's, and that worried Seabloom.

The prosecution then presented evidence of the search of the lake. Kenny would love to have been the witness and was anxious to do battle with Rohrbacher, but Seabloom's commander was called to testify. He began by describing the discovery of Mina Jensen's car and the blood in the trunk which had been found through the use of the chemical leucocrystal violet. He continued by telling the jury about search techniques, divers, and the remote operated vehicle. Kenny was pleased when the gun he'd found in the bushes by the murder scene was introduced into the trial. Testing on it had been completed. The commander testified that it matched one of the missing guns from the house and also matched the bullet found imbedded in the wall. Unfortunately, no fingerprints had been developed from the weapon. Kenny wondered if that would be a critical problem for Rogin's case. After several days, the prosecution rested, having presented all their evidence.

The defense started their case by calling Dr. Jerome Strauss. Rogin had explained to Kenny that mental illness wasn't a defense in the case, but he suspected Strauss would testify about how it was possible that Jensen had blacked out and didn't remember anything. Seabloom thought it was simply a guilty person trying to protect himself, but the defense was entitled to present whatever they wanted to the jury.

Strauss made jokes at first and didn't seem too serious until Rohrbacher corrected him several times. Seabloom could see Rohrbacher's strain by the lines that furrowed across his face. Then the doctor settled down and did a good job. Kenny didn't believe any of the psycho-stuff, but he noticed that a many of the jurors took a lot of notes during the testimony. Dr. Strauss sounded pretty convincing about something he called the amygdala hijack and how it would cause a person with PTSD to black out and not know what he was doing—even killing someone.

Rohrbacher called a second expert about the hijack and several other witnesses. He called his investigator, Samantha Carter. Kenny had never heard her testify before and looked forward to it. She was a woman with an attitude, but also a great witness. When she started to talk about two other "suspects," as she called them, Rogin erupted with loud objections.

"There is absolutely no evidence about this. It's complete conjecture on the part of the defense," he shouted.

Rohrbacher assured the judge that the defense was relying on the mental health defense. But this new evidence would show how the tension between Dan and Mina had started. The judge allowed Rohrbacher to continue the questioning. All the jurors sat up and listened. Through Sam, Rohrbacher introduced the evidence of the affair between the victim and a guy named Korsokov and about how Mina had tried to stop it.

The lawyers were arguing about every sentence that Sam tried to say. The exchanges heated up with shouting and even some personal accusations. Both fought hard, and it was obvious how committed they were to their cases. Many times the judge had to stop to calm them down and warn them about their behavior.

Dan Jensen testified last. He was vague about the details he could remember. Seabloom didn't like him. Too arrogant and upset, but in the end Jensen showed genuine grief over the loss of his wife and, therefore, caused Seabloom to wonder how the jury would react to him.

Seabloom glanced at the jury and saw they were all taking notes —a bad sign, he thought. He focused on the testimony again. When the defense had finished, he had a sinking feeling in his gut. Everything they'd offered made sense—even the new amygdala hijack idea. And since all the defense had to do was poke enough holes in the government's case to create reasonable doubt, Kenny worried.

It got worse for him after Rohrbacher made his closing argument. Kenny had watched trials before, but he'd never seen anyone as good as him. Rohrbacher used a combination of a likable personality, strong evidence, a good argument, sympathy for the defendant, and sprinkled it all with bits of humor. He challenged the jury to accept the amygdala hijack as the new but correct law about mental illness. At the end he almost cried and asked the jury to find his client not guilty.

Seabloom thought that if he ever got in trouble, he'd hire this lawyer in a second.

The judge instructed the jury on the law, and they retired to a room behind the jury box. Two deputies were posted at the door to make sure no one disturbed or interfered with the deliberations.

Three days later, the jury had finally come to a decision. Ted hurried up to the courtroom with Jackie and Sam. They met Joe, who was already there talking quietly with Dan Jensen.

"Hey, Teddy, you gave it all you had," said Sam.

"More than I thought I had."

"They've been out for three days. That's usually a good sign," Jackie said.

In ten minutes, everyone was seated in the silent courtroom. Judge Vang asked the foreperson if the jury had arrived at a verdict. An older woman stood from her chair at the corner of the jury box and announced, "We have, Your Honor."

"Hand me your verdict." The judge accepted a folded piece of paper from the juror, read it, and handed it to the clerk. "The verdict will be read in open court," the judge ordered.

The young clerk cleared her throat and pushed her glasses up on her nose. She opened the paper, studied it, and cleared her throat once again. "We the jury find the defendant, Daniel J. Jensen, guilty of murder in the second degree, signed April Smith, Foreperson."

The courtroom erupted in noise.

Over at the prosecution table, Rogin and Mo smiled briefly at each other. They were obviously happy with a win but disappointed the verdict was only for second degree instead of first degree murder. Several of the younger prosecutors who had watched Rogin try the case burst through the gate in the low wooden railing to clap him on the shoulder. The white glare from the ceiling surrounded them in light so strong it bleached out their skin color. Reporters swarmed the table and tried to talk with the team.

Dan Jensen slumped into his chair. His head flopped forward and he cried quietly. Jackie tried to pat him on the back, and she whispered into his ear. Dan didn't move.

Ted had the strangest experience. His hearing stopped. It was like he sat in a room full of cotton. Silence surrounded him, and no matter how hard he tried, sounds didn't penetrate the room. He was vaguely aware of some movement around him, but he didn't hear anything.

In a few minutes, some sounds came through to him. He thought he heard Jackie.

"Ted, at least it's only second degree. That's a huge victory," Jackie said. She sat to the left of him. "And we got to use the amygdala hijack."

"Shut up! They still found him guilty. Did you miss that part? I got beat in a murder case where they didn't even have a body. The first one in the history of the state, and I lost it."

"Hey, chill. You knew this would be—"

"I gave it everything."

"We'll appeal the verdict on the amygdala hijack issue."

"I don't care. I lost."

Jackie walked around the table to stand in front of him. "It happens. In a few days, you'll accept it and move on."

Judge Vang ordered the sentencing to occur two weeks later, but changed her mind when Jackie asked her for a special sentencing hearing that Jensen was entitled to have. Considering the high bail already set and the fact Jensen always came to court, she allowed him to remain out of custody.

Jensen unfolded himself from the chair and pushed it back under the table. He made sure that it lined up correctly. With a quick sniffle, he said to Ted, "You fucked up, Counselor. This is wrong. You know it."

"You heard Jackie. We've got a sentencing hearing for you. We'll try to get the minimum."

Dan's face reddened and he turned to face Ted, who still remained seated. "I'm not going to take this lying down. Somehow, you're gonna pay." He shook his head and hurried out of the courtroom.

Ted snorted, "Another satisfied client."

Matt and two friends worked their way through the crowd to reach the counsel table. Matt gave Ted a soft punch on the shoulder. "Hey, nice try. Here are two of my homies. Brought 'em to watch you."

"Thanks," Ted mumbled.

"It's okay. Uh, I'm sorry. Hey, gotta run." Matt waved at his father but didn't look him in the eye and left quickly.

Jackie tried once more to console Ted. When he grunted at her, she packed her briefcase and turned toward the door. "We'll work on the sentencing hearing. Maybe we could use the amygdala hijack again for that purpose. Think we got a much better chance there." She left him. Joe Kopp must have decided to bail on the funeral around the defense table, and he left too.

Soon the courtroom emptied, and even the judge's clerk picked up all the files and disappeared through the door.

Samantha sat on the right side of Ted.

"Is there more we could have done?" he asked her.

"Probably not."

"Probably?"

"All right, no."

"I wish I still drank. I could use something right now. And what about that ass, Rogin, and Maureen? They're out there telling the press how great they are."

"Don't worry about them."

"After all he's done to me."

"I warned you—don't put all your money on this one."

"I didn't want to in the beginning. It just grew on me, I guess."

"It's not the case that grew on you." She stood and assembled her papers into the accordion file.

"Huh?"

"You got yourself into this, I'm sorry to tell you. But I think you know that, don't you?"

He nodded. "It's just like the old case all over again. I can't escape it."

"Come on. Let's get out of here."

"And where am I going to go? Back to the hotel room? Laurie kicked me out, my partners kicked me out, and I don't have a job." He looked up at Sam.

"Drop the pity party and get up again."

When Ted refused to move, Sam put her hand on his shoulder, squeezed, and left him alone in the courtroom.

Chapter Twenty-eight

Four days later, Ted sat in a Dunn Brothers coffee shop on Lake Street. He'd walked around Lake Calhoun twice and found himself wandering up the street until he stopped for a latte. He hadn't been back to the firm since the trial. In two weeks he'd go before Judge Vang and try to get Danny's sentence reduced. Well, Jackie would make the argument. Ted was worn out. He'd come face to face with Mina's family outside the courtroom after the verdict. They felt sad but satisfied that the ordeal was over and that justice had been done —in their opinion. It had been painful for Ted to talk with them, even briefly.

Now what was he going to do?

Sam had been right: he had to pull himself out of the pity he felt. It was a useless waste of time. Ted would have to patch up his life once again. It wasn't fair. How many times did a guy have to screw up and get kicked in the ass? He couldn't seem to learn from his mistakes.

He watched young people pass before the window on their way to the lake. Some pushed bikes, some used skateboards, and most walked. Two girls with pink hair wrapped in buns on top of their heads passed the window, wearing loose t-shirts that were too large. Everyone wore flip-flops.

Ted heard his cell phone tinkle. He pulled it out of his pocket and saw a text from Dan: "u fuked up counselor I won't forget it." Ted deleted it and left another voicemail for Sam. He wondered how the concert had gone at the Dakota. She hadn't returned his calls, not that he blamed her. The media had finally quit harassing him about the trial. It hurt to face them, just like it had years ago. Thank God his father wasn't around. Ted had talked with Matt twice. He tried to console Ted, but underneath his kind words, Ted could feel his son's pity—worse than his own—and the disappointment he had in Ted. He saw a text from Deputy Sarah Mooney.

"stop by new info—puzzles me"

He clicked off the phone. The medical examiner hadn't been able to identify the body found in Lake Minnetonka—some unfortunate missing person who would go unnamed forever. There was still talk about digging up the landfill in Bloomington, but since the trial was over, officials questioned the expense of the effort for dubious results. The sheriff's office had shifted the search, finally, to the Mississippi River. It was always the last place to look—since it was so dangerous. Searching in the river relied mostly on luck to try and snag the body. Yesterday, against all odds, they'd found a body. Working around strong currents, they'd been able to lift it and discovered the back half of the skull missing. Once again an autopsy was ordered, and everyone revived their hopes, especially the family.

Ted stood up to shake some cinnamon in his coffee and noticed again how tired he felt. Overall, bone deep fatigue. Funny, he didn't worry about the future. Maybe because he'd been in this spot before. Instead, he just felt tired. In a few days, he'd try to call Laurie. Would she even talk to him? He smelled the cinnamon and stirred it into his coffee.

His phone pinged and he saw another text from Mooney: "you should come here now." He called her.

"Ted, you have look at this."

"Thanks, Sarah, but it's too late. The trial's over."

"I know, but there is something I missed."

Ted looked out the window at the sun. From the dark interior of the coffee shop, it looked even brighter than usual. A guy walked by with a green mullet hair style. Ted thought about taking another, aimless walk around the lake to watch the sailboats. "Huh?" He'd almost forgotten Sarah on the phone.

"It's from the Panascan."

"Look, I'm sorry, but I'm kind of busy now. My practice, you know." Did he sound convincing enough? He wondered.

"Okay. But this could change things. I'll have to notify the prosecutor's office, but I wanted you to look at it first."

He frowned. What did she have? And the last thing he wanted was to be in second place to the prosecutors. "Hey, thanks for re-membering me. Sure, I'll be there in a half hour."

He drained the latte and went out the back door to the tiny parking lot. At least he still had the Mercedes—for one more month. He climbed in and drove through downtown to the sheriff's lab. He was buzzed through the security door and walked down the hall to Sarah Mooney's office.

She was dressed in uniform and rose to meet him. Sarah hurried him into the second chair and said, "Sorry to hear about the trial. I know how hard you worked on it."

Ted shrugged his shoulders. "Sentencing is in two weeks."

There was an awkward silence until Sarah said, "Well, I've got something to show you." She folded her hands together. He sat and pulled himself up to sit beside her in front of the small desk. It was tan with plastic laminate on top. In the middle a large monitor took up most of the space. Her phone rang, but she ignored it.

His phone tinkled at he looked at another text from Dan. "my life is ruined I'm coming after you it's ur fault." Was Dan in another amygdala hijack? There was nothing to do; Ted ignored the message.

"This was created by a Panascan camera. It's something new the crime lab uses. It's got 300 megapixels of definition." When Ted didn't react, she continued, "That's a lot of 'em. It means the details are fantastic. Watch this." She touched a button on the laptop, and the images flickered until they came into focus on the monitor. The camera crawled through the Jensen house from room to room. At any time, Sarah could freeze the action or, by putting her cursor on the small arrows in the picture, rotate the images anywhere around the room, including the floor and ceiling. "This was taken by our techs at the crime scene the night of the murder."

"How does it work?" Ted asked.

"The camera lens is kind of like a fisheye. The tech holds the camera at a prescribed position to maximize the field of view. Mean-while, the lens takes in every spot in the room. Watch this." With another touch of the cursor, she was able to zoom in on any spot she chose. "The yellow plastic tents you see were set there by the investigators to mark the 'hot spots' where critical evidence was found. They're numbered to correspond with the number on the seized item so we can go back to the property room and look at the real thing if we want." She moved the cursor again, and they looked in the corners at the ceiling of the room and then came down to the floor again. Ted could see the bloody footprint and the drag marks.

"I remember this film from the trial. But the prosecutors used a DVD."

She shook her head. "I warned them. I told them to use the computer and the large TV screen to get the full effect, but Rogin said he didn't need it."

"Guess he didn't after all."

"Okay, here's what I want to show you." Sarah moved the camera from the kitchen into the hallway, past the family photos, and kept going toward the bedroom where the murder had occurred. She slowed the action. "Here it is. See that?"

"See what?" Ted lifted out of his chair enough to get closer to the screen. He watched as the camera panned over the wall where a large mirror hung. It had a wide gold frame with intricate carvings. He could almost make out the detail of the carvings—mythical creatures like dragons and knights. "A mirror?"

"Look into the mirror."

He put his face close to the monitor but didn't see anything different.

"Okay. I'll back it up and run through it with you. Here we go." She reversed the action, stopped, and came forward again. This time, she went into slow motion when the camera reached the mirror. "See the faint image? Kind of pink? It's a transfer stain."

"What's that?"

"A bloodstain resulting from the contact between a blood-bearing surface and another surface."

"Sure." Ted didn't understand but looked at the image again and, with her direction, he saw it. Very faint on the wall opposite from the mirror.

"Because it's really a reflection off the mirror, I missed it even though I've gone through this film many times. It's an image from the wall on the opposite side of the room." She stopped the film and zoomed in for a close-up. It was still faint.

"How come no one saw this at the crime scene?"

Sarah stopped and sat back in her chair. "If you remember, it was an unusually humid night. During the search of the scene, it got very hot in the house from all the people who were there. After everyone had placed the yellow flags and had seized the evidence they needed, our techs set up the camera for the final run-through. There were two films taken, prior to anyone investigating the scene and then after they were finished. But since it was so hot in there, the camera man opened the French windows in the bedroom. Since all the evidence, fingerprints, and testing had been done, it was okay to open the windows. When they did that, the cooler air caused some condensation on the warmer walls. That's what created the image you see in the mirror."

"Really?"

She leaned forward and worked on her keyboard again. "I think I can Photoshop this a little more. If I add some color tints, it should bring out the image better." She clicked on the keys until the image popped from the background. Sarah sat back with pride.

Ted peered at the faint image and could make out a smear of blood on the wall. The top was rounded with lots of thin tangled lines underneath that ran down toward the floor. "Can you figure it out?" he asked Sarah.

"The edge characteristics are poor. I've been working on it for over a half hour. But here, at the bottom it looks like someone's hair."

Ted flopped back into his seat. "Hair? Yeah, I can see those thin lines. And that stuff around it is blood?"

"Definitely."

"Oh, no."

"What?" Sarah looked at him with concern.

"I think I know where it came from." He told Sarah about the bloody wig found in a landfill.

Thoughts swirled through his mind. Should he approach Judge Vang with a motion for a new trial based on newly discovered evidence? Before he jumped, he asked Sarah. "Could you testify about this stain in court?"

"Sure."

"That a bloody wig was pressed against the wall?"

She smiled. "Sorry. Can't go that far. I can't even say it was human hair, although it certainly looks like it."

"I understand."

"And there's really another, more fundamental problem, Ted."

"What's that?"

"It goes back to what I told you the first time you were here. There are odd things that trouble me about this crime scene. This evidence simply adds to the mystery."

"What do you mean?"

"I read Detective O'Brien's statements as part of the initial preparation for my investigation. He says the body was removed in a rug or something that prevented the blood from dripping out. If that's correct, how would we get a stain that appears to be human hair on the wall? Wouldn't the body and the hair be inside the rug?"

Ted blew out a large breath of air. "Of all the hundreds of stains and evidence you've found here, only this *one* stain doesn't make sense. So, in spite of one stain, you could still write your report and testify in trial, as you did."

"Of course. I can only testify to the conclusions that I draw from those facts. I can't draw any logical conclusions from this." She smiled. "And besides, I didn't see it until now."

"I get it." He reached to his side and pulled open the door. Cooler air puffed in from the hallway. "Well, I have to run. I'm awfully busy."

"But if you combine this image with the arterial spurt, I get goose bumps. It's odd."

He looked at her face and saw frustration in her eyes.

"When an artery or the heart itself is opened, we often see what's called an 'arterial spurt' as a bloodstain. The pressure from the pumping causes the blood to shoot out like from a gun. The images are very easy to spot."

"There was one in the room, right? I remember you mentioning it."

"Yes. Here." She moved the cursor, and the camera panned through the doorway to the bedroom and along the wall by the bed. She stopped and zoomed in. "That's an arterial spurt stain."

He didn't look. "So what?"

"This one is too high. The victim was about five-four. Even if she had the highest blood pressure on record, her arterial spurt wouldn't have gone this high."

"I still don't understand."

"I don't either. That's what I mean when I say this doesn't make logical sense. The spurt should be much lower."

He got up from the chair to turn into the hallway but stopped and squeezed back into the office. "Explain that to me again." He listened for another fifteen minutes as she reviewed the bloodstains at the crime scene. A thought crept up from behind him and jumped into his brain. He discarded it immediately. But it came back again, this time more convincingly. He asked Sarah more questions and then he watched another ten minutes of the film. At the end, he was convinced that he was right—Dan Jensen was not the killer. He might have experienced the amygdala hijack, but he hadn't killed Mina.

Ted left the sheriff's lab. He didn't feel good. A headache threatened. He didn't know what to do, so he decided to head back to the firm. Maybe he could get a little paying work accomplished for a change before he was fired.

Ted drove south on France Avenue toward his office. He thought what it would be like to move into a new office and a new job. Previously, he had liked the trappings of luxury and the support staff that did so many things to make his life easier. But after the trial, Ted didn't want to go back to helping rich people get richer.

The traffic surged around Ted in all four lanes, but common to Minnesota drivers, no one honked. Too impolite. He saw Byerly's grocery store on the left hand side of the road. Behind the store stood several new rental buildings. They seemed to pop out of the ground every month. He thought he spotted Dan's truck behind him. Was the guy really crazy enough to stalk Ted? The traffic closed together again as he passed.

The thought that had struck him in Deputy Mooney's office came back again. Like cancer, it grew uncontrollably into a crazy scenario. Something so impossible, he pushed the idea away. But then Ted swerved to the left and crossed two lanes, which caused angry drivers to swerve—but not honk—at him. He turned left, drove around the lot behind Byerly's, and stopped in a visitor parking space at one of the apartment buildings. Ted got out of the Mercedes and walked to the front door. He smelled fresh-cut grass and noticed a weeping willow hanging over the man-made pond next to the door. In the light breeze, green tendrils swished across the surface of the water.

Four white columns flanked the double doors at the entrance. Ted reached for the handle, a heavy bronze one, and pulled the right door open. Inside, he scanned the list of tenants for the name Dorsch. He didn't see any.

Outside again, Ted walked across the parking lot to a second building. It was a mirror image of the previous one. White columns and double doors at the entrance.

He stepped into a cold air conditioned lobby, decorated in colonial furniture and colors. This building had a large lobby with a receptionist who sat behind a desk working on a computer. She paused when Ted approached, pushed the screen to the side, and smiled at him. Next to her a vase of red carnations contrasted with her pale skin. "Hi. My name's Betsy. May I help you?"

"Maybe," he said. Ted felt awkward standing there with the half-formed idea in his mind. What should he ask for? "Uh, do you have anyone living here named Dorsch?"

"Would you spell it?" After he did, she said, "Let me check." Betsy turned back to the screen and clicked on the keys. Her phone rang. She put a finger up in the air to indicate that Ted should wait. He walked from the desk to a nearby circle of chairs. He sat in a wingback chair covered in cloth with a pink floral pattern.

While he waited, Samantha called him, finally. They talked about her gig at the Dakota. It had gone well. Sam was sure the group had knocked the roof off the place. She laughed quickly. "They even invited us back again."

"Sorry I wasn't there. I just didn't feel very good."

"That's *exactly* where you should've been, T-man. Music will heal your soul. You still got a job?"

"For now. Regardless what the partners think, I'm quitting."

"Don't worry. You'll survive."

"Hey, Sam. Remember you questioned some of the data on Mina's phone?"

"Yeah?"

"Could you e-mail that list to me?"

"Like right now?"

"Yes."

There was a long silence. "Teddy, let it go. The trial is over. The case is over. You gotta pull your life back together again. You should be at Laurie's house—uh—your house trying to get back inside."

"I know. Just this one thing."

Samantha sighed. "Okay. Watch for it." She hung up.

In a few minutes, his phone pinged and he opened his e-mail to see one from Sam. She'd attached the list of data retrieved from Mina's phone. As he was about to open it, the receptionist called over to him.

"Sir, we do have a resident named Dorsch. I don't think I've ever seen the person. Must be very private." She stopped talking abruptly. "That's the only information I'm allowed to give you. You'll have to call up on the security phone." Betsy nodded toward a glass door to her right. Ted walked to it, and ran his eyes down the board of numbers beside it until he saw the name next to number 312. He pushed the button and saw a digital message telling him to wait. It must be signaling upstairs. The next message asked for his name or ID. He didn't respond, hoping the person would let him in anyway. Sometimes people did things like that. The door remained locked. Ted glanced back at the receptionist. She focused on her computer screen with her head half-hidden behind it. He waited.

In a few minutes a resident came out through the door. Ted depended on the fact that he was a white guy, dressed in an expensive sweater, and had silver highlights in his hair. It worked. The resident didn't even notice him. Ted jumped through the door just before it closed and locked.

As he walked toward the elevator, he scrolled through Mina's phone data. The doors opened and he read the names and web sites Mina had left on it. A site named Lynn Peavey attracted him. What was that? He stepped into the elevator. Ted keyed in the website and waited for a moment. The doors closed. As he rode up, the site opened and his breath caught.

The site listed itself as the best source for crime scene equipment for police and law enforcement. He scrolled through it and when he got to the third page, his hand shook. The caption read, "Blood Spatter Heads." Below that was a photo of three white human-shaped heads, like the kind you'd see on a mannequin. But all of them had red tops. The caption said:

> The Bludgeon Heads are available with the top ¼ composed of wax material and can be filled with blood. Now it's easy to re-create the crime scene and the bloodstains caused by the blows from blunt instruments. Great for training in bloodstain analysis. Buy three for the sale price of two if you order within 30 days!

The elevator doors parted and Ted walked down the short hall to a pale oak door with six recessed panels. Number 312. He knocked four times and finally, it opened. Although she wore a blond wig, Ted looked at Mina Jensen.

Chapter Twenty-nine

Mina fought to keep control of her expression, but Ted could see the corners of her eyes twitch and her mouth tightened. When she regained her composure, her lips curved into a slight smile, and she cocked her head to the side.

"Hello, Mina. Lots of people are looking for you."

"I suppose they are." Her hand gripped the edge of the door as she peeked out from behind it.

"Going to let me in?"

Her eyes floated up for a moment while she thought. "First, tell me how you did it."

"Luck. Laurie told me she thought she'd heard your voice at Byerly's." He waved his hand in the direction of the store. "At the time, I thought it was just her grief that caused her to imagine it. But when I talked to the bloodstain expert and saw the website on your phone for Lynn Peavey, I got to thinking about a far-fetched, crazy possibility. I remembered your maiden name and took a shot that you might be in one of these new buildings. Hiding right out in the open."

"You always were smart."

"Do I get in now? Or do you want everyone to hear about this?" He pulled out his cell phone.

Mina stepped back and pulled open the door. Ted walked in, and she shut the door behind him. He moved into a small living room area. It looked like she'd decorated it from IKEA. Bright yellow upholstery, blond wooden furniture, and unique design features. They circled around each other, trying to decide what to say. Finally, Ted started. "I don't suppose you'd tell me *why*."

She took a deep sigh that expanded her chest; then she let it out. "Maybe. But first, we've got to make a deal."

"Deal?"

"Ted, I don't think you can even imagine how difficult it was for me with Dan. He's mentally ill and violent. I lived through hell with him and finally decided I had to get out. When I suggested to him that we get a divorce, he blew up and went crazy. He almost killed me that time. Told me he'd follow me anywhere in the world to get me."

Ted thought of the amygdala hijack and started to have some sympathy for Mina.

"You know how violent he is."

"Yes. I've seen him explode. Scary."

"When he got back from Afghanistan, things really went to hell."

"The affair probably didn't help."

She dropped her head for a moment. "No. But I was lonely and desperate. I stopped it, though and told that to Danny. He got even worse. Protection orders didn't work and only made him more violent. I decided to escape in a way that he'd never try to find me. After all, how can you find someone who's dead and missing?" She looked up at Ted, and her eyes opened wider.

"What about your family? They're grieving. And Laurie. She's devastated."

"That's the hardest part, but don't you see I had to protect myself first? When I know I'm safe, I'll contact all of them in secret." She blinked. "The other big regret I have is I won't see Jon Stewart again. I really miss him. Is Dan taking care of him okay?"

Ted thought back to his years as a prosecutor and how he'd worked with many battered women who had been victims of brutal men. He began to understand what had motivated Mina. Probably thousands of other women would do the same if they had the brains and opportunity. "How'd you keep Jon Stewart quiet during all your, uh, *work?*"

"Easy. Locked him downstairs. Remember, there wasn't really any violence, but Jon would've certainly been upset with the smell of blood as I threw it around the room."

Ted backed up to a sling chair and sat down in it. On the low table next to him was a pair of Jackie Kennedy sunglasses, big round ones to hide behind. Mina sat on the edge of a couch at an angle to him. She frowned, and wrinkles creased the skin around her eyes. She was still pretty, with tanned skin and large eyes. Her explanation made sense, but then he thought about the sheer immensity of the plot and how long it must have taken to prepare for it. There were so many questions he had for her.

He thought of the money and manpower spent by police departments, sheriffs, the courts, the volunteer searchers, and his own time and struggle. Part of him felt sympathy for her; part of him was furious at what they'd all gone through in the process. The risks he'd taken and all that he'd lost as a result—including his grieving wife.

"Will you help me?"

Exactly what he was thinking—what should he do? Help or call the police? "I don't know. Tell me more."

"Well." Mina slid deeper into the couch and inched closer to him. "I got the idea from a *CSI* TV show about bloodstain analysis. I bought a book on forensics and researched a lot on the Internet. It seemed possible to create a fake crime scene. I found the site with the mannequin heads."

"How were you able do it while Dan was there?"

"He had to be there to be blamed for my death. I drugged his beer, and he was out before he finished the second one."

"You disposed of the beer bottles, which is why they weren't found at the house."

"Right."

"But Dan says he fought with another man. Then he blacked out. Who was the other guy?"

Mina frowned. "He told you that? It's bullshit. He made it up to protect himself."

"What about the blood all—"

"I had practiced in the garage with the bludgeon heads and a sheet that I hung up from the rafters. It took a long time to get the spatters just right." She flashed her killer smile at Ted. She was proud of herself. "In our bedroom I needed a lot of my blood, so I regularly used a syringe to extract some until I had enough to make the scene convincing. I stored it in the fridge downstairs by the spa because Dan never went down there."

"Almost five liters?"

"Yeah."

"Why are you still in town? Why didn't you run?"

Mina sighed and leaned back in the couch. "I screwed up. Simple as that. I'd planned so carefully for the event itself that I didn't think through what I'd do afterward. I plan to leave as soon as possible." She looked back at him. Her eyes softened. "Will you help me now?" Mina squeezed closer to him. She wore khaki cotton shorts that had pulled up to expose her tanned knees and bare legs. She touched his knee with her own. "To save me."

Ted shook his head. "I can't—"

"Do you know anything about the 'battered woman's syndrome'?"

"Yes. I didn't have any idea things were so bad with you two. Dan told me you were getting along well and had even made a commitment to start over."

"He always was delusional. Typical that he couldn't see what he was really doing to me." She moved closer to him. "In a battered woman's world, surviving is all she can possibly try to do. How can you blame me for that?" Her voice became shrill.

"What about some alternatives? Shelters and groups to help women escape from those situations. How can I ignore what you did?"

"You don't know Danny. Remember what he did in Afghanistan. What does an order for protection do? It's only a piece of paper. He would've tracked me down anywhere. Besides, those shelters don't have any security."

Ted didn't say anything. She was right.

"Let's be honest, Ted. You've failed at many things. I know about your past. This is one time you can do something to help someone. It's really a form of justice—helping me out of a dangerous situation where he surely would've killed me. It was just a matter of time before that happened. You can see why I had to do what I did, can't you?"

Ted took a deep breath and thought of what she'd said. Her words struck him hard. "I don't know."

"Please."

"Hey, what about the wig? The one found in the landfill?"

She grinned. "Pretty clever, huh? I used that to create the stains when I dabbed it along the lower wall and floor. To make it look like my body had rolled over there during the assault. Then it went into one of the garbage bags with the other stuff I had to get rid of." She stood and straightened her back. "How did you finally figure it out?"

"Dan's story never made sense to me. All the evidence certainly made him look guilty. But I wasn't convinced. Then when I met with the blood spatter expert, she told me of two 'problems' she found at the crime scene. You were almost perfect."

She smiled in appreciation.

"But you screwed up with the arterial spurt and the image of the wig on the wall."

"Yeah, that was an accident. I had to get it out of there. When I was leaving with the wig, I slipped and my hand pressed against the wall. But I could hardly see it. How could you?"

Ted explained Mooney's discovery with the Panascan.

She turned toward the kitchen. "Hey, how about something cold? Beer, mineral water?" Mina walked toward the kitchen.

"Mina, what are you doing? We're talking seriously here. Come back."

She called from over her shoulder. "Sure. Let me get my wig off first." She turned around the wall of the kitchen and must have gone to a bedroom.

Ted stood, put his hand in his pocket and felt his phone. Maybe he should at least call Sam and tell her everything. But on the other hand, if he let Mina go, who would ever know? He could give some form of justice to Mina Jensen. Of course, he would tell Laurie the truth. She'd be shocked but ultimately happy that Mina was alive. Case closed.

Ted's conscience wouldn't allow him to ignore the fact Dan had been convicted of a murder that hadn't happened. What about the justice of that? He pulled out his phone to call the police. Mina came around the corner quickly, her wig still on and a small black gun in her hand. It had a silencer screwed into the barrel. She pointed it at his stomach.

"The other missing gun from your house?" he asked.

Mina nodded.

"You can't just shoot me. How would you cover up a murder in your apartment?"

"Oh, I could figure out something. By the way, we're leaving in your car." She moved sideways to the table by the couch and grabbed the sunglasses, which she propped on her nose. "I tried to get you to see my predicament. Or at least to help me. But you're still the same failure you always were. I can understand why Laurie kicked you out."

Ted felt his face redden with his anger. "This won't work, Mina."

"Oh?" She gave him the broad smile again. White with perfect teeth. "After all, I'm an expert on creating convincing crime scenes." She chuckled and continued, "I'll just say that you attacked me if I'm ever caught. Self-defense." Mina jerked her head toward the door and scooped up a large canvas purse from the couch. She glanced around her shoulder and scanned the kitchen. She looked back at Ted. "Since you won't cooperate with me, I have no choice."

"What's your plan now?"

Mina stood several feet behind Ted. "I've saved enough to get me started. I'll get out of her and after that, I don't know for sure." She motioned with the gun for him to move. "I risked everything to escape, and I won't let you ruin it."

Ted snorted in a laugh and thought of how her actions had already ruined his life. But she had the gun. He didn't know if Mina would actually shoot, but he believed in her determination—look how far it had taken her. He edged closer to the door.

"Get going, Ted. I don't have time to explain anymore." She crowded behind him.

He thought that at least there would be people outside, and that might give him his own chance to escape. He turned the doorknob in his hand.

The door burst open, knocking Ted backward. He fell against Mina, who toppled over onto the wooden floor in the kitchen. Ted heard her grunt, and the gun clattered across the floor. He stumbled over the sling chair, tried to regain his balance, and fell into the chair. One of the wooden arms dug into his chest and hurt like hell. He twisted around to see Dan Jensen plow into the room.

He slowed long enough to spot Ted. Jensen bellowed, "Ted, I followed you here 'cause you fucked me over!" He lurched toward Ted. Jensen's anger caused him to seem larger than his real size. His face contorted in wrinkles and bright red color. Then he saw Mina on the floor. He looked back at Ted, but it took a moment for him to comprehend what he saw. Jensen's shoulders twitched and he went for Mina.

"What the hell? You bitch!"

"Get away," she screamed.

"Look what you've done to me."

"Help."

Jensen leaped on top of Mina. He grabbed her throat with his strong hands and squeezed. Ted saw her sunglasses bounce off her face and the wig shake loose. He struggled to get out of the low chair. His chest ached and he felt dizzy. Ted stood up and stumbled toward the kitchen. He grabbed Jensen's back and gave a heave. Nothing moved. Ted pulled harder, and Jensen popped off of Mina. He swiped his arm at Ted, knocking him backward. Jensen reached for Mina again.

Ted lifted his leg and kicked Jensen in the side as hard as he could. Jensen screamed in pain, let go of Mina, and got up from his knees. He turned to Ted, eyes small and red, and grabbed for him.

Ted ducked to the side and came up against Jensen on the opposite side. Ted tried to perform the neck move that Samantha had done to stop Jensen in her home. He couldn't remember it. Ted swung his fist at Jensen's face, catching him under the nose, and Jensen staggered backward for a moment. Blood gushed from his nose over his chin.

He came at Ted, swinging his fists through the air and grunting each time. Ted ducked once more, but Jensen lifted a knee to catch Ted in the groin. His world dissolved into a sharp pain, a sick feeling, and Ted collapsed onto his knees. He almost threw up.

Jensen came in again, kicking Ted in the side. With his forearm, Jensen clubbed Ted across the back of the neck. Ted's vision went out and he saw only blackness punctured by bright flashes of light as he pitched forward onto the cool wood of the kitchen floor. It felt smooth against his cheek and he wondered if he could rest there for a moment. He felt Jensen kicking him in the side. Ted knew enough to ball up in the fetal position.

At that moment, Jensen backed up and stopped kicking. Ted's lungs made a scraping sound as he gasped for breath.

Ted uncurled and tried to crawl away. He had no idea where he was going but tried to escape. Ted made it to the edge of the lower drawers in the kitchen. He felt Jensen grab his left leg and pull him back to the middle of the floor. Easier to stomp Ted in the open. Just then, Ted saw the gun and silencer where it had slid under the overhang of the drawers.

He tried to reach for it, but his arm was pinned under his body. Jensen pulled him farther from the gun. Ted rolled to the side, pulled his arm out, and made a grab for the gun. He missed.

Jensen screamed at him and jumped on Ted's lower leg with his foot. Ted kicked back, got a moment of release, and squirmed forward to reach for the gun again. This time he felt the cold metal in his hand. He wrapped his fingers around it and turned over onto his back.

Jensen's face was puffy and red. He lifted his foot to stomp on Ted's exposed stomach.

Ted raised the gun and fired it once.

Part of Dan's chest exploded in bloody flesh and gray fatty material. It splattered across the blond wood of the drawers and up onto the countertop. The force of the blow spun Jensen around to the right, where he hit the counter and bounced off to crumple onto the floor. He didn't move.

Ted dropped his head back onto the floor and gulped air into his lungs. He tasted blood in his mouth, metallic and warm. He tried to roll over onto his knees but couldn't move. He waited and tried again. This time he managed to get up onto all fours. His body felt smashed all over. He raised his head and saw Jensen lurch from side to side on his back and whimper like a baby. He was still alive.

Call 911, Ted remembered. Call 911. Luckily, his phone was still in his pocket and in one piece. He called, slumped to his side in order to lean up against the drawer beside him, and tried to clear his vision.

That's when he looked around and saw that the front door stood open and Mina had disappeared.

Chapter Thirty

One month later, Ted and Laurie sat in the Dakota Jazz Club encircled by a soft booth. The lights started to come up as the applause died down. Some of the tables emptied of people while the wait staff darted between them like fish on a reef, looking for things to pick up.

Samantha's jazz group had finished their final set, and she was about to come out from the green room to say hello. Ted sat back and felt full from the walleye dinner he'd eaten. He smiled over the table at Laurie. A small flame danced in the candle between them. It was their "first date" since the trial. Although Laurie had learned of Mina's true involvement, she was still upset by Ted's willingness to charge ahead with the case against Laurie's wishes. But now her eyes flicked up to meet Ted's and she smiled with him.

"Matt and I are going to a Twins game this Friday," he said.

"Good. He misses you—and is very proud."

"Didn't seem that way in the courtroom. Of course, I looked my worst then."

"You're the hero now." Her head dipped forward. "I can't believe Mina would do—"

"I had no idea until I talked with the bloodstain expert."

"Will they find her?"

Ted shrugged. "She said she had some money and vowed to escape. She could be anywhere."

"People have such strange secret lives." Laurie sighed. "I love her, but I'm mad, too. For what she put us all through. And now she's going to get away with it." She looked up at Ted.

"It happens sometimes."

"Hey, you two," Sam interrupted as she came up with a force of energy and excitement. Her face shone, and her forehead looked plum colored in the low light. She sat in the straight-backed chair next to Laurie. "Haven't seen you for a while, girl. Welcome back."

"Thanks, Sam." Laurie leaned sideways to hug her. "It sounded wonderful. I really liked that song that sounded kind of out of time."

"Oh, that was Dave Brubeck's *Take Five*. It sounds out of time 'cause it's written in five/four time, which—" She must have noticed the blank expressions around her because Sam stopped talking.

"You've got such a subtle sound," Laurie said.

Sam laughed. "Subtle?" She glanced at Ted. "Lot of people wouldn't call me subtle. But that's what I was trying to convey up there. I'm glad you caught it." She leaned back in the chair and raised a hand. The closest waiter came over and took her order of cognac in a snifter. "Courvoisier, nothing less, and bring me some milk on the side." Sam turned back to the table. "Where are we at, Counselor?"

"Under the circumstances, I made a post-trial motion to have the verdict overturned. With the evidence the police found in Mina's apartment, which identified her, the judge agreed. No murder occurred, therefore Danny's not guilty. Rogin and Hanrahan also agreed in the 'interest of justice' not to pursue any further prosecution."

"Generous of those two jerks."

"I haven't seen Dan since the fight." A waiter walked by with a plate and Ted smelled the remains of a grilled steak.

"Probably a good thing. Even though he didn't kill Mina, he still suffers from the amygdala hijack. That's scary." Sam wore a black suit with a bright red blouse underneath that matched a small rose fastened to her lapel. "Hey, I've got a couple questions. What about the bloody shoe print?"

"Still no explanation for that. Does it mean Korsokov was there and helped her? We'll never know."

Sam smiled again. "Smart girl. So she faked the body on the floor, pulled out the small rug from the other room, and left blood all over?"

"She did it all. Remarkable accomplishment—if it wasn't a crime to fake a crime. Left her car at Lake Minnetonka with the bloodstains in the trunk to make investigators think she'd been carried to the lake and dumped in."

"It's not fair," Laurie said. She clipped off her words. Angry. Hurt.

"No, no it isn't. But look at it this way: Teddy did his greatest work in the courtroom and finally got Danny Jensen out of trouble," Sam said.

"Even if he didn't particularly appreciate it." Ted sipped on his Diet Coke while Samantha laughed.

Sam reminded him, "Hey, you got him some kind of justice. That's your job. And you should hear the buzz around the court-house. You're gold again."

"Did Mina also plan for the amygdala hijack defense for Dan?" Laurie asked.

"No, that was our creation. But he certainly had a history of domestic trouble and assaults—that's also why she fired the gun into the wall. It created enough proof for the jury to convict him. But she didn't plan on Harrison's involvement, either. Danny told us first, and that's when Harrison started to look guilty. But it was the Pana-scan film that opened my eyes to everything."

Sam watched as the waiter set a snifter of cognac before her. When she swirled it around, it left streaks of dark brown liquid on the inside of the glass. "Do you think she was in business with Korsokov?" She lifted the glass to her nose, breathed deeply, and sighed.

Ted shook his head. "She was just leading him on. Maybe, at one time, she had some feelings for him and would have left with him, if she could have. To be murdered and disappear was so much better."

"I agree," Sam said. "But I think he was more involved with the whole thing. Did he pick her up at Lake Minnetonka when she planted her car, for instance? He'll never admit to anything, and the cops can't prove anything." Sam shook her head. "He gets to walk away again."

Laurie coughed and drank her white wine. "It must've taken her months to plan this out. But then, she was always so organized and smart."

"She had a lot of people fooled," Sam said. She sipped her cog-nac. "Hey, but you looked like pure gold in the courtroom, Teddy. That's your calling."

Ted felt warmth in his face. "Thanks." His head tilted back. "I gave my notice at the firm. I'm not going back. I decided to practice criminal law again—but this time, I'll only represent innocent people. I may do some death-row defense work for defendants in other states."

"Ted, Matt's about ready to start college. How will we afford—"

"We'll make it. I've learned that, although I need to be in a courtroom, I can't let it interfere with my family ever again. And it won't."

"It's called *balance*. I work on that all the time in jazz."

Ted looked over at Laurie.

"What happens now, Ted?" she asked.

"Well, the setbacks have taught me something. I'll build from them to get to a good place again. I'm committed to try."

"I've heard this before," Laurie said slowly.

"I know."

Sam cleared her throat. "He's going into therapy—with me. Once a week I'll whoop him upside the head when he goes off the tracks." She leaned back and laughed from deep in her body.

"You feel good?" Laurie asked Ted.

"I feel great—except for us."

She flicked back the hair that had fallen across her face, her eyes lifted to meet his, and she said, "Maybe it's time for you to come back home."

About the Author

Colin T. Nelson has worked as both a prosecutor and a public defender for many years. His stories come from the many characters and crimes he's seen over the years. He has published three previous suspense mysteries called **Reprisal, Fallout,** and **Flashover.** This series features prosecutor Zehra Hassan. While she tries to convict the bad guys, she finds herself pulled into the same criminal plots— often fighting not only to win the case, but to save herself.

Up Like Thunder introduces Pete Chandler, an investigator who travels to Myanmar (Burma) to find and rescue an American woman who has disappeared there. While he's searching for her, Pete fears for his own life and wonders if he'll ever get himself back home.

The Amygdala Hijack is part of a new series featuring Ted Rohrbacher. He's a private criminal defense lawyer who always seems to take on the most hopeless and difficult cases.

Colin is married and has two adult children. When he's not writing, he plays saxophone in a jazz trio.

Contact him through his web site at www.colintnelson.com or e-mail him at colinnelson683@gmail.com.

Made in the USA
Monee, IL
24 October 2023

45124612R00177